MW01632679

WHERE *the* CREEK RUNS

Where the Creek Runs

A NOVEL BY

Mary Abraham

For Family
and
Long Leisurely Walks in the Woods

Acknowledgments

Weaving an idea into a story and actually writing it has long been a desire of mine. In 2005 my friend, Fred Fisher, unbeknownst to him, gave me an idea. Once I started writing, he was relentless in asking me if I was getting it done, offering additional information and encouraging me at every opportunity. Thank you, Fred. And thank you also to Diane, his wife, who—after being roped into reading an early draft—has continually given enthusiastic support.

No doubt the most untiring and faithful encourager in my effort has been Jennifer, my daughter. She read—she liked or disliked. She asked questions, and sometimes when life was busy and I hadn't looked at my computer for months (or even years), she prodded me to get back to it. Thank you, Jennifer. I couldn't have finished it without you.

A big thank you to the rest of my family—to Abie, my husband, who never (not even once) complained because I was thinking about writing rather than supper; to Ralph Jr. and his wife, Carla, who have been continually interested in the progress; to my grandchildren, Ryan, Kayleigh and Thomas, who just think the whole idea sounds "neat."

Others to whom I owe an invaluable debt for their willingness to read and offer insight are my cousin, Alta Lee, and friends, Loleeta, Molly, Michelle, Ron, Joyce and Sara. Changes—for the betterment of the whole—were made because of your comments. My thanks to each of you.

Thank you, Cyndi Clark, for your wonderful work on designing the inside of the book and especially for your ready willingness to tolerate my more than occasional indecision.

To Evan Johnston, thank you for your extremely thoughtful, layered and intelligent approach to designing the perfect cover. You have been encouraging and kind and collaborative, all of which I appreciate immensely. Meeting you and working with you has been a pleasure.

Finally, a huge, huge thank you to Joe Lee, editor and consultant, who I met only two years ago. He has been incredibly thorough and amazingly patient as he guided me through this process about which I knew nothing. Any weaknesses you find are definitely not his, but are very likely areas he encouraged me to change, and I resisted. Thank you, Joe, for your continuous oversight and for becoming a friend.

CHAPTER ONE

$\mathcal{H}$ANNAH SUFFERED the sting of the whip. Her trouble had come just a few months after her sixteenth birthday. The first strike across her legs felt like hot coals flung against her flesh, pressing in, searing, burning. She had felt nauseated. Queasiness filled the back of her throat. She heaved but wished desperately not to be sick. "Breathe, just breathe," her mind's little voice whispered. She remembered gasping and her fists clenching white on the brass bed frame in front of her. She had not cried. Her eyes stared into the quilt that covered her bed, but she did not see. With every muscle tightening in anticipation of the next lash, only survival filled her senses.

Lifting her stare from the quilt, she found herself looking across the room at her father's reflection in the dresser mirror. His face was red, his jaw clenched. His neck veins protruded and small beads of perspiration glistened sanctimoniously on his forehead. His fist had turned a splotchy red and white from his crushing grip on the whip's handle. She then closed her eyes and wondered how her sister, Katherine, had endured and prayed for the courage to accept the next blow. It never came. A restraint, not before seen in her father, held back his big frame. He walked slowly from the room without speaking. Hannah, relieved to escape a second lash, sank to the floor, buried her face in the comfort of the quilt and questioned if she would ever be free of the anguish she felt.

Was it, she wondered, her condition that dissuaded him?

***

WATER SPLASHED on Hannah's feet. The cold wetness startled her consciousness and forced it into the present. It was a hot and humid summer afternoon in 1919 Mississippi, and it seemed to Hannah that the heat of the current summer was trying to out-heat all the summers that had come and gone before. She sighed deeply and shook her head in an attempt to shake free of the plunge her soul had taken. "Go. Please go away!" her heart said to the unwanted memory. The cold splash felt good and helped push away unpleasant thoughts from her mind. With all the internal resolve she could muster, she shifted her focus to the pleasantness that surrounded her. The sun was shining, and the leaves were green, and the water was clear. The dark shadows that crowded her mind gradually faded. She sat quietly on her moss-covered knoll, oblivious to Lost, the frisky, young and lovable family dog that was at that moment creating a storm of vegetation in the woods nearby.

LOST HAD left Hannah's side a short time ago to ramble through thick underbrush in the woods that surrounded the creek. The area was almost impassable for humans. He explored and romped through the thousands of weeds and scrub bushes that grew and thrived there as if they knew that corner of the world was theirs for the taking. Twigs snapped and tall grass separated as he pushed through like a big wall of water. Bright yellow and black wings fluttered rapidly up and down as a host of butterflies lit first on one branch and then on another before quickly lifting up and away from the havoc the invader was creating in their world.

Lost sniffed first here and then there as he frolicked in all directions and stopped only occasionally to give brief attention to the various scents left by critters that had recently slithered or scampered along the way. A wealth of life called the woods and bushes home. He found it all fascinating, and on occasion he unwisely investigated gopher holes where resident snakes lifted their heads, faced him squarely, and hissed displeasure. Even though he was only a puppy, he knew at those times it was best to back up and move on.

Mice scurried along, making their way to the corncrib and hoping to find remnants of grain left from years past. Brown, shiny bugs crawled over partially rotten stumps and along secret paths under the weeds. Grasshoppers jumped in every direction to avoid Lost's big paws, and a bevy of birds flew upward from the bushes while chirping strong frustration at the intruder. The rabbits wisely and quickly moved deeper into the woods to get away from the activity.

Lost was enjoying sharing life with all these creatures when suddenly his attention was drawn to one particular spot. He was energized almost as if he had discovered a gigantic bone buried just for him. His ears stood straight and his tail wagged rapidly, beating the weeds on either side—whap–whap, whap–whap, his mind on the target. Lost was strong. With all his strength, his front paws flew immediately into repetitive motion: left, right, left, right, fast, fast, faster! He was determined. He dug with powerful force. The thick vegetation was no match for him. Dirt, sticks, roots, and weeds were all airborne. Whap-whap, his tail continued to beat against the grasses, and his paws continued to dig. He was determined; determined as if his life depended on it, determined to uncover whatever was buried beneath the dark gray dirt.

With unbridled glee Lost recklessly unearthed what—to him—was a great treasure. To Hannah it would be a battering ram against the protective barrier that shielded her from a memory she tried desperately to keep buried deep inside. With the battering, she would be reminded that the past is always with us.

WHILE LOST roamed, Hannah was spending a short respite on the bank of the creek that ran through the woods behind her house. For as long as she could remember, the creek and surrounding woods had been her place of refuge. The water eased her mind by taking with it the anxiety that sometimes lingered in her consciousness, and the trees, like guardians, provided a haven completely hidden by the dense forest.

A breeze blew softly. It crossed Hannah's face with welcomed coolness. Strands of her hair lifted slightly as if following the gentle wind. A little wisp caught between her lips and stuck in the corner of her mouth. She freed the strands with her fingertips and pushed them behind her ear. She sat quietly, reflective and lost deep within her thoughts.

The many shades of green that surrounded her were reminiscent of new leaves budding in springtime. The ground was soft and felt to Hannah almost like fine velvet as she absentmindedly stroked the surface with her fingers. The knoll was just high enough that she could easily dangle her feet into the icy-cold water of the spring-fed creek, or lean against a giant old bay that had for years served as the perfect backrest. She bent her knees and gave her toes and the soles of her feet the pleasure of the moss-covered earth. She loved that particular part of the woods and the special memories that had been created there.

A FOOTPATH STRETCHED from the house, across the yard, through the trees and right down to the edge of where the creek runs through. Hannah, along with her older sister, Katherine, her little brother, Samuel, and her mother, Kate, had traveled the path many times on their way to spend fun afternoons playing in the water or relaxing on the bank.

Samuel, quiet and timid, usually stayed close to Kate—he played in shallow areas near the bank where Kate sat nearby. Occasionally the girls coaxed him out into the deep and held his middle while he kicked his feet and paddled with his hands. "Look, Mama, I'm swimming!" he yelled to Kate. His sisters laughed and giggled as they pulled him from one side to the other.

Katherine was the spirited one. She was never inhibited in word or deed. Whether they were alone or surrounded by lots of other people made no difference to her. She was daring, ever the leader. Unlike Hannah or Samuel, she never minded that the water was cold. She was the first one in. She would run the last several feet of the path and jump in, holding her legs folded tightly under her. She landed in the water like a great big ball and pushed water upward in a grand circular spray.

Hannah always hesitated and watched the water drops pepper back onto the surface of the creek. Katherine's head would pop back up, and through wet hair plastered down across her nose and mouth, she yelled, "Hannah, come on. You're slow as Christmas." Almost before she got the words out, she was bending over and disappearing underwater again. Katherine never badgered Hannah further. She might splash a tiny bit of water toward Samuel, but mostly she contented and amused herself swimming back and forth while she waited for Hannah to get wet.

Hannah's approach was different. She tiptoed in, shivering, keeping her arms folded across her chest as if that would help keep her warm while the coldness crept up to her neck. Occasionally, she cupped a little water in the palm of her hand and trickled it down ever so slowly over her legs. There might be a second handful sprinkled over her shoulders, but either way it was a slow process. Hugging herself, Hannah inched into the water little by little. After both girls were wet, the fun would begin. They spent hours searching for treasure, playing with Samuel, and swimming.

KATHERINE WAS TEN and Hannah eight at the time when there was a most memorable change in their swimming afternoons. It was then that they were unexpectedly allowed to go to the creek alone. It was hot. It was summer. It was a perfect day for swimming. The girls assumed that—as always on hot summer days—they would soon be heading to the creek. Then, out of the blue, their mother announced, "Janie's making dumplings this afternoon. I'm going to help her, hopefully learn how to make them myself."

Janie was the McMolison's cook, and both girls knew she had a reputation for making good dumplings because people were always asking their mother to bring them for church dinners. However, nothing (especially not dumplings) was important enough to stand in the way of going swimming. They were shocked and more than a little disappointed. This news was not welcome.

Katherine, frowning, turned to Hannah and whispered, "Did somebody die or something? This isn't right. I wanna go swimming."

"Don't think so," Hannah said, shaking her head and leaning close to Katherine's ear.

Their mother had always made herself available to take them swimming except on the rare occasion of something extreme like sickness or death. Since neither girl was aware of a death or sickness, they did not move. They stood there side by side looking intently at Kate. Their brows slightly furrowed and their lips parted in disbelief as they waited for her to correct her mistake.

"Come on," said Hannah after maybe a minute had passed. "Mama wants to cook with Janie. Let's just go. We'll figure out something else to do." Hannah spoke so softly that Katherine could barely hear her.

Katherine was not ready to give up quite so easily, however. She turned her head slightly toward Hannah, and through pursed lips she hurriedly whispered back, "Making dumplings on a perfectly good summer afternoon makes no sense. She can do that any old time—wintertime, raining, storming. Anytime."

Hannah wanted to plead their case against dumpling-making as bad as Katherine did, but their mother had been emphatic about her plan for the afternoon and was already pulling pots and pans from the cupboard and flour from the pantry. Hannah turned to leave the kitchen, but Katherine grabbed a handful of her dress. "Don't you dare leave. Just wait a minute," Katherine said through barely-parted lips. Her tone was low and commanding.

Hannah stood back beside her sister. They were both quiet as they looked at their mother, thinking she would surely come to her senses. Katherine and Hannah—Katherine to a greater degree—became more and more frustrated as they listened to Kate and Janie chat like two old friends. They were disappointed, and they were ignored.

"Chickens already picked off tha bone, broths ready. We in good shape," Janie said. She seemed to be enjoying having a student on hand as much as Kate was enjoying being there. Both pair of hands were white with a covering of flour dust. "Lemme get lard and some milk," Janie almost sang, as she swished the tail of her apron back into the pantry. The girls could see her backside bounce through the thin gray fabric of her dress.

Kate looked up at her daughters, who were still standing in the door of the kitchen. "Want to join us?"

"No, ma'am," both girls said in unison.

"That's *not* what we wanted to do," Katherine added, shaking her head from side to side. Her words were stronger and more sarcastic than she intended.

Kate's smile vanished. "Katherine, don't be haughty. That kind of tone is never acceptable." Then came the surprise. "But tell you what—you can go on down to the creek. If we get finished here I'll come, but otherwise, y'all watch out for each other."

The furrows in Katherine and Hannah's brows deepened, their eyes brightened, and their chins dropped. Still quiet, they stood with their mouths open.

"Now, girls, I'm putting you in God's hands. He takes care of all of us all the time, anyway, and you're old enough to be responsible."

Kate was sure about God being in control of all things, even though she was often guilty of running things her own way without checking in with Him first. Kate's Presbyterian logic was, on occasion, a little skewed—which didn't matter since she could trace her family tree directly back to Scotland. She had a heritage to be proud of, one that made her really and truly Presbyterian. Kate, the girls knew, could spring God and His sovereignty into any conversation. They had heard her. They also knew her eleventh commandment: Worrying is the responsibility of every good mother.

"Oh, thank you. We'll be fine." Katherine's words lingered in the air as she raced toward the backdoor.

"Yes ma'am, we'll be fine. Creek, here we come!" Hannah's words blended with Katherine's.

"I didn't expect her to let us go by ourselves," Katherine said as they hurried down the steps.

"Me neither," said Hannah. "Glad she's trusting today. Probably need to hurry before she changes her mind." As the girls raced toward the edge of the woods, Hannah added between giggles, "This is exciting. I mean, you know, getting to go by ourselves."

"Quit giggling and come on. We need to get clear of the yard before she thinks of some reason not to let us go." Katherine glanced back at Hannah, who was several steps behind her. "Hurry up, Hannah. Run."

As the girls reached the point where the yard turned to woods, their mother's voice rang out, "Not only is God in control of all things, but remember He sees all things as well. So behave yourselves, and if I don't get there, be home before suppertime." What they could possibly do at the creek that would constitute misbehaving was a mystery to them, but *behave yourselves* was a frequent caution from their mother so hearing it again had little significance.

"Yes ma'am," the girls yelled back. They merrily scooted down the path, glad they had escaped without having to recite questions from the Catechism that would have reinforced Kate's point on who, what, and where God was. They were soon sharing what would be the first of many wonderful unsupervised afternoons. Hannah laughed out loud at the memory.

* * *

YEARS HAD PASSED since those days of wild and innocent play at the creekside. Katherine wasn't there to add her spark to the afternoon. She had married and moved to Hattiesburg with her husband, and the girls had lost their sweet Samuel well before then. Yet the creek and woods remained much the same, a place of escape, adventure, and beauty.

The water still flowed lazily along, gently weaving around and through the ferns and tree roots that graced the bank. It was clear as crystal and appeared blanketed with a thousand tiny diamonds when small ripples caught the intermittent sunrays that peeked through the swaying branches overhead. The spring that fed the creek flowed continuously. The water eased through the swimming hole and then gathered itself into the narrowed creek that stretched into the woods on the other side.

A few buttercups lingered in a small marshy area nearby. Their butter-yellow crowns joined the little clumps of purple violets that grew here and there all along the well-worn footpath. The flowers, though small in size, boasted grand but gentle beauty with every intricate detail and, for Hannah, they were like friends faithfully returning year after year. Their very presence added comfort and delight to her special place on this summer afternoon.

Hannah's thoughts continued to be restless, her mind jumping from one memory to another. She did not want to dwell on the past, but she was having difficulty quieting it.

She yearned for the love she had known. Her body warmed with the memory. The old and grand trees that surrounded her were privy to her secrets and to theirs, but they didn't tell. Instead, they stood quietly in all their majesty. Some were tall and stately while others were short and gnarled, but all provided asylum and refuge. They sang the song of the woods as an unseen breeze floated through the branches. Hannah enjoyed the music and imagined each tree was telling a special story. She longed for a happy ending to her own.

* * *

HANNAH SHIFTED HER POSITION so she could put her feet and legs in the water. The coolness was refreshing. Even though she was completely shaded from the sun by the canopy of branches overhead, she was hot. Putting her feet in the creek immediately made her feel cool all over.

Hannah dipped her fingers in the water and flicked some toward Joseph. He laughed and, even though he was content playing with his little driftwood boat, was always happy to have her play with him. Joseph was several months past his third birthday. He had dark hair, blue eyes, and a fun-loving spirit—a little like his Aunt Katherine. He loved to come to the creek just like Samuel did when he was little, and like Hannah and Katherine continued to do through their early teens.

On that day Hannah and Joseph were home alone. Kate was taking her turn caring for Mrs. Epsy, one of the widows from the church. Mrs. Epsy had been sick, on her deathbed for some time now. She never had any children, so the ladies in the Women's Aide Society were taking turns seeing that she had proper food and care. Hannah had gone a few times to help out but found herself feeling scared and anxious when she thought Mrs. Epsy might actually die in her care; Hannah had spent most of the time sitting back a safe distance from the bed and praying for her to live until relief came. Hannah much preferred being responsible for all the chores at home while Kate took a turn.

Before Hannah went to the creek that day, she had taken a picture from her letter box. She kept it protected, hidden beneath a few sheets of yellowed writing paper. She often longed to look into the eyes of the young man in the picture. She longed to feel his touch and know the security of his embrace. The memory of his love was deeply embedded in her heart and soul. Only on days like this when she was in the house alone (except for Joseph) did she feel safe enough to face her buried emotions. Pain was always a part of loving, but the pain she felt was often heavier than she ever imagined possible. Hannah had held the picture in her hands, softly stroked it with her fingertips and, as tears filled her eyes and blurred her sight, she remembered the man who claimed her heart and introduced her to a part of herself she had not known before. Every time she took the picture from the box and gazed into the face, a sad yearning inside her rekindled. Yet she could not resist.

As she stood with the picture pressed against her heart, Joseph had called to her, "Mama, Mama, are you coming?" She blotted the tears away and put the picture quickly and carefully into the safety of its hiding place just as Joseph ran into the room where she stood. "Come on … pleeeeease?" he said. "I'm ready to go swimming."

Hannah and Joseph had now been at the creek for several hours. While she would have loved to stay safely atop her mossy knoll, she knew it was time to be starting home. Joseph had played hard. He was tired and hungry, and there were chores that had to be done before dark.

"Joseph, it's time to go," she said.

Joseph grabbed his boats and walked toward her. "I wanna take my boats home."

Hannah laid them carefully on the moss. She picked up the towel she had brought to the creek and dabbed the water droplets from his face. She tousled his hair playfully and began to dry him off. She hadn't finished when he picked up his boats and ran for the path saying, "I'm gonna beat you!"

Hannah fell into the game. "I'm coming. I'm right behind you." They scurried up the hill, winding around the trees, following the path, and were both out of breath when they reached the yard.

Lost heard them coming. He was still rambling in the woods, and by that time he had made his way up near the yard. Lost was not quite two years old. At least that was the favored opinion of those people who thought they could guess. He was already a big dog, though. Joseph could easily prop his arms on Lost's back when they stood side by side. He had a brown shiny coat with some black mixed in, and had soft rounded ears and huge feet. He loved people, loved to play, and was easily Joseph's best friend. Lost had appeared at the door about a year and a half earlier. Since only Kate, Hannah, and Joseph lived there at the time, Kate decided to let him stay until somebody came looking for him. Nobody ever did. Kate had said he was lost, so Joseph started calling him Lost. Therefore, Lost became his name.

"What's Lost got?" Joseph yelled, his voice rising with the anticipation of sharing Lost's discovery.

"I don't know," Hannah answered.

Lost had come running, his feet covered with dirt. It was obvious he had been digging. He was often digging and was as energetic about the art as any other big dog anywhere. Lost had dug more than his share of holes and successfully uprooted several decent-size trees. Hannah and her mother were always less than pleased when some of their garden plants were pulled up and left to wilt on the ground (or potatoes dug prematurely, played with, and then left to rot). What he had that afternoon was not a tree or a plant or a potato, however. He was dragging a corn sack across the yard. He tried to pick it up and shake it, but it didn't shake very well. The sack was too big, and whatever was in the bottom weighed it down so that he couldn't get it into a good shaking position. The opening of the sack was tied securely with twine. Lost ran to meet them, avoided stumbling, and gripped the sack tightly in his teeth. His tail was wagging as fast as he could wag it.

"Whatcha got, boy?" Hannah asked, reaching down to pat his head. He dropped his gift at her feet.

Hannah carried the dirty, torn, and rotting corn sack to the back steps. It had something in the bottom. She had no idea what it could be. They used sacks like it around the place from time to time, but she couldn't imagine why one was tied like this or where it had come from. While Joseph busied himself arranging his boats in a safe place on the porch, Hannah sat on a step and began to untie the twine. "Why would someone tie so many knots?" she wondered. Using a knife, she cut the twine, untied the remaining knots and cut the sack. Inside was a once-white flour sack. Rain and dirt had discolored the material to the point that the faded lavender flowers were barely visible. The flour sack was also tied in a knot; it looked familiar, but flour sacks were common. Certainly lots of people got sacks with the same design, she thought. She untied the sack and looked inside, seeing a metal box. It was old but still in good shape. Had Lost uncovered someone's buried treasure? She felt a twinge of nervousness at the thought of invading another person's privacy, but she didn't want to stop. She couldn't.

Hannah pulled the box from the sack and slowly lifted the lid. Inside was a bundle of white cloth—another flour sack that had been cut open to form a flat piece of material. It was wrapped multiple times around the still mysterious contents. She lifted the clump of cloth and began to unwrap. Even before she had completely removed the covering, Hannah knew what she was holding. As she unfolded the last layer, she gasped. Her heart ached in despair. Her throat closed so much that she had difficulty breathing. Her chest pounded; her head suddenly throbbed and she felt sick to her stomach. Before her was the device of family-shattering death. It had belonged to the one whose life had been lost. Now, suddenly, there it was in front of her, hideous in her sight and unforgiving in its history. It had been wiped clean as if innocent of its past, but in her mind's eye she could still see the wet, warm blood seeping through the chambers as it lay quietly on her sister's living room floor. The sheriff had picked it up and taken it with him. Hannah did not know he had returned it to Leaf Creek along with the body. It belonged to the dead. She wished the dead had kept it.

"I'm thirsty," Joseph called to her. Somewhere in her subconscious mind, she heard his request. She quickly replaced the white cloth, closed the lid, returned the box to the flour sack, and tied the opening even tighter than before. She put the flour sack in the corn sack and again tied the opening. She would get more twine later and redo the knots just like she had found them. She placed the sack under the house and out of sight by wedging it into a crevice between a floor joist and one of the brick support columns. She would come back later and figure out where to hide it. Just as, she knew, her mother had done.

Lost had gotten Joseph's attention, nudging him to play so that he forgot about the sack. Hannah was thankful. She didn't understand what was happening herself, at least not in a way she could possibly explain to a three-year-old. She and Joseph had been back from the creek only a few minutes, and it suddenly seemed like a lifetime. The peace and contentment she had managed to muster had dissolved into intense sadness. She took a long, deep breath. Joseph didn't notice she was shaking as she dipped water from the water bucket into his little cup.

CHAPTER TWO

THE MCMOLISON'S dogtrot style house was about four miles out from town. When the children were young, the family spent most Sunday afternoons on the big front porch that stretched from one side of the house to the other.

Samuel would play for hours with the vast supply of wooden blocks their father brought him from the mill. Triangles were stacked on squares. Rectangles stood on end. He built farms or towns or whatever suited him on any given day. Katherine and Hannah always grabbed one of the big oak rockers and rocked alongside their mother. When neighbors dropped by, adults got the chairs and children got the floor. The men gathered on one end of the porch and the women on the other. Hannah and Katherine, by positioning themselves on the steps halfway between, could listen to whichever of the two conversations seemed more interesting. Most Sundays their interest quickly waned. They excused themselves, went to their bedroom, and read a book— one of the few acceptable activities for a Sunday afternoon.

The neighbors rocked, drank coffee, sipped lemonade, and fanned. The McMolison's fan basket was full of the hand-held, cardboard-on-a-stick advertisements. Words and pictures describing various and sundry ways to improve one's life waved back and forth, stirring the air. Praying hands to the right, praying hands to the left … over and over. The church's invitation to visit followed obediently on the opposite side.

Two fans were from Fisher's Feed Store, which was for All Your Feed and Seed Needs. There were several with a picture of a thimble and spool of thread on one side and the words, "I'm A Fan of Leaf Creek Mercantile" on the other. Most, however, came from stores in Leeville, a town to the south. One or two others were advertisements from as far away as Hattiesburg.

Regardless of the messages, the fans were popular. On hot summer days everybody wanted one. They rocked and they fanned. Only the shooing of an occasional fly interrupted the back and forth of the fans, or broke the rhythmic sound of the long rockers on the weathered wood planks of the porch.

The front door opened into a hall that ran from front to back. The hall at the McMolison's was wider than most and was closed on either end. The furniture in the hall was sparse. Two never-used straight chairs with tall backs buffeted each end of a narrow pine table that sat along the wall. Tall green vases, given to Kate by her grandmother, were especially pretty sitting on the ecru-colored scarf Kate crocheted for the table. On the opposite wall and closer to the front door was a coat rack made of oak. The basket of fans sat on the floor just to its right. The hall served mainly as the place to leave hats and coats or as a pass-through from front to back or from one side of the house to the other.

Kate enjoyed the sitting room best. It was there she and her children read books while snuggled together on the green and blue upholstery of the camel-back sofa, or sang songs as they clustered around the Mason Hamlin upright piano. Playing the piano and reading were Kate's favorite pastimes. Desiring to instill an appreciation for both in her children, she insisted that Hannah and Katherine take piano lessons from Miss Velma at the church. Hannah was a little more serious about the lessons than Katherine. She practiced every day, and by the time she was ten years old, she often accompanied while the others sang.

Open windows allowed a cooling cross breeze through the sitting room on summer evenings. Flickering flames in the fireplace radiated cozy warmth on winter nights. Crocheted doilies graced the back of the sofa as well as various chair arms. Off-white lace curtains fell loosely over the windows. The room, comfortable and welcoming, was a perfect gathering place for the family.

The bedroom just next to the sitting room was Samuel's. His iron bed frame was painted a dark brown and matched the brown and blue quilt that covered his bed. Two specially selected wooden planks, perfect for shelves, were brought from the mill and attached to one wall. Kate had visualized the shelves being covered with books. Indeed there were books, but most of the space was covered with fruit jars filled with Samuel's truly special treasures. On one end was an extra-large arrowhead, too big to fit through the mouth of a fruit jar. The arrowhead had been given to Samuel by one of the men who worked at the mill. It was four inches wide and glistened in varying shades of gray, black, and brown. The colors reminded Samuel of good, freshly-plowed, dark brown dirt. To him, the arrowhead— polished so that it was as smooth as glass—was beautiful and the best of all his treasures. Next to the arrowhead, in an equally prominent spot, was a railroad spike that Samuel found one day while playing in the woods near the house. It remained a mystery as to how the spike made it to their woods because a track had never been close by. A train, bright black and shiny, looked really fine sitting on the shelf, but Samuel didn't find it much fun to play with. Of far greater importance to him were his rocks of assorted sizes, special pieces of odd-shaped wood, a fishing cork, and tiger-eye marbles of different colors.

The shelves screamed Samuel. His interests covered every inch.

Hannah and Katherine's bedroom was next to Samuel's. The sisters always slept together in the double bed that had been given to Kate and Bill as a wedding present. The bed had originally belonged to Kate's maternal grandmother. It was a cherished possession not only because it had belonged to family but also because of the lovely winding brass scrollwork that made up both the headboard and footboard. Covering the bed was a patchwork quilt made of many colors. Katherine had insisted on a pair of prints for their wall, both scenes at a circus. Red, yellow, green, and blue balloons flew high above the clowns that appeared to be dancing in front of tents painted in red, white, and yellow stripes. Red, yellow, and blue pillows were scattered across the head of the bed and filled a rocking chair that sat in one corner of the room. A vast array of colorful hair ribbons and bows overflowed a basket that sat on the dresser. The room had a vibrant and magical enchantment. There were times when Hannah would have preferred calmer surroundings, but Katherine's luster and exuberance showed through in every aspect of her life. Their bedroom was no exception.

Kate had decorated the master bedroom first. Bill wanted wood furniture. He said it would be appropriate for them since his livelihood was timber. He and Kate started together to find the perfect pieces.

They made a couple of trips to the larger town of Hattiesburg but did not find anything to their liking. Several weeks had passed when one day Bill learned from a timber buyer that a family down in Lee-ville was selling all the furniture that had belonged to their parents. Bill and Kate went to Leeville the very next day.

After spending a night in the hotel that sat on the corner across from the courthouse, they were up and dressed early. Both, anxious to see the furniture, were hoping no one else had bought it. Asking only one question at breakfast was all it took to learn all they needed to know about the location of the furniture, its lovely and long-time old home, the passing of the beloved doctor who had owned it and the daughter-in-law (from up north somewhere) who wanted to be rid of everything. Opinions were many and freely given.

Bill and Kate found the house easily. It sat just on the edge of town and was surrounded by big oak trees. The daughter-in-law, wife of the only heir, answered the door and invited them inside. She told Kate, "I want everything gone. I'm starting fresh, filling my house with every-thing new. *Everything* is for sale."

The wife's attitude was a mystery to Kate, but it explained the raised eyebrows, smirks and veiled (and not so veiled) comments she and Bill had been made privy to at breakfast. Kate smiled and responded, "You certainly have some lovely things." Then, looking up at Bill, she added, "Why don't we walk around and see everything."

Bill glanced over toward the lady and asked, "Will that be alright?"

"Certainly. I'll be in the kitchen. Look as long as you like."

When they were safely in another room, Kate, standing close to Bill's side, whispered, "It's wonderful. Every piece is perfect. Don't you think? Can't imagine why she wants to sell it all."

"Well, don't ask. If she regrets it later, that's her problem. If you like it, let's buy it."

They bought it all that day. The master bed was mahogany with large round posts and a beautifully-carved headboard. Also for the bedroom were a washstand, a white and cream washbowl and pitcher, and a chifferobe with a full-length mirror on one of the doors. Every piece was magnificent. Bill was pleased and Kate was thrilled. Kate chose fabrics in shades of grey green and ivory for their room. Green, her favorite color, seemed to pop up in everything she chose.

The trip to buy the estate furniture had been more successful than either Kate or Bill could possibly have hoped. Included were a dining table and chairs and a pie safe. The dining furniture was stained a light walnut that Kate liked. She wasn't particularly happy with the ivory and maroon-striped fabric that covered the chair bottoms, but knew she could soon recover the chairs herself. The pie safe was made of wood and painted off-white with silver tin insets in the doors. It worked perfectly in the kitchen. An iron bed, ultimately Samuel's, as well as the camel back sofa for the sitting room and a few other odd tables and chairs, were also part of the sale.

The house itself, except for the brick base for the columns on the front porch and the brick fireplaces, was made entirely of wood from Bill's mill. He chose the timber, hired the loggers, oversaw the milling and finishing of all the material, and supervised the construction. Kate chose off-white paint for the outside of the house and deep green for the trim. She even painted the front door deep green, copying the idea from a picture on a Christmas card. All the walls inside were painted off-white. The oak floors were left their natural color.

***

WHILE GROWING UP, Kate had often heard her mother say, "Cleanliness is next to Godliness." She continued to hear her mother's words;

keeping the house clean was of utmost importance, so she worked diligently to see that it was done. The inside floors and furnishings were cleaned at least weekly, more often when dirt was tracked in. Daily sweeping of the porches was a given, and at least twice each year they were scrubbed with water, white sand, and the corn shuck broom.

Before every scrubbing, dried corn shucks were pulled through holes in the broom's rectangular wooden base. The shucks were secured with twine, and the wooden handle was tightened. Buckets of water were brought from the well and white sand was brought from the big cave located a quarter mile from the house.

In the early years one of the hired hands did all of the scrubbing. After Katherine, Hannah, and Samuel were born, they loved helping, especially with the sand and the water. The children's assistance usually added extra work, but the help never minded. The children's presence made the job more of an adventure to be shared, rather than work to get finished. Most families cleaned outside floors only once a year, but Kate McMolison insisted that twice was an absolute necessity.

THE YARD IN THE FRONT was fenced. The fence of wooden slats ran across the front, turned down each side and, after passing the front porch, turned again until each side connected with the house. This area, though dirt, was swept clean with a sagebrush broom. Kate and the help used the brooms inside and out until they were worn down to a stub too short to be of much use.

The front yard, welcoming and beautiful, boasted rose bushes, gardenia bushes, hydrangeas and a few evergreen shrubs surrounding the porch. Kate enjoyed all her flowers, especially the gardenias. Their fragrance reminded her of her mother and gave her a warm wave of comfort that she always embraced.

* * *

BILL AND KATE HAD MARRIED IN 1894 and moved the week after their wedding to Leaf Creek from their home in South Carolina. Bill had heard about the abundant timber in Mississippi and set his sights on moving to the area, acquiring land, and starting a timber mill.

Kate had eagerly moved with her husband. The adventure of starting their life together in this new place had been as exciting to her as it was to him. Bill's mother had died several years earlier from pneumonia; his father had recently sold their farm, remarried, moved to a neighboring state and started a new life of his own, so Bill no longer felt ties to South Carolina. Kate, however, was an only child. Moving far away from her parents was hard for her and for them. She never dreamed she would not return within a year (or certainly two) after leaving there.

She and Bill began to establish their new life. They bought land, began building their house, built and opened the mill, planted a garden, and bought and tended animals. Summer became winter, winter became spring, spring became summer. The cycle repeated.

KATE KEPT THE HOUSE, planted the garden, milked the cow, and tended the chickens. Although she didn't mind work, all of it together was just about more than she could manage. Plus, she was not used to working alone. She liked being with other people. Kate had grown up in a family in which everybody helped. Aunts, uncles, and cousins always worked together to do whatever chores needed doing. In Mississippi, however, she was too far away for them to help her, or for her to help them.

Workdays back in South Carolina had often been long and hard, but they were always filled with lots of conversation and laughter. Kate thought about the many days she spent in the field picking beans with her cousins. The rows were long and the sun was hot, causing heat waves to shimmer over the distant vines. There was always some kind of race going on—which of them could fill their bucket the fastest or which one of them could get to the end of the row first. Some days they broke corn. Some days they dug potatoes. None of the days were bad, as long as they were all together.

KATE SMILED as she thought back to the watermelon patch with all the green vines running low and covering the ground. She remembered stumbling, sometimes barefoot, over uneven dirt as she and her cousins followed her uncle around watching him thump every melon. A hollow sounding thump, a creamy yellow bottom, and the quick cut of the stem with his pocketknife meant get the melon—regardless of its size—to the wagon. The older boys carried the bigger ones. The girls and the younger boys carried the smaller ones.

A dropped melon would burst wide open on the ground. It happened occasionally. Sweet red meat clung to the broken and irregular pieces of green rind, little black seeds peeked from their windows or lay scattered where they fell, and tiny rivers of juice trickled over the surface of the powdery ground. Dirty hands scooped up juicy red meat from the pieces that landed meat side up and clean. The melon was hot, but it still tasted good.

Kate missed having help, but even more she missed sharing laughter and time with family.

* * *

TIME PASSED. BILL WORKED long hours. His time at home became less and less. He liked the feel of success. By the end of the first year he had twenty men working for him. He liked hearing "yes suh" and "no suh" and "sho' boss" and having the men do exactly what he said. The enjoyment of power began to settle in and take root.

Bill was proud of the mill. He was proud of his involvement in the church and the community. He had a beautiful wife who efficiently managed their new home. To his way of thinking, things were good.

Those first months in Mississippi saw both Bill and Kate working hard. They were building their new life together, but they were, without realizing it, doing so separately.

Chapter Three

After supper one night a year and a half or so after moving to Leaf Creek, Kate, exhausted from her never-ending chores and disappointed that her husband was gone from home so much of the time, followed Bill to his chair in the sitting room. She didn't sit but stood in front of him.

"What is it? What are you doing?" Bill said, looking up at her with a questioning frown.

Kate answered without hesitation. "Bill, I'm glad the mill is doing well. Your hard work is really paying off. That's all good. I'm really glad. You know I am, but it seems like I never see you. I miss having you here, at home. Plus, I need your help. I can't keep the work around here caught up. Mostly though, it just seems there are a lot of days I barely even see you at all."

His thoughts went immediately to business. "I know, I know. I miss being home too, but I can't be everywhere, and right now I've got to keep pushing things at the mill. You've just got to understand. It's already important to the community, and I'm gonna make it even more important." His voice grew loud. He was emphatic, and his tone more sharp than Kate was accustomed to hearing. He looked directly at her. "You do understand that a lot a men depend on me for their jobs?"

Kate's feelings were hurt. It was unusual for Bill to speak to her in such a harsh and uncompromising manner, but she kept her composure. She pulled a stool close to his knees and sat down. "Oh Bill, I know you're working hard, and I know you're providing jobs, but I still need you here, need to see you … sometime. Can't you plan a little time at home?"

Bill turned abruptly in his chair, crossed his legs away from her and knocked a doily to the floor. He sighed an irritated sigh as he reached to get the doily, but he did not say anything.

Kate sat straight. "Why aren't you saying anything?" Then, a bit louder and more confidently, she said, "You're gone so much these days. I don't ever even know if you're going to be here at all. And like I said, in addition to wanting to see you, I really need help with some of the work. I can't get it all done. I don't mind it, but I can't get it done." Kate stood but didn't move away from his chair. Looking directly at him, she added, "It seems to me … at least I was hoping we could do some of it together."

Bill leaned back in the chair, looked up at her, and listened, but his mind stayed elsewhere. The fact that Kate was asking him to spend time with her never registered with him, or at least he didn't allow it to register. Instead he responded by immediately making plans to hire help. In a year and a half he had become the largest employer in town. He looked up at Kate, his brow furrowed. "A lot of men and their families depend on me—there's no way I can spend a bunch of time working around here at home," Bill said half to himself and half to Kate.

Kate sighed deeply and sat down in the chair next to him. "But, Bill …"

He looked over at her. "I know. I know. It has taken a lot of work to get things going, here and at the mill. Now it takes a lot of work to *keep* things going. You're right. You can't do it all. You shouldn't have to, but like I said, I have to be at the mill and out in the community. I have a lot to do."

Kate, not sure what her husband was thinking, sat quietly. Although she was enjoying the comforts that came with his success, she wished they did not come at the expense of their lives together.

With his eyes suddenly open wide, Bill sat straight and clapped his hands together. "That's it. Don't know why I haven't thought of this before. I'll get you some help. With my success it'll be good for you to be able to do whatever you want to do, whatever women do—sew, read, visit—whatever." Bill leaned forward, turned slightly sideways and faced Kate. "Yes, you need to take on the proper role. Our reputation in the community depends on you too."

"I don't mind the work," Kate interjected. "I just can't get it all done, so I thought if you could be home at least some of the time, we …"

"Appearances are important, very important," Bill interrupted. "The solution is to hire hands. Hire hands to take care of everything."

Kate, though disappointed, said, "Okay, I guess so, if you think that is what we need to do." She stood, sighed, and looked absent-mindedly into the fireplace.

"Kate, don't act like that. Look around you. You do realize you have a nice house, nice furniture? All this is because of my mill, me and my men working hard and my money."

"Yes, I know," Kate said softly, hating his prideful talk.

* * *

THE MCMOLISON'S way of life was quite customary in those days. Most of their neighbors led similar lifestyles. They all had gardens to plant, animals to tend, meals to prepare, and floors to scrub. There was, however, one significant difference that soon set the McMolisons apart. The difference was their help. It wasn't long before they had three full-time hands working at their place. This extravagance was far and away out of the ordinary. No other family had ever considered having so much help, even if they could. A couple of families in town had one maid. Other families shared so that they had help one or two days a week. Some took their dirty laundry to the home of one of the coloreds that took in washing and ironing. Then others had help only when some special occasion like a wedding or a funeral came along. But the McMolisons had help all of the time and for everything.

FRANK WAS THE FIRST. He was originally hired by Mr. McMolison to help clear the land where the mill was built. Frank had spent his life going from one white man to another doing whatever odd jobs were available. The mill job was the best opportunity he had ever had, and he worked hard to keep it. He was quiet and conscientious. He enjoyed his moonshine, but it never got in the way of his work. Frank never grumbled. While he was on the job, he was always working. Bill McMolison noticed.

Bill didn't say anything. He stayed above any type of familiarity with his workers. He maintained a rigid "I'm the boss, you're the hired hand" attitude. He hired men and expected them to work. That was pretty much the extent of his relationship with them. The only thing the hire could expect was his pay or what was left of it after his credit at the mill's store had been deducted.

"I sure hate to lose you at the mill, Frank," Bill began. "This arrangement may be temporary, but right now Mrs. McMolison needs help around the house. I need you to help with all the work on the outside. We have a garden. We have one cow, but we are building a barn so we can get a few more. The horses and the wagons need looking after. Mrs. McMolison also has a few laying hens. We pretty much have a small farm. Your work will include whatever is needed to keep things running smoothly." He turned and then, almost as an afterthought, said, "I'm looking for someone to help her on the inside, too."

"Yes suh, Mista Bill, wherever you need me. And, Mista Bill, if you don't mind my saying, I can get you some inside help if you really thinking on the idea."

"Okay. Who did you have in mind?"

"Well suh, my wife has been working for the same woman for over twenty years, up to recent. The woman's name was Miz Page. She was getting pretty old long time ago. Anyways, it's been now about a month ago, poor thing had some kinda twitching spell, lived just about two days before the Lawd took her on. June Ellen ain't had no work since. She'll do a real fine job for your wife, and I'd be much obliged. We sure could use the work."

"Tell her to come to the house in the morning to meet Mrs. McMolison. Come about seven-thirty. I'll be there too. Mrs. McMolison and I will meet her then. As a matter of fact, you plan to come on tomorrow and start work at the house."

"Yes suh. Mighty fine."

JUNE ELLEN APPEARED PROMPTLY at seven-thirty the following morning. She knocked gently on the back door. Frank was there, too, but he waited over near where the barn was being built. Kate went to the door and greeted June Ellen with a warm smile. "Good morning, come on up on the porch." June Ellen eased from the steps onto the edge of the porch. "I understand you worked for the same lady for a long time. What all did you do for her?" Kate asked.

"Mostly everything that had to do with the cleaning," June Ellen answered. "I kept the house up real good and washed and ironed clothes. Did a little cooking, but have to be honest with you, my cooking ain't the best."

"Sorry to hear you say that. The kitchen is not my favorite place either. But I appreciate your honesty; so let's see how things work out. You can start today if you would like."

"Thank you, ma'am. I'll do you a good job. You won't be sorry."

June Ellen and Frank were both dark brown. They were not dark black like some of the other coloreds working at the mill. June Ellen was five feet eight inches tall and big boned. She was not fat, but she was big, and she was strong. She had not mentioned that she plowed with a mule and chopped firewood in her previous job. She had gained amazing physical strength doing such heavy work and now moved furniture and cleaned as if she was working around furniture in a dollhouse. She was opinionated about how things should be done, and if Kate disagreed she responded with "yes um, yes um, that's fine." As time went by, most everything was being done June Ellen's way. Kate didn't mind. She was pleased as long as things were clean and orderly. June Ellen liked clean and orderly as much as Kate; she just went about it in her own way.

June Ellen hadn't been working quite two weeks when Kate

brought up cooking again. "Your work is great, June Ellen, but I do wish you could cook. How is it you grew up around all those cooks and didn't learn more about cooking? I thought all y'all were good cooks."

"I don't like to cook, Miz Kate. Not that I don't know how. And if that's what you want me to do, I'll try more of it, but it's like I told you before—I ain't never done much cooking for nobody but Frank, and I sure enough don't wanna start."

"That's okay. It was just wishful thinking on my part," Kate said. "You help me when I need help and it'll be fine." Then Kate added jokingly, "I'll just keep wishing. Maybe a wonderful cook will appear. Wouldn't that be nice?"

Kate didn't know it at the time, but June Ellen also thought that would be really nice, and if the McMolisons would go for it, she had just the person for the job. June Ellen had never known a family with more than one colored working in their house, and she certainly didn't want to jeopardize her own job, but just maybe the McMolisons were different.

"Miz Kate, I don't know what you and Mista Bill got planned for help around here in the house, and out in the garden and the barn when it's finished. I do know there'll be a lot to do what with all the animals to tend and wood to get chopped and brought in. I've been thinking. I can keep everything clean, and help with the canning and with everything else you need me to, but I was thinking. You may like to have a cook. You could have a real cook, and I know somebody. You'd like her a lot. I can ask her if you want me to. She just moved back thisaway. She's been staying down around Leeville the past year. She was helping to take care of her poor mother up till the time she died. She came back here last week and is just now starting to look for some work."

"Oh, June Ellen, I don't know. The idea sounds wonderful, but I don't know if it's the right time for us to hire anyone else. I'll mention her to Mr. McMolison and see what he thinks."

The opportunity to hire someone to do the cooking, "to add to their house staff," as Bill phrased it, was an excellent idea. He said the mill was doing even better than he expected, that they could afford to hire someone else, and it would be good to have more help in place when they started their family.

JANIE ARRIVED the following day, and June Ellen was right. She could cook! Janie was a little shorter than June Ellen and a little darker and a lot heavier. She was polite but immediately took charge of her new kitchen. She asked Kate what she wanted cooked but was constantly offering suggestions even as she asked. After surveying the supplies in the pantry and in the smoke house, she helped Kate make lists for the market. There were some items essential to a well-run kitchen, and the McMolison kitchen was lacking.

Janie was fun, always smiling and always busy. Everyone needed to stay clear unless they intended to help. Her apron's bib strings looped over her head, and the waist strings were crossed around her back and tied in the front. The strings were just barely long enough to meet back in front and be tied in a secure little knot. Her hand-wiping cloth stayed snugly tucked under the string at the waist.

Kate had always considered herself a fair cook, but she quickly learned from Janie there was much more to cooking than she had ever known. Janie made all kinds of bread and pastries and her fried chicken had the best-ever crispy fried crust.

Janie had been with the McMolisons a few weeks when—on a day she was frying chicken—Kate came into the kitchen to help. "Grease *pertinerly* hot enough," Janie said, when Kate offered to coat the pieces with flour.

Kate coated each piece and put them in the skillet to fry. Almost immediately she forked a thigh and turned it, then a leg, then the wishbone. Only a few minutes passed before she started the process again.

Janie was close to having a conniption. "Don't play with it. Just let it fry," Janie said sternly without thinking.

"Yes ma'am," Kate responded with a hint of wit and sarcasm. "Dear Janie, would you like me to get out of your way?" Kate was laughing and her eyes were twinkling.

Janie dusted her flour-covered hands together over the biscuit-making bowl and answered with her own bit of sarcasm, "You can stay, Miz Kate. Just don't fool around with my chicken."

Kate did not like any part of getting a chicken from the chicken yard to the frying pan anyway. She wanted no part of wringing a neck or plucking a feather, so she told Janie the kitchen was totally hers on those days. Janie was not really so fond herself of the process, but she did it. The selecting and cleaning had to be done if they were to have fried chicken.

Certainly a more pleasant task was baking, and on many days, the family enjoyed the delicious smell of cake or bread baking. Being close to the kitchen for hot bread or cake was a treat not to be missed. She made cobblers with whatever fruit she had available, huckleberries, dewberries, apples, or peaches. Apple peel most always hung from her knife in continuous little spirals, finally dropping into the scrap bucket. Peach peels, not quite as cooperative, most always broke into at least two pieces before falling to their resting place.

Janie came early every morning. She gathered up stove wood and brought an armload into the house. Within minutes she had a fire burning and the stove heating. By the time it was hot, the biscuits were ready to bake, ham or sausage was in the skillet, and grits were cooking. Janie left the kitchen occasionally to help June Ellen and vice versa, but on most days, she was cooking or getting something ready to cook. She canned and cooked vegetables, cracked and shelled pecans, and washed hundreds of pots and pans. Almost singlehandedly she prepared three meals a day and cleaned up after each one. Kate helped when needed or when she wanted to. She had never enjoyed cooking, but learning from Janie was fun.

* * *

BILL SUGGESTED that Frank and June Ellen move into a little house back in the woods on the property. "Be good to have a man close around on the nights I'm gone," he said.

Frank and June Ellen had never had a house of their own but rather had lived with June Ellen's sister and brother-in-law. Now they had the little property house. The house had not been lived in for a number of years. After the previous owner's wife died, he had moved to another town to live with his daughter.

The porch had mostly rotted boards. Vines were growing in the window openings. Critters had taken up residence, and a few straggly bushes were overgrowing what had once been the yard.

June Ellen and Frank were thrilled. The house and yard would be perfect in no time. They fixed it up and made repairs with lumber brought from the mill.

Chapter Four

KATE WROTE WEEKLY LETTERS to her parents in which she described in great detail the business her husband was building, the number of men he hired, their house, what she had done that day and her plans for the next. With a letter finished, she walked to the box beside the main road, put her letter in and lifted the flag.

Kate, always anxious to hear from her parents, opened their letters the minute she took one from the box. She read as she walked back toward the house. Often she stopped on the front porch, sat in the swing or on one of the front steps, read and delighted in every word.

She refolded the paper. "Mother, I wish you were here. I wish *y'all* were here," Kate said aloud. Her heart brimmed with thoughts of her parents. She wished desperately she were not so far away from them as she read the letters filled with news about her hometown and the people she had left behind.

"We miss you and we love you always, Mother and Daddy," were words that always closed the last line.

She held the pages next to her heart. "At least hearing from you helps to bridge the long miles between us. It's not as good as seeing you, hearing your voices, or feeling your hugs. But it's good. I love you."

THEN ONE DAY, two and a half years after the move to Leaf Creek, a letter arrived from Kate's childhood preacher. In it he described the accident as gently as he could.

Dear Kate,

I do hope this letter finds you well. It is one that gives me great sadness to write.

Your parents' wagon overturned near the river crossing. Something, most probably a snake, must have spooked their horse. The wagon left the road, and one of the wheels hit a big rock, breaking the wheel off the axle.

Kate could hardly believe the preacher's words. Her heart began to race as she fearfully continued reading.

The wagon was upside down next to the riverbank, and your parents were thrown out. They were on the ground near the overturned wagon. Mr. Moses, your folks' neighbor ... I'm sure you remember him ... well, he came upon the accident when he was on his way into town. I'm so sorry, Kate, but he said there was nothing he could do. Your parents were both already dead when he found them. He didn't think it had happened too long before he got there, so he didn't think they suffered.

The details he included in the rest of the letter were almost lost between the tears that filled her eyes and the numbness clouding her brain.

Kate, I'm so very sorry to be sending this news. Since there was no family close by, at least none I knew of, the church folks took care of all the funeral arrangements. Mrs. Moses selected the clothes. I personally selected the scripture and the hymns for the service. The burial was in the church cemetery.

I will look after things here until I hear from you. And anytime you can come, I will go with you to visit the graves.

If there is anything else we can do here, please let us know.

May God comfort you as only He can.

Blessings,
Jonathan Whitefield

Kate instantly felt like a tissue paper version of herself. All the support parts that usually kept her standing faded away. She slumped to her knees and tried to breathe, but suddenly her chest and lungs felt as if they were in a vice grip. The pressure was heavy. It was hard to get air in and out. Kate looked toward the sky and then back at the paper. She was irreparably crushed by the news before her. With an intense resolve, she crumpled the paper as if turning it into a small wad would kill the news written on its surface. "Both already dead, both already dead." The words pounded in her heart and mind. She straightened the paper and tried to smooth it by rubbing it between the thumb and index finger of both hands. She slowly lifted herself to her feet and once again allowed her eyes to see the terrible message she had just received. The words were the same.

Her heart ached and she yearned to be home in South Carolina. She desperately wished to feel the arms of her parents wrapping her in their love, but as her mind grasped the news, she knew that would never be. She would not visit them. They would not visit her. The finality was impossible to think about. Her heart held the reality at bay, but her brain gradually allowed layers of the truth to sink in as her heart and mind began to cope.

The death of her parents left her with a sadness that burrowed into the recesses of her soul. With time and the birth of her own children, she thought about them less frequently, but the loss left a void that was never filled.

***

KATE HAD LOST HER PARENTS. She now had family of another kind. She had Janie, June Ellen, and Frank. They could never replace her mother and father, but being surrounded by them made the news easier to bear.

Friends, too, helped Kate cope with the surreal news and the loneliness. Christine, Laura and Edrie were the three she spent the most time with. Christine and Laura lived on neighboring farms and Edrie lived in town. Together, they quilted, stitched, and chatted one afternoon each week at Edrie's house, in an extra bedroom where the frame could be left in place until a quilt was finished.

Christine, running late, came hurrying in one early June afternoon. "I've got more squash than I can manage. The vines seem to be multiplying, and squash are everywhere. I shoulda just stayed home, but here I am. Can y'all use some? Please say you can."

"Land sakes, no. Not me," Laura responded emphatically. "We've got squash bearing more than ever before. A good year for squash, I guess."

"We have plenty too," Kate chimed in. "I've taken some over to the Epsey's."

"Well, if you're sure you have more than you need, I'd like to get some from you before you give them all away," Edrie said, jumping into the conversation.

"They are yours. Come tomorrow and we'll pick all you want," Christine replied, now speaking as emphatically as Laura had.

"Forget squash," Laura said. "I'm noticing some of the stitches are getting too long. We need to all pay attention to what we're doing." Laura never minded expressing her opinion even when being critical of one of her friends. The others usually listened and took what she said with a grain of salt, but looking closely at their work that afternoon, they agreed more than a few stitches needed redoing.

"Okay Laura, keep us straight," Kate said laughing. "By the way, have y'all been by The Mercantile lately? They have a whole lot of new fabric, some really pretty, I thought. I bought three pieces." Kate sighed and added, "I don't know when I think I have time to sew with all the garden coming in, but I'll get to it at some point."

"Good you bought it," said Edrie encouragingly. "You have to buy it when you find it and then sew it when you can."

The women chatted incessantly while they quilted, and over time they discussed almost every possible topic. Laura, unlike the others, wasn't shy about bringing up personal matters, even about her husband. She never criticized him, but she didn't seem to mind talking about what he did in bed (and what he didn't do that she wished he'd do). The other three just listened and were often too embarrassed to look up from their stitches.

Kate knew she would never share anything personal or negative about Bill. Home life should be private, she felt, and protecting it was proper and essential.

***

"BEEN HERE NEARLY THREE YEARS. Hard to believe," Bill said to Kate as they sat beside the fire. He had come home earlier than usual, and they were sharing what by then had become a rare evening together.

"It is hard to believe." Kate watched the flames flicker. A piece of firewood burned into two pieces, fell into the ashes and spread chunks of red over the embers below.

"Just think about it. I've got the mill and it's going so good I need to hire even more men than I have now. That's something, really something. Can't believe it myself sometimes."

"It is," Kate agreed. "It's truly a blessing it's done so well."

"And the church. Now that I'm an elder, got to keep on top of things there."

"I know, but you'll do a good job. I know you will," Kate said encouragingly. She had no idea what prompted his unexpected sharing but was glad for it, regardless of the reason.

"And the best thing for our future is my election to the county board of supervisors."

"What do you mean, the best thing?"

"Oh, nothing much. Just always good to get to know more people."

Bill knew being county supervisor from the Leaf Creek area would give him opportunity to become friends with other supervisors around the county. He was confident he had all the qualities to become the leader. He had a commanding presence, charisma, and could speak to anyone about anything. He planned for his influence to become significant from county line to county line and beyond.

"Always good to know more people," Bill repeated as he settled deeper in his chair.

Bill had no intention of telling Kate he had aspirations for a higher political office—state representative, maybe governor. As far as he was concerned, women had no business trying to understand political matters.

"It is good to know people," Kate agreed. "Helps us to care about them. At quilting yesterday Laura was telling me about a poor family whose house burned, lost everything. I was thinking we—"

"That's too bad. Do whatever you think. Buy 'em some things." Bill stood. "I'm going to bed. Got to be gone early in the morning."

Kate watched him walk from the room. She knew already and was seeing once again that Bill's increasing power, control and prestige not only consumed his interests, but were also eating away at the fiber of their relationship. He spent little time with her and rarely showed interest in her days. His focus on himself, on his successes, continued to cause her concern.

She sat and watched the slowly dying embers in the fireplace. "Why do I let him trigger me to feel so uneasy and sad?" she wanted to say aloud. Feeling upset at herself, her thoughts continued: "Long days, long nights, he's away. No explanation." His frequent absences began to gnaw at a suspicious side she didn't even know she had.

Kate never discussed her concerns with Bill. Instead, she continually tried to suppress her anxious side. Rather than speak out, she gradually built a strong wall of quiet.

Within a few years they shared a bed but little else.

***

"IT *WILL* BE GOOD to have help when we start our family."

Kate thought about the declaration Bill had made back when he was justifying hiring help. In God's providence, the family arrived as he planned. It was almost as if the children knew they were to be born into this world only after the mill was up and running, the house was built and—most important—the help was in place and waiting on them.

Janie and June Ellen served as midwives for all three McMolison children. The firstborn was Katherine in 1898, then Hannah in 1900, and finally Samuel in 1903.

With every delivery the two women attended Kate's needs with confidence. Janie always said, "Getting children born is a natural thing. The Lawd planned it this way, and He'll see to getting us through it." June Ellen agreed.

Bill missed all three deliveries. He was busy; the mill needed him; the church needed him; the county needed him.

Chapter Five

*I*T WAS JUST AFTER DARK on a fall night in 1907. The moon was not quite full but glowed brightly enough to cast a glow over the front yard and into the edge of the woods. The trees between the house and the road stood tall and black against the softly-lit ground that surrounded their trunks. They stood guard like faithful soldiers protecting the perfect night. Kate, Katherine, and Hannah sat in the bench rocker on the front porch. The rocker, big enough for two adults, was perfect for one adult and two small children. Kate rocked with Hannah on one side and Katherine on the other.

Kate was a wonderful storyteller. That night she told them all about the great flood, about Noah and his family, and how God saved them along with two of each kind of animal. "Just think what it would be like to be completely surrounded by water," Kate began her story. "The water would be constantly lap, lap, lapping at your door." Kate sang the last few words and patted the girls' legs in rhythm as she sang. "Noah had to get all those animals inside before the rain came and started the lap, lap, lapping." Kate was patting the girls and singing again.

"Let's see if we can get some of the really big animals inside first." Kate's voice deepened: "Thump, thump, thump, thump. Here come the elephants and … look! See there, on the back of one, is a little white rabbit." Slowly she continued, "Thump, thump, thump. Here come the elephant's big feet crossing into the ark. Can you see them?" Kate's voice became lighter and high-pitched: "Listen to all the different birds, chirp-chirp, chirp-chirp. They happily sing as they fly inside." Then Kate added, "See the bluebird riding with the rabbit? I bet those two will be friends the whole time they are inside."

Hannah and Katherine snuggled closer to their mother when she suddenly, gruffly, and loudly had lions in the rocker with them: "Rrrrrrrr, rrrrrrrrrr. Rrrrrrrrr, rrrrrrrrrr … the lions roared with all their might!" Kate said in her deepest and most majestic voice. "Mice scurried in between the feet of the lions," she added next, as she ran her fingers quickly down the girls' legs. Both giggled and grabbed their mother's hands. It made Hannah feel squeamish to think of a mouse running down her leg, but the story continued: worms slithered and monkeys swung from one rafter to the next. "Sometimes the monkeys hold hands and swing together," Kate added. "I see one clinging to the neck of a giraffe. He says it's really fun way up there and calls his friend to join him." Kate turned her voice into her best screeching and squealing monkey sounds, and the girls laughed at the thought of swinging from a giraffe's neck.

Kate's voice softened and became more serious. "Noah, his family and all the animals are now inside. God closed the door. He made them safe. The rain is starting." Kate peppered the top of their heads with her fingertips. The pretend raindrops continued for several seconds. "The water lifted the ark right off the land, but Noah and all the creatures were happy and dry." After the story was over, the three sat quietly and continued rocking. They listened to the sound of the crickets making lively conversation in the night air.

HANNAH FELT HER MOTHER SIGH as she leaned against her side. Looking up, she could see tears in Kate's eyes. "Mama, are you crying?" she asked.

Katherine quickly looked into her mother's face and leaned in closer, trying to provide comfort. Both girls knew their mother was sometimes sad. During those times she would be very quiet, and although she never failed to give them her attention, they knew it was sometimes hard for her to laugh and have fun. On that night she had suddenly slipped into a sad place, and tears filled her eyes before she could stop them. Hannah and Katherine had seen their mother sad before, but had not often seen her cry.

"I'm fine," Kate said, wiping her eyes with the back of her hand. Then, with an arm around each girl, she hugged them tightly, patted them, and said, "It's late, time for bed."

Once they were in bed, Kate came in to listen to their prayers. "Dear God, please bless Mama and help her to not be sad," Hannah prayed.

Tears again began to mist over Kate's eyes, but the room was almost dark, so neither Hannah nor Katherine noticed. "Good night," Kate said as she kissed each girl on the forehead. "I love you."

"We love you, too," were the sweet words that floated through the darkness.

THE STILLNESS OF THE NIGHT, broken by the constant chirping of the crickets, had robbed Kate's heart of all lightheartedness and peace. The chirping was a lonely sound that reminded her of Samuel and his last terrible night. The night and the sounds brought melancholy that weighed down gladness and smothered her joy.

Kate wished for her mother. It had been several years since the death of her parents, yet she often longed to tell her about Katherine and Hannah … and about her precious Samuel.

"I need her wisdom. I want her comfort. I want her." Kate's silent words burst from her heart. Tears rolled down her cheeks, and choking sobs filled her throat.

Truths weighing heavily on her mind left her with incredible feelings of weariness, but she was determined to protect her family. "I'll keep the secrets for the sake of my girls. I'd never tell anyone that Bill is not everything they and the rest of the town and county think him to be."

Kate crawled slowly into bed and pulled the covers close under her chin. As her head sank into the pillow, she said to the stillness around her, "Life is not what I thought it would be, not what I planned."

The slight but familiar squeak of the front door filled the hall. Kate's sobs ceased. A nervous tightness filled her chest, and she tried to steady her breathing. She prayed her husband would think she was asleep; she desperately hoped he would have no reason or desire to wake her. She hated and loved the man coming to her bed.

HANNAH AND KATHERINE had heard the soft sobs of their mother as they lay quietly in their bed. They knew she stayed sad about losing Samuel. They did too. Their shoulders touched, providing a sense of comfort as they each waited for sleep to come.

Hannah kept thinking about the story Kate had just told them. "God kept Noah's family safe." The words pierced Hannah. "*Why didn't you keep Samuel safe?*" She almost screamed at God out loud before she caught herself. Remembering Samuel so frightened made her angry, nervous, and scared all over again.

Hannah's heart pounded as she thought back to that fateful night. Samuel was barely three, and even though she was only five at the time, the memory was embedded deep in her mind. She and Katherine both still had nightmares in which they relived the terror and heard the trembling voice of their little brother.

It was the night of the family's deepest and darkest secret. It was the night from almost a year before, the night never to be spoken of but impossible to forget.

* * *

YES, IMPOSSIBLE TO FORGET. A partial moon had glowed that night, but the house was dark and quiet. Everyone was home.

"Mommy, Mommy," Samuel had called from his room adjoining the girls' room.

Hannah and Katherine, awakened by his call, rushed to get to him before his cries woke their parents. They knew their father often got mad at Samuel, demanding he do nothing wrong, demanding he act grown up. He had whipped him once for leaving one of his arrowheads on the floor. As little girls, their father had never been so harsh with them. They didn't understand why he was so hard on Samuel.

What they did know was they would do their best to protect their little brother any time they could. On that night they had not gotten to him in time.

"Samuel, be quiet. Hush that noise," their father bellowed as he crossed the hall into Samuel's room with their mother close behind him.

"Bill," she spoke softly, hoping to calm him, "I will see about him. Please go on back to bed."

"No, I'll do it. He's got to learn he can't be screaming out in the night. If he has wet himself again, he's got to learn better. I can't be having a boy of mine growing up a bed wetter." His voice was loud and filled the whole house.

"Please, Bill," she pleaded. "Please don't. Please. He's just a little boy." Kate rushed to grab her baby, but Bill shoved her to one side and snatched Samuel up and into his arms. He headed down the hall and out the back door.

Samuel cried and called, "Mommy, Mommy!"

Hannah and Katherine were frozen, unnoticed, against Samuel's bedroom wall.

"Oh, Bill, NO! NO! What are you doing?" Kate screamed.

Hannah and Katherine had never heard their mother raise her voice to their father before. They eased into the open hall, where they had a moonlit view of their father holding Samuel over *the open well*. "You stop wetting the bed, or I'll drop you in and you'll really be wet! No son of mine can be wetting the bed," Bill shouted into Samuel's fear-filled face.

As Hannah and Katherine saw their father holding Samuel with outstretched arms and heard his hateful words, their knees buckled. They crumpled into a ball on the floor with their eyes closed and their hands over their ears. They could not bear the distressing screams of their baby brother's fear. They were helpless and they knew their mother, too, was helpless.

"Bill, *stop*!" Kate screamed. She reached for Samuel. As she did, Bill took one hand from Samuel to push her away. Samuel slipped from his grasp just enough that he hit his head on the brick edge of the well. In horror and panic, Kate screamed again: *"Stop. What are you doing? Give him to me.*" With trembling, fear-filled arms, she reached for her baby.

Terror pulsed through Bill's soul as he pushed Samuel into his mother's arms. "Here, you want him?" he shouted wildly. "Here, take him. Keep him quiet."

Bill rushed back inside. The realization that he had almost dropped his son into the deep well caused a fear with which he was unfamiliar. He hurried to get back into bed and slid deep under the covers, hoping to hide from the reality of what he had done. He had made his point and there would be no further discussion, but at what cost? His attempt to justify his action seemed futile, even to him.

The covers did not help. He tossed and turned. Over and over he asked himself, "Why? Why? How could I. Too horrible." When he closed his eyes he saw the darkness of the well. He saw the fear in Samuel's eyes, but he did not get out of bed. He did not go the short distance across the hall. He did not say, "I'm sorry." He felt regret and repeatedly asked himself why … but his pride held him in place.

Bill sunk deeper into the covers and tried to console himself. "I'm his father. I have to teach him to be a man. Starting tomorrow I'll do better. I'll be a better father."

He heard the clock strike every quarter hour as he waited for daylight.

KATE HUGGED Samuel to her chest and watched Bill disappear into the house. She then sat on the back step with Samuel in her lap and embraced him tightly. His cries changed to intermittent sobs, and his head rested safely against her bosom as she rocked side to side. With every breath, she said, "I'm so sorry. So, so sorry. It's gonna be alright. I love you."

A light came flickering from the edge of the woods. Although Kate couldn't see, she knew immediately it was Frank or June Ellen. It was both; once they were close enough to see Kate sitting there on the step holding Samuel, Frank held back. June Ellen came up to the steps. "What're you doing out here, Miz Kate? Something wrong with our baby?"

"Just a little accident. I think he's fine," Kate answered.

June Ellen leaned over. "Sweet boy, you don't need to be out here in the middle of the night." She gently pushed Samuel's hair off his forehead and then started to run her fingers across his temple toward the back.

Samuel grabbed her hand. "No. It hurts."

"What'd you do? Let June Ellen see."

Kate spoke up. "I think he's okay. Just bumped his head."

June Ellen held the lamp up and pushed Samuel's hair out of her way. "No wonder we heard you scream. You got a big old nasty lick. Bleeding's 'bout stopped and I don't see swelling."

"I'll get it cleaned and get him back to bed," Kate said softly. "Thanks for coming. Tell Frank thanks too. Y'all go on back home."

"Are you sure? Don't you want me to help?"

"No, no," Kate answered quickly. "He's okay. Be sore for a day or two." She leaned over and kissed the top of his head. "All of us need to get to bed."

"Okay then. Night, Samuel. See you in the morning. We'll get Janie to make you something special, whatever you want."

"Night," Samuel said softly.

HANNAH AND KATHERINE were still crouched in the corner of the hall when their mother came in carrying Samuel. She saw them and, with Samuel still in her arms, she tucked them back into bed, kissed them and said, "Everything will be alright." They were not sure things would ever be okay again, but they both knew she wanted them to be.

Kate washed the cut on Samuel's head. She lovingly changed him into dry clothes, covered the damp spot on the bed with a piece of oilcloth, and covered the oilcloth with a dry cotton sheet. She tucked Samuel in.

"Mommy, Mommy, stay with me. Please stay," he said.

"Yes, I'm staying. I'm right here with you," she whispered softly while gently brushing his cheek with her hand. Kate knew her staying might anger Bill, but it didn't matter to her. Samuel had just survived a more terrifying experience than she would have ever imagined possible. Bill had had outbursts of temper, but what just happened to her family that night was inconceivable to her. Kate's heart raced and beat so violently it pounded her eardrums. Her whole body trembled as her shaking hands eased the quilt up and over Samuel's little frame.

Kate knew Bill had scared even himself. She could still see the fright and horror that filled his face when he pushed Samuel into her arms. The realization that he had almost dropped his only son had terrified him. She hoped the incident would bring back some of his humility and gentleness, but the anger and rage which filled her throat and chest at that moment made it hard to breathe and smothered the slightest thread of sympathy or forgiveness.

Kate eased down on the bed beside Samuel. She gently stroked his forehead and rubbed one of his arms with her still-quivering hand. Samuel drifted to sleep and, finally, Kate settled enough that she, too, dropped off to sleep. She awoke a little before dawn. The events of the night came into her heart and mind like a crushing flood. It took a second, but she realized she didn't hear breathing. She felt for the little chest beside her and was suddenly trembling again.

"Samuel! Samuel!" she cried with breathless shrillness. The tension in her chest and throat erupted violently and prevented the loud scream she'd intended. She grabbed Samuel into her arms. "Samuel, wake up!" She shook him gently at first and then more vigorously. "Samuel! Samuel!"

Her mind slowly grasped that shaking him and calling his name was no use. His body was limp. It was still warm but draped across her like a rag. Kate dropped to the floor with his little body across her lap and held him tightly to her chest. She rocked back and forth and sobbed. Her voice was paralyzed in her throat. She was paralyzed. She could not make a sound. She could not move from the floor. All she could do was hold and hug her baby as tears ran down her face and into the strands of his hair.

"No, no. God, please, no … no not my baby. How can this be?" She asked the question, but knew she didn't want an answer.

JANIE, UNAWARE of the previous night's events, had arrived before dawn. A fire was burning in the stove and breakfast was almost ready.

Bill hadn't slept. He knew Kate never returned to their bed, and although he was glad she had stayed with Samuel, he wouldn't tell her so. "I'll be sure she knows she can't keep on coddling him if he's to grow up strong," he thought. "I'll tell her exactly how it is going to be. Any son of mine must learn to be a man." He planned his instructions to be the first thing he said to her.

It was still mostly dark in the house. The sun was just coming up when Bill stopped in Samuel's room on his way to the kitchen. The sight in the shadows before him was incapacitating. He stood numb. Before him on the floor were his wife and his lifeless son, the son who only a moment before he was going to make a man. "What happened? What are you doing?" he screamed.

"He's not breathing. I just woke up and he's not breathing." Kate could barely get the words out.

"Not breathing. What do you mean? Why didn't you call me? Samuel! Samuel!" Bill yelled as he grabbed his son from Kate's arms.

Realizing there was no life in the little body, Bill gently laid Samuel back across Kate's lap and knelt on the floor in front of her. Hannah and Katherine, awakened by the shouting, ran into the room and dropped to the floor beside their mother.

"What's wrong? What's wrong with Samuel?" they both asked.

Kate didn't answer. She put one of her arms around them the best she could and continued to hold Samuel with the other. They rocked together.

Bill stroked Samuel's face and rubbed his legs. "He can't be. He just can't be." His voice was barely audible. He slipped sideways from his knees to a sitting position on the floor and sat with his head in his hands.

Janie heard the crying and the shouting and hurried to find out what was wrong. When she entered Samuel's room, her knees went weak and her lungs would hardly work. She rushed to Kate's side, reached over her shoulder, touched Samuel's face, and felt his chest. Then she screamed, "Oh Lawd! Lawd, help us, help us please! Lawd, you took my baby. Why? You gave us this precious life. Please don't take it back. Not now, not now. Oh God, please, Oh God, not now."

BILL LIFTED HIMSELF FROM THE FLOOR. He stood for a long moment without speaking. Then in a soft voice he said, "We have to make preparations." Kate glared up at him. Without her uttering a sound, Bill knew Kate was laying the blame at his feet.

He walked slowly from the house, went to the mill and, once there, took great pains to choose the best available lumber to make the little casket that would hold his only son. Into that casket would go his heart, and with it his chance to love his son the way a father should.

The truth of those last twelve hours was almost more than Bill could bear. He would try to bury it, but he knew he never could. On his way back home from the mill he left the main road and drove down a secluded logging road. When he was well out of sight, he stopped the wagon, got out, and walked to the nearest tree. With his back against the trunk, he slid all the way to the ground. He held his face in his hands and sobbed. In the midst of a flood of tears, his voice rang out, "Please forgive me, Samuel. Please forgive me. I'm so sorry."

"COME ON, Miz Kate," Janie said lovingly while reaching to help Kate and the girls from the floor. Janie took Samuel in her arms and was hugging him when June Ellen arrived.

"Lawd, what's happened? Have mercy. Help us, Lawd." She looked at Kate. "What happened? He was fine." Kate didn't answer.

June Ellen dropped to the floor beside the bed, buried her face in the covers, and continued to sob pleadings to God. Hannah and Katherine moved to her. They knelt, one on each side with their little white arms around her strong, dark neck. Instinctively, June Ellen encircled them with her arms and drew their little frames close to her own.

After praying, June Ellen lifted herself to her feet. "Come on, girls, come with me. We'll get you dressed and then see about something to eat."

They dressed. They made their bed. They went to the kitchen where food was already prepared. Grits, eggs, and bacon—food they usually enjoyed—was prepared, but it was impossible to eat. Each girl was too full of sadness. They sat crying softly. Neither of them spoke of what had happened during the night.

June Ellen hugged one and then the other. "We'll make it, we'll make it," she kept saying. "We'll make it. Lawd Jesus gonna take care of us."

June Ellen left the girls just long enough to go tell Frank about Samuel. She knew he was probably milking Betsy, one of the two milk cows. She walked across the yard and into the front of the barn. "Frank? Frank, where are you?" she called.

"Here. In Betsy's stall. What're you doing out here?" Frank yelled from the low milk stool where he sat coaxing milk from Betsy.

"It's awful. It's awful, Frank. Our Little Samuel's dead. Miz Kate found him this morning." June Ellen leaned against the barn wall and dissolved into uncontrolled sobs.

"*What?!?* Can't be! What are you saying?" Frank asked, not wanting to believe what he'd just heard.

June Ellen wiped her face with both hands, rubbed her hands down the sides of her dress and then lifted her dress tail to blot away lingering tears. "You need to stop what you're doing soon as you can, and go tell the preacher. He'll get the word out."

"Something more happen last night?" Frank asked.

"I don't know." June Ellen stood shaking her head slowly. "I just don't know. Nobody said if it did. I gotta get back to Hannah and Katherine. This is an awful day. Gonna be an awful few days. Lawd help us."

Frank, devastated, stood in disbelief, and June Ellen headed back toward the house.

Betsy continued munching hay in the trough in front of her. Her tail swished sideways to shoo a fly. "Gotta get you milked." Sadness soaked Frank's words as he patted Betsy's side and lowered himself to the stool. "How could it be? How could it be?" he kept repeating. His insides wept.

With the milking finished, Frank saddled one of the horses and headed into town to find Preacher Echols.

CHAPTER SIX

61

THE UNDERTAKER in Leeville sometimes came to Leaf Creek to prepare a body for burial. Other times friends did the necessary tasks of bathing, dressing and laying the deceased out appropriately.

Kate did not want the undertaker or friends. She wanted to take care of Samuel herself. It was the final thing she could do for her baby. With Janie's help, she bathed his little body and washed and combed his hair. Janie felt a nervous glance from Kate when she saw the abrasions on Samuel's neck and the deeper cut on the side of his head. "What's this?" she asked quietly as she ran her fingers through Samuel's hair.

"He fell, bumped his head last night. He was fine. I held him for a while and he was fine—I *thought* he was fine." Tears filled Kate's eyes and her voice broke.

"I'm sure he was, least so far as anything you could do," Janie assured her.

"Let's get his clothes on," Kate said hurriedly, not looking up.

The two women dressed Samuel in his white Sunday shirt, navy blue pants, brown leather belt and white socks. Janie felt something was terribly wrong, but neither of them said another word.

Once Samuel was cared for, Janie turned her attention to Kate. "I'm heating up plenty of water for you to have a bath." Janie knew warm water would not lessen Kate's grief, but she hoped it might provide a small measure of comfort.

Kate was numb and silent as she went through the motions of dressing. She felt dazed and wished desperately to wake from the horrible reality in which she found herself, but the nightmare wouldn't go away. It was real. Her baby was dead.

June Ellen had laid out a navy blue dress. Kate slipped her arms into the sleeves and began mechanically to button the front. The belt, made from the same navy fabric as the dress, buckled easily around her slim waist. Kate hadn't made the dress with mourning and funerals in mind, yet she was putting it on to mourn—to mourn her own son.

"Whate'er My God Ordains Is Right" tried to push its way into Kate's mind, but she pushed back. She pushed against the words with her whole being. Nothing seemed right, nothing at all. Haltingly, the words continued to filter in: *My Father's care is round me there; he holds me that I shall not fall.* "I don't feel anything holding me," Kate thought. "I'm falling, caving in. It hurts all over. Strength? Where is it? Where are your everlasting arms?" Kate pleaded. "You promised them. Please, please how can I ever understand?"

Kate finished dressing and did the best she could to prepare for what was coming. She felt certain that Bill's overpowering desire to appear strong and capable, regardless of circumstances, would not change even in the midst of so horrible a time. She knew, too, that without question, he would expect his entire family to stand strong together (even though at that moment, Kate didn't care about Bill's expectations or feel like meeting them). Her baby was dead, and all she wanted to do was collapse to the floor in darkness and cry. She wished she could scream at Bill or at God or at somebody, but she couldn't. She could barely breathe.

KATE DIDN'T KNOW that Bill, too, was completely shattered. He was weak, vulnerable and scared. She would never know, because he would never tell her.

She didn't know that right then he was still in the woods on his knees, bent over so completely that his face touched the straw. He cried, "Why God, why? Samuel barely slipped. It can't be my fault. I beg you, let me somehow know I didn't kill my son. Please God, please!"

Lifting his face toward the sky, he shouted, "Oh God, hear me! My family's in the middle of an awful time, the most difficult you could send. Please, God, please help me get through this." Then bending over with his face near the ground and his forearms holding him, he cried again, "I trust you. I do. I want to. Help me now, today. Help me to get myself together. Help me be strong."

Deeply broken, Bill lifted himself to his feet and leaned again against the tree. "I've got to get myself together," he said to himself. "Can't let anyone see me like this. I must be stable and strong. I can't crumble. I can't."

He walked to the wagon, drank a few sips of water from his water jug, and then soaked his handkerchief. After wiping his face with the cool, wet fabric, he folded it over his reddened eyes. He brushed straw from his pants and straightened his shirt. With some measure of proper appearance regained, he lifted himself onto the wagon seat, gently tapped Pete's back with the reins, and weakly double-clicked his tongue against his teeth. Pete began to pull the wagon toward home.

Bill sighed hard, and with deep resolve he pledged to leave his grief-filled angst in the woods. People would be watching to see his response in the face of tragedy, and he wanted them to see stoic strength—not the shattering weakness that filled his being. He would stand beside his wife and daughters, and together they would mourn with dignity during this difficult time. He would be strong, as expected. Kate, Katherine and Hannah would be ever polite, as expected, and ever silent—also as expected.

JANIE AND JUNE ELLEN set about putting the kitchen in order. "I can't say 'cause I don't know why, but Miz Kate was out back with Samuel in the night," June Ellen whispered with great concern.

"Whatta you mean, outside? Where?" Janie stopped wiping the stove and looked straight at June Ellen.

"On the back step. Miz Kate was just sitting there, holding him."

"How come you were out there in the middle of the night?" Janie asked.

"We heard loud crying. Sounded like Samuel. Like something was wrong, so we came fast as we could," June Ellen answered, still in a hushed tone.

"What happened?"

"Don't know. Miz Kate just said an accident, but he'd be okay. Did have a right big skinned place on one side a his head. Didn't see lot a swelling though, and bleeding had 'bout stopped far as I could tell."

Janie stood dead still, frowning, eyes squinted together. "What happened then? What'd you do?"

"Miz Kate was just sitting on the step holding Samuel and rocking side to side. I asked if I could help. She told me everything was fine, said go on back to bed. Hated to leave her, but she told me to go. Didn't seem like she wanted to say anything else. Just saying this to you, nobody else."

JANIE WENT TO DRAW WATER from the well to refill the stove reservoir. When she lifted the well cover, she noticed spots on the edge of the opening—spots she had not noticed the day before. Thoughts raced through her mind, unimaginable thoughts. "Blood? Is that blood? How did blood get on the well underneath the lid?"

She stood there and thought about what June Ellen had told her and the cut she had seen on Samuel's head. Her heart pounded. Janie snatched the cloth from under her apron string. She wet it and began to vigorously scrub the spots. She scrubbed until they were just barely noticeable. She—like Kate, Katherine, Hannah, June Ellen and Frank—would remain silent.

THE HOUSE QUICKLY FILLED with people. Everyone brought food; no one would think of coming empty-handed. Janie and June Ellen kept order and were careful to cover each dish with a clean kitchen towel, the edges tucked securely beneath to protect from flies.

Platters of fried chicken arrived first. Drumsticks were Samuel's favorite pieces. Hannah spotted several on one of the platters. She imagined Samuel easing by and sneaking one when no one was looking. He often slipped into the kitchen when Janie was frying chicken. Janie pretended she didn't see him, but she always left the plate close to the edge of the table so hc could easily reach it. While making a big fuss about her chicken disappearing, Janie would look everywhere for the chicken leg and Samuel would laugh. Hannah's heart sank as she thought about Samuel never sneaking or laughing about chicken ever again.

Next came a lady bringing a big pot of chicken and dumplings. Katherine looked at Hannah and said, "She must not know about Janie's chicken and dumplings, or else she's mighty brave to be bringing 'em."

"Right," was all Hannah could manage in response. She was too sad to care.

Kate's quilting friends brought peas, butterbeans and deviled eggs, some cut sideways, some lengthways. The sideways oncs weie tipping over, causing the top of the stuffing to mash and get messy on the plate. "I'll prop 'cm with pickles," Janie said as she took the plate and opened a jar of her homemade pickles.

One of the schoolteachers came in carrying a ham. Boiled potatoes with white gravy and white rice with brown gravy arrived next. A chocolate cake, a syrup cake, a coconut cake, three chocolate pies and two egg-custard pies appeared.

Katherine and Hannah watched the parade of people and the parade of food. If they hadn't felt so sad, the sight might have been comical. Instead they just stood, watched, and wondered who could possibly feel like eating. They certainly didn't. Their mother always took food to other people's houses when somebody died, but the girls had never imagined what it looked like. They desperately wished for the mountain of food to go away and to have Samuel back.

THE WAKE WAS SCHEDULED FOR TWO O'CLOCK. It was a few minutes before two when Mr. McMolison called the girls into the hall from the kitchen. "Are y'all ready? It's time." His voice cracked.

He hesitated. The muscles in his jaw twitched as he clenched his teeth in his effort to maintain composure. "It's time," he said again. "It's time for us to be in the sitting room. Your mother and I will stand together near Samuel, and the two of you stay near."

Katherine and Hannah were silent. They held hands as they followed their parents down the hall and into the sitting room.

Kate and Bill entered first, the girls close behind. A desk had been moved into the hall to make room for the table holding the casket. People were everywhere. The room was abuzz with whispers. People stood and began to gather around Kate and Bill. They ultimately formed a line. Katherine and Hannah wondered at first what they were lining up to do but soon realized every person was going to speak, shake their father's hand, hug their mother and—to their dismay—hug them as well.

Even worse than being hugged repetitively, some people didn't bend quite enough, causing the girls' faces to land in belly buttons or other undesirable places. They learned quickly to turn their heads to one side or the other. They were used to being hugged, but this was different. Neither liked what was happening. Some people hugged too long, some too tightly. Others squeezed. Both girls were anxious for the line to end almost before it got started, but peering out the front window, they could see the yard full of people and a line that looked endless.

Mrs. Cain was an especially large woman. When Katherine spotted her, she escaped by saying she needed to be excused. She hurriedly left the room, ran down the hall, and out the back door. Hannah, though dreading the fat that was about to envelope her, stood quietly. Just as she expected, Mrs. Cain leaned over and pulled her close. Through layers of flesh and ruffle-trimmed cotton, Hannah heard her muffled words: "Oh darling, so sorry." At least Hannah thought that was what she said. She wasn't sure, as her face was squished into a very large bosom that smelled strongly of lavender.

Katherine watched from the door and returned only when Mrs. Cain had left the house and was well out into the yard. "Whew," she said as she took her place beside Hannah. "How was it?"

"Wasn't fun," Hannah replied somberly.

Hannah wanted to follow the people out, run around the house, and hide in the pantry next to the kitchen where Janie and June Ellen were working. She knew she couldn't, though, as her father would not approve. He would say that leaving was not proper behavior. Then, too, she felt bad that she did not want to stay in there with Samuel. She stood close to her mother, and Katherine stood close to her.

ALONG WITH THE HUGS CAME CONDOLENCES, most sounding crazy to Hannah and Katherine. Mrs. Perkins patted Katherine's shoulder and whispered, "It's gonna be okay."

"No, it's *not* gonna be okay!" Katherine yelled silently. She wanted to knock Mrs. Perkins' hand off her shoulder and tell her Samuel was dead and that it was not okay.

Soon came Mrs. Echols, the preacher's wife. She wore a blue dress and black lace-up shoes. Her hair was pulled into a tight bun on the back of her head. She had been in line a long time and was finally getting a chance to offer her best words of consolation. "Samuel's so happy up in heaven with Jesus," she said.

The girls had always liked Mrs. Echols, but on that day she sounded as confused as everybody else. Mrs. Echols, after all, wasn't standing beside *her* little brother, dead and in a box. *They* were. It was their little brother who was dead, and they had no information about Samuel being happy in his new circumstance. And even if he was happy, *they* were not. But they answered politely: "Yes, ma'am. Thank you."

The yard and house were both still full of people by late afternoon and all of them wanted to speak and hug. The girls stayed in their proper place but were glad when their mother suggested they sit on the sofa and rest a bit. They were glad for the reprieve from standing and thought it would be a respite from being consoled. Some people did skip them, but most did not.

"The Lord knows best. You girls be big and strong for your mother," said Mrs. Lamb, the lady from the bank, as she hugged them both at the same time. "I know you will miss Samuel, but always remember he is with God and in a better place."

All both girls felt like doing was crying, and they wondered just how all these people came to know so much about what was going on with Jesus and Samuel and God anyway. The only thing they knew was that they wanted Samuel back with them, and not lying in a wonderfully-made, fine wooden box on a table in the sitting room.

Kate stood dutifully beside Bill and continued to warmly greet each person, even though all she wanted to do was run to her bedroom, close the door and scream, "Why, why, why?"

Bill, dressed in his dark gray suit and white shirt, was somber but warm as he, too, successfully masked anguish. He firmly shook the hand of each man that came, and he responded with kind words of appreciation to the women. He thanked each person for the kindnesses being shown his family and nodded his agreement with those who shared wisdom about God's will, about God giving, and God taking away.

Kate's fists clenched at the repeated words about their all-knowing God. God's sovereignty had always been her resting place, but hearing about it over and over on that day coupled with "precious in the sight of the Lord is the death of His saints" made her chest tighten in anger. Embracing the comfort and truth of the Word seemed far away. She wanted God to know Samuel was precious to her—very precious— and she wanted him back.

Katherine and Hannah watched as the people streamed past the open box with Samuel inside, every person saying something. Katherine leaned her head toward Hannah's ear. She whispered, "Did you hear what Mrs. Peavy said?"

"No, what?"

"He looks peaceful, as if he's asleep."

"What does she mean? He doesn't look like he's asleep to me. Why would anybody dress up, lay flat with their legs straight out and their arms folded over their stomach, and then get in a box to sleep? Samuel sure wouldn't. She's loony."

"How sweet and natural he looks," said yet another lady. She and a companion stood looking at Samuel for what seemed an eternity. They looked down into his face, shook their heads from side to side ever so slowly, and dabbed tears from their cheeks with handkerchiefs. They kept speaking back and forth to each other. "He's just so natural. It's a blessing."

Hannah and Katherine had thoughts of their own: "It's not natural. He can't open his eyes, he can't talk, he can't breathe, he's completely still, he's dressed in his Sunday shirt and pants he *never* liked to wear, and he's lying in a box on a table in the house. Something is not right about these people." They wanted to scream and let everybody know there was nothing natural at their house on that day.

Toward the end of the wake, the girls were standing near their parents again. They overheard Mrs. Bexley talking to Kate, saying, "He is beautiful, Kate, looks like an angel. God probably already has him singing in the angel choir."

The girls looked at each other with knowing eyes. They started to whisper at the same time. "She doesn't know what she's talking about," Katherine said first.

"She must think God puts wings on people and turns them into angels," Hannah replied. "Even if He did, Samuel wouldn't want to sing in a big ole choir."

"I know. The only time he liked to sing was when he was with us." Katherine replied more loudly than she intended. Kate glanced her way with her eyes a bit squinted and her mouth offering a pursed-lip smile. It was a look of caution both Hannah and Katherine were famil-iar with, but it didn't matter. Mrs. Bexley hadn't heard the comment as she continued to share her knowledge about God and angels.

Kate stood straight, her hands waist-high in front of her, being held by Mrs. Bexley. She smiled slightly, listened patiently and remained quiet—though every part of her wanted to lash out just like her girls had done. Unspoken words pounded her insides. "God doesn't need Samuel," she thought. "He doesn't need anything, but I do. I need my little Samuel back."

Chapter Seven

"WHEW. THANKFUL we have cold weather," the girls heard Mrs. Clara Jones say (she was one of the church ladies). "Sure helps keep the body. Hot weather can take a toll in a mighty big hurry." Mrs. Jones was always organizing. She was flitting around, fluffing chair cushions and straightening doilies. Katherine and Hannah had heard their mother refer to her often when the women were planning any activity that involved life at the church. She was in charge of everything from making schedules to caring for the sick to being sure the crocheted scarf on the pulpit hung straight. If a member had a question about anything at the church, they knew to ask Mrs. Jones.

"Yea, the cold is good," a second lady answered. The girls knew her as Miss Polly. "It's cold in here now," she said as she pulled her coat tighter around her plump middle. "Gonna get colder tonight when the temperature drops. We need to be sure there's plenty blankets for the people sitting up with the body."

"Oh, you're right. We do. I'll ask June Ellen to get a couple for us," Mrs. Jones replied, as she stood near Samuel. Her hands were on her hips as she looked around the room. "Don't want to forget anything. Bill said the service will be at the church tomorrow morning at eleven o'clock."

"That'll be good," responded Miss Polly, who was most always jolly. She laughed a lot and spent more time with the children than with other adults. When she helped each year with the Christmas pageant she made everything fun. She didn't mind pretending to be one of the animals, braying like a donkey or baaing like a sheep. As a wise man or shepherd, she stood straight and tall and joyfully encouraged the children to do the same. Katherine and Hannah loved Miss Polly, and they knew she had loved Samuel. She had gotten on the floor and helped him be one of the sheep for the last pageant. She seemed different to them on this day—she wasn't laughing, but that was good because they didn't feel like laughing either. Nobody did.

"I'm sure Preacher Echols and the deacons already know the plans," said Mrs. Jones. "I'll check with them to be sure." She looked around the room again. "Think everything's back straight. I'm going to find June Ellen. Need to get blankets before I forget." Mrs. Jones left the room and disappeared down the hall.

Realizing the fireplace would remain dark and cold just as their insides seemed to be, the girls retreated to the kitchen and found warmth and refuge in the space behind the wood stove. Sitting on the floor with their heads propped against the wall, they dozed for a time as adult voices continued to hum though the house.

* * *

THE NEXT DAY WAS extremely cold. More food was brought to the McMolison's kitchen. Two ladies from Leaf Creek Presbyterian's Ladies Aide Society came with two colored women. They took over the running of the kitchen so Janie and June Ellen could go to the funeral.

For the funeral Kate wore a black dress made of soft wool. It buttoned in the back, had a standing collar, and two pleats from the shoulders to the waist in the front. The skirt reached her ankles and had a slight fullness beginning below her knees. The long sleeves were secured at the wrist with five small fabric-covered buttons and fit easily under her black full-length wool coat. She was glad to have the veil. It fell from the wide brim of her black felt hat, and helped hide her from sympathetic or curious eyes. Except for three small black felt flowers adorning one side, the hat was plain.

Bill also wore black. His suit was three-piece and made of wool, as was his knee-length topcoat. The perfect knot of his black and gray four-in-hand tie was snug against the collar of his white shirt. His trousers were cuffed and fell just to the top of his black shoes. The only hint of color was the tiny blue feather tucked in the band of his black wool Homburg hat.

Katherine and Hannah did not wear black. Katherine's dress and matching coat were dark forest green and Hannah's were navy blue. Their coats reached almost to their ankles, but for extra warmth June Ellen wrapped their shoulders with wool shawls. They all rode together in the wagon to the funeral. Mr. McMolison drove and Kate sat beside him on the bench seat. Katherine and Hannah sat on the floor of the wagon bed close behind their parents, and Frank, Janie and June Ellen sat at the very back with their legs swinging down. Not a word was spoken.

The family held hands as they walked down the aisle. The preacher went first, followed by the four men carrying Samuel. The casket was small. Two men could have carried it easily, but Bill did not want to show favoritism between the four men who served with him as elders at Leaf Creek Presbyterian. They each wore dark suits, dark ties and white shirts. A bundle of pine boughs with pinecones still attached almost covered the entire top of the little casket. Blue and brown ribbons secured the branches and dropped to either side.

Staring at the casket, Hannah felt as if she might smother just imagining what it must be like for Samuel. She knew he would not like being closed up in there. He would want to cry and kick to get out. She wanted to cry and kick too, but she couldn't. Her left hand was in Katherine's and her right hand was nearly squeezed white by her mother. All she could do was keep her feet moving forward.

The church was quiet except for the piano music. Miss Velma played "Jesus Loves Me." Preacher Echols led them to the first pew on the right side of the church. Hannah and Katherine sat motionless, Katherine beside their father and Hannah beside their mother. Janie,

June Ellen and Frank stood in the balcony. Their hearts were breaking just like the hearts on the front row, but the church didn't have seating for coloreds. They had to stand out of the way, and that was in the back of the balcony.

It was warm in the church. Fires had been burning in the little wood stoves since early that morning. Preacher Echols and the deacons did what they could to make everyone as comfortable as possible. The pews were full. Leaf Creek Presbyterian was not accustomed to being the focus of most of Greene County, but on that day it was. Mr. McMolison's status in the county meant anyone of importance (and others not so important) had come. "I'm sure people will want to come. We need to be ready," he'd said to Preacher Echols the day before. To Bill, the thought of an overflowing church was somehow a thread of pleasure in the midst of this sadness—he saw it as a tribute to him and his family.

Horse-drawn buggies and wagons filled the churchyard. People wrapped in blankets from head to toe came from all over the county. They had endured perhaps the coldest day of the year to be present at the sad occasion. Preacher Echols, thin and short in stature, felt large and important upon seeing the crowd and seized the opportunity. His role as pastor of the church where every influential person in the county had assembled energized him, and his size belied his deep, strong voice.

"The Lord is my shepherd, I shall not want," he began. He looked straight at the family there on the front row and continued reciting the twenty-third Psalm. His clear, confident words filled the sanctuary. He went on to talk about Jesus preparing mansions in heaven and taking the sting out of death. He quoted some man named John Jasper who said Jesus came and died to make the graves of his children nice and smooth for them to pass through.

To Hannah, that thought sounded nice but a little strange. She couldn't help but wonder how someone would pass through a grave, especially after all the dirt was piled on top.

Katherine was barely listening. She sat looking at her father's hands clasped together in his lap. She remembered them hugging her, though not in a long time. Her thoughts were confusing and muddled. She wished he would put his arms around her right then, but at the same time she kept seeing Samuel grabbed up and crying. Everybody stood and sang "What a Friend We Have in Jesus." Katherine couldn't sing. The lump in her throat was too big. She wanted the music to stop and the preacher to be quiet. She didn't want to leave Samuel, but she wanted to be back home.

Hannah couldn't sing either. She stood with her hands clutching the back of the pew in front of her. She kept thinking, "If Jesus was my friend, why did he take Samuel like He did?" She desperately wished for things to be back to normal.

During the singing of the last verse, Preacher Echols started walking back down the aisle. The same four men who carried Samuel inside the church picked up the little coffin and followed him. Bill reached for Katherine's hand. Katherine grabbed Hannah's with her other hand. Kate gently blotted tears with her lace-edged white handkerchief before pushing the handkerchief into her right hand. She breathed deeply and reached for Hannah's unclaimed hand. The family eased from between the pews and followed.

Since the graveyard was only a quarter of a mile down the road, the men kept walking, carrying Samuel's casket between them. Everybody followed. It was colder than when they had gone inside. The wind blew against their faces, but they walked on without a word between them.

Once in the graveyard, the family stood near the hole. It was deep and dark. Hannah couldn't think of leaving her little brother in that cold, dark space. She grasped Katherine's hand and clung to the side of her mother.

Bill, standing next to Kate, continued his posture of strength, although it was becoming more and more difficult. The weight bearing down on his heart and lungs was almost more than he could keep controlled. His breathing was shallow. "Got to hold it together," he kept saying to himself as he squeezed his eyes closed in an effort to keep tears from spilling out. Bill looked again at the little casket. "I'm so, so sorry, Samuel. Please forgive me. I never told you, but I love you so much."

Janie, June Ellen and Frank stood back behind the white mourners. Katherine thought they were too far away to see the darkness where they would be leaving Samuel, and they should be glad. She wished she were standing with them.

The preacher started again. "When one of God's children dies, his soul is received and accompanied by the blessed angels." He talked on for another minute or two, but Hannah focused on God's angels. She felt a tiny bit of comfort for the first time since Samuel died. It made her feel better to think that angels were taking care of him and loving him and that if he wet the bed, nobody would be mad. In fact, they would probably just fan his sheets dry with their wings, and no one would ever know. That thought made her heart feel better. She continued to dwell on the angels, even after the dirt was thrown into the grave and over the wooden casket. As she remembered the words of "Jesus Loves Me," she visualized Samuel in one of the mansions. Jesus and the angels were there. The streets were actually made of gold, and pearls were on the gates. It was a beautiful place, and Samuel was happy.

Chapter Eight

BILL FOUGHT HARD to push the guilt and grief away. As he ran from the anxious void that haunted him, he accepted an appointment to the board of the Leaf Creek Bank. He pushed for increased mill production, added extra travel days to Leeville, assumed new committee responsibilities, and off-handedly explained away many overnight absences from home. The constant striving brought him little comfort.

Kate knew that he was trying to escape the painful reality that constantly gnawed at his conscience. He never shared one sorrow, one pain, or one fear. Alone, he faithfully nursed the contrition and blame that simmered in his psyche.

Kate, too, was struggling. She was certain the accident with Samuel had been just that (a terrible accident), but she still blamed Bill for the raw pain that lingered in her heart. Part of her felt sad for him, but a lot of her was angry. She needed and wanted to share with him the pain she knew they both felt, but his aloneness left her alone.

They never spoke about Samuel.

THE BUSYNESS BILL SOUGHT filled his every waking minute. In Leaf Creek he began to push plans for a new school. He worked with the architect and chaired the committee to raise the necessary money.

Two years after Samuel's death, the children of Leaf Creek moved into a four-room, two-story structure with a wood-burning heater in every room, by far the nicest school in the county.

During that same period of time, Bill read an article in the *Christian Observer* about a company in North Carolina that was building factory-made church pews. The picture of the pew end, though black and white, spurred his desire. With easily-obtained church approval, he ordered solid oak pews with curved armrests and a carved cross centering the rounded top. The old homemade wood slat pews were uncomfortable. No one would object to getting new, nicer, more comfortable ones. Securing the necessary funds was a major step, but Bill was unwavering in his effort. Only a year and a half passed before they had the entire amount.

He was instrumental, too, in the oversight of maintenance at all the Leaf Creek churches—Presbyterian, Baptist, Methodist. He sent crews to work whenever and wherever work was needed. Bill did whatever he could, important or not, to avoid being idle. The townspeople marveled at his unselfish and tireless efforts. They didn't know about the inner festering ache that drove him.

GRAVEYARD CLEANING DAY had always been important to the community. It took on new meaning for Bill after Samuel's death. Cleaning had been done two or three times a year, but he introduced the idea that it should be done monthly—at least in the spring, summer, and fall. He was content to skip the winter months; weeds didn't grow, and the few leaves that fell were quickly blown away by the winter winds. With his leadership, monthly cleaning was implemented almost as quickly as he suggested it. The fellowship was good, the graveyard was clean, and Bill was busy.

To Kate it was obvious that Samuel's death was the driving force behind Bill's efforts, but if anyone else suspected, it didn't matter. No one talked about it.

On those days, Bill, Kate, Katherine and Hannah worked to clean Samuel's grave, and other people would do the same for their loved ones and friends. Most everyone had at least one family grave, and many had several to care for.

As each family arrived, the mules were unhitched and led to a distant shade to spend the day. Usually the animals stayed put, but on a workday in late spring of 1909, they grew restless and began to ramble off in different directions. Everyone was working and talking and paying no attention to them.

Katherine, having finished her sweeping, talked Hannah into playing hide and seek. While Hannah stood facing one of the big old oaks with her eyes closed, Katherine set off to find the perfect hiding place. She listened to Hannah's countdown as she ran from one tombstone to the next ... fifty, forty-nine, forty-eight. She first squatted behind one of the biggest of the tombstones, but then changed her mind when she spotted the clump of bushes on the other side of the food wagon.

"Eighteen, seventeen, sixteen," Hannah continued. Katherine raced toward the food wagon and crouched comfortably behind a bush just as the words, "Two, one ... coming, ready or not!" rang out

Katherine picked the thickest bush, sat down behind it, and settled in to wait. After perhaps thirty seconds, she was ready to be found (or at least for Hannah to get close enough that the anticipation would be exciting). In order to check on her sister's progress, she lifted herself to her knees, found an opening in the leaves, and peered through the limbs. She didn't see Hannah. She couldn't see anything but the brown side of a mule. She stood up, looked over the bush, and saw the mule's head bobbing slightly over a big pot of peas. She hollered, "Get away! Go! Go!"

Katherine ran around the bush, waving her arms in the air. The mule paid no attention to her. She began to yell, "Mama, Mama, a mule's in the peas. A mule's in the peas!" Everybody looked toward the wagon where all the food had been left. Hoes and shovels dropped to the ground as the men and women ran toward what was meant to be their dinner. Usually everyone was respectful of graves, but not in such a time of emergency. Graves were stepped on and grave markers jumped. Long skirts rustled and blue overalls ran from every corner.

"That's my pot of peas. Get that mule away from there," Hollis

Smith yelled. Hollis was a big man, probably near two hundred seventy-five pounds, but he ran with as much agility as any of the other men. He yelled again, "Get that mule outta there!" The seams of the faded blue denim that stretched tautly over his wide girth strained to hold together, and the white sweat rag that hung from his right pocket flopped up and down with every step.

Bill, running alongside Mr. Smith, said, "Hollis, that's what everybody's trying to do. We'll get him." The mule, suddenly aware of all the commotion, looked up, then turned and trotted quickly away before any of the men got to him.

None of the other food had been touched, so there was still plenty to eat—just one less pot of peas. After the few minutes of hysteria, Hollis started laughing. He picked up the big straw hat that had blown off his head as he ran. He knocked it against his thigh a couple of times to brush off loose dirt that clung to its brim and, still laughing, he plopped the hat on his head and said, "Well, I can say one thing. That mule knows a good pot of peas when he finds one. He's 'bout licked it clean." Laughter filled the air. A couple of the men left to round up the wayward animals, and everyone else returned to work, all with a smile and a chuckle.

"We'll be telling our grandchildren about the mule in the peas," Mrs. Polly said to Kate as they walked back across the graveyard to where they had been working.

"Probably so, Polly," Kate answered. "Certainly added some excitement. I'm just glad all the mules didn't stop by the wagon for dinner." She laughed again as she visualized the mules all gathered around for a proper dinner on the grounds.

Those days in the graveyard found Bill doing any manual labor needed. He went from grave to grave lending a hand. He worked as long and as hard as any other man and longer and harder than most.

The large ruffled brim of Kate's blue poke bonnet shielded her whole face from the sun, but by slightly tilting her head she could watch. She could watch as Bill worked without rest. As she watched, she wondered how much sweat would his pores have to release and what else it would take to provide a soothing salve for his soul. Kate, on her knees, inched around the little stone that marked Samuel's grave. She washed dirt stains from its base and pulled weeds that had grown up the sides since she was last there. Katherine and Hannah swept the grave and then played with the other children until the adults finished the work. The fellowship was good. Bill laughed and talked right along with everyone else, but Kate knew he was desperately striving to bury the guilt and pain that weighed on his soul. She wondered if it would ever be healed.

MARTHA ECHOLS PULLED WEEDS from the graves of people who had no kin present. She had moved to town with her husband when he became pastor of Leaf Creek Presbyterian, and since they had no family plots, she assumed responsibility for the unclaimed graves. She stood, hand on her waist with her fingers pointing backward. She arched her back in an effort to stretch out the stiffness that had settled in her muscles. She walked up beside Kate. "Some days I think I am getting too old to do all this bending over. I get so stiff."

"I know. Me too," Kate responded as she bent over to brush loose dirt and grass from the bottom of her dress.

Looking across the graveyard at Bill, Martha shook her head slowly from side to side and said, "I tell you, Kate. Your husband is remarkable. I know you are proud of all he does. He works so hard. You know he is the one that keeps us all going. You know that, don't you?"

Kate looked at Martha and smiled. "That's kind of you to say, Martha. Thank you. He does work hard, but just look around. Everybody here is doing something. Everybody is working together. That's what makes these days special."

"You're right of course," Martha answered. "Every project requires a leader, though, and we are blessed to have such a faithful and good one in your husband."

Kate smiled again. "Thank you," she said softly.

"I'm in need of a cup of water. Can I bring you one?"

"No. Thank you, though. I'm about finished here. I'll walk over and get some in a minute." As Kate looked in the direction Martha walked, she could see Katherine and Hannah playing hopscotch in an area yet unclaimed for graves. Not far to their right was Bill, who continued to shovel with as much determination and speed as his body would allow.

Kate lifted the tail of her apron and wiped away droplets of sweat that were trickling down from her temples. She leaned against a tree, watched her husband, and reflected on all Martha had said to her. The man Kate saw was vastly different. She saw torment. She saw guilt. She saw the person she blamed for the death of her child. She saw someone she loved … and wanted to be loved by. She straightened her apron. "I don't know what I think or feel anymore. Why think at all? I'm tired," Kate wanted to say aloud. Her thoughts were mixed with a deep sigh. She pushed herself away from the tree trunk and walked to join Martha at the water bucket.

* * *

KEEPING UP APPEARANCES continued to be of utmost importance to Bill. He was crushed and broken on the inside, but on the outside he maintained a notably distinguished look just as he always had. He wore a three-piece suit except in the heat of the Mississippi summer. Beautifully designed platinum and gold cufflinks with intricately engraved centers and platinum borders adorned his cuffs, and the gold chain of his pocket watch looped down the front right side of his vest. June Ellen washed, starched and ironed his shirts until they were smooth and crisp, and Frank polished his shoes until they shined and reflected like newly-silvered mirrors. Bill never left home without checking himself in the full-length mirror of the chifferobe, squatting slightly to get the full view. Bill was tall. His six-foot two-inch frame, slim stature, his clothes, and his full, slightly-graying beard all served to give him the prominent appearance he desired.

Chapter Nine

IT WAS LATE SEPTEMBER 1914. The girls had been home from school only a few minutes when they heard the front door slam. It was their father, home earlier than they had ever known him to be before. He had just learned a tent revival meeting was about to take place nearby. His voice echoed through the house.

"I need everybody in the dining room. Hurry. Everybody in here now. I've got to get back to the mill." He grabbed a leftover biscuit and piece of fried meat from the pie safe. He pulled the biscuit open, pushed the meat inside and took a bite. Crumbs, completely ignored by him, dropped to the floor. The urgency of his mission seemed to be masking his usual, mostly-proper decorum.

He swallowed. "Listen and listen carefully." He started to lift the biscuit toward his mouth for a second bite but stopped. With his elbow bent and the biscuit about chest-level he began emphasizing every word with emphatic hand gestures. The half-eaten biscuit went up and down and side to side. More crumbs fell. "That tent meeting that's going on just down the road—*don't get near there.*"

Kate's eyes narrowed. She tilted her head slightly forward and to the right. "What tent meeting? Don't tell me another one of those things is here." She closed her eyes as she inhaled deeply. Then, with both hands on her hips, she rapidly pushed the air from her lungs with a loud whish.

"Well, I'm telling you. Tents going up. It'll be starting in a day or two. Just stay away."

"Don't worry. We won't be going near." Kate, hands still on her hips, looked over at Hannah and Katherine. Her eyes widened and her chin lowered as she said, "You both understand? Right?"

"Yes ma'am. We're not going anywhere," the girls answered.

Bill walked toward the front door. He turned when he heard Katherine say to Hannah, "Wonder what all the fuss is about. Sure they're just regular people out there."

"Katherine, now you listen to me, I don't—" Kate began, but Bill stepped back into the room before she could finish.

"Katherine, Hannah, have you heard what I said?" Bill's voice thundered across the room. "I don't want to hear of you going in that direction *at all*. You have no business there, so none of your shenanigans."

"Yes sir," Hannah said softly.

"Katherine?"

"Yes, sir. I understand," Katherine said, a little less convincingly.

Their father's voice mellowed slightly. "Look, those meetings are not good, not appropriate for us. I don't want you there. That's all you need to know. Do *not* go near that place. Do you hear me? I mean it. Don't go near."

Kate sighed. "Oh me. Can't believe they're setting up so close to us."

Bill, not acknowledging that Kate had spoken, continued, "Those people are outsiders." His words grew loud again, and the last bite of biscuit was directed at the girls' faces as he pumped his hand toward them. "They come into our county and take advantage of ignorant people that don't know better. Set up those tents out in the middle of nowhere, hold their meetings, get people worked up in a frenzy with outlandish talk and their loud goings-on." He shoved the last bite of biscuit into his mouth and called out, "Janie, bring me a glass of water. I've got to get going."

"Yessuh, coming," came the voice from the kitchen.

"I know some folks go just to have someplace to go, but it's just about more than I can stand to think about. I was told they had a snake out there last time, handling it, handling *poison* like that. Makes no sense," Bill continued.

"Really? Why would they have a snake? That's really scary." Hannah shivered at the thought.

Janie handed Bill a glass of water. He tilted his head backward and drank half the glass before answering. "The preachers tell people not to worry. If they're bitten, just pray and the bite will be miraculously healed." His tone dripped with sarcasm.

"Will they be healed?" Hannah asked.

"Not likely." Katherine chimed in as she gave Hannah a 'you should know better' look.

Bill finished the water, put the glass on the table, wiped the back of his hand across his mouth, and picked up where he'd left off. "If they're not healed, the preachers blame the person or his family for not having enough faith—or the right kind—or their prayer wasn't earnest enough, or some foolishness like that. Crazy. I don't want them around here."

"You can be sure we're not going near," Kate assured him.

Halfway out the front door, Bill turned to them and added, "Plus the preacher is everywhere, up and down the aisle screaming *repent, repent, repent*! Today is the day, may be your last." Bill's voice softened a little. "And he is right about that part, but no matter. We don't have any business getting anywhere near."

"They're not reverent. I know that," Kate said, shaking her head.

"No, they're not. Just people traveling around saying that it's a church, wailing up and down the aisles, and taking people's money. That's what they're doing, saying they heard the call and getting rich off the poorest people around here."

Bill let the door slam behind him, still talking. "I'll be glad when the week is over, and they've gone back to wherever they came from." His words rang into the yard as he descended the steps.

***

HER FATHER WAS RIGHT. As it turned out, the tent, taut and white against the blue sky, was set up just out from Leaf Creek in a pasture not far from the McMolison's home. It was not on McMolison land to be sure, but even so, neither Kate nor Bill was particularly pleased.

Hannah thought it unusual for her mother to express her feelings quite so strongly, but on that subject, she seemed to be in total agreement with her father.

The tent meeting event being called a church service had been especially distasteful to people like her parents. Like most Presbyterians (actually Baptists and Methodists too), they were traditional in their church service, dignified in their church behavior, and worshipful with their church language. Clothes, plain or fancy, were freshly washed and ironed for Sunday, and Sunday dinner was often cooked on Saturday. Children running in the sanctuary were scolded. Children playing up on the chancel where God's Word was front and center knew to hide before getting caught. The church house was God's house. Reverence was a priority. The preacher occasionally got fiery, even awakened a dozing elder once in a while by hitting his fist on the pulpit, but dignity prevailed even in those times.

Her father had been clear. She and Katherine were to keep a safe distance from that tent meeting.

KATHERINE'S DISTANCE GREW SHORT, HOWEVER. She met Stephen at the Mercantile. He had stopped in to buy a shirt, and Hannah, Katherine and Kate were in town to shop for material. Katherine had been asked to sing a solo at the next week's chapel program at school. Chapel was held weekly, and different grades took turns being in charge. Two or three Bible verses or a hymn (or both) were always included. Hannah and Katherine sang at church all the time, but never a solo.

Katherine didn't seem to mind though. At sixteen she was still game for most anything. "I'll choose a hymn I already know—maybe 'His Eye is on the Sparrow.' That one sounds good. I've done it a bunch a times before. I'll just stand on the stage and sing it." Like always, she talked as if it would be no big deal. "I want a new dress, though, to wear for the program."

"A new dress? Why do you need a new dress?" Kate asked.

"I'm sure it will make me feel prettier. I'll be more confident and I'm sure I'll sing better," was Katherine's ready answer.

"Okay," Kate said, giving in to Katherine's reasoning.

"Lavender. I would like a lavender dress," Katherine added.

"Why do you want lavender?" Hannah asked her sister. "Only old ladies wear lavender." She couldn't imagine why her vibrant, extroverted sister wanted to wear such a boring color.

"I just do. Lavender's a pretty color." Katherine lifted her chin, cocked her head to one side, and flipped her hair with her hand.

"Hannah, do you want to go with us? You might find some material too," Kate asked.

"Sure, but it *won't* be lavender," Hannah said emphatically but cheerily.

Katherine looked back at Hannah, pushed her lower lip into a pout and batted her eyes playfully.

Hannah hooked her arm in Katherine's elbow. "Come on. Let's go get your *laa-veen-der* material," she said with the best southern flourish she could manage.

HANNAH AND KATHERINE WALKED hurriedly into The Mercantile. "Good morning," they said in unison as they entered the sprawling store. Rectangular-shaped wooden counters were wall to wall and piled high with the necessities of life. Kate entered close behind them.

"Good morning. How are y'all today?" Mrs. Mac, the owner, greeted them warmly. Mac was short for McKenna, but no one called her Mrs. McKenna. Many years before, her husband had shortened McKenna to Mac. He didn't like Dora Imogene, her birth name. He never said exactly why, except the name was far too common for someone as pretty and sweet as she was.

Kate looked through the materials and visited with Mrs. Mac.

Hannah was admiring hair ribbons when Katherine suddenly grabbed her elbow and shook it hard. "What are you doing? Trying to shake my arm off?" Hannah frowned as she looked around at Katherine.

"Shhhh. Look over toward the men's things. See him? I've never seen him before. Have you?" Katherine whispered, close to Hannah's ear.

"I don't know. I don't think I've ever seen him either and I definitely think I'd remember," Hannah whispered back as she gazed across the store. "Guess now you need something from the men's department?"

"That's what I was thinking," Katherine answered as she started easing in that direction.

The man was browsing in the shirts several counters over on the other side of the store. Hannah watched as Katherine calmly and casually walked toward the stranger.

Hannah, unnoticed, walked closer to get a better look. She could see he was probably not much older than Katherine and was dressed more neatly than most of the boys around Leaf Creek. His creased and cuffed pants were dark blue and ironed. His shoes were brown leather lace-up oxfords. Even the street dust that had blanketed them could not hide the polished shine beneath. His shirt was a light tan color and also crisply ironed. The sleeves were rolled about halfway up his arms and the top couple of buttons at the neck were unbuttoned, exposing tanned skin. The hours since shaving had given him a shadow of a beard; his eyes were sky blue and his hair sandy-colored … not blond, not brown, but a shade in between. He was ruggedly nice-looking, not handsome in a smooth perfect sort of way like his clothes. Instead— his features were strong, and his manner radiated confidence.

It was obvious that Katherine was attracted to what she saw.

KATHERINE SAUNTERED over to the shirt counter—to the end opposite the stacks of shirts. She picked up a pair of overalls and turned them in her hands, as if considering a purchase.

"Buying overalls? Those look a mite big for you." The voice was strong and self-assured.

Katherine looked up. "Oh, hi," she answered in an unnaturally timid voice.

"Hi back." He smiled at Katherine and appeared to totally forget the shirts he had been looking through. "Do you work here?"

"Oh, no. I don't. I'm just here with my mother and sister."

"So you're buying overalls?"

"Actually, no. I was just looking around." Katherine walked toward the shirt end of the counter. "We're here to buy some dress material. Looks like you're buying shirts," she said as she traced buttons on one of the shirts with her index finger.

"Thinking about it but really just looking to see what I can find in this town of yours."

"Guess that means you're not from anywhere around here?" Katherine questioned.

"Guess it does." He smiled teasingly. "And you? Do you live here?"

"Just out from town a little—not far." Katherine waved her hand in the direction of home. "That way."

"Oh, I'm gonna be out that way the next few days," he said with a smile that caused Katherine's heart to quicken.

"Really? Not much in that direction but woods and pasture and cows. Where would you be?" Katherine said in a slightly mocking, largely flirting manner.

"I'm here to preach for a few days. We're just finishing putting up the tent and getting ready. Why don't you come?"

Katherine's heart was suddenly in her throat and her mind raced as she sought her answer. "I would love to. I really would, but I don't think I can, not this week at least, maybe another time." Katherine desperately wanted to say something that would encourage the possibility of seeing him again. "Will you be coming to Leaf Creek again?"

"I'm sure—someday. We go from place to place all the time. Are you sure you can't come to the preaching? We usually have refreshments after. You could tell me more about what you do around here."

Katherine sighed. "I can't." She looked at the floor and spoke softly. "Papa doesn't let me go much at night, and the truth is he doesn't let us go to places where preaching is not in churches." She held her breath for his response; no way was she going to tell him all her father had said.

"Well, okay then. Let's think of something else. I know you live that way." His head nodded in the direction of the McMolison's and the tent. "And what is your name? Mine is Stephen. I'm thinking I might need your opinion on one of these shirts if I decide to buy one."

"Katherine," she answered, barely able to contain her excitement.

"How far is it to your house? Would your father mind if I came by?"

"Probably. But I could meet you somewhere." Katherine suddenly felt flushed and nervous as she realized how forward her suggestion had been. Her mother would definitely think her behavior improper and un-ladylike.

"I can do that. Where can we meet?" Stephen answered enthusiastically.

"There's a sharp bend in the road on down from where your tent is—toward my house. A big magnolia is in the curve. We could meet there."

"I'll find it. Should get there around nine. That okay?" Stephen smiled, raising his eyebrows questioningly.

"Yes, fine." Katherine nodded and returned his smile. Her heart beat wildly with excitement as she agreed to the forbidden plan.

"Till tonight then." He strolled toward the door, then turned and waved as he left the store.

HANNAH, back at the ribbon counter, watched the exchange between Katherine and Stephen. They were both smiling. After Stephen was outside, Katherine walked briskly back to Hannah's side.

"Oh, Hannah, isn't he wonderful? I'm going to tell you something, but you can't tell."

"Okay," Hannah responded matter-of-factly.

Katherine glanced around the store to see if anyone was close enough to hear.

"What is it?" Hannah persisted. "You know I don't ever tell our secrets, and no one can hear you anyway. Nobody else is even in here except Mama over there with Mrs. Mac." Hannah was getting a little perturbed at the caution her sister was taking.

"I know, but this is really, really secret."

"*Okay*, I said. Are you going to tell me or not?"

Katherine moved very close to Hannah and whispered in her ear, "His name is Stephen—and he is one of the tent preachers here for the tent meeting."

Hannah gasped and her eyes widened. "Oh no, Katherine, you can't do whatever it is you're planning. You know we'll both be in trouble."

"It's okay. We've got a plan. Don't worry. Just be normal. Did Mama find the material?"

"Who's got a plan?" Hannah started to ask, but Katherine was already walking toward their mother.

While Hannah's heart raced with anticipation of what might happen in the coming days, Katherine was already over at the fabric counter where Mrs. Mac was showing Kate two bolts of lavender material. "I like that one," Katherine said, pointing to one of the bolts without giving much attention to either. Katherine's thoughts were elsewhere. She suddenly had little interest in which of the two fabrics was chosen—she was in love.

CHAPTER TEN

HANNAH SPENT EVERY NIGHT that tent revival week worrying. Katherine spent every night slipping out to meet Stephen. Hannah held her breath while Katherine managed her forbidden tryst by crawling out the bedroom window after their parents' door was closed for the night. Just in case their mother (or worse, their *father*) peeked in, Hannah put pillows under the covers where Katherine was supposed to be. Hannah knew that if Katherine got caught, they would both likely be on the receiving end of their father's whip. It hung on a nail on the back porch. He had used it on Katherine before when she crossed him, either by molding truth to fit her circumstance or offering unsolicited comments that she described as opinions (but which he described as backtalk). As a result of her lack of judgment, Katherine had occasionally suffered whippings that left whelps on her legs and backside.

Hannah couldn't keep herself from thinking about the day she remembered as one of the worst of those times. As she waited for Katherine to return home one night from her rendezvous with Stephen, she relived the day. She was seven and Katherine nine. It was on a Sunday morning at church. The two girls sat side by side on the family pew.

Katherine leaned slightly toward Hannah, nudged her with her elbow and whispered, "You want a piece?" Katherine's hand was in her lap, palm down. A little piece of yellow could be seen when she lifted her index finger.

"*No*. Put it back in your pocket before Mama or Papa sees it," Hannah whispered quietly through clenched teeth and barely-parted lips.

"Chicken," Katherine whispered with a slight shrug of her shoulders. She eased her hand into her pocket and successfully unwrapped a piece of Juicy Fruit gum.

"Katherine, don't," Hannah said under her breath as Katherine successfully folded the stick of gum four times before slipping it into her mouth. For several seconds she let the gum sit still on her tongue.

"All stand," Preacher Echols said. "Let's begin this morning by singing 'All Hail The Power of Jesus' Name.'"

Katherine thought it seemed a safe time to chew since her father and mother both stood tall above her. She was enjoying the sweetness of the gum when she realized her father was looking around her mother and down at her.

"… bring forth the royal di-a-dem …" Katherine sang with all her might. She pronounced every syllable, all the while moving the gum so it could be swallowed.

Later, when Sunday dinner was almost finished and Katherine was thinking the gum had escaped her father's notice, he looked at her and said, "Katherine, were you chewing gum in church?"

"Oh, no sir," Katherine answered him quickly and confidently.

"Don't lie to me, Katherine. You know lying makes things worse."

Hannah was frozen, eyes toward her plate. Her heart pounded.

Kate, fearful of what was coming, interjected, "Katherine, please. Did you have gum, or was it just maybe that it looked like you had gum when you were singing?"

"Kate, she wasn't *just* singing. I saw her," Bill said harshly, all the while staring at Katherine. "How can you tell me you didn't have gum? Come here to me," he said sternly.

Katherine stood and walked close to his chair, close enough that he reached into the pocket of her dress. He pulled out a stick of unwrapped gum and a wadded-up gum wrapper. "What's this?" he snarled, holding the crumpled wrapper at the end of her nose.

"That's from another day."

"Another day? It's from this *morning*," he yelled. "I saw you. Lying has consequences. It's an abomination." He grabbed her by the hand and pulled her toward the back porch.

Hannah and her mother, seated at the table, were silent and dreaded the next few minutes. The lashes that afternoon resulted in bloody oozing from Katherine's torn and abraded flesh. Disobedience of any kind resulted in consequences, but defiant lying shot them to the nth degree as far as Bill McMolison was concerned.

TOWARD HIS CHILDREN, Bill had never been lenient, but Hannah knew that to Katherine, Stephen was worth the punishment if it, in fact, came.

Hannah watched each night as Katherine gingerly crept out of their yard and disappeared down the road. She lay awake, waiting for her to return. She was nervous about the risk Katherine was putting them both in but anxious to hear all about her romantic adventure. When Katherine was safely back home that first night and had changed places with the pillows, Hannah eagerly listened as she described in detail everything about the evening and about Stephen.

"The road bed felt cool and smooth, like glass. It's hard and slick like," Katherine began. To muffle the sound, the girls pulled the covers over their heads and whispered.

"Why are you talking about the road? Don't tease. I don't care what the road feels like, Katherine. You know I don't, and I know you don't either. Tell me what happened," Hannah said, her hushed voice filled with exasperation.

"Well, you asked me to tell you everything," Katherine said jokingly.

"Oh stop. You know what I meant."

"Okay. Well, I walked to the big magnolia, the one in the bend of the road. You know where I mean. It's about halfway to where the tent is set up, and he was there. Just like we planned," Katherine said dreamily.

"What happened then? Come on, tell me. It'll be morning if you don't get on with it," Hannah said impatiently.

"Oh, he is *sooo* wonderful, just like I knew he would be. We sat by the road and just talked. He's not at all like what Mama and Papa tried to say about tent preachers. I mean some may be what they say, but not Stephen."

"So tell me, what about him? What's he like really—besides good-looking? I know that part."

"Well, he is sane, not crazy. He's wonderful, not awful. He's kind and thoughtful, not just taking advantage of people. He's all good things—nothing like they said."

"And he's good looking," Hannah added again.

"That too. But he's so exciting to talk to. Knows about lots of different things. He is perfect."

"What are you going to do?" Hannah asked, fearing Katherine's answer.

"I'm going to meet him again tomorrow night," Katherine answered firmly.

"You're gonna get us both in trouble."

"No, I'm not. You're not going to tell anybody, and I'm sure not, so how am I going to get us in trouble?"

"Did you tell him why you're coming out in the middle of the night?"

"I did, a little, and I think he understood," Katherine answered thoughtfully. "I hope so."

They were both quiet for a moment before Hannah asked, "Other than explaining why you had to meet in the night, what did you talk about?"

"Everything. We talked so much I don't even remember hearing crickets or anything."

"What about? You've been gone for two and a half hours," Hannah reminded Katherine.

"Books. He's read lots of books, even more than we have, and he's been all over to different places. He's been to Louisiana and Alabama and lots and lots of places in Mississippi." Katherine had rarely been out of Greene County, so she soaked in every particular that Stephen shared.

Hannah didn't know it at the time, but the die was cast for Stephen too. He had been as smitten with Katherine as she'd been with him. Nothing would stop their clandestine late-night meetings; she would have to remain quiet and calm that entire week and in the weeks to follow.

On Wednesday, Katherine returned breathless and more excited than she had been the previous two nights. "He's great. Everything's gr—"

"Shush," Hannah said as she held the covers for Katherine to slide under. "You're talking too loud. Get under here."

Katherine scooted under the covers as directed, then reached for Hannah's hand and placed it over her heart. "Feel how fast my heart is still beating?"

"Okay, I feel it," Hannah said impatiently. "What happened? What did he do? What did y'all do? Quit stalling and tell me." Hannah withdrew her hand and folded her arms comfortably in front of her. "You can swoon later."

"Well, he took my hand in his, and it was so warm and soft. I felt my whole body tingle. He wasn't saying anything. I just looked out toward the road and didn't say anything either, but I could feel him looking at me."

"Did he kiss you?"

"No, but I wanted him to." Katherine sighed deeply. "I really wanted him to."

"So what happened then?"

"We just sat with the moon shining down. He stroked my wrist with his thumb as he held my hand. Oh, Hannah, I do love him," Katherine whispered softly.

"You just met him four days ago. Can you love somebody in four days?" Hannah said skeptically. "He sounds really great, but what are you going to tell Mama and Papa? You know they'll kill you and probably me too when they find out."

"I'll figure out something when I have to. I know one thing for sure: I'll do whatever I have to, regardless of what Papa says, because I know he just doesn't understand," Katherine answered confidently.

On Friday night Stephen hugged Katherine and pulled her close. Their hearts beat into each other as the full moon radiated down and made the lips of both even more desirable. They knew their time together needed to end, and they parted with plans for the future.

Katherine had successfully sneaked out and back in every night that week and no one was the wiser except Stephen, Katherine, and a very nervous Hannah (who was almost sick from anxiety). Hannah had enjoyed hearing Katherine's stories, but she dreaded even the thought of what would happen if their father found out. Katherine would be punished for her actions, and she would be punished for knowing and not telling.

The whole mood of their house would take a grave turn.

<h1 style="text-align:center">Chapter Eleven</h1>

After the revival ended, Stephen returned to Leaf Creek often, almost every week. The trip took a day and a half from his house to theirs. He was quick to say he didn't mind, that Katherine was worth it.

It was never quite explained to Mr. and Mrs. McMolison just how Katherine and Stephen met. Kate remembered seeing him at the Mercantile. She had certainly noticed that Katherine was giving more attention to the young man than to the lavender material they had gone there to buy.

Hannah's throat got dry and her palms damp each time Katherine was asked who he was and where she had known him.

Katherine, however, showed no signs of anxiousness. She was evasive and responded to their mother's questions with a polite shrug of the shoulder and increased interest in whatever came into her mind. Katherine did not want to tell either of her parents she had never seen him before their shopping day, and she especially did not want them to know he was connected in any way with the tent meeting.

Kate never pressed Katherine for additional information, however. Stephen seemed polite, pleasant, and well-mannered. She was pleased for Katherine to have the company of such a fine young man.

STEPHEN'S LAST NAME was Neal. Katherine had said something that day at the Mercantile which led her mother to think he was from somewhere around Leaf Creek and, on that particular day, was on his way to visit relatives further down in the county. Bill McMolison knew a Neal family that lived one county over and decided on his own that Stephen must be one of them.

It was after one of Stephen's visits that Bill announced, mostly to himself, "The Neals over in Perry County are good people. Only Neals I know of around these parts—must be Stephen's family. They have a sawmill. Dealt with them some few years ago; honest, hard-working and very successful." He seemed especially pleased when recalling the successful part.

During the weeks of Stephen's first visits, half-truths and little white lies were left unchecked. No one actually told a lie, but no one corrected any of the half-truths, either. Even Bill never pressed Katherine or Stephen for additional information. Apparently having Neal for his last name was all the credit Stephen needed, at least for the time being.

Bill unexpectedly agreed without hesitation that he would make Katherine a good husband. After all, she was nearly seventeen. It was time for her to get married. Most importantly, he knew from dealing in timber himself, that if she married a man in the sawmill business, she would be provided for in the manner he deemed suitable for one of his daughters. He was ready to give his blessing to this young man who had a good name and had asked for her hand.

***

THE TENT MEETING was in early fall of Katherine's senior year of high school. By the second week of December, Stephen had rented a room at the boarding house. When his preaching schedule permitted, he would stay several nights in Leaf Creek. On those days Stephen waited for Katherine just outside the school.

"Wish you were through with school. I wait all day for right now," Stephen said on one of their first afternoons after getting engaged.

"I'm sure you've filled the time with something exciting,"

Katherine said, smiling.

"Not as exciting as you," Stephen replied. "It's so warm and pretty today. Why don't we take the long way home?"

"You mean circle down through the woods to our big oak?"

"That's what I was thinking."

They strolled through the woods to an old oak that stood amidst hundreds of pines. "This is one of my very favorite places," Katherine said as she dropped her books, sat down, and propped against the trunk.

"I know. I like it too. It's beautiful out here." Stephen eased down and sat cross-legged in front of her. "Katherine, you know I love you. I want a home with you and for you to be the mother of my children."

Katherine reached for his hands and spoke softly. "Me too. That's what I want too. I love you."

"You know we have to tell your parents the truth. I mean, they think I own a sawmill. We have to fix that. We can't just keep pretending."

"I know, but not yet. Let's wait a little longer. Please? It's almost Christmas, and I have to finish school. You really don't know how Papa can be. Let's please wait." She looked intently into Stephen's eyes. "We'll tell them. We have to. Just not yet."

Stephen stroked her cheek with his hand. "Okay, if that is what you want. We'll wait." He patted the straw next to where he sat. "Why don't you move right over here?"

"Okay," Katherine said flirtingly. She held her skirt securely over her knees as she slid away from the tree and to Stephen's side.

Stephen eased his hand around Katherine's shoulders and gently pulled her backward onto the shiny amber-colored new straw that had fallen all around the long rows of pines. They lay side by side on the sun-warmed pallet. "Katherine, I love you—I love you so much," he said as he turned his face and body into hers. "I want to marry you right now, right this very minute."

"I know. Me too," Katherine said as she buried her face in his chest. Desire for each other drew them in a way they had not allowed before.

Stephen caressed her face with his hand and gradually moved his gentle strokes downward so that Katherine wished desperately to be one with him. She ached for every touch, but she was determined to be true to her wedding night dreams. She covered his hand with her hand and held it still.

"No," she said reluctantly. "I can't. We can't."

The desire they felt was difficult to restrain, but Stephen loved Katherine and like her, wanted no regrets. Their inner voices rose against the line they crossed, but neither Stephen nor Katherine wanted there to be a need for the voices to get louder.

DURING THE CHRISTMAS HOLIDAYS Stephen was in Leaf Creek to spend several days with Katherine. He had barely been there half a day before Mr. McMolison started talking timber and sawmills. Stephen said little, just nodded and listened politely. He tried to steer the conversation toward horses, gardens, Christmas, anything he knew something about—but it didn't work. Before he knew it, he had a commanding invitation to go to the mill and was hearing Mr. McMolison say how anxious he was to show him around.

Stephen was anxious too, but for a completely different reason. He knew, even as he grabbed the reins of his horse, slid his left foot into the stirrup, lifted his right leg easily over the shiny, chestnut-brown coat, and settled into the saddle, that his trip to the mill would very likely expose the truth.

KATHERINE, AFTER HEARING HER FATHER insist to Stephen that he go with him to the mill, felt more anxious than she'd ever felt in her life. She watched from the doorway as the two men rode out of sight. Unable to do anything but wait for what she felt certain was about to happen, she hurried to the bedroom to find Hannah.

"Hi. What are you doing? I thought you and Stephen were going into town," Hannah said as she tied a ribbon onto a Christmas present.

"We were, but Papa started talking about today being a perfect time for him to show Stephen the mill. I'm scared—scared about what is about to happen. I tried to tell him we wanted to go to town, but he just kept saying how anxious he was to get to know Stephen better. You know how Papa can be." Katherine plopped down on the bed, scooted into the center and put her face in her hands.

Hannah pushed wrapping paper and ribbons to the foot of the bed and sat down beside her sister. "Oh, Katherine, I'm sorry. Stephen will be okay, though. I'm sure he will."

"I know what's gonna happen. Stephen doesn't know anything about timber and sawmills and stuff. Papa will figure that out real quick. I know he will. And then when Papa asks him, Stephen will tell the truth. There's no telling what Papa will say or do." Katherine picked up a piece of the red ribbon, wrapped the ends around fingers on both hands, and pulled it back and forth as she spoke. "He'll be furious. You know he will."

Hannah slid her arm around her sister's shoulder. "Please don't worry. We'll do whatever we have to. Stephen loves you. You love him. That's what's important. Remember that."

"I can take it, whatever it is. I have before, but Stephen has never seen how bad things can get when Papa gets mad." Tears filled Katherine's eyes. "He better not hurt him. He better not. I'll leave, Hannah." Katherine straightened up and turned her face toward Hannah. "I really will."

"Please don't say that. Just wait. We'll figure something out. I wish Mother knew, though." Hannah spoke soothingly, her right hand now gently rubbing Katherine's back.

"I couldn't tell her," Katherine said, mumbling almost inaudibly into hands that were again covering her face. "You know I couldn't." Tears spilled down her cheeks.

THE TWO MEN RODE SIDE BY SIDE. Their conversation was mostly of a general nature—the weather, their horses, Stephen's trip to and from Hattiesburg and such—but upon arrival at the mill Mr. McMolison could restrain his curiosity no longer.

Stephen barely had both feet on the ground before Bill was pointing to stacks of logs, some at least six feet high. "That's a pretty sight, isn't it? Logs that fine always look good to a timber man." Bill spoke proudly as he led the way into the mill. "Most days I get 250,000 to 300,000 feet through here. What do you do on a good day?"

Stephen's heart began to pound and his throat tightened as he attempted an answer. "Sir," he said, his voice soft with uncertainty, "what feet are you referring to?"

"You must be kidding, son. Is it that you do so much more you don't want to tell me? That's fine. I appreciate modesty," Bill continued. "You got a lot of men working to bring the logs in?"

"No sir, I don't, and I really don't know about the feet either."

Bill stopped walking. He turned so that he was face to face with Stephen. "What do you mean? Did your father not teach you the workings?" Bill's forehead wrinkled and his eyes narrowed to a near squint.

"It's not my father. Sir, I'm sorry. I don't know how it was you came to think so, but my father doesn't have a mill."

Suddenly Bill realized Stephen not only did not own a mill, he knew absolutely nothing about timber. The truth raced into Bill's mind. "Board feet means nothing to this boy," he thought. "I might as well be talking about pigs' feet or any other kind of feet for that matter." He stepped close to Stephen's face.

"Why did you tell me your family is in the timber business?" Bill asked through grinding, clenched teeth.

"Well … I mean … we—or I, I should say … I don't think I did, sir …" Stephen said, trying his best to sound calm.

"Sure you did. Why else would I think you were one of the Perry County Neals?"

"Sir, nobody meant to cause a misunderstanding. I mean I think it sort of just happened." Stephen took a step backward, but Bill immediately stepped forward, putting his face within inches of Stephen's. His breath was hot on Stephen's face, and his eyes bored into him.

"What exactly do you mean? Who are you? What do you do?" His face turned red and his voice quivered with anger. "You deceiving my daughter?"

"No, Sir, I …" Stephen sidestepped in an effort to put a little distance between himself and Bill McMolison. He ended up with his back against the mill wall.

"You're what? *What?* Tell me."

"Mr. McMolison, I love Katherine. I never meant for you to think

I'm something I'm not. I just …"

"Don't talk to me about love. You've been lying for months. Love, lying—they don't go together," Bill said as he pushed his index finger against Stephen's chest. "If you're not from Perry County, where are you from? What do you do?"

"I met Katherine, sir, in early September …"

"Okay, September. *Where* did you meet her?" Bill stepped back a foot or so.

Stephen took a deep breath. "Mr. McMolison, I met Katherine when I was here for the revival meeting out at the tent. I'm one of the preachers."

Bill froze. For a few seconds he stood with a fiercely angry stare. Stephen could hear the breaths that came through his flared nostrils. "You *snake*," he said through clenched teeth. He was screaming on the inside, but his harsh and uncompromising words were whisper quiet. "Leave my mill. Leave *now*. Never see Katherine again. Go home. Do you understand? Go today."

His face grew redder and his neck veins bulged. He picked up a discarded piece of wood, one and a half inches thick, and snapped it as if it were a small twig. The overall-clad, sawdust-covered mill workers couldn't hear the words, but they could see the outrage in every gesture. Bill's arms flew up, his right index finger again aimed in Stephen's face, and the broken pieces of wood were flung with such force that they bounced off a wall and back against one of the saws. The parting words in Stephen's ears were, "You're a liar, a fraud. Imposter, get out of my sight, get out of my sight now."

Stephen said no more. He mounted his horse and rode quickly toward the boarding house.

"LISTEN. THAT'S PROBABLY PAPA," Hannah said as the sound of fast-paced horse hooves drifted into their bedroom.

The girls heard footsteps cross the porch and the front door slam. "Katherine." A pause, and then much louder: "*Katherine, come here*! Where are you? Come here, *now*." There was no mistaking the anger that coated their father's words.

"Stay here," Katherine said to Hannah as she wiped the tears from her eyes.

"Are you sure? I'll come with you," Hannah said hesitantly. She wanted to support her sister but did not want to face their father.

"I'm sure. Stay here. I caused this, but I'm not sorry." Hannah hugged a pillow to her chest as Katherine started toward the hall where their father waited.

Kate came from the sitting room where she had been reading. "Bill, why are you screaming? What on earth is wrong? Where's Stephen?"

"Just wait. You're about to find out more than you want to know. Your daughter's been lying and up to no good. *Katherine,* where are you. I said come here."

"Sir?" Katherine said as she walked into the hall.

"Bill, whatever it is, please don't be so loud. We have company." Kate stood, bewildered, looking from Katherine to her husband and then to Hannah, who had slipped into the hall behind Katherine.

"We don't have company. At least he better be gone. I told him to leave." Bill looked directly at Katherine.

"You what?" Kate gasped. "Why? What's going on?"

Bill stared at Katherine as his rant began. "No daughter of mine will ever get hooked up with something like that! Do you understand me? Do you? You obviously don't care about yourself, about your family, about our reputation, about our honor ..." He turned his back toward Katherine and took a few steps before turning swiftly and pointing his finger at her. "What about your own reputation, your honor? Did you think of that when you were getting involved with that man, bringing him into your life, into our home? What's the matter with you?"

"Bill, tell me what's happening? What are you talking about?" Kate pleaded.

"I'll tell you—or maybe Katherine wants to tell you," Bill bellowed into Katherine's face. "You've been raised better, raised to act Christian. You've gone behind our backs, been dishonest, disrespectful, and acted as if you have no integrity and certainly no honor. You bring shame on all of us." Bill slammed his fist on the table. "What else have you done? You better not have gone and gotten yourself messed up by that boy."

Hannah eased up beside Katherine. Bill shifted his gaze toward her and asked, "Did you know about this? Did you?"

"Yes sir, I did." Hannah responded quietly.

"Sure you did. You're as guilty as she is."

"Papa," Katherine said, speaking for the first time as she looked first to her father and then to her mother. Kate stood with a look of disbelief and horror on her face. "Mama, y'all please try to understand. I love Stephen. I want to marry him. I'm sorry it's like this. I never wanted it to be this way. I knew you would be mad. That's why I didn't tell you. I was going to tell you after Christmas. I'm sorry, I really am. Stephen isn't like what you think. Please give him a chance. Don't send him away. I want to spend the rest of my life with him. I am really, really sorry for letting you think something that wasn't true."

"No you're not," Bill said, glaring at her.

"Papa, I love him and he loves me. We've made plans."

"Katherine, why? Why are you doing this?" Kate asked sorrowfully.

"We love each other. And y'all liked him till you found out he preaches in tents and doesn't own a sawmill. That's not right. It's not fair."

"Don't be insolent," Bill cautioned sternly. "This is a bad situation and you know it."

"Papa, please."

"Don't talk about *please* anything. I told him to leave. He knew I meant it. He never should have been around here in the first place. You know that. Don't talk anymore about it. It's over."

Katherine was silent but vowed to herself and later to Hannah, "He is not going to stop me. I will marry Stephen. Maybe here or somewhere else, but I'm getting married. To *Stephen.*"

Chapter Twelve

Bill clenched his fists and spewed his unrelenting diatribe when he spoke of the ridiculous infatuation, but the whip stayed on the nail. Katherine focused on finishing high school with her three classmates, relished her occasional clandestine time with Stephen and joyfully (in spite of her parents) made secret wedding plans. The household was civil but stiff.

Katherine, figuring Sundays to be a little more peaceful than any other day of the week, chose a Sunday night supper in mid-February to gingerly announce her plan. "Papa, I know you've been disappointed in me and I'm really sorry," she said. "I really am, but please try to understand how I feel about Stephen."

Her father stopped eating. He glared across the table at her. "Don't start with that again, Katherine."

"I have to because I want to marry him when I finish school and I want you and Mama there. Or here—that is, if you will let me get married here. Having a wedding here is what I really want to do. Will you let me?" She spoke quickly, not wanting to lose her nerve. Her parents stared at her.

"Oh Katherine," Kate said, her eyes instantly filling with tears. "We don't really know him. What about his parents? Who are they?"

"Katherine, I don't like any part of this." Bill looked daggers at her. "And I'm a good mind to tell you if you're gonna act this way, then just go. Go do what you think you gotta do. Go marry that man, whatever he is. Go now since you think you know best for you and don't care what's best for us, for your family."

"Bill, what are you saying? Katherine can't leave," Kate said, her voice more pleading than commanding.

"Well, if she's just going to do whatever she wants, she can certainly leave and just get on outta here."

"Papa, please try to understand. I don't want to leave. I want to be here with y'all, at least till I finish school. But I want to marry Stephen and he wants to marry me."

Bill paused and looked at her. Angrily he said, "I know you think you can leave after you finish school anyway and do whatever you want to do, but I assure you it won't be as easy as you seem to think." He turned and took a few steps toward the door, then ran both hands through his hair. "You're too headstrong for any of our good—yours or ours. Do what you want, wherever you want. Don't expect me to be happy about it." He hit the back of one of the dining chairs, sending it skidding under the table, and left the room.

KATHERINE GRADUATED from high school in mid-March. She planned to be married in April. The two months between February and the wedding found every member of the McMolison family in varying states of emotion. Kate cried some days and laughed others as she, Katherine and Hannah planned for the upcoming nuptials. Hannah shared excitement with Katherine, supported her mother with understanding, and maintained a careful calm around her father.

SPRING FINALLY ARRIVED, bringing with it the day of Katherine's wedding. It was April 1916, and just as Katherine wished, she and Stephen were being married on the family's front porch. White dogwood blooms filled the woods that surrounded the yard, and purple wisteria hung like huge clusters of grapes from the big oak tree that hugged one end of the porch.

Hannah buttoned the last button on Katherine's dress. "You look beautiful," she said.

"Thank you for always being here for me and helping me. I have the best little sister in the world." Katherine hugged Hannah and added, "I love you."

"I love you back, and I'm so happy you found Stephen. I really like him—a lot."

"Oh darling, you do look gorgeous. I just want to tell you again that all I've ever wanted is for you to be happy," Kate said as she entered the room.

"I know," answered Katherine. "I am happy. Please don't worry."

"Well, I think it is almost time," Hannah interjected. "Are you ready?"

"I'm ready," said Katherine without hesitation. "Let's all walk out together."

The three were smiling as they stepped onto the front porch. Katherine took her place beside Stephen. Kate and Hannah walked to where Bill stood at the end of the porch.

Hannah's smile grew bigger and brighter as she saw the happiness that radiated from her sister's face. She was captivated by the desire she saw in Katherine's eyes—a desire of one for another bound together by the security of love. "It'll be me one day, standing there with someone perfect," Hannah daydreamed silently ... until she was forced to the present by her parents' whispered conversation.

"It's a perfect day for Katherine. The weather is lovely, and she is so happy, Bill," Kate said. "Please be happy with her."

"I'll be happy when this is over. Katherine never should've put us in this situation. I mean there are three or four preachers here ... at least that is what they're claiming. We don't really know who or what they are."

"Bill, please don't say anything," Kate urged.

"I'm not gonna say a thing. I'm through saying—just want to get on with it. I'm going to give her away just like I'm supposed to or rather watch her be taken," he scoffed. "That'll be the end of it."

"Bill, shhhh. Please be quiet." Kate whispered.

Without acknowledging Kate further, Bill walked to the center of the porch, stood beside Katherine, and nonchalantly said, "You look pretty."

Katherine took her father's arm and smiled. She was determined that not even his cool demeanor would steal away the joy on her special day.

The couple stood between two large gray urns filled with magnolia leaves and wild honeysuckle, exchanged their vows, and pledged their love to one another. After the ceremony, guests surrounded them with congratulations, compliments and best wishes for their future. Bill McMolison shook Stephen's hand without comment.

ONLY THE CLOSEST of kin had been invited. It was too difficult, Mr. McMolison had instructed, to explain who and what Stephen was. "The fewer who come, the better," he said with a tone that left no room for discussion.

With the official pronouncement of marriage over, Bill grabbed Kate's elbow, leaned into her ear and under his breath said, "Who is that man anyway that married them?"

"Another one of the tent preachers, one of Stephen's friends. He's Baptist, I think."

"Well, he's not the Leaf Creek kind. And it's obvious he's not Presbyterian, not orderly or dignified."

Kate locked eyes with him. "*Stop* talking about this right now."

"I guess they're married," Bill replied, ignoring her. "Who knows? I woulda never thought we'd find ourselves in such a sad state."

Kate tried to smile. "Bill, don't call attention. I'm sure everything is fine. Here, have some punch," she said, handing him a cup. "Go visit with the guests."

IF BILL HAD DOUBTS about the authority of the preacher who performed the ceremony, he said nothing more, and when the time came, he allowed Katherine to leave with her new husband. He gave her a quick hug and said, "Take care of yourself." He turned immediately and went inside the house.

"Got to assume they are legally married, but who knows when dealing with people like that," Bill said that night, continuing his ruminating at the supper table.

"I know. I understand how you feel," Kate said softly. "I feel sad about the way things happened too, but now we've got to quit worrying about the past. Think about how happy Katherine is. That's what's important."

Bill scooped up peas and a piece of tomato with his fork before responding. "Well, I still say it would have been much better—and much more favorable in the eyes of God—to be married by a real preacher."

"He was real, Papa. I'm sure he was real. Stephen wouldn't have had him if he wasn't," Hannah said, timidly entering the conversation.

"Really? How do you know?" Bill cocked his head to one side, opened his eyes wide, and looked at Hannah.

"Well Stephen seems nice, and Katherine was so happy today." She looked toward her mother and added, "That's what we want, isn't it?"

Kate nodded, but her father spoke. "I want her happy. You think I don't? For sure I want her happy. I just don't know how she can be. One thing I know, you better never pull such a stunt. I won't tolerate another insult like this in my family. Won't tolerate more disrespect and disobedience. Remember that."

The following week, there was a brief announcement about the union in *The Herald,* the county paper. Mr. McMolison had thought it most important that folks know Katherine was married and living in Hattiesburg with her husband. Printing a proper wedding announcement, he felt, would cut down on the gossip about where she was and why she had left home. In order to control exactly what was printed, he wrote the article himself. The only assistance he accepted was Kate's description of Katherine's dress. Otherwise, only minimal details were included. There was nothing personal about Stephen. The officiating preacher was not identified.

Katherine Jane McMolison Weds
Stephen Harrison Neal

Miss Katherine McMolison of Leaf Creek and Mr. Stephen Neal of Hattiesburg were united in holy matrimony this past

Saturday afternoon at the home of the bride's parents. The bride was given in marriage by her father wearing a sweet white lace-trimmed dress. Matching lace and pearls adorned her veil and her bouquet was a single magnolia blossom. The vows were exchanged amidst urns of flowers that made the setting lovely for the occasion. Relatives were in attendance and enjoyed refreshment of fruit punch and butter cake following the ceremony. The couple will make their home in Hattiesburg.

Bill never picked up on the fact that the announcement sounded as if *he* was the one wearing the sweet white lace-trimmed dress; no one thought it a good idea to bring that detail to his attention. He dropped off the article himself at *The Herald* office on his way to the monthly meeting of the Greene County Board of Supervisors.

Chapter Thirteen

$\mathcal{A}$ FEW MONTHS after Katherine's marriage, Mr. McMolison invited Kate and Hannah to accompany him on one of his trips to Leeville. Bill was up for reelection to his Beat Three seat on the Greene County Board of Supervisors, and his friend, Mr. Stokes, was up for reelection in Beat One.

Neither Kate nor the girls knew much about county business. Bill didn't talk to them about his trips. He considered business to be solely for men and saw no value in receiving input from women. Kate, although sometimes feeling lonely and isolated, did not give his attitude much thought because his was the same as that of most men. Her focus was on her family, her home, and her church.

Kate, aware it was time for the supervisor election but unaware of her husband's long-term political agenda, was surprised by his invitation but pleased at the same time. "It would be nice to get away for a few days," she thought.

Hannah was less pleased about making the trip, but said nothing. She didn't want to irritate her father or disappoint her mother. "The trip might be fun," she encouraged herself. She knew it was election time and that many people from all over the county would gather at the courthouse in Leeville (and at the hotel where they would be staying).

She had never been, but she'd overheard enough of her father's conversations to know that election days were also social days. Her father usually went alone on his out-of-town trips. Whatever the reason he'd invited her and her mother this time didn't matter to her; she would get ready, be quiet and go. Her mother was looking forward to getting away for a few days. She would too.

He asked them on Saturday, meaning they had three days to get ready. He wanted to leave bright and early Tuesday morning, the day of the election.

November sixth, Election Day, dawned bright and clear, and even though it was late fall it was comfortably warm. Hannah packed her coat in the trunk she and her mother shared. "Hope we don't need all these clothes. Why take so much?" Hannah said to her mother as she folded another dress.

"We don't know about the weather. Could stay warm but may get cool. And I don't know what all we'll be doing." Kate waved her hand toward the dress Hannah was holding. "Get a sweater to match that dress and your hat and gloves," she instructed.

"Got it, but hope it stays warm so we won't need all this heavy stuff."

"Me too, but you never know. Better safe than sorry, as my mother always used to say," Kate said with a smile.

Kate had been to Leeville a few times during the early years of her marriage. She and Bill had attended a night of a revival at the Presbyterian Church, and they were also in town when they bought the estate furniture. She and Bill stayed with friends from the church while attending the revival but at the hotel for their furniture-buying trip.

"I'm excited we're staying at the hotel. It's really lovely. I'm glad for you to see it and be there," Kate told Hannah as they closed the lock on the trunk.

"Guess it'll be fun since I've never been," Hannah responded with only a small hint of enthusiasm.

"You will enjoy it. I know you will. The hotel is right across the street from the courthouse, close to where all the people will be. I'm sure Bill will be busy. We can do whatever we want to, walk around, visit the shops." Kate grew more excited as she encouraged Hannah.

"I'm sure I will," Hannah answered half-heartedly. "Wish Katherine was here to go with us."

"I do too. But we'll have fun. Hope the weather is nice enough that we can sit on one of the hotel porches. They're beautiful, Hannah. Porches wrap around three sides. Lots of rocking chairs, big oak limbs draping over. You're going to love it too," Kate said, continuing her effort to get Hannah excited.

"I *am* excited, Mother. You don't have to keep trying to convince me. I know it'll be nice. Not sure how much fun it'll be, but that's okay," Hannah teased Kate. "I do want to go. I've never stayed in a hotel, so that'll be fun."

"Okay, sweet daughter, just wait. Just wait till you sit on the porch, sip tea, listen to the birds and watch the squirrels scamper through the limbs of the live oaks."

"Sounds wonderful, a whole lot like what we do all the time here." Hannah smiled at her mother, cocked her head to one side and raised her eyebrows.

"Oh come on. You're being hopeless. Sound like Katherine. Go call Frank to carry the trunk outside." Kate smiled back at Hannah and shook her head side to side.

If it was too cold to be outside, Kate knew there would be a welcoming fire in the massive fireplace of the hotel parlor. It would provide a cozy and equally-inviting place to visit, watch people, sit, and relax, but she could see her teenage daughter had been encouraged as much as she desired to be, at least for the time being, so she decided to let the lovely parlor and the fireplace be a surprise.

Kate, however, was getting more and more excited as she thought about the time away. It had been several years since she had accompanied her husband out of town, and she had certainly not traveled anywhere without him.

FRANK LOADED THE WAGON. He was cheerful as always, but especially so on that particular morning. Janie and June Ellen were also hurrying around with a hum on their lips. Who could blame them?

They had plans to enjoy the next three days as well. The family would be away. Frank would take care of the animals and do the usual outside work. Janie and June Ellen would take the opportunity to turn and fluff the feather beds, air the quilts, and give the kitchen a thorough cleaning. Without the family, however, there was no one to care for and no need for a schedule. The time was theirs. Janie and June Ellen looked forward to the freedom of an empty house, and so did Frank. Even though his chores would not change much, he would be free to do them whenever he wished—except, of course, for milking Betsy and Lila. They were milked first thing every morning, and that would not change.

Bill took Kate's hand and helped her into the wagon. She sat on the bench beside him, and Hannah settled down on a pallet of quilts behind them. She brought two books and planned to read as they traveled. Katherine had sent them to her for no special occasion, just a special treat. Hannah was confident they would not be dull since Katherine had said they were two of her favorites, and Katherine never favored anything that wasn't exciting.

Hannah opened to page one of Sir Arthur Conan Doyle's *The Adventures of Sherlock Holmes*. Hannah loved mysteries. The second book, *Beautiful Joe* by Marshall Saunders, rested on the quilt beside her. Katherine sent *Beautiful Joe* because she knew that of all the books she and Hannah had read together, Hannah's favorite was *Black Beauty*. "Perfect day for a mystery," Hannah thought. "And Katherine said this other book has some sad parts. I don't feel like reading sad today." She turned the page and started on an adventure with Mr. Holmes.

Bill asked Hannah about her books. He asked Kate if she was comfortable. He actually sounded interested, concerned. His air of gentleness sparked in Kate a memory from long before, reminding her of the man she married.

Hannah and Kate were glad for the way their trip was beginning. They were grateful for the glimmers of softness in Bill's demeanor and did not want to say or do anything to trigger a change. The majority of the trip that lay ahead would be very public and, therefore, all conduct—his and theirs—would need to be exemplary. It would be easier if all three were happy.

Before getting on the main road to Leeville, they stopped at the Leaf Creek School where the local voting was taking place. Mr. McMolison's name was on the ballot but unchallenged. No one in Leaf Creek would think of running against him. He had been Beat Three supervisor for several years, and everyone in the beat wanted it to stay that way. He took care of every person and family in the beat as much as the office allowed. He was strong and forthright. His commanding presence demanded results, and no one in Beat Three wanted to lose his influence. The three stopped only long enough for Bill to cast his vote, and then they turned their wagon toward Leeville. Bill wanted to get there in time to have at least a few hours to campaign for his longtime friend, John Stokes.

Unlike Mr. McMolison, Mr. Stokes was opposed in his bid for re-election for supervisor in his beat. His opponent, an inexperienced upstart named Levi Pierce, had actually made substantial inroads among the people in Beat One. Pierce had been away to college and had just recently returned home to "better the community." He had learned a bit of savvy during his time away, and there was talk that it was paying off as he made his play for the supervisor seat. In addition, he had lots of male relatives who were all registered to vote.

Mr. McMolison was having great difficulty understanding how the men in Beat One might actually vote for this new kid. In his mind, "the boy was not even dry behind the ears. How could they lose the experience of his friend, John Stokes?" He mulled the thought over and over. It seemed to him that the people of Beat One had lost all common sense if they did not reelect the man who had already proven himself and done great things for the county. After all, Stokes was a man much like himself. He was strong and honest. He was a man of integrity, a man with a family, and a man with proven business savvy. Above all, he was a good church-going man. It didn't hurt either that he was a Scotsman and Presbyterian. Yes, he was truly a man much like himself.

Not only did Mr. McMolison want his friend to win for his friend's sake, but also for his own. He needed Stokes to stay in a position of leadership. His own goal of moving up in the political world would be greatly jeopardized if Stokes were not in office. In order to bring his political ambitions to reality, Bill needed friends in as many high places as possible, friends who he knew would give him support and would do whatever was necessary when the time came, whatever was necessary to secure his victory.

Bill McMolison, continuing to mull over his political goals, was happy that—at least so far—his plans for the day were falling into place. His wife and daughter, looking the perfect part, were with him. They had gotten an early start, he had voted, and they were well on their way to Leeville. In addition to helping Stokes, he would have the opportunity to begin showing the entire county that he was a family man, a qualification that would be important as he took steps to attain a more prominent and ultimately state-level office.

Once in Leeville, Kate and Hannah could rest and freshen up before joining him on the courthouse lawn where they would be together and be seen on and off throughout the evening. While he waited for them, he planned to grab a bite to eat and go straight to the voting area where he would begin encouraging everyone to vote for John Stokes. He wanted to waste no time in doing what he could to help get his friend elected. The stakes were high for both of them.

* * *

HANNAH READ FOR A LITTLE WHILE and then slid down onto the pallet of quilts. She snuggled into a comfortable position and began to doze. Half-asleep, half-awake, she listened to the clop-clop, clop-clop, clop-clop of the horse's hooves on the dry hard dirt of the road. She had no trouble visualizing the slight puffs of dust that wafted up and around the horse's ankles with the recurring steady gait. Upon opening her eyes, she took in the majestic beauty of the bright blue sky overhead. An occasional white fluffy cloud interrupted and added spectacular grandeur of its own. Green swaying pine tops stretched far above and appeared to reach the white puffs of softness. The view reminded Hannah of scenes on Christmas cards, scenes of abundant, lush greenery on freshly-fallen snow. With ease, Hannah soared to the treetops. She rested in the soft, white down and allowed her mind to take her to places she had known only in books. Clop-clop, clop-clop.

THE TRIP PROVED to be delightful. There was little conversation. Kate rode quietly beside her husband, only speaking if he spoke. Her thoughts began to take her to the days of their courtship.

They were in high school together in South Carolina. He was popular and handsome even when his thin leather football helmet covered his thick dark brown hair. She, too, had been popular and had received attention from a number of the boys in her class, but the attention Bill gave her claimed her heart. He wooed her masterfully. He brought her flowers, took her on Sunday afternoon rides and con-fidently, but gently, kissed her. They talked of future plans, plans that included marriage, family and building a business. She was drawn to his enthusiastic ambition. It was exciting, and it included her. She remembered when he first told her about the timber opportunity in Mississippi, about other men working for him and them getting rich. It would be an exciting challenge. At that time he talked to her about what they could do in life together. He shared every thought, and she listened. Never did she feel even the slightest cause for concern.

She recalled her wedding day. Her heart and his had been alive and bursting with love—a love, she had been certain, would be perfect and permanent. On that day, she did not know the man her husband would become.

Sometimes now she felt more dead than alive, continuously strengthening her shield of quiet. As Bill's prominence had grown, his desire for more and more of the same had grown. He was successful in business. He controlled every group of which he was a part. His high regard for his own importance gradually broke the structure of their lives. She still loved the man she married, but he had mostly disap-peared into a world of work infused with ambition and, by that time, poisoned with ever-growing guilt.

Kate was saddened by the loss of the love, excitement and passion they had once shared. Even more, she was sad not to know the constant, secure, respectful love that years of marriage should bring. She was sad, too, to admit to herself that she had grown into a current state of mere endurance. She knew, though, she couldn't change the person she had become, at least not by herself.

In those early years she had responded sometimes with fear and sometimes with anger. She had been fearful of losing his love and then angry because he caused her to even think about it. Occasionally she asked questions, most times she was quiet, and on a few occasions she attempted indifference. She did whatever seemed best for her and best for her children. The uncertainty of his response on any given day made her role a tiring one.

On that day she felt peaceful. She was completely content to sit quietly and enjoy the ride. Whatever the past had held or the future would hold, she wanted to savor the moment, and the moment was delightful. She, like Hannah, was enjoying the splendor of the day.

HANNAH WAS WIDE AWAKE and propped against the side of the wagon when they rounded the final curve that led into Leeville. Two big houses surrounded by oak trees sat back from the road on the left. On the right was the Presbyterian Church. A beautiful big oak tree hid portions of the church, but Hannah could see that it was painted white, and through the limbs she could see parts of the steeple and the green and purple stained-glass windows on either side of the front door. The surroundings were a lovely welcome. A short distance beyond the church, the overhanging trees gave way to the town and open blue sky.

It was just before noon. After riding a little further, they could see that the big hand on the courthouse clock almost covered the small one. The hands of the clock were black and easy to see against the cream color of the building. The courthouse was bigger than any building in Leaf Creek. There were at least nine or ten steps leading up to the main door. Tall windows crossed the front and sides. People were milling around everywhere. Hannah was getting a glimpse of Election Day in Leeville for the first time. The activity looked exciting. She thought the trip might turn out to be fun after all.

Chapter Fourteen

ʜANNAH PEEKED INTO THE HOTEL DINING ROOM. There were three large round tables, each with a lazy Susan laden with all kinds of vegetables, fried chicken, chicken and dumplings, and smothered steak. The vast quantity and varieties of food reminded her of Sunday dinner on the ground at church. People were seated at all the tables. Her father did not sit. Instead, he walked around every table and greeted every person.

"Hey George, how's it going today? You're voting for the right person, aren't you?" Bill slapped him on the shoulder and moved on. The next man stopped eating long enough to shake hands. "Beautiful day, Ruskin. How's your family?" Hannah listened as her father moved around the room calling most every man by name. There was Walter, who was worried about how things were going with the voting. Then there was Lloyd, who wanted to know if something more could be done about the road conditions. "We're sure gonna try," her father had answered. He asked each one something personal, and most every time he asked their thoughts about the election. If someone mentioned Levi Pierce, Bill responded with, "He's so young, doesn't have the experience of Stokes. I advise you to think long and hard before you vote him out."

He reached over one man's shoulder, grabbed a piece of chicken, and told Kate he would wait for them on the courthouse lawn. He walked through the kitchen and out the back door. It was obvious he knew all the help; the cooks and servers were more than accommodating to him. If he wanted to walk around the table and reach over shoulders for chicken, it was apparently fine with them. It was clear to see he had frequented their dining room and kitchen many times before.

Kate and Hannah, both famished, were delighted to sit and enjoy the meal before them. They'd had just enough time to freshen up before hearing the ring of the dinner bell, a signal that let everyone know the food was ready. They sat at a table with eight other people, most who seemed to know each other. Some of the men were local. Other men and their wives were in town for the election and staying at the hotel just like they were—all staying in order to be present for the vote counting.

Hannah was fascinated. She had never eaten at a table with a lazy Susan before. Kate, who had, waited for others to take the lead. Several of the men started at the same time. As they began to serve their plates, Hannah and Kate did the same.

HANNAH WAS SEATED in the chair directly across from a man who began eating first and did so swiftly. The activity at the courthouse was cause for most of the men to be in a hurry because the election was foremost in everyone's mind. When the server addressed Mr. Smith after refilling his tea glass, he didn't say anything—he just pushed his chair back, got up, and left. The server who spoke to him quickly replaced the dirty plate with a clean one, put a knife and spoon to the right of the plate, and a fork and clean napkin to the left. With a quick flick of her wrist, she brushed some wayward crumbs from the chair bottom with her hand. Within a few seconds, the place was ready for the next hungry guest.

Hannah was intrigued by the speed and graceful ease with which the server carried out her duties. She was a small colored girl, almost frail and not built at all like Janie or June Ellen (who were both large with soft laps, big arms and even bigger bosoms; Janie, honestly, was fat). This girl was slender, and it seemed strange to Hannah to see a colored girl so thin. Her skin was different, too—a much lighter brown than either Janie's or June Ellen's. She was friendly but quiet and did her work in almost a cat-like fashion, quickly and purposeful. Hannah liked her but didn't know why—maybe because she was pretty and graceful. She was different from any colored person Hannah had ever known.

As Hannah continued to watch, the most handsome boy she'd ever seen took the empty chair across from her. He was dreamy, an absolute fantasy. His hair was black like coal and his eyes were as blue as the sky—bluer than the sweater he wore. To Hannah, he was flawless. She had never seen a boy so perfect in Leaf Creek. In her stricken state, she forgot to drop her gaze. Within seconds, the eyes belonging to the exceptional specimen sitting directly in front of her were staring back. There was a faint smile on his face. Hannah felt her heart in her throat, and she was certain every person in the room could hear it beating.

She felt her face begin to flush and feared it was turning a dark shade of red. She knew she would never be so fortunate as to turn only a flattering shade of pink. "What can I do," she wondered. She felt beyond humiliated. "I don't want to look stupid. Where is Katherine when I need her? She would know what to do." Kate, seated to Hannah's left, was oblivious to her predicament. She was engaged in conversation with the lady on her left, and the man on Hannah's right was talking about the war in Europe with whoever was next to him. Hannah looked in the only direction she could, which was down at her plate. The corn, peas, rice and chicken were all still there, but she was so mentally distracted she wasn't hungry anymore. She moved the food around on her plate with her fork and finally took a small bite of rice. She sipped her tea and occasionally pretended to be looking out one of the front windows, as if she just had to pass the time while she waited for her mother.

Within a few moments, the colored girl appeared and refilled her tea glass. She lingered beside Hannah's chair for an extra minute and asked softly, "Miss, do you need anything?"

Hannah wondered if the girl had been watching and knew she definitely needed something (a distraction, at least, if nothing else). She was relieved to have somewhere to turn her attention.

There was no way for Hannah to know just how completely the girl understood what was happening, no way for Hannah to know about all the talk and all the dealings that went on in that dining room. The server beside her chair knew. She knew more than Hannah could have ever imagined—because she worked there every day. She overheard conversations as she scurried around the dining room serving tables, keeping glasses full and place settings clean. She overheard conversations because as long as she did her job, most people treated her as if she weren't there, couldn't hear, or was not capable of understanding their discussions. She lived in the Quarters along with all the other coloreds, so every day she not only heard the talk in the hotel dining room, she heard all the gossip that crossed the tracks from the white side of town. She learned a lot about many people … and that included a few things about the young man seated directly across from Hannah.

He was the heartthrob of every white girl near his age (and some who weren't). He had charisma that seemed to disarm every lady regardless of age, and after going away to college he was in command of the room every time he entered. He had grown up coming to this dining room with his family, and the colored girl had grown up serving here. Although he usually paid little attention to her, she had suffered through two personal encounters with this young man who'd caught Hannah's fancy.

The first was when they were both about thirteen. She dropped a platter of chicken. He snickered and loudly said, "You clumsy half-breed nig—" His father's hand had clamped like a flash over his forearm. John Stokes quickly stood. He jerked his head up and sideways, motioning for his son to get up. He then led Thomas Stokes just outside the door, outside the hearing of the other diners but not far enough away that she didn't hear. While she picked up chicken pieces and wiped crumbs from the floor, she heard his father tell him to never say anything like that to her again. Did he understand? Mr. Stokes's tone was surprisingly harsh, she'd thought. Mr. McMolison had walked close to the door and listened to what was said before walking away. It was a strange occurrence that the colored girl—named Rosie—wouldn't fully understand for several years and Thomas never would.

The second encounter she had with Thomas Stokes was two years later, when they were both fifteen. Thomas suddenly saw Rosie through different eyes. He saw a beautiful, fully-developed girl with smooth, light brown skin and lovely dark brown eyes. The sight of her stirred a desire in him he couldn't ignore. He followed as she left the hotel one evening.

"Hey, Rosie, you headed home?"

"Yes, it's not much further," she answered politely.

"Did you have a hard day at the hotel?"

"It wasn't bad."

"Slow down, Rosie. Let's talk for a while."

"I really can't. I need to be getting home." Rosie's heart quickened with anxiety and fear.

"Oh, come on. You can stop and talk for just a little while."

"I really must be going home. My grandmother will come looking for me."

"I know your grandmother. She knows me. She won't mind if we talk for a little while." Thomas stopped his wagon on the street, got out, and walked toward her. They were at the edge of the woods. "Wait up."

Rosie had never before been bothered, but she knew that some of her friends and many of their mothers were used for learning by the young white men (and just plain used by the older ones).

"Come on, Rosie, we're old enough to know each other better."

Rosie backed away, but he grabbed her arm. She stood still and closed her eyes as he began unbuttoning her dress. "Mr. Thomas, please don't. Please don't do this."

"Why? It'll be fun."

She tried desperately to think of something else until he left her, but his searching fingers and heavy breathing made that impossible. Before he reached the flesh he sought, a wagon stopped on the street a few feet away. Thomas was completely oblivious until his name rang out in the darkness. It was his father, Mr. Stokes, who had apparently come looking for him.

Mr. Stokes spoke firmly through clenched teeth: "Thomas, get in your wagon and go home. *Never* touch Rosie." He did not say that he would deal with him when he got home or anything else that a father might say to a son in such a situation. Instead, he turned to Rosie and said, "Are you okay?" It occurred to Rosie that what Thomas was doing didn't upset Mr. Stokes as much as who he was doing it to.

"Yes sir," she managed to answer, as she stood frozen against the tree behind her.

Mr. Stokes turned toward his wagon, and as he lifted himself up and onto the seat, he called back to Rosie, "Button your dress, and get in the back of my wagon."

He drove her home in silence. She got out of the wagon, looked up toward the face that was staring straight ahead and quietly said, "Thank you."

John Stokes said nothing. Rosie heard the double click of his tongue and the reins pop the back of the horse. The horse pulled forward, and by the time Rosie reached her front door, the sound of the wagon wheels turning against the dirt was barely audible. Glad to be safely home, she walked inside. The words *never touch Rosie again* rang in her ears. Why would Mr. Stokes have said that, she wondered?

Rosie's grandmother had heard the wagon and was standing at the window when Rosie walked inside. "Why is Mr. Stokes bringing you home?"

"He was." She hesitated. "I mean he came. He came …"

"Rosie, what is it? Tell me. Is something wrong?" Her grandmother turned to face her.

"It's just that when I left the hotel tonight, his son followed me …"

"Followed you? You mean Thomas? Thomas followed you? Why?"

"Yes ma'am. I don't know why. He was suddenly there. He started to …" Rosie stopped mid-sentence. "I don't know where Mr. Stokes came from. Somewhere on the road, I guess." Her voice started to quiver, and tears filled her eyes. "I was scared. Nothing like that has ever happened to me before."

Her grandmother hurried across the little room and grasped both of Rosie's upper arms. "Started to what? What happened?" Her breathing quickened as she looked deep into Rosie's eyes. A troubled frown covered her face. "Tell me what happened," she demanded. "Are you alright?"

"Yes ma'am. It's all okay, really. Nothing happened. Don't worry."

Her grandmother loosened her grasp and hugged her tightly with both arms. "Oh, my dear, precious Rosie, are you sure nothing else happened? You would tell me, wouldn't you?"

"Yes ma'am, but nothing happened. I promise."

"Where did you say Mr. Stokes was?"

"I don't know. He just appeared. Guess he had come looking for Thomas." Rosie wiped tears from her cheeks with her fingers. "I'm glad he was there."

Her grandmother pulled a handkerchief from her dress pocket and handed it to Rosie. "Here, baby, use this. Come sit with me—just for a spell." She took Rosie's hand and led her to the sofa where they sat side by side. "Now tell me everything. What did Mr. Stokes do?"

"He told Thomas to go home and to *never* touch me again. Then he told me to get in his wagon, and he brought me home. I was scared, so I don't know for sure, but it seemed like Mr. Stokes was upset because it was me Thomas had stopped. Why would that make a difference?"

Her grandmother turned sideways, clasped Rosie's fingers in her hands, and rubbed the back of Rosie's hands with her thumbs. "Like I've told you, child, we don't always get answers. I'm just thankful he came along. Mr. Stokes will take care of Thomas. He won't bother you again."

"How do you know?"

"Doesn't matter. I just feel pretty certain Mr. Stokes will take care of it. Go to bed and try to put tonight out of your mind."

HER GRANDMOTHER had been right. Almost two years had passed with barely a nod from Thomas. She served him when he was in the dining room, but few words were exchanged and no eye contact was made. Today eye contact was being made, not with Rosie herself but with a new girl she had never seen before. Rosie lingered near Hannah's chair, continuing to offer tea refills even when they weren't necessary.

HANNAH LOOKED UP at the friendly face and managed a slight smile. "Thank you," she said quietly. Hannah continued to sip tea as inconspicuously as she possibly could. The peas, corn, and chicken stayed on the plate. She had gotten nervous. There was no way she could eat. When Kate finished, they excused themselves and headed for the courthouse lawn. The jet-black hair, the beautiful blue eyes, and the perfectly-shaped lips were left at the table, but every detail of the boy was stored away in Hannah's memory. Her father had said everybody was to go to the courthouse, and she would keep watch in the crowd for the blue sweater.

Kate and Hannah strolled around the lawn. Banners with candidates' names hung from trees. Men and women were handing out ribbons and cards that encouraged votes for their favorite. People were gathering from all over the county. Some brought chairs from home, while others spread blankets and quilts on the ground to serve as pallets where ladies sat, slightly leaning to one side as they propped on one hand, their legs with dress-covered knees bent and pointed in the opposite direction. Lemonade was available to purchase along with coffee, cake, and cookies. Hannah and Kate found Bill. He kept them close by his side as they walked around the courthouse lawn looking like the perfect family. He greeted everyone, always introducing Kate and Hannah and always putting in a plug for John Stokes. All the politicking struck Hannah as a lot of bluster. She was glad when he suggested they might enjoy mingling in the crowd on their own.

They visited with two sisters, Ethel and Muriel, from the eastern part of the county. They too would be spending the night but were staying with relatives. Their group of four, as they explained, was made up of the two of them, Muriel's husband, and Ethel's son. Ethel added that her husband was overseas somewhere in the war. "He was with one of the first groups to leave the United States, and I worry so for him." She sighed deeply and said, "I hope and pray daily for his safe return." Tears filled the women's eyes.

Hannah was interested in her story and felt sad for her and her son, Ernest, but when the woman suggested that Ernest might show her around and introduce her to some other young people, Hannah wanted to move on. She politely declined, saying she hoped to get her mother to take her shopping.

KATE WAS AMUSED. She had not considered going to the stores quite so soon but was not surprised by Hannah's request. Both of her girls enjoyed going to the Mercantile in Leaf Creek. She surmised that Hannah was thinking the stores there in Leeville would have larger selections. What Kate didn't know was that Hannah's true motive for declining Ethel's offer was back in the dining room. He had blue eyes, black hair, perfect lips, and a blue sweater—none of which Ethel's Ernest could claim.

AT SIX O'CLOCK the polls closed and the official counting started. It was already dark. Lanterns glowed in all the courthouse windows. The traditional bonfire was lit, warding off the chill of the night air. Hannah enjoyed the festive atmosphere in spite of the fact she had not seen the handsome boy wearing the blue sweater. She wished desperately Katherine were there, because she would have loved to tell her about him.

The crowd began to thin soon after the polls closed. Folks from the outlying areas had to get home to take care of livestock. Townspeople hung around for another couple of hours, after which time most of the women went home as did about half of the men. The other half gathered in the halls of the courthouse and waited until every vote was methodically counted one by one.

Hannah and Kate went back to the hotel. Bill had not wanted to leave the room where the count was going on, so Kate asked the kitchen help to pack a supper for him. They most willingly packed more food than he could possibly eat. Kate and Hannah carried the generous supper along with a quart fruit jar filled with tea across the street and into the courthouse. "Sir," Kate addressed one of the men standing near the door. "Do you know Mr. McMolison?"

"Sure I do. Most everybody around here knows Bill. You need me to get him for you?"

"I would appreciate it. Thank you," Kate responded.

Bill soon came from one of the side rooms into the hallway. His greeting was pleasant. "What did you bring me?"

"We brought you some supper, thought you might get hungry before the night is over," Kate answered him cheerfully.

"I'm hungry now. Thanks for bringing it. I need to get back where the count is going on. I don't think anyone involved would do anything dishonest, but it's best to stay close by. Every candidate has at least one person in the room." Bill seemed happy to stand and chat a few minutes, and Kate was glad for the friendly exchange with him. He seemed more like the man she married than he had in a long time.

"We'll probably walk back over to the hotel. It's getting pretty chilly outside, and most of the women seem to have gone home," Kate said.

Hannah added, "And there is a huge fire burning in the fireplace. If it's okay with you," she said, looking at her mother, "I'd like to sit by the fire and read more of my book."

"Sounds nice," said Kate. "I'll join you."

Hannah continued to hope the young man from the dining room might reappear. She knew she would have no chance of seeing him if she went to bed. Sitting by the fire in the parlor seemed the best option.

"Thanks again for bringing supper," Bill said with a final wave. "The counting probably won't be finished until the morning hours, and I won't be in till it's finished." He walked inside but called back from halfway down the hall, "Y'all go on to bed."

Chapter Fifteen

THE ELECTION WAS OVER. It was the morning after, and Bill was up and dressed early even though he had not gone to bed until the wee hours of the night. Kate and Hannah had retired around ten-thirty, but he stayed until the count was complete. The margin had been a close one, but his friend was victorious. They could relax, celebrate, and continue plans to run the county.

Bill headed to the dining room to get breakfast. Stokes met him there, drank coffee and rehashed the events of the day before while Bill ate buttered biscuits and ham. They visited with everyone in the room, now politicking for the future with increased confidence and a celebratory air. The smell of cigars and pipes filled the room. Smoke wafted toward the ceiling, sometimes in puffs and sometimes in little intermittent circles. Jake Gordon, the banker, leaned his chair back against the wall and poked in the bowl of his pipe. "Last night was a good night for Greene County," he said, looking at McMolison and Stokes. "We got you two back in office. Now it's up to y'all to move things forward."

Bill walked over to Jake. "Man, I appreciate everything you did to help us," he said. "You can be sure we'll both work hard." Bill then turned to James Walley, the sheriff. He gripped the sheriff's right shoulder with his left hand, looked him in the eyes, and firmly shook his right hand. "You know you can always count on my help. I want this to be a safe county, so you be sure to let me know if there is ever anything I can do."

"Shore will. I'll keep that in mind," the sheriff drawled as he pulled a chair out and sat down where his plate waited on the table. While mixing two soft fried eggs into a serving of grits that covered half his plate, he added, "Sometimes a little extra help is just what I need." Every man in the room understood the unspoken meaning. White robes weren't necessary; money, knowing the right person and an occasional additional incentive (physical or otherwise) was all it took. Coloreds need to stay in their place; whites need to do what's right. Bury secrets when necessary. It was a small group, but its numbers did not matter. It determined the county's activity. Money, the promise of power, threats, silence, whatever it took to advance their purpose—all came into play at one time or another. McMolison and Stokes both had strong voices.

Washing down the last bite of grits with what was left of his coffee, the sheriff pushed away from the table. "Got to get on with the day. Y'all take care now." He took his hat from one of the knobs that stuck up on the back of his chair and walked toward the door.

John Stokes was still making his rounds. He stopped Sheriff Walley to shake his hand again. "Remember, we want a safe county."

"Got it," Walley said in response.

Both Stokes and McMolison repeated the backslapping and handshaking with every new man walking through. Big white coffee cups were filled and refilled. The atmosphere was electric. Future political ambitions included being elected to a higher office, and if those aspirations were ever realized, one could only imagine how much greater the celebratory air would be. One thing was sure: both men, with ambitions intact, had plans to find out one day in the near future.

***

FINDING THE DINING ROOM filled with men and smoke, Kate and Hannah opted to sit on the front porch. The sun had already burned last night's chill from the air, and the sky was clear and beautiful.

They each settled into one of the big rockers. Kate enjoyed the peacefulness of the early morning. Hannah was glad to be on the porch for a completely different reason. She could see most of downtown. She hoped to get another glimpse of the handsome guy from the day before.

The same colored girl was working again. "May I bring you something to the porch?" she asked. "It won't be a full breakfast, but maybe some tea or coffee with biscuits?" Hannah couldn't help but think again about how different she looked and sounded from the coloreds back home.

"That would be lovely," Kate answered. "We were not sure we would be able to eat since the dining room is full."

"Yes ma'am, it's full this morning. The men are still celebrating." She left them but returned shortly with orange juice in tall glasses. The juice was fresh-squeezed, and a small orange wedge was placed on the rim of each glass. The girl also brought hot tea and a plate of biscuits with pieces of ham tucked inside.

The tea service was in the Baby Rose design. The background was white with pink roses and tiny green leaves scattered all around. The service included milk, lemon slices and sugar. Hannah had never seen anyone use milk in hot tea before. Her mother always drank her tea with only a little sugar. Hannah decided to try a little of everything. She added sugar, then a touch of milk to her cup. The lemon slices were pretty, so she squeezed one into her milky tea. Her heart sank with embarrassment as she looked at her curdle-filled cup. "Oh no, what happened?"

"Don't worry. It's fine. We'll get another cup," Kate said reassuringly. "Lemon and milk don't work together very well. I should have thought to tell you."

"I'm sorry. This looks awful. I can't drink it," Hannah said timidly.

The colored girl appeared quickly, almost as if she had been watching. She served Hannah another cup of tea, lifted the cup of curdle-coated tea from Hannah's tray, walked to the end of the porch, and poured the contents over the banister. Hannah, more appreciative than the girl would have imagined, smiled and said, "Thank you."

AFTER FINISHING THE TEA and biscuits, Hannah and Kate strolled down the side street and visited the Little Variety Store. There was not much of interest to buy, but they enjoyed browsing and visiting with the lady who owned the shop. She was a bit plump and plainly-dressed but was jolly and chatted endlessly about whatever came into her mind.

"Good morning! Y'all come on in and look around. *Law* me, I thought it was gonna be cold today. I wore this long-sleeved dress, and now I'm about to burn up. Course I've done a day's work already, been cleaning the shelves. Think I'll just sit and cool off."

"The sun has warmed things up a lot," Kate offered in response.

"Are y'all in town because of the election yesterday?"

"Yes we are."

"Election Day is always some big day round here, lots going on and people to see. I had to cook extra 'cause some relatives came. They got up early this morning and left. I was happy to see them, but I was really glad they left." She got up from her stool and adjusted a doll that was leaning sideways on one of the shelves. "I like 'em straight, don't want any of my little girls falling over." She laughed. "My name is Pearl Smith. I pick out everything you see in here, been doing it for over twenty years." She picked up one trinket and then another, either moving them around or being sure Hannah and Kate saw them.

"It's nice to meet you, Pearl. I'm Kate, and this is my daughter, Hannah. We're just browsing around today while my husband finishes some business."

"Well, y'all just look to your heart's content." Pearl's smile covered her face. "I'm getting lots more stuff in sometime next week or the next if y'all are back this a way. I'll be here if the Lord's willing and the creek don't rise," she said with a chuckle.

KATE AND HANNAH agreed that meeting Pearl had been fun. Their hearts were laughing as they left.

The Main Mercantile was their second stop. That store was much like the Mercantile in Leaf Creek. The merchandise was similar, but with a bigger selection. Kate found material she considered purchasing.

"Look at this beautiful deep green velvet," she said to Hannah as she flipped the bolt over so that a piece draped down the side of the counter. "This would make a lovely Christmas dress."

"That's pretty and it's your favorite color. You should get it," Hannah encouraged her mother.

"Well …" Kate sighed, continuing to admire the fabric. "I could make the dress, but I'm not sure I would ever wear it—most too dressy for church. I'll think about it and come back by the store before we leave town if I decide to get it."

Knowing it was near time for the dinner bell, they returned to the hotel.

AFTER EATING DINNER, Kate chose to go back to their room to read and nap before the get-together with the Stokes family. They had been invited to join the Stokes for supper, and the plan was to go sometime around mid-afternoon.

Kate and Hannah had briefly met Mrs. Stokes the day before. She, looking the part of the perfect wife and mother, had been busy at the side of her husband. Even though their husbands were very close friends and fellow supervisors, Kate had only been with Mrs. Stokes two previous times. The first had been years before, not long after Kate and Bill moved to Leaf Creek. She didn't remember the occasion, and the second had been at her precious little Samuel's funeral. Mrs. Stokes had come with her husband to offer condolences.

Kate was pleased to have the opportunity to know Mrs. Stokes. She thought if they could become better acquainted—or even friends— perhaps it would be a reason to accompany Bill on future trips. She was enjoying this time away from home. It was going well, and if circumstances allowed, maybe she would be invited to come again.

Instead of napping, Hannah had gone back to the front porch. She would certainly not run into the blue sweater if she closed herself up in the bedroom. She knew the sweater was probably hanging in a wardrobe by then, but she was certain she did not need it to recognize the magnificent vision if he appeared. She continued rocking, hoping, and watching just in case.

THE TIME NEARED to leave for the visit with the Stokes family. Hannah did not look forward to the evening. As she dressed, she dreaded it more and more. "Nothing will be fun about sitting with four adults," she thought. She was certain they would not talk about even one thing she would be interested in; the men would talk politics, and the women would speak of roses, cakes, and crochet. Not one of these subjects was of interest to Hannah. Feeling sure she would be trapped for the whole evening, she grimaced. "And I'm sure I'll get the same old questions: "How old are you? What grade are you in?" She didn't think adults knew any other questions to ask.

Hannah would much prefer to stay around the hotel and check out whoever came in, but she did not have a choice. She had to finish dressing. Her mother always encouraged her to look her best, regardless of the occasion, and her father, of course, expected her to.

Hannah hurriedly pulled some of her blond curls up and fastened them with the jeweled comb Katherine had given her for Christmas. She changed into a pink dress and matching sweater. The dress had a lovely gathered skirt and a scooped neck that was just low enough to reveal that she was no longer a mere girl. She looked at herself in the mirror and thought, "Pretty dress. It's a shame to be wearing it with no hope of seeing anyone—at least no one important—just old people." She took in a slow deep breath, held it briefly while she admired herself, and then let it out quickly with an audible sigh. "Oh well, might as well get started so I can get it over with."

Once she had finished dressing, she thought again of her father's expectation that she look her best, smile, and be polite. "Okay, I've almost done the look-your-best part. Now I'll go sit, smile, and be polite." She was feeling more and more frustrated just thinking about the evening ahead of her, but her dreary attitude and frustration did not show. She looked beautiful. Her radiant white skin, smooth as porcelain, glowed with a hint of pink on her cheeks and lips. She smiled sweetly and told her parents she was ready and would wait for them downstairs in the parlor.

Chapter Sixteen

M R. MCMOLISON HAD THEIR WAGON brought around to the front of the hotel and they were soon on their way. The Stokes lived only two miles out of town, so the trip was a short one. To Hannah it seemed they arrived in only a very few minutes, far too short a time for her. It was four in the afternoon when the three of them—Bill, Kate, and Hannah—pulled their wagon into the Stokes's drive, and all Hannah could think about were the boring hours ahead of her.

"Evening, Mista McMolison." The colored man spoke first to Bill before nodding toward Kate and Hannah and addressing them with a polite "Ma'am." He seemed to come from nowhere and met them as they entered the short drive leading from the road to the house.

"Evening to you, Lisha," Bill answered. "How've you been?"

"Fine, mighty fine," Lisha answered. "I'll take ole Pete here and give him some of my good *Lisha care* while y'all have your visit. He'll be fit and ready for the trip home tomorrow."

Lisha took the reins and led Pete away from the house. Pete had been in a stable in town, but now it was obvious he would be getting a little extra special attention.

The steps were steep and the porch was long. It was painted gray. There was a swing at one end. Rocking chairs, also painted gray, were in groups of two on both the swing end and the other end. Flower urns were sitting beside the columns at the top of the steps and at the end of the porch. There was not much in the way of flowers growing in the urns, but then it was November.

Hannah thought of their house back home. "Our house is nice, probably the nicest in Leaf Creek, but this house is certainly bigger," she thought. "Mr. Stokes must own two mills … or maybe he owns the whole forest and the mills." Hannah was suddenly looking forward to seeing the inside of the home. At least being in pretty surroundings would help to make the afternoon and evening more tolerable.

The door opened, and Hannah almost gasped out loud. Her legs went suddenly weak, and she choked on air she wasn't even sure was there because it felt as if her lungs were barely working. All she felt in her chest was a flutter. When she wiped a strand of hair from her eyes, she realized her hands were damp. She gained enough composure to put them against the skirt of her dress to dry them. She smiled politely as Mr. Stokes introduced her and Kate to his son, Thomas. He was not wearing the blue sweater, but a cream one instead. His eyes were just as blue, his hair just as black, and his lips just as perfect as they had been the day before—when she sat directly across the table from him in the hotel dining room. His smile was sure and confident.

Kate responded first: "It's nice to meet you, Thomas."

Hannah followed her mother's lead: "Yes, it is nice to meet you." She hoped the slight quiver of her lips didn't show.

Now Hannah knew the evening would be more interesting and exciting than she'd anticipated. With concentration and effort, she was able to breathe and to talk. She hoped her breathing appeared calm and that her sentences were complete. After visiting with Mrs. Stokes for a few minutes, she began to feel a little calmer, although her heart was still near her throat and her mouth was dry.

AT THE HOTEL THE DAY BEFORE, Hannah had not gone unnoticed by Thomas. He had been as aware of her across the dining table as she had been of him. Her beauty had definitely gotten his attention. The pretty face was new to him, and he wondered where she had come from. He saw the blond curls that fell softly around her shoulders and her green eyes drop from his gaze to her plate. He had grown up in that town and knew everyone—he would never have missed someone like her. He knew that she had been aware of him, too, and he enjoyed it. He was accustomed to being noticed by girls, but he loved the fact that Hannah was demure and seemed to want to hide her face in her plate. Thomas lost no time in finding out from the hotel staff that Hannah was her name and that she was the daughter of his father's best friend. He knew the McMolisons were to eat supper with his parents. He would definitely be home.

Mr. Stokes invited the McMolisons into the parlor. Mrs. Stokes suggested they have tea and visit before supper. She offered milk, sugar, and lemon with tea that she served in white cups with gold rims.

"Oh no," Hannah thought. She knew she didn't want milk, but she couldn't remember whether it was proper to put sugar in the tea before lemon—or lemon before sugar—or if it mattered. "No, thank you. I like mine plain." (She really didn't, but saying otherwise was safer.)

Hannah was nervous and desperately wanted to make a good impression. "Please, God," she prayed silently. "Just help me. Help me not to say something silly. He's so together. Help me be together. Help me not sound stupid. Just get me through this evening. I don't have any trouble talking to boys back in Leaf Creek."

She kept telling herself this boy was no different, just maybe a little older. "Just need to be more like Katherine," she thought further. "If she were here, *she* wouldn't be nervous. She would laugh and talk and ask whatever questions she wanted the answers to." Hannah tried to encourage herself, but she continued to nurse what felt like a thousand butterflies. "Maybe I could just pretend to be Katherine or act like her." The thought spun in her head, even though she knew Katherine would tell her she was being crazy; Katherine's advice would be to just be herself and have fun. Hannah took a deep breath and felt a little calmer just as she realized she was hearing her name.

"Hannah." He, Thomas with the blue eyes, the jet-black hair and perfect lips, was saying her name. "Hannah." It sounded wonderful.

"What is wrong with me? Get yourself together," she told herself.

She had never before responded in such a way to anything, especially not her name. She managed a slight smile and softly answered, "Yes?"

"Would you like to skip out on these adults for a few minutes? One of our cats had kittens about a week ago. They're in the smokehouse right beside the back porch. It will be dark when we finish supper, but we can see them now. What do you think?"

Kate smiled, so Hannah assumed permission was granted. After all, they were only walking down the back steps and about thirty feet to the smokehouse. She stood, and Thomas led the way and opened the smokehouse door. The smell of smoke, salt meat, and canning supplies filled her senses. There in one corner was a large wooden box. The bottom was covered with an old and faded blue blanket, and snuggled in the folds of the blanket were little kittens. They looked like furry balls, all curled and nestled close to their mother. He picked one of the purring creatures up and handed it to Hannah. She held it close, feeling the softness on her neck. The mother cat protested loudly with several shrill meows.

Hannah loved cats, kittens, dogs, and puppies but had never had any of her own. Mr. McMolison had always forbidden his children to have a pet of any kind. There was no clear reason, except because he just said so. Thomas picked up a second kitten and stroked it gently. "We haven't decided on names," he said. "Maybe you can help."

Hannah and Thomas started suggesting to each other names for each kitten. "What do you think about Boots for the black one with white feet?" he asked.

"Wel-ell," Hannah replied, drawing the word into at least two syllables, and added, "I guess that seems obvious. Boots is a perfect name." She was proud of her answer. The words had all come out without a stammer. "What about Smokey for the gray one?"

Thomas laughed and said, "Seems we have come up with two original names. What do you think?"

Hannah laughed with him. "We have. Maybe the other gray one can be called Soot or Sootsy if it happens to be a girl." They both laughed and continued to stroke their now-fidgety kittens until Mrs. Stokes called to them that supper was ready. They set the kittens next to the mother cat, making both cat and kittens happy.

The trip to the smokehouse may have caused anxiety for the felines, but it had served to calm Hannah a bit and give her a little confidence. She was completely enthralled by her handsome host, and she very much wanted the time to go well. Even the boring, tiresome talk of political strategy was bearable since it was intertwined with an occasional wink from one of Thomas's blue eyes directly across the table from her.

In addition to politics, the conversation included timber prices, the mills, church and, of course, family. Learning about the Stokes family was what Hannah was most interested in. She was particularly anxious to hear any story that involved Thomas. She learned that he was actually in school in Oxford, at a place called Ole Miss. At that time he was in his first year and had come home to help with the election. He wasn't old enough to vote but was tasked with spending time with his friends and their families in an attempt to sway them toward voting for his father. Hannah was eager to learn anything she could about him, though she already knew in her mind he was perfect. She had never spent time with college guys before, but if Thomas was an example of one, she was certain she liked them a lot.

Mrs. Stokes also talked about her other children—two were older than Thomas and one was younger. The older two (a girl and a boy) were both married. The son had been in town the day before for the election but had already returned to his own home in the next county. The daughter had two small children and lived in north Mississippi. The younger child was another son. He had just turned sixteen, was a junior at the high school, and on that night was at school for play practice.

Hannah had a sudden pang as she realized Thomas had a younger brother that was her age, or maybe even a few months older. Hannah wished Thomas were the youngest son, the one still living at home. There might be some chance of seeing him again. "How old is Thomas?" she wondered. Her father had never let her go on a date. But as she thought about the possibility, she knew he would never consent to her being with someone older unless … "Maybe, just maybe, since

Thomas is the son of Mr. Stokes (Papa's best friend), then maybe he might," she thought. Then Hannah caught herself. She realized she was daydreaming right there in front of her parents, as well as Mr. and Mrs. Stokes and, most of all, Thomas. She felt herself blush, even though she knew no one could possibly know her thoughts. After all, she had been listening attentively and politely as Mrs. Stokes shared her stories, one of which included the fact that Thomas was only fourteen months older than his younger brother. That was good news.

Suddenly Mr. McMolison announced, "It's time for us to be on our way."

Hannah wilted inside. "Why," she thought, "does Papa want to go home early tonight? Of all nights, this is the worst. He never seems to think that way when he is away alone, at least he doesn't hurry home." She had hoped for another little interlude with Thomas. She was certain that his eyes, peering across the table during their meal, had told her he had been thinking the same thing. Now her father had cut it all short. There was nothing she could do but extend a polite, "Thank you for a wonderful evening," get in the wagon, and go to the hotel.

She left the house wondering how she could possibly manage to see Thomas again.

CHAPTER SEVENTEEN

THE FOLLOWING MORNING Bill, Kate, and Hannah headed home. Clop-clop, clop-clop. Pete pulled the wagon toward Leaf Creek.

Hannah was quiet as she stretched out. She did not read. She did not want to; she meditated on her own fairy tale. Filling her mind were blue eyes, black hair, a wonderful smile, and a handsome face. Filling her mind was Thomas. She relived naming the kittens with him, receiving the winks from him and hearing her name spoken by him. She fanaticized about visiting him at Ole Miss. He would introduce her as his girl. Hannah, thinking back on her sister's wedding, thought maybe she would marry on the family's front porch just as Katherine had done. She even designed her wedding gown and reveled at the glow in Thomas's eyes when he saw her in it. She felt his gentle caress on her skin, heard his confident voice—hushed and romantic—saying her name and smelled the slightly spicy fragrance that came with his presence. She imagined and pored over every detail of the beautiful face and body that now owned her consciousness.

Once home, routine returned. In school Hannah shared her days with the same friends, boys and girls, with whom she had spent countless days in the past. Words like *humdrum, boring, unsophisticated,* and *dull* summed up her thoughts about all of them. How had her feelings changed so quickly? She had never been a pretentious person (or didn't think herself to be), but being in Leeville and with Thomas made everything and everybody she had known before look and seem different. She liked her little taste of the world outside Leaf Creek, and she wanted more.

HANNAH WAS ANXIOUS to tell Clara about her trip and especially about Thomas. Clara was her best friend and the person she confided in since Katherine was no longer around. Clara had never been out of Leaf Creek except to visit a relative that lived somewhere down on the Gulf Coast. That trip had been the biggest thrill she had ever experienced. She had told Hannah at length all about the beach, the waves, and the sea gulls. Hannah had listened attentively, so she reasoned, "Now it's Clara's turn to listen, and Thomas is far more interesting than water and birds. I can hardly wait to tell her!"

Hannah described in detail everything about Thomas including his clothes, his beautiful blue eyes, his jet-black hair, his winsome smile, and the wink at the family supper table. For a few minutes Clara listened patiently, but when Hannah showed no interest in walking with her down by the school where she thought some of the local boys might be, her interest quickly waned.

"Well, he sounds great and all, but he is not here." Clara's tone was more impatient than she had intended so she added, "Oh, I'm sorry. I didn't mean to cut you off. I'm sure he's wonderful, and I hope you get to see him again, but right now I want to go by where some of the boys are shooting basketball. Chris Graham told me he would walk me home if I waited for him. I need to go. Come on, Hannah. Come with me. A bunch of the boys will be there."

"No, you go on. I'm going home." Hannah's feelings were hurt that her friend had not been more interested in the most important thing she had ever had to tell her. She told herself that Clara couldn't understand anyway, because she had never met anyone as special as Thomas. As Hannah walked home, she calmed her frustration with Clara by thinking of how excited Katherine would be to hear her news. The hard part would be having to wait until she came home again.

Two weeks passed. Hannah was hoping her father would include her and her mother on another of his trips to Leeville, but so far he hadn't. He had made at least one overnight trip back to the county seat since their return, but had gone with only a moment's notice, at least to Kate and Hannah—he simply announced one morning that he would be away for a day or so. Frank saddled his horse, and he promptly left. Hannah never stopped to think that even if her father had taken her with him, she likely wouldn't have seen Thomas, as he would have been back at Ole Miss. Even so, she thought of him continuously and held tightly to the hope of seeing him again.

A week later, a letter arrived. Hannah came home from school to find her mother, along with Janie and June Ellen, in the kitchen and looking a little smug. Hannah was directed to the shelf of the pie safe on which she found a letter with the return address, "Oxford, Mississippi." Her heart was aflutter, and her smile was so big it could easily have absorbed all three of the smiles coming her way.

Kate knew Hannah had been attracted to Thomas the night they had supper at the Stokeses'. She also knew Hannah had been more interested in the mail the previous three weeks than she had ever been before. Hannah had, more than once, mentioned Thomas and naming the cute kittens. Kate never thought cats were what Hannah was most interested in, and her response to seeing the letter made her certain.

What everybody was thinking did not matter to Hannah. Nothing mattered but the letter in her hand. Kate, Janie, and June Ellen laughed as she ran to her room.

November 18th

Dear Hannah,

I had planned to write you as soon as I got back to campus, but because of some extra required reading and studying, I've let a few days get by. I missed an examination in my algebra class while I was at home. It was necessary for me to complete the make-up work as well as keep up with my current assignments. It is really cold here so staying inside to study is ok.

I enjoyed meeting you and your family. I want to thank you for helping me name the kittens. I'm sorry you didn't get to tell them goodbye before leaving. I had hoped you could. Perhaps I can bring one of them to see you sometime.

Speaking of coming to see you—I will be home for a few days around Thanksgiving. I was thinking of coming to Leaf Creek on Friday if that is ok with you and your family. You probably don't have time to write me before then. I will plan to come, and if you're going to be away or if for any other reason this plan is not good, I suppose I will learn when I get there.

I hope this letter finds you doing well, and I shall look forward to seeing you.

Best Regards,
Thomas

Hannah read the letter a second time and then a third. She lifted it to her nose and smelled it although it didn't smell of anything in particular. She read it again. She held the letter against her pounding heart, refolded it, placed it in her letter box and then took it out again. Excitedly she ran down the hall and into the kitchen. "He's coming! He's coming here to visit!" She jumped up and down and spun around. She hugged her mother, spun around again and then stopped dead still. Hugging the letter to her chest, she looked at her mother. "He can come, can't he? Papa will let him come?"

"We'll see, Hannah. I hope so," Kate responded.

June Ellen chimed in, "Well, it's a good thing he's coming here 'cause I need to check him out," she said with a laugh. Every person in the room knew she was only pretending to joke. She would definitely have her say when it came to any boy showing up to court Hannah.

Janie agreed, "That's for sure."

"Y'all will like him," Hannah said with a lilt in her voice as she skipped from the kitchen.

Kate took a deep breath and made a moaning sound as she exhaled. "I'm glad to see her so happy," she said to Janie and June Ellen. "But she's so young."

"She's 'bout old enough to be thinking on such things," Janie said matter-of-factly as she wiped off the table where she had been sifting flour.

"I know. I know," Kate agreed. "Thomas seemed like a nice young man, and I can see why she liked him. He was incredibly cute and charming, but you know Hannah hasn't dated, and he has already been away at college. I'm sure he has had lots of experience."

"It's normal, Miz Kate. Don't worry. She's a smart girl. She'll be fine." Janie spoke confidently. June Ellen, holding in her lap a bowl of long green beans, never stopped snapping, but she looked up and nodded in agreement.

"Well … hope you're right." Kate poured hot water into her teapot. "I knew Hannah really liked him the night we had supper with his parents. I just hope she doesn't get swept off her feet. His father is a friend of Bill's. I liked him, too. I just don't want her to get hurt." Kate's thoughts almost ran into each other. She rocked the teapot gently back and forth before pouring tea into one of her china cups.

"Let's just take a day at a time, Miz Kate. It's plain to see Hannah is on top of the world," June Ellen, still snapping beans, chimed in. "I think it'll be a bad thing if you start to talk about all your worries."

Janie added, "We'll fix all Hannah's favorite things. It's gonna be a real good day when he comes. And we'll surely check him out while he's here."

Young love was exciting to be around. They could all three see that Hannah was smitten and would do everything possible to make Thomas's visit as perfect as possible.

KATE, UNSURE OF HOW BILL would respond to the news of Thomas's visit, thought it best if he heard it quickly and heard it from her. She was sure Bill would think he should have been asked and not told—and even surer he would not like learning he was the last in the household to know. She thought too that if he became angry, she would like the opportunity to smooth the situation before he confronted Hannah.

Kate rehearsed her words and made plans to broach the subject that evening. In her mind they didn't have a choice as to whether Thomas would come or not. He had sent word that he planned to visit, and the only way to stop him would be for Bill to meet him in Leeville and tell him not to come. That thought was not acceptable to Kate. It would not only be rude, it would be terribly disappointing to Hannah. She knew she would just have to tell him and then deal with his answer, regardless of what it turned out to be.

In the sitting room after supper Bill pulled a chair close to the fire, sat with his hands folded across his stomach, tilted his head backward against the chair, and closed his eyes. Although his posture did not encourage conversation, Kate sat near him. "Bill," she said softly.

"What is it? I thought I could just sit here peacefully for a few minutes," he answered stiffly.

"And you can. It's just that I want to tell you something first." Kate answered him more boldly than she thought she was able.

"Well, okay. Tell me."

"Hannah received a letter from Thomas Stokes today."

Before she could continue, Bill opened his eyes, looked toward her and asked, "What is he writing her for? I thought he was away at college."

"Yes, actually you're right. He is away at college. He attends Ole Miss, but I'm sure you remember the two of them meeting the evening we had supper at the Stokeses'. It appears they enjoyed each other's company. He wrote that he plans to come for a visit soon, sometime during his Thanksgiving holiday."

"Sounds fine to me. He's a nice kid, good family." Bill tilted his head back and closed his eyes just as they had been before Kate spoke.

No flare-up, no untoward comments, no outbursts of emotions. Kate was mystified by her husband's uncharacteristic response. She said nothing more. She could only assume that his positive attitude was because Thomas was the son of his friend, Mr. Stokes.

Relieved, Kate reached into a basket that sat on the floor beside her chair. She picked up crochet thread, hooks, and a partially completed doily. She leaned fully against the back of the chair as she breathed an undetected sigh and with the little hook, she began to nimbly pull the off-white thread into the pattern. The warmth of the fire felt especially friendly now that she had good news to share with Hannah.

Chapter Eighteen

KATHERINE AND STEPHEN had not been back to Leaf Creek since their wedding the previous spring. The whole family eagerly looked forward to their Thanksgiving visit.

Bill tried not to show anxiety or enthusiasm, but he asked Kate more than once what time Katherine had written that they might arrive. He didn't like Stephen, and he didn't like his daughter being married to him, but he loved Katherine, and on that day he wanted to see with his own eyes that she was okay.

Stephen and Katherine arrived on Wednesday. They planned to be in Leaf Creek for Thanksgiving Day and then start back toward Hattiesburg before mid-morning on Friday. Stephen hoped for them to make the same time going home as they did on their trip coming down to Leaf Creek. Barring unforeseen problems, they would recover the forty-five miles in two days, getting home by Saturday night. Stephen used to make the trip on his horse in an easy day and a half, but in the wagon, he planned on fifteen to twenty-five miles a day. Twenty-five was optimistic and required good weather, good roads, good horses and no breakdowns. Stephen stayed optimistic and had good horses, but daylight hours were short that time of the year, making unforeseen travel problems more difficult to handle.

Bill walked with Kate and Hannah down the front steps and into the front yard to greet Katherine and Stephen. Almost as quick came Janie, June Ellen, and Frank from around back of the house.

Tears of happiness brimmed from Kate's eyes as she hugged her daughter. She took Stephen's hand, shook it gently and said, "Welcome."

"Thank you, Mrs. McMolison," Stephen responded without hesitation.

"Good to see you, Katherine." Bill put one arm around her shoulders and pulled her toward him in a semblance of a half hug. Katherine responded by hugging him with both her arms.

"I'm so happy to see you—seems like it's been forever," Katherine said giddily. "I've missed all of you so much." She wrapped Hannah in the tightest possible embrace and held on. She then moved to Janie, June Ellen, and Frank, encircling each one unreservedly with arms of love.

Meanwhile Bill turned his attention to Stephen. He shook his hand and said, "We've really missed Katherine. Appreciate you bringing her to see us."

"Yes, sir." Stephen looked into Bill's face. "I'm glad we were able to come, sorry we haven't been able to come sooner."

Bill did not acknowledge Stephen's last statement. He abruptly turned toward Frank. "Help them get their things in the house and then take care of their horse and wagon." He was sharp and cold and left no doubt that he was not ready to let any of them, especially Stephen and Katherine, forget his disapproval of them.

"Yez suh, sure will, happy to," Frank answered with a smile and a quick step toward the wagon. Frank knew the hostility was not meant for him, and if it was possible to temper the choleric tone of Mr. McMolison's words, he wanted to try.

Bill got on his horse and rode off toward the mill. Kate put her arm around Katherine's shoulder as they walked up the steps and into the house. "I'm sorry, Katherine," Kate said softly. "Give him time. I'm so glad to see you. Let's not let anything spoil your visit."

"We won't. I'm so excited to be home even if it's just for a little while. I miss you, but you know Papa does make it hard." Katherine squeezed her mother's hand and added, "Let's not think about anything but good things right now. I want to hear all the news around here, and I can hardly wait to tell you all about our house and Hattiesburg and our church—about everything."

Janie and June Ellen headed around the house toward the back. Hannah and Stephen followed Kate and Katherine inside. The remainder of the afternoon was spent working on Thanksgiving dinner. Katherine and Hannah chopped celery and onions for the cornbread dressing. Janie worked to get all the feathers off the turkey. June Ellen washed turnip greens that would be cooked the following morning, peeled sweet potatoes for pies, and boiled cranberries for sauce. Kate gathered linens, china and silver from different chests and cupboards. "I love having everybody all together. It's wonderful," Kate almost sang as she moved around all the work being done. Even Stephen was in the kitchen. He sat in a chair enjoying the warmth of the stove as well as the happy sight before him.

"Katherine has written us a little about your new church. Do you like being there?" Kate asked Stephen.

"Yes, ma'am. Glad I'm not traveling like I used to. And the people have been wonderful to us. Of course, you know Katherine started there first."

"It's a Baptist church, right?" Kate asked.

Stephen laughed. "It is and Katherine fits in fine, but she's still Presbyterian."

Kate grabbed a knife to help with the peeling and the chopping. "Baptist is okay. Known some really fine people who're Baptist."

Katherine smiled and said, "And we do too, a whole church full now. Tell them, Stephen, how it was you came to be the pastor at Pine Grove."

"Thought you've written all that. They don't want to hear it again," Stephen replied.

"Well, I wrote some but not everything. Can't write everything in a letter," Katherine answered. "I was going to the church when Stephen was still traveling. The preacher was pretty old. He was gentle and kind and wonderful. I really liked him a lot—made me sad when he got sick. It was very sudden. Said it was a stroke. He didn't live long." She frowned and her voice softened. "Really a sad time for everybody there."

"So you started going with Katherine and preaching for them?" Hannah asked while pulling strings off another piece of celery.

"Well, it wasn't quite like that," Stephen answered.

"Almost like that," Katherine corrected him quickly. "Stephen had preached for them a few times and when their preacher passed away, it seemed almost a given to them that Stephen would become their new one. Tell them about your visit with dear sweet Mr. Curry."

"Oh, I don't know, Katherine. Not sure they want to hear all the details." Stephen picked up one of the celery stalks and began to eat it.

"Careful. We need that for dressing," Katherine teased. "Now tell them about Mr. Curry, just about your visit the day after the funeral."

"*Yes ma'am*." Stephen looked at Katherine and laughed, answering as if following an order. "Mr. Curry is probably the oldest member at Pine Grove. He's not well and not able to get out much."

"It was the *very* next morning after the funeral," Katherine said.

"Katherine, chop your celery. Let him tell us," Hannah commanded.

"Just helping. I'm his help mate—remember?"

"We remember," said Hannah firmly. She looked back at Stephen. "Now, go on and tell us." Everybody was laughing.

"Well, I went out to Mr. Curry's house to check on him, and while I was there he began to talk to me about becoming the new preacher."

Katherine interrupted again: "As it turned out a couple of the other deacons had already been out to visit him and together they had made their plan."

"That's pretty much the truth of it," Stephen agreed. "I arrived at Mr. Curry's. He leaned back in his rocking chair. He was kind of a sad sight, really. He'd lost a lot of weight. His khaki pants and his shirt were so big, there was room for the man he used to be. He was truly frail, but his eyes sparkled as he lifted his maple walking stick, pointed it at me … and said I was to be the new preacher at Pine Grove."

"Amazing isn't it?" Katherine added. "No committees, no nothing."

"Does sound a little different from what we are used to," Kate agreed. "Was that it?"

"Well he told me he already prayed about it, that the Lord gave him a quick answer. He was sure it was the Lord's plan and added that I had till I got home to pray about it, so I should think about praying quick."

"Sounds to me like the Lord had you right where He wanted you," Janie said as she pulled a big skillet of cornbread from the oven.

"The congregation voted the next morning and that was it," said Katherine. "I told Stephen that the elders in the Presbyterian Church here would still be planning a time to meet to begin the discussion to make a decision."

"I guess that may be true, but we mustn't make too much fun," Kate said a little stiffly. "I'm just glad it has worked out and you are both happy."

THE FOLLOWING DAY the family gathered for Thanksgiving dinner. After all the food was prepared and served, Janie and June Ellen left for their own homes. Kate made sure they each took generous portions of everything. The bounty from the McMolison kitchen filled three tables that Thanksgiving, as it did every holiday.

Conversation during the McMolison's meal was rather bland. Nothing more exciting than the weather was discussed. The family had barely finished eating when Mr. McMolison pushed his chair from the table, stood, and announced that he had business to attend to at the mill. It was Thanksgiving Day. Everyone knew the mill was closed, but no one spoke up.

Bill rode away on his horse. He rode toward the mill but passed it by. Only a mile farther, he turned into a little farm. The house, unpainted, sat some fifty yards back off the main road. Bill rode around to the back and stopped. He lowered himself to the ground and threw the reins around a fence railing. Through the screen of the backdoor, he could see her waiting on him. Her chin was lowered into her chest, her head tilted against the door facing. A cascade of strawberry red curls fell loosely over her shoulders.

Unbridled desire coursed through him as he crossed the porch. She eased the screen door open, allowing her loose robe to part. The exposed bouquet of desire was ready and waiting for his touch. He ran his hand under the robe and pulled her warm softness tightly to him. Her lips found his. Uninhibited passion filled the Thanksgiving air.

She, waiting on a husband who was fighting in France, was always available to her visitor, and he, feeling entitled, sought the robust lovemaking she afforded him. He demanded discretion to protect his reputation. She needed discretion to avoid the humiliation that would result from being unfaithful to a soldier currently fighting in the Great War.

NO ONE AT THE THANKSGIVING TABLE cared to know where Bill was going except maybe Kate, and even she was not sure she really wanted to know. Her thoughts about his whereabouts were fleeting. She was looking forward to a delightful afternoon with her girls.

Stephen went for a long walk and then settled into one of the comfortable rocking chairs in front of the fire. His head dropped against the back of the chair, his eyes closed, and his lips parted slightly. He dozed for the remainder of the afternoon.

Kate, Katherine, and Hannah cleared the table. "I just wish y'all could come see where we live and meet some of the people in our church." Katherine poured a fresh cup of coffee. "You'd love it, and I'd so love having you." She spooned sugar into the cup, the spoon clicking the side of the cup as she stirred.

Kate sipped her coffee and laughed. "I'm sure we would. We'll get there one of these days."

"I've got some great news, too, don't I?" Hannah said, looking over toward Kate.

Kate, smiling broadly, leaned back in her chair. "I would say you do."

"Well?" Katherine, with raised eyebrows, cocked her head sideways.

"It's this boy I met." Hannah clasped her hands in front of her, fingers splayed outward. "He is *sooo* handsome, has black hair and blue eyes." Hannah barely took a breath. "He's the son of a friend of Papa." Her hands tightened around each other and excitedly moved side to side. Hannah didn't stop talking until she had recounted every detail including naming the kittens and receiving dinner table winks.

"He's really wonderful, isn't he, Mama?" Hannah added, glancing at Kate.

"He does seem very nice, certainly is charming." Kate grinned, her head tilted to one side.

"Oh, Katherine, he is really so wonderful." Hannah was standing by that time and hugging her own shoulders as she turned slightly from side to side. She dropped to her knees beside Katherine's chair, gripped her arm and said, "He's coming tomorrow afternoon. Can you please stay? I really, really want you to meet him."

"I would love to meet him, but I don't think I can this time." Katherine reached for Hannah's arm. "But let's go figure out what you're going to wear."

"You'll help me look good. If only I could always know what to say, what to talk about, like you do," Hannah said wistfully.

"Don't worry so much." Katherine cupped Hannah's face with her hands, shook her chin from side to side and joyfully said, "Just be your sweet self. Relax and have fun."

"Easy for you, always has been. I wish I could be more like you," Hannah sighed.

"No, you are perfect the way you are. Wear that new yellow dress you showed me. He won't be able to resist you."

Kate listened happily to the exchange between her two daughters. "It's such a joy to have you here, Katherine—wish you could come more often."

"Me too, but it's a long way, too far to come very often. Good we like where we live and Stephen likes what he does. He's really happy as pastor." Katherine lifted her shoulders, pursed her lips, widened her eyes and in a higher voice said, "And I actually like being the pastor's wife. Amazing, I know."

Kate put her cup on the table and took Katherine's hands in hers. "I have to tell you that I'm sorry for the things I said about Stephen and the way I acted during the weeks before your wedding."

"I love you, Mama, and I understand. I really do. It was my fault too. I disobeyed you, and …"

Kate stopped Katherine mid-sentence. "No need to rehash those days. I just wanted you to know I'm sorry, and I really like Stephen very much."

"Thank you. I'm glad you're getting to know him. I wish Papa would at least try," Katherine lamented. "Probably be a long time. If he ever does."

"It may be, but don't worry. Your father loves you and even if he doesn't admit it, he can see that you and Stephen love each other very much. He'll be glad of that."

"I hope," Katherine said as she turned her coffee cup in circles on the tabletop.

"Katherine," Hannah spoke emphatically, "Stephen didn't make this trip because he was anxious to be here with all of us. He came because he knew you wanted to come. Papa knows it. That'll count for something."

"Yes," said Kate. "I'm sure it will. Now let's not worry any more about it."

* * *

HANNAH ATE ONLY A BITE of breakfast. Butterflies took the place of hunger. The Friday after Thanksgiving had finally arrived. Thomas was to soon be there.

"I'm just too nervous to eat." Hannah, elbows on the table, repeatedly tapped the center of an egg with her fork. She was jittery and her throat was dry. "What if he doesn't come?"

"I'm sure he'll be here. Stop worrying," Katherine said. She tightened her lips together, widened her eyes and cocked her head to one side.

Breakfast finished and goodbyes said, Katherine took Stephen's hand and climbed onto the wagon. She waved, smiled, and yelled back at the family, "Just remember, we have an extra bedroom. I want y'all to come see us." Katherine pointed her right index finger at Hannah.

"Have fun today, and write and tell me all about it! Love you."

After watching the wagon until it disappeared around the bend, Bill went to the mill but said he would be home for dinner. Kate went to the kitchen with June Ellen and Janie, and Hannah went to her room where her butter-yellow dress and sweater waited for her. She dressed. She waited. Her blond curls, full and springy, bounced as she nervously paced from window to window and peered at the empty road.

Then, finally, it appeared from around the curve—the horse-drawn wagon bringing Hannah's perfection came into sight. Hannah's heart was pounding. "Calm, be calm," she told herself. "Don't act like a silly little girl." She took a deep breath. She smoothed her dress with her hands before walking gracefully and confidently out the front door and onto the porch.

There he was in front of her, as beautiful as he had been three weeks before. His leg stretched for the ground, causing the fabric of his pants to pull tightly across his thigh. Hannah could see long, lean muscles before her. Again her heart was aflutter, but her composure was intact.

"Hey, Hannah, I hope it was okay for me to come," Thomas said cheerfully as he walked toward the porch. His head was held high, his chin was up, and he looked directly at Hannah as he walked toward her.

Frank rounded the corner of the yard at the perfect time. June Ellen had told him to be watching. "I'll take care a your horse."

Thomas turned toward Frank and said, "Thank you," as he walked up the steps and onto the porch. "Hi," he said again, his blue eyes looking down into hers.

Hannah, smiling, spoke for the first time. "Hi, I'm really glad you could come." She tilted her head a little to the left. "I would have written if there had been time," she said softly.

Bill arrived. He shook Thomas's hand, patted him on the shoulder, and said in the friendliest manner, "It's good to see you, glad to have you here for a visit."

Again, Kate could only figure the reason for Bill's warm hospitality toward a young man visiting Hannah was that the boy was John Stokes's son. Whatever the reason, however, she was thankful for it.

"Everything smells delicious," Thomas said as he pulled a chair out for Kate and then for Hannah. Fried chicken, mashed potatoes, vegetables and biscuits filled the serving bowls and platters. For dessert Janie had made her delicious and beautiful chocolate cake. The five layers dripped with chocolate fudge icing as Kate served each piece on her good crystal plates.

"Best chocolate cake I've ever had," Thomas said minutes later, quickly scoring points with everyone in the household.

HANNAH AND THOMAS sat in the swing on the front porch. The noonday sun had warmed the skies so that being outside was both comfortable and inviting. Thomas suggested a walk, but Hannah, with hesitation, declined.

"It's so very pleasant sitting here swinging. Let's just stay here if that's okay," Hannah replied. She liked the thought of taking a walk, but she knew it would not be considered appropriate by her mother. The only place to walk was into the woods, and this visit was his first to their home. She didn't want to do anything to cause her parents or Janie or June Ellen to disapprove or be suspicious. She certainly did not want to do anything that would provoke her father. His attitude regarding anything to do with Thomas Stokes had been surprisingly positive, and she wanted to keep it that way.

Hannah sat on one end of the swing, and Thomas sat on the other. "That was a great meal, my favorite food," Thomas said as he pushed the floor with his foot, causing a gentle swinging motion.

"Mine too, and Janie's a really good cook." Hannah took a deep breath. "I may have eaten too much."

"I don't think so. You barely ate. I watched you," Thomas teased.

"Did you?" Hannah teased in return. She smiled. "Tell me about college. Is it hard?"

"It is, but I like it. Lots to do, lots of friends."

Hannah's spirits depressed a little as she wondered if the friends included lots of girls. "What do you and your friends do? Anything fun?"

"Sometimes, but we study a lot too. I want to go to medical school in Atlanta so I've got to keep my grades."

Hannah was quiet. She thought she had heard of Atlanta but wasn't sure. She was certain that wherever it was, it was a long way from Leaf Creek. She decided to just listen and worry about the future another day.

Thomas continued: "Enough about me and school." He playfully nudged her foot with his. Hannah felt the flutter in her chest. He reached over and gently placed his hand over hers. The touch was warm and soft, kind and gentle. His fingers soothingly massaged her hand and wrist and then, ever so subtly, the caresses intermittently transfused her dress and met her thigh. Hannah felt herself tingle with sensations she had not known before. She was certain she was feeling the signs of love.

For Hannah, the day had been wonderful, and making things completely perfect was Thomas saying he would be home for three weeks during Christmas break. "I would like to see you again," he said. His words were music to Hannah's ears and filled her with a rush of excitement. She felt as if she was receiving the grandest Christmas present ever. "I will write to you as soon as I get back to school," he said softly.

"Okay, that will be great. I'll look forward to hearing from you." Hannah managed to look directly into his eyes as she spoke.

"Well, I best be getting on the road. I told Mama I would try not to be too late." He reached for Hannah's hand, lifted it to his lips, and kissed the back tenderly. "That's to remember me by until we meet again." He smiled, made a slight bow toward her, turned and walked toward his wagon.

"I don't need a reminder to remember you," Hannah said to herself as she watched him climb up into the wagon.

"Goodbye. See you soon," Thomas called to her as he drove off the McMolison's farm.

"Bye," Hannah called back. "Have a safe trip."

It was still early afternoon when the wagon disappeared around the curve. Hannah watched it until the last bit of weathered wood was gone from her sight.

Chapter Nineteen

THE NEWS WAS ALMOST too good to be true. Mr. McMolison asked Kate and Hannah if they would like to accompany him to Leeville. The monthly meeting of the county board of supervisors had been postponed from the first Monday to the third Monday in December. His plan was to leave early on Monday morning and not return home until Wednesday morning or maybe even Thursday morning.

Kate and Hannah were happy to be included in another trip. The reason for the postponed meeting or the additional business mattered little to either of them. Kate looked forward to staying at the hotel and was excited at the thought of doing a little Christmas shopping in the Leeville stores. She thought, too, that she might even find some fun items for their tree at The Variety Store, and seeing how Pearl had decorated the little store for Christmas would have to be an interesting experience.

Hannah agreed that staying at the hotel and shopping would probably be fun, but most importantly—and definitely most exciting—was knowing the trip would coincide with Thomas's Christmas break. She wrote him at once to let him know of the unexpected plans.

THE TRIP TO LEEVILLE was a chilly one. The sun shone brightly, but the high for the day was only fifty degrees. After arriving at the hotel, Hannah and Kate quickly sought the heat of the big roaring fire that greeted them. Several people, mostly men, were standing around talking. A couple of them smiled and nodded toward Kate and Hannah as they continued their conversations.

When the dinner bell rang, most everyone moved toward the dining room. Hannah and Kate moved closer to the fire where orange and yellow flames licked the sides of the fireplace. A new supply of wood, old and green, had recently been added. Popping, frying, and sizzling filled the room. The fire was warm and the familiar sounds were welcoming. Kate and Hannah were dressed warmly, but their feet and hands felt frozen. They stood with their backs to the fire for several minutes. Feeling the heat directly on the back of their legs would be wonderful but both resisted the temptation to lift their skirts. After standing a few minutes, they each sat on the edge of one of the big overstuffed chairs closest to the fire. With hands extended and palms toward the heat, they gradually began to thaw.

The light-skinned colored girl, the one they had met on the previous trip, appeared with a cup of hot tea for each of them.

She smiled and said, "Merry Christmas. Nice to see you again." Hannah and Kate, appreciative of the warm drink, returned her smile.

Kate said, "I don't think we learned your name when we were here before."

"My name is Rosie," she answered politely.

Hannah, encircling the warm cup with her cold hands, was thinking again as she had on her previous trip, "This girl doesn't look at all like the coloreds I know back home. Her skin is the color of coffee with lots of milk mixed in, rather than dark brown or almost black. She talks differently, too, saying words that sound kind of like a mixture of colored, country white, and town white."

Kate added, "Well, Rosie, it is nice to meet you, and thank you for the wonderful cup of tea."

"Yes ma'am," she said, and was gone as quickly as she came.

Mr. McMolison stayed at the hotel just long enough to have their things unloaded and carried to the room. "I'm meeting Stokes at the courthouse to discuss some business. We'll have the girls in the kitchen send dinner over for us," he said to Kate as he left the hotel. "Y'all do whatever you want to."

Kate and Hannah planned to eat in the dining room a little later. For the time being they were content to sit quietly in the refuge of warmth.

The hotel was especially inviting. There were large bowls of fresh greenery filling every possible space. A Christmas tree stood in one corner, almost reaching the ceiling. It was covered with red, silver, and gold balls and popcorn garlands. Tinsel draped from the branches and a silver star adorned the very top. Candles burned in numerous brass candlesticks placed here and there. Oranges, apples, pinecones, sweet gum balls, holly branches and red berries had been added to every available space. Beside one of the smaller arrangements, a large Bible—opened to the second chapter of Luke—was propped up so that the text was easily visible. A beautifully crocheted cross was lying across the page. The room was warm and peaceful.

"Oh, it's wonderful just to sit here. If people could meld into their surroundings, these would be my choice. I feel like I could stay forever." Kate enveloped her words with a contented sigh and nestled deeper into her chair.

"It is really nice," Hannah agreed. "And I'm finally getting warm." The whole of the surroundings, the beauty of the decorations, the warmth of the fire, and the plushness of the chair that encircled her were all great, but the most important thing was missing. Her thoughts were of Thomas and the possibility of spending time with him, maybe time with him that very evening. The thought made her feel giddy: "his beautiful blue eyes, jet-black hair, perfect lips … and Christmas. It would be magical."

After being thoroughly warmed and refreshed, Kate left the hotel to visit some of the stores. Hannah declined. She did not want to take a chance on missing Thomas. Instead, she climbed the stairs to the room. From there she could keep watch. Her vigil would not be noticed.

THE LARGE CLOCK above the main doorway of the courthouse was visible from most anywhere on Main Street. Hannah pulled a chair close to the window so she could sit while she watched the black hands as they eased around the grayish white face on the cream-colored building. She began to feel her dream unraveling. Hannah wondered if perhaps Thomas had not received her letter in time. Even worse would be that he had gotten the letter but had changed his mind and did not want to see her. As her mouth became dry and her heart rate quickened, the hands of the clock moved on around until the time approached four o'clock. She stood, leaned forward, and pressed her forehead against the windowpane.

From her second floor window, Hannah had a perfect view of most of Main Street, the side street, the courthouse lawn and the courthouse clock. There was no sign of Thomas in any direction. "Where, oh where is he?" She grew more concerned and more anxious.

Then suddenly she saw him. "Oh, there he is! There he is!" she said aloud, although no one else was in the room. It was a little after four o'clock. Excitedly, she glanced in the mirror, pulled a wayward curl up, and fastened it with a comb. She looked back out the window and saw him walking across the courthouse lawn—walking in her direction. She reminded herself that there had been no specific time set for his arrival (except in her imagination) and after all it was still afternoon. Her heart quickened with anticipation. Hannah checked herself again in the mirror, then hurriedly made her way down the steps. She wanted to be sitting casually in front of the fire when he walked in. She certainly didn't want him to suspect that she had been anxiously staring out the window for hours.

"Hi," Thomas said as he walked through the wreath-clad front door. He walked toward her, smiling. "How was your trip? It's cold out there today," he said casually. No reference was made regarding the time by either of them. Thomas stood for a few minutes with his back to the fire, his hands behind him.

Thomas continued to warm himself, occasionally turning sideways. To Hannah it was as if her prince was on a revolving pedestal, turning slowly so that she might receive pleasure from viewing all angles. As she allowed herself to the edge of fantasy, the only thing better would have been if she were on the pedestal secured by his embrace and revolving slowly, ever so slowly, with him.

Thomas turned from the fire and said, "Hot chocolate would be good. Would you like some?"

Hannah, partially lost in her fantasy, managed a response. "Sure, that sounds good."

He ordered two cups of hot chocolate and then sat in the chair closest to hers. A settee sat empty in the group of chairs around the fire. Hannah scolded herself for not thinking to sit on it. There would have been room for Thomas to sit right next to her. She would not make that mistake again, she thought to herself.

"How long have you been here?" Thomas sat on the edge of his chair, elbows on his knees, holding his hot chocolate with both hands.

"Oh, not too long. Just a little while, actually. Mama went to do some shopping."

"It's Christmas!" Thomas said jovially. "Shopping's important—right?"

"Absolutely," Hannah answered, laughing. "Guess that's where most everyone is. It's certainly empty in here right now."

"It won't be for long. 'Bout time for the stores to close, plus it's almost time for supper." Thomas leaned toward Hannah and whispered, "I like it this way."

Hannah felt herself blush. She looked into the fire, lifted the hot chocolate to her lips, and sipped.

"You heard what I said. Are you gonna just leave me hanging?" Thomas's whispers were a little louder than before. He cocked his head to one side and smiled.

Hannah lowered her cup. "Me, too. I like it too," she said softly.

THOMAS JOINED KATE AND HANNAH for supper at the hotel. Thomas, not at all timid, asked, "Mrs. McMolison, did you find a lot to buy in the shops?"

"I really didn't buy much today, just looked. I did get a few ideas." She smiled and looked toward Hannah. "I'll go back tomorrow."

"I'll go with you tomorrow," Hannah offered.

"That's always fun, always like to have you with me, but I may need a little while alone again," Kate said playfully.

"It's that time of year, Hannah, and you don't want to keep your parents from shopping," Thomas said, continuing the slightly mysterious festive tone Kate had started.

"Now, Thomas, how long will you be home?" Kate asked, changing the subject.

"About three weeks. Seems like a long time, but the time always passes so fast. Maybe I will get back to Leaf Creek for some more of Janie's chocolate cake. Tell her again it's the best I've ever had."

Kate smiled. "I'll tell her."

A man sitting on the other side of the table suddenly spoke loudly, getting everyone's attention. "The war's bad. It's bad over there. Washington has got to do something."

Thomas answered thoughtfully, "Yes, sir, it sure sounds mighty bad. I hope President Wilson can do something soon."

Thomas sounded sensitive and caring. Hannah watched her mother and could tell she was impressed.

Once the topic of war had come and gone, Kate asked Thomas about church. "The little white church on the right as we come into town—that's where your parents are members. Is that right?"

"Yes ma'am, First Presbyterian," he said. "That's where I was raised, where I'm still a member."

"Such a lovely church. I attended a revival there once, a very long time ago," Kate said pensively. "It was wonderful."

"You'll have to visit again. My parents are always here and would love to have you, and when I'm here, I would love to have you." Thomas glanced toward Hannah as he finished.

After supper Thomas suggested Hannah get her coat and gloves. "Walking around downtown might be nice. I know it's almost dark, but there are some decorations we can still see."

Kate gave her permission, adding, "That will be fine, just remember not to be gone too long." Kate had thoroughly enjoyed her conversation with Thomas. She was glad to see him as not only a handsome and charming young man, but one of apparent intelligence, integrity and thoughtfulness as well. She felt sure he could be trusted with her daughter.

HANNAH SLID EASILY into cadence beside Thomas as they walked down the steps, down the walkway, and then down the street away from the hotel. Darkness prevailed except for the dim rays of a few gaslights on the street and some kerosene lanterns in the windows. The night was perfect. Hannah could not remember a more perfect night or day in her entire life. She had been to a few picnics and even two dances where she talked and sometimes flirted with the boys in Leaf Creek. One had even kissed her while a bunch of her classmates watched. It had been so quick his lips had hardly touched hers, but he had won his dare.

"Penny for your thoughts," Thomas said, nudging her shoulder with his.

"Delicious supper, beautiful night," Hannah answered. She would never want him to know that all she was *really* thinking about was him and being kissed by him.

"Supper was good. Enjoyed talking to your mother too. She seems really nice. And you have a sister?"

"Yes. She's married and lives in Hattiesburg. She's fun. Wish you could meet her."

"I'll look forward to it. I'll ..."

Hannah interrupted, "Look! Let's look in that window." She walked over to the front of the drugstore, dimly lit with a couple of gaslights. A black toy train was silent on its track, but it was surrounded with small, decorated trees, fake snow, lots of Christmas packages and Santa Claus. "Reminds me of my little brother." She hadn't intended to mention her brother, but the words spilled out before she stopped them.

"I didn't know you have a brother. How old is he?" Thomas, having always liked trains, continued checking out the display as he asked the question.

"I don't." She hesitated. "At least I don't now, but I did. He died when he was little, an accident. He had a black train, didn't play with it, but it still reminds me of him."

"I'm sorry." Thomas's words were quiet and kind. "There, look there in the general store window at the bells and the elves. They look happy to be out and about."

"They do. Makes me feel happy just looking at them." Hannah had a sudden pang of worry that she may have sounded too childlike, unsophisticated or silly. Remembering Katherine's instruction to just be herself may be fine for Katherine, she thought, but I need to think before I speak.

They passed the *Herald* office. Mr. Osco was still sitting at his desk near the front window. His lantern burned brightly and gave him the light necessary to do the task at hand. He never looked up, was never aware of their passing. At that moment, Thomas slid his hand into Hannah's coat pocket where her own hand was pushed in snug and warm.

Hannah's heart quickened. Thomas stopped walking—as did she—since his hand was holding hers. He pulled their clasped hands from the pocket, took her hand in his, and gently removed her glove. His warm hand clasped hers with no barrier between, just his skin touching hers. As he softly whispered, "I'll keep you warm," he gently leaned into her and bent his head just enough that his lips, so tenderly, met hers. His lips did not linger but quickly pulled away and with a squeeze of her hand, he said, "Let's walk a little more."

Hannah's head and heart were spinning. She liked everything that had just happened. She wished it had not happened so fast. Within a few seconds she had gone from having her gloved hand crammed into her pocket to having a bare hand being held with warmth and soft tenderness. She had gone from her fantasy of what Thomas's touch might be like to feeling the sensations of having his body fully, though briefly, incline into hers. His soft lips met hers gently, yet fleetingly. His kiss was nothing like the schoolyard quick kiss she had received on a dare. Thomas's kiss was real. The warm hand holding her hand was real. There was no dare involved. In fact, Hannah was feeling more real than she had ever felt before in her life.

Thomas had left his horse and wagon behind the courthouse. "Let's walk this way. I really need to check on my horse. Kinda dark, but I think we can see well enough."

"Sure," Hannah agreed. Any route was fine with her as long as his warm hand held hers.

They turned right, walked past the courthouse, and into the rear area where the horse waited. It grew darker as they walked away from Main Street. There weren't any lights burning behind the courthouse, but it didn't matter to them. Their eyes quickly became accustomed enough to the dark that they could see where they were walking.

The horse was fine. Thomas rubbed his face, gave him two or three pats on the side with the palm of his hand, and offered him water. Hannah and Thomas then sat on the back of the wagon. This time would be their additional few minutes alone before heading back to the hotel.

* * *

SHE KNEW BETTER. She wanted to do better. She did not seem to be master over her own will. She wanted and was allowing what she shouldn't. The bed of the wagon was covered with a quilt. It was all so easy. Hannah sat in the wagon with her back leaning against one of its sides. Thomas sat beside her but faced her. He ran his right index finger around her face, soothingly touched her ears, and then caressed her lips. Hannah responded completely. She was no match, nor did she desire to be, for the resulting pleasure of the apt and able hands of Thomas. Unstoppable passion rose from the wagon bed into the night air. It was a first for both of them. Hannah had never given herself before, and Thomas had never been the recipient of a virgin's gift.

The experience gave Thomas added and unexpected pleasure. Although he didn't understand why, he felt unforeseen humility and a surprising desire to protect the one lying in his arms. For the first time in his life he felt misgiving, almost wishing he had shown restraint. Even in the midst of his self-serving behavior, he understood this girl had given all but could not possibly yet realize the magnitude.

Thomas slid down beside Hannah and guided her head onto his chest. His fingers eased strands of hair from her face. "Are you okay?" he whispered.

"Yes," she answered so quietly that Thomas barely heard.

"Are you sure?"

"Yes," was Hannah's only answer. The night was quiet.

"Maybe we should go," Thomas said after a few minutes.

Hannah eased off the back of the wagon. She straightened her clothes. Thomas took her hand in his. "You're special, Hannah—maybe the most special girl I've ever met. You're so real. Being with you means a lot to me. I want to see you again."

"I want to see you too," Hannah said softly.

"Maybe you can come to Oxford sometime."

Everything had been said. Thomas put his arm around Hannah's waist and pulled her close to his side as they walked silently to the hotel.

Thomas kissed Hannah lightly and quickly on the lips. He then squeezed her hands in his and said, "I will try to come to Leaf Creek sometime between Christmas and when I go back to school."

Hannah looked into his eyes. "I hope so. I hope you can." Thomas left and walked back toward the horse and wagon and quilt from whence he had just come. Hannah stood and watched him. She suddenly felt tightness in her throat and chest as if she were watching a part of herself walk away, a part she could never retrieve. She loved the figure walking into the shadows and that was all that mattered, though. Hannah methodically climbed the stairs to the second floor and disappeared around the upper column.

* * *

ROSIE WAS IN THE HOTEL KITCHEN. She had stayed later than usual to help with the extra Christmas preparations. From the kitchen window, she had watched Hannah and Thomas come into the dim light of the street from the darkness behind the courthouse. She had no way of knowing what had unfolded in the shadows, but she wondered. The thought gave her a hollow feeling inside. Rosie had seen Hannah's shyness and obvious inexperience. She had also seen the gleam in Hannah's eyes when she first saw Thomas across the table on Election Day. She knew that Thomas—with his good looks, charm, and wealth—would be hard for even an older, wiser, experienced girl to resist.

As Rosie watched the couple approach the hotel, she thought back to the time five years before when he had called her a clumsy half-breed nigger and to the time he stopped her on the road. The curious part that she still didn't understand was Mr. Stokes's reaction. He was adamant on both occasions that Thomas leave her alone.

To Rosie, the name-calling had almost been the worst. She had been embarrassed when she dropped the chicken, and then in front of everybody Thomas had made fun of her. She'd cried that night when telling her grandmother what happened. "Why would he say something like that?" she'd asked. "Why did he make fun of me? He's never been mean to me before." In the quiet of the sleeping hotel Rosie recalled her grandmother's words as if they had been spoken only yesterday.

"Sometimes people—white and colored—do mean and bad things. It seems for no reason except just because they can. It wasn't your fault. You did nothing wrong."

"Well, I hate him. I don't want to serve him ever again." Rosie remembered her own words.

"I know that seems like a good idea, but it's not. You'll just keep feeling bad inside. Just do your job the best you can, and everything will be okay."

"I just don't understand."

"We don't always understand and we don't always get answers, but it sounds like Mr. Stokes took care of things so that it won't happen again."

Thinking about that day still caused a wave of embarrassment to circle through Rosie, but her grandmother was right. She was never again called an unkind name. Rosie, though, breathed an audible sigh. *"I was just stopped on the road home."*

ROSIE'S MOTHER HAD DIED when Rosie was born, and through the years she had often asked her grandmother for information about her mother as well as her father. She had become accustomed to her grandmother's way of not giving full answers to her questions. In fact, if she even knew whom her father was, she never told her. When Rosie asked, her grandmother always said, "You're you, and you're special. Most important thing for you to remember is that you're one of God's children. Always hold your head up high, work hard and do what's right."

Mr. McMolison, who was Mr. Stokes's good friend, had made regular visits to her grandmother's for as long as she could remember, and he always brought money that her grandmother accepted. Her grandmother would never explain, except to say, "He's a nice man. He's helping to look after the widows and the orphans." His stopping by their house had puzzled Rosie, and meeting Hannah made it puzzle her even more. After the name-calling episode she had even more questions, and they had stayed with her.

She would never be told that her mother had her own key to the back door of the hotel. She would never be told that the key was used many times, not for work but for secretly easing into the room belonging to a man from the northwest part of the county. Rosie knew her mother was a cook at the hotel by day, but she had never been told her mother was mistress to one specific gentleman from Leaf Creek by night.

CHAPTER TWENTY

*H*ANNAH WAS WRAPPING Christmas ornaments in tissue and Kate was packing them in the same storage crate that had been used for as long as Hannah could remember. There were ornaments that had been especially for Samuel and others especially for Katherine. She and her mother had shared memories when they decorated the tree and they were doing it again as they put things away. Hannah held up a wooden bell on which Samuel had printed an S. "He was so proud of this."

Kate smiled. "I know," she said sadly. "Sometimes I—"

A sudden knock on the door interrupted her. Hannah put Samuel's ornament in the crate. "I'll see who it is."

"Somebody must be having trouble on the road," Kate said as Hannah walked from the room. "Frank's here if they need something."

Hannah opened the door.

"Surprise!" Thomas said with a big smile. "Hope it's okay that I came. I wanted to see you before going back to school and I didn't have any way to get you word."

Hannah would have been thrilled if he had grabbed her and hugged her. His visit was the best week-after-Christmas surprise she could imagine. She restrained herself, responded with an equally big smile, and stepped back. "Sure, come in."

He leaned over just enough to brush her cheek with a kiss. Her heart fluttered. "Thomas, my mother is right there," she whispered, waving her hand toward the sitting room.

"Well, okay. Later then," he said under his breath just as Kate entered the hall.

"Thomas, what a lovely surprise. Come in."

"Sorry I couldn't let you know," he replied.

"That's okay. Did you have a nice Christmas?"

"Yes ma'am, we did. I go back to school the week after New Year's and I wanted to come before I go back."

"Hannah, maybe Thomas would like a piece of chocolate cake. As I recall, he said Janie's was the best he had ever eaten."

Hannah looked at Thomas, raising her eyebrows in question.

"Sounds great. I'd love a piece," Thomas answered without hesitation.

After eating cake and lavishing compliments on Janie's baking, Thomas, speaking softly, said to Hannah, "You wanna go for a walk outside?"

Hannah's heart skipped beats with the anticipation of being alone with Thomas. "Sure. Sounds great. Let me tell Mama. She's packing the last of the Christmas ornaments."

As they walked together into the sitting room, Hannah said, "Mama, if you'll wait to finish, I'll help."

"I think it's finished. We were about through earlier, so all I've done is pack the last few." Kate stood with her hands on her hips and smiled. "How was the cake?"

"It was great, better than last time … if that's possible." Thomas returned Kate's smile. "Can I help you with that? Put it up somewhere for you?" Thomas pointed toward the crate of ornaments.

"Oh no. It's fine. We'll take care of it later," Kate answered.

"Since the weather is so nice, we thought we would walk outside," Hannah said, trying to sound as matter-of-fact as possible.

"Sounds lovely. The sun is shining but it is cool. Better get your coat."

"I will."

"Nice to see you again, Mrs. McMolison, and thanks again for the cake. It's worth coming for," he said with another grin that he flashed toward Hannah.

Hannah grinned back and nudged his shoulder as they crossed the porch. "So you came for cake?"

"Well, it's awful good," he said, smiling down at her as they rounded the opposite side of the biggest oak in the yard.

Hannah paused and leaned against the tree. Thomas fingered her curls and stroked them gently behind her ear. "Wish school wasn't so far away, so I could see you more."

Hannah lifted her eyes to meet his. "Me too," she said softly.

"Wish I could come back next week before I go back to school, but I don't think I'll be able to. We've got a bunch of relatives coming from out of town and Mama always thinks I should stay around while they're there." He sighed and reached for Hannah's hands. "So … just know if I'm not here, I'll be thinking about you."

Nearing time for him to leave, Thomas pressed his fingers to his lips and then to hers. "I want to kiss you," he whispered, "but your mother may be watching."

Boldly, with her heart racing, Hannah whispered back, "I'm willing to take that chance."

Gently, Thomas's lips met hers and lingered ever so briefly. "Bye for now." He stroked her cheek and tugged playfully on one of her curls. "I'll see you soon as I can."

* * *

OVER A MONTH HAD PASSED since Thomas had been in Leaf Creek. Hannah was feeling anxious. She had not heard from him since he returned to school. She yearned to see him, to have him once again take her hand in his, to have him slide his arms around her shoulders and to feel the warmth of his embrace. She continued the daily routine of going to school, going home, doing chores, and going to church. Nothing had much meaning or was exciting anymore. Only thinking of Thomas gave her pleasure. As days passed, she became more and more uneasy. She longed desperately to hear from him.

179

It was almost the end of January. The school day was over. As Hannah walked her usual route home, the cold winter wind stung her eyes and whipped her coat. She wrapped her wool scarf around her mouth and ears and held her coat with both hands so that it was snug against her. She was not thinking of the cold, however. Like every other day since Christmas, her senses were consumed with thoughts of Thomas.

She climbed the steps to the front porch and crossed in front of the swing, the swing where he first took her hand in his. The familiar squeak filled the hall as Hannah opened the front door. She walked straight to her room. There, on her bed propped against the pillows, was a letter—a precious letter.

Kate had watched her daughter become more and more melancholy since Christmas. She didn't know that the relationship between Hannah and Thomas was anything other than platonic, but she was certain Hannah's low spirits were because she had been wishing desperately to hear from him. She'd placed the letter on Hannah's pillow.

Hannah's heart began to beat faster, and her eyes widened with excitement as she picked up the envelope and saw Thomas's name in the return address area. She opened it quickly and carefully, then read every word. She reread it again more slowly to make sure she did not miss even one little thought.

January 18, 1918

Dear Hannah,

I'm sorry I didn't get to see you again after New Year's. I really wanted to get to Leaf Creek again, but I couldn't. The relatives came and they stayed the whole week.

I hope you and your family have had a good start to the New Year. I thought of you and wondered how you might be spending New Year's Day. As I said, we had relatives. It was fun but it did keep me from doing some of the things I had hoped to do—such as seeing you.

I am now back at school. Sorry I haven't written before

now. My classes are hard. I suppose I'm going to have to really study this semester. I did pretty well last semester so guess I need to keep it up.

I will probably not be home again until around Easter. I will not be there but a few days but hopefully it will work out that I can come see you. I will be thinking about you and remembering our special evening together.

I want to hear what's going on with you, so be sure to write to me and tell me all about life in Leaf Creek.

Always,
Thomas

After reading and rereading all the words (which were neatly written with rounded letters that slanted a little to the left), Hannah meditated on "wanted to visit you," and "such as seeing you," and "our special evening together" in particular. "It was ours," and "it was special." Hannah thought the evening was special, and now she knew he thought so, too.

Her heart was lighter, and her world was right. The power of only those few words changed her whole inner being. She felt new; she felt amazing. Hannah began immediately to pen her letter back to Thomas. She wanted to write it that very evening, but even if she did, she would wait several days before mailing it. He had waited a couple of weeks after returning to school to write her. She would wait at least that long to write him. On that night, though, she would enjoy writing and rewriting her letter. It would have to be perfect.

February 10, 1918

Dear Thomas,

I was glad to get your letter and was sorry, too, that you were not able to visit me in Leaf Creek again before you went back to school.

It sounds as if your schoolwork is really keeping you busy. I can't imagine how hard it is, but I'm sure you'll do well in all your classes.

It has been cold and windy here. We even had icicles hanging from the roof after it rained last Tuesday night. They always look so pretty glistening in the early morning light, but of course by late morning they had melted away.

My classes are going well, nothing particularly exciting. Actually it has been a little hard to concentrate. I keep remembering our time together. As you said in your letter, it was special. I'm happy you thought so, too. I hope Easter will come quickly. I'm anxious to see you.

Must close. It is getting late. Write again soon.

Fondly,
Hannah

Hannah signed sincerely, but since it was nearing Valentine's Day, she had a minute of boldness and changed to fondly. She dated her letter February tenth, the date she would leave it for the mail carrier.

***

THE CALENDER THAT HUNG on the McMolison's pantry wall had a different picture for every month of the year. Hannah flipped January over and was caught up in the romantic beauty of the February picture. A collage of red hearts with white lace borders, pink roses, white curling ribbons, and dainty little bluebirds filled the page. To her, love was in every corner, just like love was in every corner of her heart. She considered going to The Mercantile to buy a red heart to send to Thomas. "No, I can't. Probably seem too forward," she thought.

Thomas's Easter visit was all she could think about. She felt joyful and happy but frustrated with herself for feeling so tired. She had been a bit sick to her stomach for two or three weeks and couldn't seem to get over it. The symptoms seemed less severe at times, but they wouldn't go away completely. "I have to be well by Easter. Nothing,

nothing, nothing can get in the way of a perfect day with Thomas," she said to herself.

Even though Hannah looked forward to Thomas's Easter visit, she really hoped to hear from him on Valentine's Day. She thought he might receive her letter then—that was her plan—but she wasn't sure it worked since she had no idea how long it took for mail to go from Leaf Creek to Oxford.

February fourteenth arrived. Thoughts of Thomas reading and rereading her letter swirled in her head as she made her way to school. She found a valentine on her desk. It was signed "Secret" and nothing more. She was glad she didn't know who put it there; if she didn't know, she didn't have to answer. Her heart belonged to someone else.

She was glad when school was over for the day. Her walk home was more energetic than usual in anticipation of finding a valentine from Thomas. She so wished one would be waiting for her. Hannah pulled the door closed hurriedly and a little harder than usual. Knowing her mother would put anything special for her on her bed, she walked straight to her room … but the pillow was bare. The mailman had come, but there was no valentine. She felt tired and stretched across her bed for a nap. "He probably hasn't had time to get my letter, plus he's been too busy with school to even think about Valentine's Day," she thought. "Ole Miss is hard, and he wants to do well. Doesn't have time for much besides studying." She contented herself with the reminder that he had already explained the difficulty of college life to her.

February and much of March ticked on by. The mailman came day after day, and Hannah was disappointed day after day because there were no more letters from Thomas. She continued to console herself as best she could with the thought that he was studying hard.

She often reread the earlier letter from Thomas and looked forward to his Easter visit. Her excitement was dampened only slightly by the fact that she could not get her energy back. She had never been so tired before, and it was frustrating. All during February she had taken a quick nap right after school, but even with the nap she was ready for bed when the time came. Janie and June Ellen had noticed and were getting concerned. They didn't say out loud what was on their minds, but they had seen the signs many times before. Kate, too, was concerned but remembered hearing a friend say that some teenagers need more sleep than anyone else. She calmed her worry by thinking Hannah must be one of those teens.

KATE FELT THE MARCH wind blow against her face and through her hair as she walked from the hen house. Frank was a little under the weather, so she had insisted on helping with some of the outside chores. "I'm being blown asunder being out here with y'all," she said to the chickens as they scurried around her. She threw a handful of corn into the air so that it fell fan-like across the dirt of the chicken yard. Cackling, clucking, and fluttering, the chickens quickly snatched and pecked the feed and scratched the dirt.

"It's cold and the wind really is going to blow me away," Kate said, still talking to the chickens. "We'll soon have warmer weather, though, and green budding out all around. I like all the seasons, but spring's the best." The chickens answered with more enthusiastic clucking and cackling as they clustered over the grain and continued pecking and scratching.

The main yard would soon be filled with blooms. The pink azaleas, white bride's wreath, and yellow forsythias would all burst with color about the same time. Pinkish-purple blooms of two redbud trees would join the yard's spring explosion of color, and the woods would soon be white with dogwood. Kate inhaled deeply as if to take in the beauty she anticipated.

The wind was getting stronger. Both Kate and the chickens were ready to get inside. Leaning forward, she braced against the wind as she walked to the chicken house. After putting the feed bucket in its place on a shelf above the nests, she turned and leaned her back against the wall. In spite of the joy of anticipating the beauty of spring, she couldn't quite shake the nagging feeling that something may be wrong with Hannah. Her daughter was nauseated and tired a *lot* these days, and Kate's concern was mounting. She wondered whether it was possible for Hannah not to know enough to be worried.

She couldn't believe what she was thinking. "It can't be. Just can't be possible." Her thoughts reeled in a direction she desperately did not want to go. Sure, Hannah was still tiny, but that was no comfort. Kate herself hadn't shown while expecting for the first four months, and the same could be true for Hannah. Still leaning against the wall, she bent over and covered her face with her hands. "I just can't think this," she whispered in the quiet. "Hannah would never ... could never. It's just platonic with Thomas. Just platonic."

ANOTHER LETTER FINALLY arrived. Hannah opened it with the frenzy of a baby calf at feeding time. She had the previous letter memorized, and the excitement of getting this new one was evident in every fiber of her being. The letter was brief, though—really brief. It included something about not much time, lots of studying and so forth, missed her, was really, really anxious to see her ... and how he would be visiting her in Leaf Creek the day before Easter Sunday. That was only two and a half weeks away! Hannah could hardly wait and burst into the kitchen.

"He's coming! Thomas is coming the Saturday before Easter!" Hannah squealed to her mother, Janie, and June Ellen, all of whom were in the kitchen. "Isn't that great?" Hannah was clutching the letter to her chest and moving her shoulders side to side in a rapid rocking motion.

"That's wonderful," Kate said with as much enthusiasm as she could muster with the underlying worry that was burdening her.

"Sure is," Janie and June Ellen chimed in. "We'll cook up a special dinner." They were worried, too, but didn't want Hannah to know.

KATE'S THOUGHTS were in turmoil. She sat alone in the stillness of her bedroom. The only sound was the chirping of birds outside the open window. She opened her Bible and started to read one Psalm and then another:

The Lord is our refuge and strength a ...

But her mind stayed crowded with worry. "What does Hannah know about men, about men with women? Surely she and Katherine have talked," she thought. Kate could only hope Hannah had learned something from somewhere; she, of course, had never discussed the subject with either of her daughters. Proper ladies did not discuss such matters but learned what they needed to know (or at least learned what they learned) after getting married like she had done. Kate held her open Bible to her chest and sighed deeply. Occasionally overhearing Janie and June Ellen boldly laugh and talk about pleasing their men—and their men pleasing them—had taught her that there was a lot she didn't know. She had been far too embarrassed to ask them questions and even more embarrassed at the scenes she imagined from their spontaneous uninhibited exchanges. From their conversations, she had come to know one thing was definitely for sure: there was a lot more that went on in some beds than others.

Kate closed her Bible and sat up straight. "Today, the important thing is what Hannah knows. Oh Lord, if she knows a lot, please don't let it be from experience," she prayed.

THE FOLLOWING MORNING after Hannah left for school, Kate sat quietly at the kitchen table. As she drank a second cup of tea, June Ellen broke the silence. "Miz Kate, Janie and I are worried about Hannah. Something just don't seem right."

Janie added, "Yea, Miz Kate, have you thought 'bout how tired and all she's been?"

Kate did not respond immediately. She held her teacup with both hands, tilted it slightly toward her, and looked thoughtfully into the dark red brew as if answers would appear on its surface. After a few moments she answered, "I know." Although their comments made the knot in her stomach tighten, she was thankful for their concern and support. "I think Bill has plans to go to Leeville tomorrow," she added. "I'll talk to her while he's gone."

"That'll be good," June Ellen encouraged her.

Kate refilled her cup with tea. She sat quietly while the two women worked around her.

Janie patted and rolled dough and June Ellen refilled the water reservoir in the stove. They both said, echoing each other, "It's gonna be fine,

Miz Kate—whatever happens, she'll be fine. We'll all see to it. You just need to talk to her and learn what it is we need to be seeing to."

Janie's dark hands, covered with flour, worked the cream-colored dough. She pinched off a piece about two inches in diameter. Then, with the dough in the palm of one hand, the fingers of the other hand turned it until it was round and smooth and perfect and ready for the biscuit pan. June Ellen was at the well, easing the bucket down into the hole until it hit the water. The work continued, but their hearts and minds were on Hannah and the conversation that needed to take place.

Kate pretended to be asleep when Bill came home that night. She wished for someone to talk to, but it could never be her husband. She couldn't begin to imagine what he would do if he knew her suspicions and concerns. She couldn't or wouldn't tell him anything about Hannah until she absolutely had to tell him. He did not make any attempt to wake her. He, no doubt, had been taken care of elsewhere. Kate felt almost thankful for whoever she was.

Kate couldn't sleep. Her mind would not settle, and her brain spun with scrambled *what ifs*. If her suspicions proved true, Hannah's life would be changed forever. Kate inhaled deeply. She crossed her arms over her body and gripped her shoulders with her hands. As she stared into the darkness above her, she became more aware than ever before of the regular rhythm of Bill's breathing. He was sleeping peacefully while she was neither sleeping nor peaceful. Anger began to well up inside her.

"Bill, we should be doing this together. Our daughter's probably in trouble. I don't know what we're facing, but here I am to figure it out all by myself." Kate wanted to scream at him. "Why do you think we have to be perfect? We're not. None of us, not even you." Kate unintentionally moaned aloud as she remembered the contempt he had expressed for others who were no guiltier than he.

Not caring if she disrupted (in fact wanting to disrupt) the pleasant slumber beside her, she turned abruptly to her left side and gave the sheet an extra hard tug. Bill turned slightly and adjusted the covers over his shoulders but otherwise gave no notice to Kate's aggressive movement.

Kate gazed intently in the direction of her open window. The full moon was bright over the big pecan tree that stood not more than thirty feet away. The silhouette had a majestic quality as it stood tall and proud against the night sky. Kate could see the outline of the rope swing and smiled as she remembered the hours of play she had enjoyed with her children. "Oh, how I wish I could turn back time," she thought. With a deep breath, she rolled onto her back. "But I can't. Those days are gone. Hannah's not a little girl anymore. She is not waiting to be pushed in the swing. But she's … she's … she's still my little girl. Oh, Hannah, dear Hannah, what have you done?"

The hours of the night passed slowly for Kate. The mantle clock in the sitting room struck four times. It wouldn't be daylight for two more hours. Sleep, wished for, wouldn't come. She rolled onto her back and pulled the sheet up close around her neck. She clutched it with both hands and held it snugly under her chin. She was frowning at whatever might be in the space above her. Her chest tightened as she recalled her conversation with Janie and June Ellen, and dread filled her. Could the concern about Hannah possibly be true? "No. No, it can't be," she thought over and over.

Just before daylight a glimmer of well-being spread through her. She was comforted by a truth: the Lord would give the strength to take the next step. Whatever Hannah faced, she would face it with her.

Chapter Twenty-One

KATE SEARCHED FOR THE RIGHT WORDS. "I've got to just ask her. I don't want to scare her, but I don't have a choice." She kept going over possible scenarios in her mind. "She'll be alright, but I hate to think about what she may be facing." Then: "Maybe we're wrong," Kate added internally, trying unsuccessfully to convince herself.

The following afternoon Hannah stretched out on her bed for an after-school nap. Kate walked to the door of her room. "My beautiful princess," she thought. "Lord, I'm so anxious about this situation. Please give me wisdom and all the right words." She leaned against the door facing as she prayed. Her hands were damp and her mouth was dry.

Hannah, sleeping quietly, was on her side with her knees bent and pulled up against her chest, her arms hugging a pillow in front of her and her blond tresses glowing as the last rays of sun shined through the west windows and danced across them.

Kate moved to the side of the bed and sat gingerly on the edge. She gently stroked Hannah's forehead and hair with her hand.

Hannah opened her eyes and gave her mother a sleepy smile. "What is it?" she asked.

"I just want to talk a minute," Kate responded.

"Is everything alright?" Hannah turned more onto her back, so she could focus better on her mother.

"Hannah, you have been so tired of late. And you've had those few times of feeling sick. All of this has me a little worried about you."

"Oh, I'm sure I'm fine, Mama. We did a lot of extra stuff at school today. We're doing a lot every day, so I just feel like taking a nap when I get home. I'm fine though, really I am."

"Hannah, what about your monthly times? Are you alright? You haven't mentioned needing anything in quite a while—not since before Christmas, I think."

Hannah was wide awake by now. Her mother's words were startling. She sat straight up, legs folded Indian-style. Both of her hands flew up and covered her mouth. Her heart began to race as she wondered what her mother was asking. She had given little thought to her "time of the month" because it had not always been exactly the same.

"What do you mean?" Hannah stared into her lap.

Kate reached for Hannah's hands. She held them softly in her own. "I just want to be sure you're okay. You've been especially tired."

"But I'm sure I'm fine."

In the gentlest possible tone, Kate continued: "Do you remember when you had your monthly last?"

Hannah felt as if her heart would explode from her chest. She didn't know enough to put all the pieces together, but she couldn't keep her mind from racing back to the night in the wagon bed with Thomas. "Is it possible that one time like that could mean …?" She couldn't let herself actually think the word. Her heart pounded harder. She couldn't tell her mother about that night. The truth would disappoint her terribly. Nice girls just didn't do what she'd done.

Kate saw the anxiety in Hannah's eyes. She put both arms around her and hugged her tightly. "Hannah, honey, is there anything you want to tell me?"

Tears filled Hannah's eyes. The night that she had relived a thousand times, the one that seemed so very special … suddenly filled her with shame and dread.

Kate wiped the tears from Hannah's face with her hand and took her daughter's hands in hers. "Tell me, sweetheart," Kate said softly.

Hannah took a deep breath, then recounted to her mother some of the events of that evening in Leeville that special evening, which were surrounded by Christmas and holiday beauty and cheer. "I didn't know it was going to happen. It just happened," Hannah sobbed. "He held my hand and then he kissed me and … I didn't know."

"I know, honey," Kate said soothingly.

"He said I was special and he wanted to see me and …" Hannah struggled to get words out between her jerking chest and flowing tears. "What am I going to do? Do we have to tell Papa? He'll be so mad."

"I should have talked to you. I'm so sorry." Kate pulled Hannah against her shoulder and stroked the back of her head.

Kate's heart was pounding too. As she ached for Hannah, she, too, wondered what their next step would be. "Oh, my dear Hannah, I don't know just what to say or what we will do. But what's done is done."

With that, they both cried. "Whatever happens, I love you and I'll be with you," Kate whispered. "We don't know for sure if … let's wait until we have answers before we try to think what to do." Kate dried her tears and handed Hannah a handkerchief.

The transgression had been revealed, and the reality of the possible consequence had been shared. It would be a secret between the two of them for at least a few more days.

It was a rare occurrence for Kate and Hannah to travel alone, but months before they'd gone on a day trip to visit Kate's aunt in a neighboring county. Kate decided that she and Hannah would again make just such a trip the following week. She'd never met the doctor in Beaumont, but she did know that one was there—and that he had an office in the back of the drugstore.

* * *

THE BIG WOODEN DESK was covered with a variety of items. There were glass bottles, papers, and a black tube with a silver disc on the end. The roll top could come down and cover everything up, but on that day it was up and exposed all the clutter.

"Hello, I'm Dr. McLeod," the doctor announced as he entered the room.

Kate and Hannah were both comforted by his kind demeanor and soothing voice. Kate thought he might be in his fifties, as his hair was graying and he was a little on the heavy side. He sat down and tilted back in his wooden chair. His fingers were laced together and rested comfortably on his stomach. He acted as if he was settling down for a visit with old friends. Hannah relaxed slightly, too. Maybe he was only going to talk to them.

"I'm Kate McMolison, and this is my daughter, Hannah." Kate sounded more in control than she felt. Hannah nodded and tried to smile as Dr. McLeod turned to acknowledge her. "I'm not sure just how to explain our reason for coming. It's … difficult. Hannah's monthly time is late, and we—she and I—need. She and I need to know …" Kate's voice trailed off. She reached to take Hannah's hand. It was damp with nervous sweat, just as her own were.

Dr. McLeod sat forward in his chair. He spoke gently. "Hannah, tell me a little about how you've been feeling."

"Just tired a little and sometimes kind of sick, but I'm fine." Hannah wished she could make herself truly fine just by saying it.

"Well, I need to examine you a little," Dr. McLeod continued. "We just need to see what's going on. It won't hurt. If you will remove your clothes and lie there on the table under the sheet, I'll be right back." He walked out of the little office and closed the door behind him.

Hannah felt horrified. So did Kate—she'd never subjected herself to the hands of a strange doctor (or to any doctor for that matter). Yet there she was with her daughter in a strange room with a man that only a few minutes before was unknown to them. She had no choice, however. She had to trust her instincts and proceed down the path they were on. It was their only hope of learning sooner rather than later if her concerns were warranted.

Hannah lay frozen on the hard, sheet-covered table. She was not cold. The room was actually warm. No breeze was getting around the window coverings. She was scared, more scared than she had ever been. Kate stood close to her side and held her hand. Kate, too, was scared. She was hot, and her heart pounded.

There was a quiet knock on the door, followed by Dr. McLeod entering. "Are you ready for me?" he said.

Hannah couldn't imagine saying yes, so she said nothing. It didn't seem to matter. He came into the room. She felt her throat start to burn and tears fill her eyes. She saw the creek on the back of her eyelids; she would swim for a while, maybe forever. She held her breath and closed her eyes and tried to shut the world, the metal, and the unfamiliar hands out of her mind. But she couldn't. The hands felt big and the metal felt cold. Both were impossible to ignore. Dr. McLeod lifted the sheet and pressed all around her stomach. Her teeth clenched, her right hand squeezed her mother's hand, and her left hand gripped the side of the table. She didn't open her eyes. She couldn't look at the face of the man whose hands were everywhere she wished they weren't.

Dr. McLeod finally finished the examination. He took Hannah's hand and helped her sit up. As she sat wrapped in a sheet with her feet dangling above the floor, he spoke. His voice was soft, but to Hannah and to Kate it thundered into their ears and hearts. "You are fine, but you're expecting," he said. "You're going to be a mother. Just remember, you are not the first girl this has ever happened to. Others have made it, and you will too." None of his words were comforting. They were rather like a foreign language flowing through the air. Hannah and Kate both wanted to flee.

Dr. McLeod stepped out of the room again to give Hannah time to get back into her clothes. She dressed though she couldn't remember doing it. She felt numb. Hannah's mind was completely consumed by Dr. McLeod's words. Her head was whirling. "What do I do?" was all she could think. She felt as if everything was in a haze.

Before they left Dr. McLeod's office, he said, "There are homes—special homes—where you may go to live until your baby is born. They provide help, any kind of help you need, and I would certainly be glad to—"

"Thank you, Dr. McLeod," Kate said firmly, cutting him off mid-sentence. "Thank you so much for seeing us and for all your help.

Right now we just need some time. What do we owe you for today's visit?"

"Fifty cents. You can give it to the druggist out front. He'll take care of it for you. You're welcome to stay here for a little while if you want to. I need to ride out into the county to see a couple of people. I'll be leaving shortly. Be gone most of the afternoon."

"Thank you," Kate managed to answer again although her chest felt tight and her breath short. "We really need to get started home."

"Well okay, if you're sure." Dr. McLeod cupped Hannah's chin in his hand and added, "Remember to send me word if I can help you in any way."

Hannah lifted her eyes briefly. In halting words barely above a whisper she answered, "Yes sir. Thank you."

"Thank you," Kate said a third time. "We really need to be going. We have several miles to go." The finality of the doctor's words had caused every muscle in Kate's body to tighten. His expression was kind and his words were gentle, but the reality he had confirmed was weighing heavier and heavier in her heart. She tried to push away the nervous tension with a deep breath, but she was anxious to get outside. Her mind was troubled with the mention of homes for unwed mothers. She knew that sending young girls away was most often the way these situations were handled, but she couldn't imagine sending her child away, especially not at a time like this. She wouldn't.

"I understand," Dr. McLeod was saying. His voice was lost somewhere in the swirling emotions. "I am here if you need me. Just send word."

Hannah and Kate walked dazedly from Dr. McLeod's office and down the dimly lighted, narrow hall and through the opening in the counter that led back into the main part of the drug store. They stopped at the little window behind which the druggist stood. He was pouring a yellow-colored liquid into a brown bottle. He finished quickly and screwed the black cap into place. Kate handed him two coins. He smiled as he voiced a soft thank you. There was no attempt at being jolly. He seemed to sense the time was not right for lightheartedness. Kate managed a smile as she turned to walk beside Hannah toward the door that would take them back outside and into the world they had to face.

Hannah tried to breathe deeply but had a hard time. Her palms were sweaty, but she was cold. She couldn't stop her body from trembling as she and Kate walked from the drugstore.

In utter silence, Kate and Hannah lifted themselves into the wagon. Pete pulled forward and started down the road toward home. "Whoa," Kate said as she pulled gently on the reins. The wagon had just rounded the first bend. They were no longer visible to anyone or to anything other than the wildlife living in the woods. Kate brought the wagon to a stop. Tears flowed from Hannah's eyes and ran freely down her cheeks. In an attempt to control the sudden rush, Hannah covered her face with the palms of both hands. Kate gently grasped Hannah's hands in her own. She pulled them away from her tear-stained face and kissed her forehead. Kate's arms enveloped Hannah with a hug of unconditional love.

Hannah sobbed, "I didn't know girls who got in trouble—girls like me—were sent away," she said feebly. "Where would I go? What will happen to me? Will I ever come home? I'm scared. I'm so scared."

"You're not going anywhere," Kate said softly but emphatically. "I don't know just what the future holds, but *I will be with you*. We'll do whatever we have to do *together*."

"What am I going to tell Papa, and what about Thomas? Maybe Thomas will help me," Hannah replied, her thoughts a flying circle of emotions.

"We don't have a choice. We have to tell Bill. That's not going to be easy, but we'll do what we have to do."

Kate straightened herself on the wagon seat, picked up the reins, slapped them softly against Pete's back and made a soft double clicking noise that let Pete know it was time to move forward.

Hannah felt full of shame, and her heart was heavy. Her thoughts twisted in a thousand directions. She wished desperately for Thomas, but she worried about what he would think. "What would he say? What will he do?" She was afraid of his reaction, but she wanted him to know. She was thankful for her mother … but she wanted Thomas.

She needed him to share this news with her. She needed his comforting, strong arms to support her. She needed to hear him tell her everything would be okay. The baby was theirs together.

Hannah and Kate were mostly quiet as they rode home. Both were deep in thought as they tried to cope with the questions that burdened their minds, the biggest one being how best to tell Mr. McMolison.

Chapter Twenty-Two

KATE ANGUISHED OVER how to tell Bill about Hannah. There were no best words. She knew she had to just say what she knew. She waited until the day after their trip to see Dr. McLeod, as neither she nor Hannah felt strong enough for anything more that day.

The following morning after Hannah left for school, Kate mustered her courage. Bill sat at the end of the dining table drinking his second cup of coffee and reading the most recent *Old Farmer's Almanac*. He looked up when Kate sat down in the chair to his right. "What is it?" he asked before she could say anything.

Kate had decided it best to take a straightforward approach. She could remind him that Hannah had not been feeling well, that she had been unusually tired and that she'd been concerned about her for some time, but broaching the truth in little steps wouldn't change the facts and would likely frustrate him. Her resolve to get the conversation behind her forced the words from her lips: "Bill, we have a situation with Hannah. She's fine, but she is in a bit of trouble."

"Bit of trouble?" Bill looked up and frowned. "What are you talking about?"

"Hannah's expecting a baby. Please, please try to be calm. Please don't do anything rash," Kate pleaded. Her voice was soft and low.

"You know she is not—"

Bill interrupted before she could finish the thought. "Rash?" he said harshly. "Don't tell me how to respond. Just tell me what on earth you mean?" He pushed his chair from the table, stood, and looked down at Kate. "Are you sure? How do you know?"

"I'm sure," Kate answered, but didn't stand up or look up.

Bill's anger grew as his questions ran into each other. "Who? Who did this? Who is the father? What does she *mean* doing something like this? I can't get this family straight from one mess before there's another one!"

"Bill, the father is Thomas … John Stokes's son. It happened while we were in Leeville before Christmas." Kate kept her voice soft, hoping to soften his wrath.

Bill stared angrily down at Kate. He said nothing, threw the almanac down hard on the table and stormed from the house.

That afternoon when Hannah got home from school, her father was waiting for her.

The strike from the whip landed across her legs. She felt the burn. Her fists were white as her hands clutched the bed frame tightly. He bellowed, and his words were as scorching as the whip. Hannah figured there were probably sentences in the rage as he yelled, but all she heard were just words, some repeated over and over.

"I can't *believe* what you've done!" he roared. "After all I've done to give you the best of everything, all you and Katherine do is bring dishonor on our family." He paused to inhale, as if to fortify his lungs to continue. "Humiliated … disgraced yourself, disgraced all of us. What did you think? Consequences to sin … here we are … your action changes your life, changes all our lives." His anger boiled. "My political career may well be in shambles because of the situation you have yourself in. You have *us* in."

Except to say, "I'm sorry, I'm really sorry," Hannah remained quiet. She knew there was nothing she could do or say that would help the situation. She could not change what she had done, and she could not walk away from the circumstance in which she found herself. She was expecting a baby, and a child, she knew, was forever.

"*You're sorry*. Kinda late for that, don't you think," her father shouted scornfully. "I'll need to resign as elder in the church because of what you've done. I'm supposed to have my children under control. You're far from it."

Hannah thought of Katherine and her baby brother. They had both endured pain and humiliation at their father's hands, and neither of them had brought it on themselves as she had done. From deep within she mustered the courage to withstand whatever lay before her and to be strong not only for herself, but also for the baby now growing inside her. Thoughts of Thomas brought feelings of apprehension and faint hints of comfort. She wished for his warm arms to hold her as they had during their special evening—but what she *really* wished now was that she had not allowed him to hold her at all. Her mind was reeling. She didn't know what she wanted. She stood with her eyes closed and braced for the second blow.

Her father raised his arm with whip in hand ... then lowered it slowly to the floor as if an unseen restraining force had surrounded him. Without speaking, he turned and walked from the room. The tail of the whip dragged along the floor and followed obediently behind him. He said to Kate, "I will handle this." He walked out the front door.

The skin on Hannah's legs was reddened with a white-centered whelp-like area, but there were no broken or bleeding places. Kate hugged her daughter. "The Lord will give strength for whatever He brings our way. We have to trust Him and take one day at a time."

Hannah had heard those words many times before, but the problem was bigger this time and was personally *hers*. She felt worse than ever before in her life. "If the Lord's gonna help me, I need Him to hurry," she thought. "Mama says 'trust Him.' I'll try, because what else can I do? I don't have a choice. I surely can't walk away." Just thinking of the future was overwhelming.

Janie came into her bedroom. Standing beside Hannah's bed, she said, "I've been talking to God about you. I know He knows it all, what you need and everything, but you still need to talk to Him." Hannah, sitting on the bed in front of her, leaned her teary face against Janie's round front.

Between sobs Hannah said, "I don't know. I've messed up so bad."

"We all mess up. It's what you do with the mess that matters," Janie said, stroking her fingers through Hannah's hair. "Let's talk to Him again, together." Janie dropped to her knees beside Hannah's bed and gently pulled Hannah down beside her. "Lawd, you took care a David and Moses, and they did some right-awful things. Help this child, too. She just made a mistake. She's sorry, and we need you Lawd, to give your mercy. Yes, Lawd, show us the way, please show us the way."

Hannah wished everyone could love her like Janie and June Ellen and her mother. As she listened to Janie pray, she hoped God would do like Janie asked—and especially hoped He would see fit to use Thomas to take care of her.

***

THE FOLLOWING MORNING, Bill McMolison headed to Leeville. "Whoa, whoa," he said to his horse as he came to a stop in front of the hotel. It was almost dinnertime. He knew his friend John Stokes would be there soon, if in fact he was not there already. Even though Stokes would not be expecting to see Bill on that day, it would be only a short time before the two men would be together in a meeting as unplanned as the reason requiring it.

Bill climbed the steps to the hotel and walked inside. Several men stood talking in the far corner of the entrance hall. They were as close to the dining room as they could get without crossing Miss Tildy's invisible line. Miss Tildy owned the hotel, and her rules were enforced. The regulars, waiting for the bell, knew exactly where they could stand. Although Stokes was often allowed liberties, on that day he was standing and waiting with the others.

Bill entered the group. He extended his hand to each one. All of the usual pleasantries were exchanged. "How are you today?" "Did you have a good ride?" "How's the family?"

Stokes spoke first, "I didn't think you were coming back this way until next week. Anything special got you here today?" The bell rang, and the men all moved into the dining room.

As they each chose a place to sit, Bill said to Stokes, "You got some time after we eat? I need to talk to you. It's important."

"Sure. Always got time for you, my friend," Stokes said as he reached for the bowl of potatoes directly in front of him. The dinner conversation was brisk.

"Wasn't that a good rain we had yesterday, slow and soaking," an overall-clad farmer stated. "Came at a good time, too. Just got my peas in the ground."

Bill McMolison, sitting just a couple of seats away, responded, "That's good. Always glad to have a good rain. Didn't get but a few sprinkles up our way."

Joe Turner, in town to buy supplies, chimed in, "Y'all think we gonna get outa the war soon? What ya think President Wilson's going to do?" He sat with both elbows on the table, his right hand clasping the fork that shoveled food to his mouth and his left closed around a biscuit. He looked around the table, waiting for everyone's opinion.

"Don't rightly know, but he needs to do whatever it takes to get it done with and get out from over there," the pea farmer said emphatically as he bit off the pointed end of a pie-shaped piece of cornbread.

John Stokes had just bitten into a fried chicken thigh when the war was brought into the discussion. He swallowed quickly, wanting to get in the next word. "I agree. Wilson really needs to try to find a way to put a stop to that mess over there. From what I've been able to learn, our boys are in bad, bad conditions." He barely took a breath before continuing. "We need to keep our eyes on things here at home too. I met *The Man* last week," he said, referencing Governor Theodore Bilbo, "and he sure has our best interests at heart. You know he's a south Mississippi man, don't you?"

The owner of the feed store joined the group just in time to make the final declaration: "Yep, he is, and he's a good one. We need to see that he stays governor and hopefully send him to Washington one day. Sure need some right-thinking men up there."

The group stayed away from the topic of religion, although it would probably have been pretty safe. Most of the men present (if not all) were in agreement about the church, and most of them would add they were striving daily to live according to the teachings in the Bible. Bill was a master at navigating those conversations. Regardless of his personal life, he always expressed like-mindedness and stayed above the fray. The fact that he often had a mistress only one floor up from where they sat was a well-kept secret. His actions were discreet and, amazingly, never became public knowledge.

BILL MCMOLISON AND JOHN STOKES finished eating, left the hotel, and headed across the street in the direction of the courthouse. "Let's walk on around toward the back. What I want to talk about is pretty private," McMolison said as they walked. They turned down a side street and away from where people were milling around. Ironically—and unbeknownst to them—they walked toward the very spot where Thomas had parked his wagon on that December night. They rounded the side of the courthouse, and Bill came to a stop. Stokes paused and looked around. Then he faced Bill and asked what was on his mind.

"Stokes, we've been friends a long time, been through a lot together," Bill replied. "I'm in town today because we've got a problem, a personal problem. We've had problems in the past that we've had to take care of, but this one is different. It's different because it involves my Hannah and your Thomas."

Stokes frowned. "What are you saying? What do you mean, *problem with my Thomas*?"

Bill looked him square in the eye. "Hannah is expecting."

Stokes stepped closer. "*Expecting*? What do you mean expecting?"

Bill said nothing, his expression intense and grave.

"Are you talking about a baby?"

When Bill still didn't respond, Stokes took a step back. His mouth fell open. "A baby?" he said aloud, as if asking about something from another planet, something he couldn't quite comprehend. "A baby," he repeated harshly. His brow furrowed into an even harder frown, and his voice suddenly had an edge in it as if the reality of what Bill McMolison was saying had finally registered.

"Yes, that's what I mean," Bill said wearily. "Apparently they were together when we were in town just before Christmas." He made every effort to keep the conversation civil; behind the court-house or not, Bill did not want an outburst in downtown Leeville. "We just need to think of a plan for their sakes and ours. I know Hannah and Thomas are our first priority, but we also need to keep our political futures in mind."

"Are you sure she's expecting, McMolison?" Stokes asked. "*Really* sure?"

"Yes, I'm sure," Bill snapped. "She and Kate have already been to a doctor up in Beaumont."

"Does Thomas know?"

"Hell, I don't know. Probably not—I just learned myself."

"Well, what are you thinking of doing? Thomas has school, Bill. He's planning to go on to pharmacy or medical school somewhere, and a wife and baby would ruin everything."

Bill resented Stokes's comments and the tone in which they were delivered. He wanted to forcefully remind him that a baby would not be easy for his daughter, either. He managed to keep his cool for the moment and said, "I'm here because I thought we could work this out together. I'd hoped you would help me come up with a good solution, a solution that would be agreeable to everybody. Kate refuses to send Hannah away, and I don't feel right to make her. The truth is I don't want her to go somewhere else, either. But listen to me, John: it will be best if the baby can be born with a proper name. If it's not a bastard child, that would help. After it's born, I'm think-ing we can find a family somewhere away from here to take it, adopt it, and then …"

Stokes raised an eyebrow. "You told Hannah and Kate any of this?"

"No, but they'll both do as I tell them. You know you can be sure of that fact."

The words hung in the air for a long moment. "Now don't take me wrong, Bill, but is Hannah sure about the baby belonging to Thomas?"

Bill felt his jaw tighten. The mere suggestion made him angry; he wondered how his friend could ask him such a question. He wanted to point out that Hannah didn't have any experience, that Thomas got them to this point—which was the truth—but the only thing he said aloud was, "Yes, she's sure and it does take two."

Stokes met Bill's gaze. "Yeah, I guess you're right." He inhaled and puffed his cheeks and lips out as he exhaled. "Well, just got to fix it. Don't need people knowing 'bout this, either."

Bill knew he'd already had a night to come to grips with what had happened. Stokes had had only a few minutes, and the news was obviously hard for him to hear. Bill had already considered the negative impact the situation could have on both their political futures, and a fractured friendship between them would only make things worse. As Stokes absorbed the news, Bill, keeping his composure, spoke quietly but firmly. "Look, John, Hannah had never been with a man until Thomas. Things got out of hand that night during Christmas when we were in town. Maybe you need to talk to Thomas."

"I'll do that," Stokes replied, his eyes hard now. "He'll be home later this week for Easter. Some Easter we'll have," he said disgustedly. He looked away from Bill and kicked a pinecone against the courthouse wall. "I'll talk to him the night he gets home. If everything is as you say, I'll arrange for them to be married at my house on Sunday afternoon. I'll be sure, too, that the preacher knows to keep quiet."

"Okay," Bill said after a moment. "That's what we'll do. I'll wait to hear from you."

"Hannah needs to stay with you and Kate," Stokes replied. "Meaning I need for you to remember that Thomas will be going back to school to finish his school year. I suggest, too, that from the beginning we plan for this marriage to be for the sake of the baby *only*, and that everyone understand that it will be *annulled* after the baby is born. I'm sure you understand that I don't want anything to stand in the way of Thomas's future plans. And, McMolison, you also have to understand that in a few years, he'll want an untarnished girl for his wife."

Bill was getting mad. He was truly galled that Stokes had spoken of Hannah with such disparaging implications. He felt like punching him hard in the face with his fist, but he took a deep breath, shook his friend's hand, and agreed that the arrangement would be temporary. Then he started back to get his horse and head home. He had accomplished what he came to Leeville to do, and a plan was now in place. Hopefully his efforts would preserve honor for both families.

Chapter Twenty-Three

*H*ANNAH'S HUMILIATION overshadowed everything else in life. Her heart exploded with embarrassment when her father told her and her mother about his trip to Leeville to see Mr. Stokes.

While eating supper, Bill leaned forward with both forearms on the table, one on either side of his plate. Left on his plate was one lone bite of cornbread, currently soaking up residual pea liquor. Looking first to Hannah (who sat to his right) and then to Kate on his left he said, "I went to Leeville today and spoke with John Stokes. You know, Hannah, he and I have been friends a very long time. We respect each other and both want to do what is in the best interest of both our families."

Hannah's stomach was suddenly in her throat. She let her fork slip from her fingers and onto her plate. She leaned back with both hands in her lap. Feeling her whole body quiver and tears about to surface, she sat rigidly, looking down. The thought of what he had done gripped her with apprehension.

Kate felt her chest tighten, but she leaned forward, toward her husband. "Bill, what are you saying? In the event you've already made some sort of decision, Hannah needed to know—"

"Look Kate, I did what had to be done," Bill growled. "Hannah didn't need to know anything and neither did you."

Kate clenched the muscles in her jaw, tightened her fists, closed her eyes and sighed deeply. Hannah sat rigidly, her breathing becoming difficult.

With his hands gripping the armrests of his chair, Bill continued. "We talked and I explained the situation. Stokes lamented what had occurred and expressed great concern regarding Thomas and his ongoing education. He said that whatever is decided, he will *not* allow the decision in any way to be a hindrance to Thomas's future."

"Oh, I can't believe this! What about *Hannah's* future?" Kate replied, a slight edge in her voice now.

"Hannah should have thought of that before getting in this mess," Bill snapped. "And don't you go making things harder. Just cooperate."

Kate closed her eyes for a moment. Then she settled her posture and calmed her tone. "Tell us what else you talked about."

"He, as I expected, wants to do the right and honorable thing." Bill looked in Hannah's direction with a quick nod of his head. Hannah didn't see the gesture; she still sat with her chin down. "He will talk with Thomas when he gets home for the Easter holiday, explain the circumstances to him, and they will come here on Saturday so that we can all talk together."

Hannah had never heard her father conduct business, but she imagined that this was what it must sound like: his thoughts, his commands, his plans, and his decisions rolled forth, one after the other. She couldn't move. She lifted her face and stared at the center of the table. Her throat was tightening even more and her teeth clenching together so that no words were spoken, but they were there. "I've got a baby growing inside me, mine and Thomas's," she wanted to say. "It's *my* baby. We're talking about my baby."

Hannah thought things couldn't get worse until her father added, "Stokes is going to set up a nice little wedding for Sunday afternoon. Then, after the baby is born, the marriage will be annulled. By then we'll have found a good home to take the baby. He's gonna be on the lookout for a couple over in Alabama, and I'll reach out to some contacts up in North Mississippi."

Before leaving the table, Bill added, "You can't return to school in your condition. It's against the rules. Even though school will soon be over for the year and no one knows about your problem yet, they soon will if you continue going to class. That would just mean further damage to your reputation. My reputation as a member of the school board would suffer as well."

Bill then turned his attention to Kate. "You plan to go talk to Mrs. Satcher on Monday after the wedding." Mrs. Satcher, as Hannah knew, was the school principal. "Be honest but discreet when you speak with her. We need to do everything possible to stop rumors and speculations."

"What exactly are you thinking I should tell her?" Kate asked, the very hint of sarcasm in her tone. Bill either didn't catch it or chose not to acknowledge it.

"You'll think of something," he said. "They're in love, wanted to get married. We're pleased to have Thomas in the family. We understand about married students not being allowed to attend school, but we gave in. She'll finish her work at home. You know what you need to do—just do it, and as soon as possible." Bill pushed his chair back from the table and stood. "We all understand what has to be done, right?" Neither Kate nor Hannah answered.

Satisfied with the conversation, Bill walked from the room and out the front door. As soon as Hannah heard the squeak of the door opening and the thud of it closing, the tears that had been stinging the back of her eyes surfaced and streamed down her cheeks. Kate knelt beside her chair. Their tears mingled.

Hannah wanted to scream as loud as she could. She, before her father's announcement, had been trying to think of the best way to break the news to Thomas. She didn't know what he would say or do, but she'd thought it would be their moment. It would have been private, at least, whether good or bad.

Kate was not totally surprised by her husband's actions, but in this circumstance it had not occurred to her that he would make such extreme plans without at least telling them first.

TURMOIL PERVADED THE MCMOLISON home. Only Janie and June Ellen seemed to keep their wits about them. The only time they came close to forgetting their place was when they heard Mr. McMolison say the baby would be given away. The thought was unthinkable to them and threw them into a frenzy. Pots were jerked from shelves, cabinet doors slammed, and a side of bacon was pulled from the smokehouse ceiling with a force that brought the hook and a few splinters down with it.

Janie stomped around the kitchen muttering, "It ain't like there's no means to take care of it. There's plenty everything around here, and anyway, you can't just be giving your baby away like it's some kinda pound cake or something. It ain't right. Babies are part of your soul. They're a gift from the Lawd. Our little Hannah may a made a mistake, but don't make her pay for it for the rest of her life." Janie grabbed the flour can from the pantry shelf, opened it, and set it on the worktable with a thud, all the time shaking her head. A mist of white puffed up before settling back down, covering the tabletop. Still shaking her head, she snatched the ever-present rag from her apron string and began to clean up the mess the layer of fine flour had made. "Ain't right," she said under her breath. "Makes my insides knot up just thinking about her having her very own flesh somewhere she don't even know where it is."

Kate listened as Janie and June Ellen made their points over and over, and Hannah overheard the conversations more than once. She took their sentiments to heart, knowing that in her case they were right. The thought of giving her baby away became more and more unimaginable. "But what can I do? What can I do?" she thought. The questions crowded into her mind. "Right now I've got to get through the next week, and the next, and … oh, I can't think about all of it."

Angst filled Hannah's being during the days that followed. If it were not for the gentle love and support of her mother, Janie, and June Ellen, she was not sure she would have survived.

"The Lawd don't bring things to us 'less He brings the strength to meet it," Janie told her more than once.

Hannah heard the same words from her mother, but she never felt strong. "I know y'all are right, but I need extra," Hannah sobbed to Janie.

"Oh child, He'll give it. He will," Janie answered confidently.

June Ellen put her big dark arm around Hannah and said, "The Lawd's timing is just right. Maybe it don't seem like it, but it is."

"Yea, that's for sure," Janie added. "A baby is a special gift." She turned to the stove to stir the soup she was making. "You, sweet Hannah, just got the cart before the horse." She continued stirring but looked around so that her eyes met Hannah's. "Just you remember, mamas need to take care a their own, less the Lawd takes 'em and they can't."

"That's the truth, and we gonna help any way you need us," June Ellen said adamantly, as if the women somehow had the final say.

* * *

THOMAS ARRIVED HOME FOR EASTER and had barely gotten in the back door when he heard his father calling his name. "Thomas, come to the sitting room."

"Yes, sir. I'll be right there," Thomas replied, his voice echoing through the house.

Thomas entered the room, and Mr. Stokes closed the door. Without saying hello or asking if the trip home had been okay, the senior Stokes said, "Sit down. We have something to discuss." His tone was stern, his face hard.

Curious, Thomas said, "Yes sir. Okay." He sat in a blue striped wingback, the first chair he reached. He leaned back, hands in his lap with fingers casually laced together. He looked up at his father. "What is it? What's going on?" The most important thing he could imagine was some political maneuver or business dealing. If there was a grave situation involving the family, his father would include his mother in the conversation. So Thomas wasn't alarmed.

Mr. Stokes's style was as direct as that of Mr. McMolison. He stood three feet from his son and glared down at him. "Thomas," he said, "have you had relations with Bill McMolison's daughter, Hannah?"

Thomas's heart suddenly raced. He wasn't nearly as concerned about his father learning that he'd been intimate with Hannah as he was *the reason* he had found out. The question caused Thomas to sit up and move forward to the edge of the chair. He placed his hands palm down on his knees. "Well, I … what's this about?" His mind raced back to that night in December.

Mr. Stokes took a few steps to the right, then turned abruptly. Once again he faced his son. "It's not a hard question. You either have or haven't. Which is it?"

"Yes, sir. I did, just one time." Thomas had hoped to see Hannah again and recapture the passion of that December evening. Hearing his father's question made him know, however, that something far differ-ent was about to unfold.

"One time," Mr. Stokes said loudly. "One time." Both arms waved upward and out. "Guess you're finding out that's all it takes." He walked across the room and leaned against the mantle.

Thomas pushed to his feet, where he stood with his elbows bent and palms up. "What do you mean, *one time*? What are you talking about? What's going on?"

"She's *expecting*."

Thomas backed into his chair and sat down heavily, the wind driven from him. "Expecting?" Thomas repeated, as if he really didn't know what the word meant.

Stokes paced across the room and back again, stopping once again in front of Thomas. Thomas did not move, but looked up at his father as John Stokes emphatically said, "Yes, Thomas. *Expecting*. That's what I said. She is expecting a baby—*your* baby." He started to turn away but stopped and said, almost as an afterthought, "that is, unless you think she may have been with someone else?"

Thomas rubbed his thighs with suddenly damp hands. He felt defensive for Hannah when he responded, "No, sir. No, sir, she had never been with anyone else. I know she hadn't."

"Well then," Mr. Stokes began, "I hope you see what you've done. You've really messed up and put your whole future at risk." He sat down and pulled his chair close to Thomas. Without waiting for an answer, he continued. "I think Bill and I have come up with a plan that will help with the problem. It will give us an immediate solution and will keep your life and Hannah's from being ruined."

Thomas wondered what his father meant. His head spun as he tried to fathom the news of a baby. "Sir?" he questioned. His father felt almost too close, so Thomas leaned back in his chair.

Stokes gave no attention to Thomas's response. Sternly, he continued: "You will marry Hannah—"

"*Marry* her?" Thomas popped back up and walked to the mantle. "Not sure I want to be getting married right now."

His father let out a scoffing chuckle. "Right. Well, it's too late now. You're gonna do what's right."

"But why? You said you and Mr. McMolison had a plan to take care of everything."

"And we do, but when the baby comes it needs to have a proper name. It will be a Stokes, but then when it's adopted it'll take the new parents' name. I'll see that the marriage is annulled, and that will be the end of this mess."

Mess. The word rang in Thomas's ears. He didn't want to be getting married, but he knew Hannah was probably getting the same instructions he was getting, and things would go worse for her than for him. She wouldn't be leaving it all behind and going back to school.

Mr. Stokes walked toward the door. "Now that I know the truth for sure, I've got to go tell your mother. Just remember—your college will not be interrupted. *That's* the important thing." He left the room and closed the door behind him.

Thomas plopped down in the chair. He dropped his head against the tall back and bit a piece of rough skin from near his right thumbnail. "A baby," he said to himself. He stared at the ceiling. "I can't blame Father or Mr. McMolison for coming up with a plan, but I can't believe that they—even the two of them—didn't give me and Hannah a say in the matter." He paused, keeping his voice down. "I mean, I don't want to be married and I *do* want to get back to school, but you'd think they might have at least discussed it with us." He stood, walked to the front window and gazed, unseeing, at the azaleas that were glowing with bright pink blooms. "No—not our fathers. They're not going to discuss anything with us. They make the decisions. We're just puppets. They pull the strings."

WITHIN A FEW BRIEF MINUTES Thomas went from a carefree college student arriving home for the Easter holiday to a young man learning he was soon to become a father (and even sooner a groom). In the same breath his father declared that he would become *not* a father or a groom. As the plan rotated in his mind, his father reentered the room, already talking.

"You and I will go tomorrow to Leaf Creek," John Stokes said. "That will give you a chance to talk to Hannah before getting married. On Sunday, Mr. and Mrs. McMolison and Hannah will come to our house. We will have a quiet ceremony in the sitting room. Of course it'll have to be in the afternoon. Church is in the morning, but we'll do it as early as possible so you can get started back to school."

Thomas turned to face his father. His father's words sounded sterile, matter-of-fact. "This is all so unreal. I'm just thinking that …"

Mr. Stokes crossed the room until he was directly in front of Thomas. "Look at me, son," he said firmly. "I need to be sure you realize what is at stake here. We will do everything just as I have told you. Don't get any different ideas."

"I'm going back to school. I mean, I want to go back to school, and I'll get married just like you say, but I was thinking that maybe I …" Thomas' words were quiet and calm.

"Nothing for you to think about, son," Stokes said, in a tone that left little doubt that the plan was set in concrete. "Bill and I have thought everything through, thought about what we ought to do, and what will be best for everyone."

* * *

HANNAH LAY AWAKE. It was Friday night before Easter. She wanted to sleep but couldn't. Her thoughts rolled feverishly into one another. As she imagined what seeing Thomas would be like, all she could think about was what he was going to say and what he was going to do. Being discussed by her father and Mr. Stokes was humiliating.

Every time she thought about the fact that they knew what she had done, a hot flush rushed through her.

She clasped her hands together under her chin, lay on her left side, and pulled her knees close to her chest. "If only Thomas will say he will be here, that he will help me," she whispered. Her hands tightened around each other as she wondered if she would even get to talk to him. "Papa and Mr. Stokes will probably do all the talking, and it will be *to* Thomas and me, not *with* us." Her thoughts remained fractured as she relived every moment she had spent with Thomas and imagined the unknown scene that was still to come. She imagined possible scenarios for their future, but she knew that no matter how much she wished things were different, Mr. Stokes and her father would have their way.

IT WAS EARLY AFTERNOON when the two men arrived at the McMolison's. Hannah sat quietly on the sofa, her hands again clasped tightly together. Her heart pounded wildly as she waited inside with her mother while her father went out to greet Thomas and Mr. Stokes.

The men walked into the room. Hannah looked up. "Hello," she said, barely above a whisper. Her eyes met Thomas's eyes only briefly before she looked back at her lap. In spite of her circumstances, she was still drawn to the beautiful blueness in his eyes that she had so often dreamed of.

"Hello," Thomas said softly. He took a step toward the sofa, but Bill McMolison grabbed his elbow and motioned for him to sit in a chair across the room.

Hannah's jaw tightened at her father's gesture. "I want him close to me." The sentiment filled her heart, and she wished she could scream the words at her father.

"Let's all sit down," Bill McMolison said, ignoring her, as he sat in one of the chairs near the sofa. Kate moved to the space on the sofa beside Hannah.

The grip on Hannah's throat felt tighter every minute. She wasn't sure she could continue actual breathing. Waiting for a sentence of life imprisonment would be easier, she felt certain.

Hannah glanced up and found Thomas's eyes on her. He dipped his chin and smiled slightly. The warmth and kindness in his gaze eased her apprehensiveness. She wished desperately for him to touch her, to hold her hand, and tell her he would be with her whatever came.

The two elder men did the talking, however. Mr. Stokes leaned forward, elbows on his knees, his fingers interlaced, except for the index fingers that touched each other and pointed outward toward Hannah. "Hannah, I'm sorry for this situation, and I hope you know we're going to do everything we can to make it right for everybody." He sat back in his chair, crossed his legs, and rested his hands comfortably on the chair arms.

"Hannah?" Her father looked at her, his tone instructing her to answer.

"Yes, sir," Hannah managed, glancing for a brief instant toward Mr. Stokes.

Bill sat on the edge of his chair. "Is everything set for tomorrow? The wedding, I mean."

"I called our preacher, explained the situation. He's coming and Mrs. Stokes is making a little cake or something."

Kate reached over and put her hand on Hannah's arm.

John Stokes uncrossed his legs and leaned forward. "Main thing is Thomas's education. Can't let anything get in the way. Hope y'all all understand that."

"That's right. Everybody understands," Bill McMolison replied. He looked quickly to Hannah and Kate, and Hannah saw warning in his eyes. They were to remain quiet. The look told them, and they did.

"Second important thing is this baby has a proper name and family," Stokes continued. "We'll have the wedding tomorrow and then start to work on finding it a home. Think that covers 'bout everything." And with that, he stood to leave.

Hannah rubbed the skirt of her dress with damp hands. She didn't say anything. She wasn't sure she could get a word out of her constricted throat even if she thought she would be heard. Her father had made it clear that in his mind, she had forfeited all rights to be included in making plans for either her baby or getting married. She knew her father's primary objective (as well as that of Mr. Stokes) was to make the dishonorable appear honorable.

She felt the two men taking everything away from her—her marriage, her groom, her baby.

"I think that gets it. I believe we have things under control," Bill said, and stood.

Hannah wanted to shout, "It's me! It's me and my baby y'all are talking about! This isn't just some business deal." She wished Thomas would say something, but he, like she, had remained quiet.

John Stokes and Thomas were at the door to leave when Thomas hesitated and looked at his father. "If it's alright, sir, I'd like to talk to Hannah. We'll walk outside if that's okay."

"I guess. Go on, but make it quick. We need to get going." Mr. Stokes gave a sideways and unsmiling glance toward Hannah.

Thomas stepped toward her and held out his hand.

Hannah, glad for the hand, lifted herself on legs that felt like mush. Thankfully they held her up, and she walked out the door in front of him.

They walked silently until they reached the big oak. Knowing they dare not go any farther, they stopped on the other side.

Hannah looked up into Thomas's face. "I'm so sorry," she said, her voice quivering.

Thomas took her hands in his and spoke softly. "I'm sorry, too. It's my fault, and I don't feel right about leaving you like this, but I've got to go back to school. It's almost the end of the semester. I have to go. My father would never forgive me if I didn't."

"I know, but you'll be back," Hannah said. It came out in more of a question than a statement.

"Hannah, I'm so sorry to have to tell you, but I'll be staying at school through the summer. I wish I could be here, wish I could see you every day."

Hannah felt her heart sink. Her hands tightened on his. "Oh no. Does that mean you won't be here at all?" Hannah's voice was quiet and pleading.

"The plan is for me to finish a year early and go on to pharmacy or medical school, whichever one works out, but I'll come when I can. You know you're really special to me. You know I care about you a lot, and I want to be here when I can. It's just going to be hard with my father wanting me to go to school and stay there."

She stood holding the hand of the man she was to marry the following day. She wanted him to hug her, to hold her tightly and tell her he would be with her forever and that they would be a family. The hug came, but the words never did.

"I'll write," he said. "I promise I'll keep in touch so I can know how you're doing. And I want to know about the baby."

"It's *our* baby, Thomas," her eyes piercing deeply into his.

"I know." He put his arms around her again. "You do understand I have to go to school. My father would never let me do anything different. But I'll at least see you tomorrow." He kissed her quickly on the lips. "It's our wedding day."

Hannah began to steel herself against the fact that even if he cared for her or for their baby, the pull of his father and the life he had planned for himself was of greater importance. It was a bitter realization.

THOMAS WAS QUIET on the ride home. Seeing Hannah had stirred him through and through. Thoughts of her filled his heart and his mind. "Beautiful, sweet, genuine … innocent until I met her. What have I done?" he wanted to say aloud. He'd noticed that her dress seemed tight at the waist, and he wanted to rub his hand across where his baby was growing. He had wanted to hold all of her and tell her he would be there for her. Instead he told her he wasn't even coming home for the summer. Thomas's heart hurt. He groaned at the memory.

"What is it? What's wrong?" his father asked.

"Thinking about Hannah having a baby. I can't believe it. Don't think I ought to leave her to do this all by herself."

"She's *not* all by herself," his father said loudly. "Don't even think about changing plans. You're going back to school. That's final. If you do something stupid, you'll regret it."

Thomas didn't answer. "I can't leave Hannah to do this alone." His silent thoughts collided one on another. "She's scared and innocent. I'm the one that's not innocent, yet I'm the one that's fleeing." He gripped his fists tightly together and pushed the ball of clasped fingers into his lips. Thoughts continued to whirl in his head. "There's no telling what Father would do if I don't do as he says. I'll have to do what he says. How could I help her if he takes everything away from me?"

"Just remember you're doing the decent and honorable thing," John Stokes said as if reading his son's mind. "You're giving the baby a name. Hannah should be thankful."

"But what then?" Thomas thought but didn't say. "What is decent and honorable after that? Leaving and going on with my life? Decent and honorable hardly seem the right words to describe what's happening." Even as he was shrinking from any thought of standing up to his father, the emotions at war in his heart and his head had Hannah on one side and his father on the other. He knew he had never been (and would likely never be) strong enough to argue against his father. At that moment, the only words to cross his lips were, "Yes, sir."

* * *

THE STOKES AND THE MCMOLISONS gathered at one o'clock on Sunday afternoon in the Stokeses' parlor. The room was dusted and clean. Doilies covered chair arms and fresh flowers were on the end tables.

"I have a little something for you, dear," Mrs. Stokes said, greeting Hannah with a forced smile. She handed her a small bouquet of two roses and a cluster of brides' wreath. "I'm sorry but those are the only roses I have."

Hannah smiled. "They're really pretty. Thank you."

"Yes, thank you." Kate gently squeezed Mrs. Stokes's hands. "I appreciate your doing this."

"We need to get started," John Stokes said, his voice blaring through the room. "Thomas? Where's Thomas?"

Hannah's immediate thought was that he'd disappeared. She felt a streak of panic rush through her.

"I'll get him. He was finishing getting dressed," Mrs. Stokes replied.

Hannah relaxed a bit when Thomas came into the room. Dressed in a dark blue suit, white shirt, and a red and blue tie, he looked to Hannah more handsome than ever. Her heart quickened, and for a brief second she forgot her condition.

The slight tightness of Hannah's dress was barely noticeable. The pink fabric framing her face made her glow in a way that reminded Thomas of her innocence and sweetness. He walked to stand beside her. He took her hand in his.

"Until death do us part," she said. "Until death do us part," he said. "I now pronounce you husband and wife," the preacher said.

As soon as the preacher pronounced them husband and wife, Mr. Stokes said firmly, "Thomas, you need to go. You'll miss the train back to Batesville."

Mrs. Stokes spoke softly to her husband: "John, why don't you give him a few minutes. I think he has time. I've made coffee, and I have cake."

"No, he needs to get going," Stokes barked. "If he wants cake, give him a piece to take with him."

Thomas squeezed Hannah's hand and kissed her lightly on the cheek. "I've got to change clothes. Don't want to wear this back to school." He waved his hand down the front of his jacket.

"Yes, okay. I guess you do." Hannah looked up into his face and attempted to smile. He squeezed her hand again.

Kate appeared at Hannah's side. "Are you okay?" her mother asked.

"Yes, ma'am. I'm fine," she answered, but what she really wanted was to hide from all that was going on around her. Everybody was being properly polite, stiff, and stilted. Even though her mother stayed close and guided the conversation with Mrs. Stokes, Hannah felt awkward. She felt as if all eyes were on her, seeing her as conspicuous, defiled, and horrible. "I'm not horrible," she wanted to scream, but she couldn't, even if the circumstance allowed. Her throat was far too tight and dry.

Hannah's heart felt as if a vice grip was crushing in. She wanted to be home. The vows took only a matter of seconds. The whole affair couldn't have been more than ten minutes. The preacher had said a few words during which Mrs. Stokes sniffled quietly until Mr. Stokes bumped her arm, instructing her to stop.

The baby—her baby—was never mentioned by a grandparent or, even worse, not once by Thomas. Mrs. Stokes handed her a piece of cake.

"Thank you." Hannah looked at the cake but feared she would be sick if she tried to eat a bite. She broke a piece off with her fork and moved it around on the plate. "Until death do us part," Hannah repeated the words in her mind. "Not this time," she thought. "What have I done? I'm married—even married to a man I love—but why? Honor? It was not Thomas's idea and not even mine. Honor? It's flawed honor."

Hannah was nauseated. Feeling hot and sweaty, she put her plate on a side table, eased out the front door, walked across the porch and sat down on the steps. Being sick right there in the Stokeses' house would make her even more embarrassed. Plus, she didn't think she could bear hearing Mr. Stokes say another word. All she had heard him talk about was Thomas's school and being glad to get *things* taken care of.

"I just want to go home," she was saying aloud as she sat with her elbows on her knees and her face in her hands.

"Hannah, I'm so sorry things have to be this way, but I don't have a choice." She looked up when she heard Thomas's voice coming from above her. He put his hand on her shoulder and said, almost too quietly to be heard, "I've got to go. I'm sorry." He sat on the step beside her. "What are you doing out here?"

"I just needed to come out for a little bit."

"Did I tell you that you look beautiful today, baby and all? *Our* baby."

"Thank you. You look really handsome too. I wish you didn't have to go."

"I know. Me too. I'll be back and see you somehow. Right now I probably need to get going before my father realizes I haven't left. I'll check on you when I can."

"Does he mean it?" Hannah wondered. She wasn't sure that he was sincere about coming back. She wanted to believe with her whole heart that he did.

Their lips met gently and softly. Thomas looked into Hannah's eyes and wiped a tear from her cheek with his thumb. "I'll be back," he said. Then he walked down the steps and was gone.

Hannah didn't move from the step. She looked after him through her tears but said nothing. She couldn't imagine feeling more alone than she did at that moment. Her chest felt so heavy breathing was difficult. A minute later, she stood up and looked off into the distance. This time she spoke aloud.

"Here I am, married to Thomas. He's gone. I'm alone. We're alone, but he'll check on us." She rubbed her hand over her stomach. "I hope."

Chapter Twenty-Four

KATHERINE AND STEPHEN had not been present for Hannah's
wedding. They didn't even know about it until it was over. Kate wrote
Katherine weekly, and in an early April letter, she wrote as much about
Hannah and Thomas as she felt comfortable including. She added that
Hannah was doing okay, but if they could come for a visit, it would
mean a lot.

Katherine wanted to go to her sister immediately after learning
about her condition, but Stephen had been sick with the flu. Not only
did they wait until he felt strong enough to travel, but they waited to
avoid the risk of spreading the flu to her family in Leaf Creek. Stephen
had recovered sufficiently by late April to preach the Easter services at
their church, but it was not until the first week in May that they made
the trip to Leaf Creek.

Upon their arrival at the McMolison's Stephen went straight to bed.
His bout with the flu had robbed him of much of his stamina.

Katherine went straight to Hannah. Hugging her and then clasping
her hands around Hannah's, she held her close as questions tumbled
from her lips, "How are you? How do you feel? I'm so sorry I couldn't
get here sooner."

"I'm fine. I really am, but I've missed you so bad. It's been awful,"

Hannah said, tears filling her eyes.

"Come on. Let's go talk like we used to. I want you to tell me everything."

The girls barely got through the bedroom door before Hannah started to cry. "I'm really glad you're here. I messed up bad. It's so embarrassing and humiliating."

"I'm so sorry I haven't been here with you, and you've had to go through this. Did Papa make it really hard when he found out? What did he do?"

"He got the whip, but just one lash. That's not the worst part, though."

Katherine leaned against the brass post of the footboard. "What do you mean?"

"He told Mr. Stokes about the baby before I could tell Thomas." Hannah's eyes spilled a flood of tears that wet her cheeks and then covered her fingers as she attempted to wipe them away. "I've made trouble for everybody. I don't know what to do."

Katherine pulled Hannah to her. Short, intermittent sobs burst against her chest as Hannah held tightly to her hug. Salty wetness soaked Katherine's shoulder and the side of her neck, causing strands of her hair to stick in a clump to Hannah's face.

Katherine took Hannah's shoulders in her hands and gently separated herself from her. She patted the side of the bed. "Here, sit down." They sat on the edge of the bed they had shared. Their weight pushed down the mattress. The squeak of the springs was familiar, almost comforting. "It's still there—that same old squeak, I mean," Katherine said, and smiled as she reached for Hannah's hand again. "We've been right here together, squeak and all, through hard times before. And we will get through this together. I may not be right here beside you, but you know I am with you in my heart. Every time the bed squeaks, you remember that I love you, and I will be with you any chance I get."

"I will. I love you, too. Thank you for being here. I know what I did was wrong, and I let everybody down," Hannah whimpered through tear-stained lips.

"Don't cry. Go wash your face. Let's get Mama and go for a long walk in the woods. Being outside will do all of us good."

Katherine had never met Thomas, but on that day she wasn't sure she liked him. In fact, she was mad at him for not being at Hannah's side. It was obvious that he owned Hannah's heart, and his presence would have made things much easier for her. But it sounded like Mr. Stokes's influence over his son was powerful and would more than likely dictate Thomas's responses. Time would tell.

STEPHEN AND KATHERINE returned to Leaf Creek for another visit around the first of August that year. It was during that visit that Stephen, surprisingly, was more favorably accepted by his father-in-law. Mr. McMolison actually lingered after meals and spent time asking Stephen about his church in Hattiesburg and about the weather on their trip down. The reason for his change of heart, however, become apparent as they planned to leave for home.

"Let's take a quick walk out toward the barn," Bill said, and patted Stephen on the back and waved his hand toward the barn. "I've got a little something I want to show you."

Stephen looked at Katherine. She widened her eyes, pursed her lips, and lifted both shoulders. She mouthed the words, "I don't know."

Hannah had told Katherine of the proposed arrangements for the baby during the May visit, but neither had accepted that her baby would actually be *given away*. Katherine had told Stephen what her father was planning and he, too, couldn't believe it would really happen.

The two men walked to the far side of the barn. Bill stopped and turned to face his son-in-law. "Stephen, I need you to help find a suitable home for Hannah's baby."

"Sir, I don't know," Stephen said, not prepared for the conversation.

Bill paid no attention to Stephen's reservations. "It'll be good if you find someone farther away than Hattiesburg."

Stephen was silent, but it didn't matter. Bill continued: "I have someone looking over in Alabama, and I'm gonna check in Louisiana too, but if you know people up in north Mississippi, say, that would be really good. I'm counting on you to help me with this, son. It's important we find a couple and a good home … and soon."

"Yes sir. I'll see what I can do." The words came from Stephen even as he knew in his heart that he could never help give Hannah's baby away—at least not unless she was the one who asked for his help.

Chapter Twenty-Five

*I*T WAS A BRILLIANT September day in Leaf Creek. The sun was shining brightly and sent heat waves, hot as those in mid-July, into the air. Hannah sat with her mother under one of the shade trees hoping to catch a little breeze. She had been feeling bigger, hotter, and more uncomfortable in every way.

She had received two letters from Thomas, one shortly after the wedding and one in late July. The letters were only a couple of paragraphs long. He wrote about school, mostly describing his English literature and American history courses. He explained that both classes required a lot of reading and left him little time for anything else. He added that he hoped she was okay, that he wished he could see her … but he never mentioned the baby. He included a picture of himself in the July letter, saying it was a copy of the one in the previous year's annual and how she might like to have it. He was right. She was thrilled to have it. For several minutes she longingly searched his face, remembering the first time she saw it and wishing with her whole heart to have it close enough again to feel the warmth of his skin. She traced the photograph with her fingers. The lips, cold to her touch, did not diminish her memory of the warm, soft, tender lips that kissed her. As she placed the picture in her box alongside the two letters, she hoped she would someday feel his touch again.

Hannah wanted to keep the picture on her dresser table but knew if her father saw it, he would not approve. Suddenly, tightness spread across her stomach along with a fleeting pain. She gasped.

Kate looked up from the book she was reading. "What is it?"

"I don't know. My stomach felt a little funny, kind of tight, but it's gone. Could this be the beginning? Is it starting?" Hannah asked her mother. She suddenly felt afraid.

"We will see," Kate answered calmly, although her insides churned with butterflies as she thought of the experience that lay before her daughter. "I think we should go inside. You can walk around or lie down. If it's time, we will know soon enough."

The tightness came again and again. Hannah's stomach became board-like more and more often. She grasped the bed on either side of her, and said, "It hurts. It hurts so bad. Is it supposed to hurt like this?" The pain increased every time the tightness came. She didn't cry out, but thought, "I can't cry. It's all I can do just to breathe. The room is so hot."

"Try to relax, Hannah." Kate spoke calmly even though her heart was beating fast and she was almost as damp from nervous anxiety as Hannah was from giving birth. "Let me get Janie and June Ellen. I'll be right back."

The clock struck midnight. Kate, June Ellen, and Janie had been at Hannah's side for the past seven hours. All were waiting and each was doing everything possible to console Hannah and make her as comfortable as the situation allowed.

Frank kept the wood stove burning so there would be plenty of hot water. The extra rags, towels, and blankets had been clean and ready for days.

One or another of the three women wiped Hannah's face a hundred times. They rubbed her aching back, her arms, and her legs. Janie said over and over, "Child you gon' be fine. Ain't easy, but you can do it. Just you breathe and relax. Your baby's on its way. Just think a that precious little baby that's coming."

"I don't wanna think," Hannah said between contractions. "It hurts.

I just want it over." She grimaced and grabbed the bed hard. "Ohhh-hhhh …"

Mr. McMolison had gone to Leeville that day and would be there at least overnight. He had met with John Stokes and the other members of the board of supervisors earlier in the evening. A second dark-skinned mistress had years before taken Rosie's mother's place. She stayed with him long enough that night to soothe him to slumber, and now he slept peacefully in his room. He had no idea his home in Leaf Creek was not at all as tranquil as he was.

At home his wife sat anxious and worried, and his daughter endured the stress of pain.

By four a.m. Hannah was exhausted, but she pushed hard. She didn't want to push, but she knew she had no choice. She heard Janie's voice time and again telling her to push, that it was almost over.

Kate held her right hand and June Ellen held her left. Hannah squeezed them hard and tried to do as Janie asked. "It's here, the head … itsa coming." Hannah heard Janie's words somewhere in a fog. Then, suddenly, it *was* over. Hannah felt something else, but now it didn't hurt. Janie was speaking again: "Everything's fine, fine. It's a boy. It's a *perfect baby boy*. Thank ya, Jesus."

Crying filled the room. Janie wrapped the precious new arrival in a blanket and handed him to Kate, who then placed him across Hannah's chest. Hannah felt unbelievably content. She was so tired, yet she felt a special comfort in the gently squiggling bundle atop her. The only other sensation that registered in Hannah's fatigued mind was the cleansing rags in the able, gentle and loving hands of Janie and June Ellen. Kate sat at Hannah's side and stroked the damp hair from her daughter's face, and wiped away as well the tears that fell from her own eyes.

The midwife from Beaumont had been in Leaf Creek for the past day and night. She had come to assist a young wife in the delivery of her first baby. On one of her previous trips, she had stopped by to see Hannah. Dr. McLeod had requested that she keep tabs on the girl from Leaf Creek and let him know how she was faring. She knew that Hannah's time was getting near, so she dared not return to Beaumont without checking on her.

It was mid-morning now, and Hannah was resting quietly. The knock was soft. Janie barely heard it. She answered the door and, realizing it was the midwife, Janie's pride kicked in. She would be pleased to show off her handiwork. She greeted the midwife warmly and escorted her to Hannah's room where they found both mother and baby sleeping peacefully.

"It's a beautiful scene, isn't it?" the woman said to Janie. "Everything looks like you did a perfect job." Janie was beginning to like her. "Even though I wasn't here I can still fill in the paper for the birth certificate if you would like me to. Why don't I check on the baby, and then I will be on my way. Dr. McLeod will be pleased to hear that Hannah had her baby and that both are fine. You did a good job. I will tell Dr. McLeod they are in good hands."

"Hannah." The midwife touched Hannah's shoulder and quietly called her name. Hannah roused slightly, opening her eyes, squinting. "My name is Jackie. I'm from up in Beaumont. You've got a mighty fine baby here. I can fill out the paperwork for a birth certificate for him. I just need some information from you." Hannah felt incredibly tired, but she awakened enough to answer the necessary questions. Kate and Janie were both poised to fill in any blanks.

"What is your full name, Hannah?"

"Hannah Caroline McMolison." She paused. Then: "Stokes."

"I'm sorry. What was the last name again?"

"S T O K E S," Kate said, spelling the name. "Stokes."

"And the father's name?"

Hannah answered this time: "Thomas Stokes."

"Is there a middle name?" the midwife continued, writing on her piece of paper.

Hannah felt a nervousness spring to her heart as she realized she did not have the answer. She didn't know if the father of her baby had a middle name.

"His name is … it's just Thomas Stokes," she responded. She gave the Stokeses' current Leeville address. Then she admitted she didn't know where the baby's father was born.

"Have you thought about the baby's name?"

"Yes," Hannah answered as she thought back over the many hours she had spent considering names. Naming a girl would have been easy; naming a boy had proved more difficult. "Should he be a namesake for his father?" she wondered. "No, probably not. What about my father? No, my father wouldn't like it even if that was what I wanted—which I don't." He needed a name, though; the midwife was waiting to write it down. Hannah smiled as she thought to herself, "Since there are no men on earth to choose from, maybe I better think about names that God has a history of being partial to. We can both use all the help we can get." It was time for a decision. Hannah's thoughts spun in her head. "Joseph David," she answered confidently, remembering two men from the Bible. "His name is Joseph David Stokes."

Janie chimed in with the time of birth, and Kate answered the remaining questions. Hannah drifted back to sleep as Kate made an additional request: "Please ask that the certificate be sent to us here in Leaf Creek. Will that be a problem?"

"Not at all. Give me the address, and I will be on my way."

Janie saw Jackie to the door. She even thanked her for her trouble. This was one midwife she actually liked.

* * *

BILL RETURNED from Leeville later in the day. Kate met him at the door. Excitedly she told him, "Bill we have a beautiful grandson. He was born early this morning."

"Is Hannah okay?" Bill asked matter-of-factly.

"She is! Yesterday, she—"

"Is the baby okay?" Bill interrupted.

"Yes, Hannah is tired, but she and the baby are both fine. Come see them. He's beautiful, Bill."

Bill headed toward the kitchen rather than toward Hannah's room. "Don't you want to see them?" Kate asked in disbelief.

"You've told me they're fine. I'll check on 'em later," he replied as he walked on through the house and out the back door. Kate worried that Bill only went to Hannah's room two, maybe three times during the next eight to ten days that she was confined in bed. She worried, too, that when he questioned Hannah about how she was feeling, he never took much notice of his new little grandson beside her.

232

Chapter Twenty-Six

THOMAS WAS HOME the day Mr. McMolison came to tell his father that the baby had been born and they needed to expedite the finding of a suitable family. Sitting around the supper table that evening, Mr. Stokes said to Thomas, "Bill let me know Hannah had the baby, so I'll start working tomorrow to get your marriage annulled." He took an exasperated-sounding deep breath as he stabbed a pork chop and vigorously cut it with his knife. "Finally, you can forget all this mess and get on with your life."

Thomas's heart rose in his throat. "What is it?" he asked. "A boy or a girl?" He stopped eating for the moment, his fork balanced between his fingers, the tines resting on his plate. He straightened slightly and with raised eyebrows, he looked anxiously at his father. The news fell hard in the pit of his stomach, giving him an unexpected surge of excitement.

"It's a boy. I think that's what he said." Stokes looked squarely at Thomas. "It doesn't matter. Everything is taken care of, or at least it will be."

"John," Mrs. Stokes spoke softly, "a little baby boy—don't you think we might just see him?"

"*No*, you're not going to see him and neither are you, Thomas.

That's not a good idea. Don't think about it. Bill and I are handling everything. Only reason I told you is so you would know we'll soon put all this behind us." Stokes's tone was sharp, and he punctuated his words by angrily jabbing his fork into another bite of pork chop.

"I think I'll ride over and check on Hannah," Thomas said with a glance at his mother. "You know, at least see if she is alright or if she needs anything."

Stokes didn't let his wife answer. "No you won't. I don't want you getting involved. Go back to school tomorrow and forget this ever happened. It's not for discussion."

"What's it gonna hurt for me to just ride over to Leaf Creek?"

"Thomas, are you having trouble hearing me today? If you know what's good for you and your future, you'll do what I tell you." Stokes glared at Thomas, pushed his chair from the table, stood, and strode from the dining room.

* * *

"I'M SORRY, THOMAS. He thinks he's doing what's best. I don't know … maybe he is. We need to do as he says," his mother said calmly.

"Why? Why do I need to do what he says? I want to go see about Hannah." Thomas's voice was low but emphatic. "I want to go see my baby. I *have* a baby. You have a grandbaby and he's telling us we can't even see him? How does that make you feel? Tell me, Mother, do you feel good about what's happening?"

"Thomas, please. You know it's not that easy. Please think about what you're saying and doing."

"What I'm doing so far is not right. You know it isn't." Thomas stared at his mother, pushed his chair hard away from the table and spoke harshly. "He thinks he has all the right answers to everything."

"Thomas, please. He's your father. Please just do what he says." Now her voice was hushed and pleading. "If you don't, I'm afraid he will make you drop out of school, or worse, not let you return home. Please just do as he says. Maybe you can see Hannah later."

Thomas stood and slung his napkin down on the table. "Sure, right, and that may be too late. You know as well as I do what he and Mr.

McMolison are planning." He gave his chair a strong push toward the table. "I have a son I may never meet. How can you think this is okay?"

Mrs. Stokes took a moment to respond. "It's not that I like anything that is happening, or think any of this is okay," she said quietly. "I just don't want things to get worse. I love you, and I would love your son, but your father is thinking about your future and what is best for the baby. Please do as he says."

"Maybe, Mother. Maybe I'll do what he wants for the time being. But don't keep taking his side. Don't keep talking about what is best for me, best for the baby, best for Hannah. She and I should have had a say. But my father—and hers—didn't give us one."

"Thomas, I know this is hard but don't be disrespectful—"

"Why? I know I did wrong. Hannah and I both did, but I feel disrespectful and what's more … I feel *disrespected*. I'm sure Hannah does too. I'm going to bed."

* * *

THE FOLLOWING MORNING Thomas was up early and waiting in the dining room when John Stokes came in for breakfast.

"Morning, son. Beautiful day," he said, his voice chipper and smile wide. "You have a good night?"

"Not really, sir. I mean with what's going on, how could I?" Thomas became angrier as he spoke. "For that matter, how could you? How could anybody?"

"Watch it, Thomas," Stokes replied. His eyes quickly went to slits. "You're about to step over the line. You ought to be thanking me, not sitting around sulking and whining."

"I just want to go to see Hannah. That's all. I want to see my baby."

"Well you're not going, and don't ever let me hear you say *my* baby again." Stokes stepped forward menacingly. "What's it going to take to get through to you?"

"I just want to do what's right by Hannah. Tell me what it would hurt for me to ride over there and come right back? I sure don't see the harm."

Stokes stepped forward, his face close to Thomas's face. He put his right index finger into Thomas's shoulder and pushed so hard that Thomas had to step backward to keep from falling. "Don't see harm?" he bellowed. "Well let me tell you." His father's finger bounced repeatedly into his shoulder. "*Forget* that girl over there. Don't even think about going to Leaf Creek, and that's *final*. You are going to school *this morning*. Do you hear? This morning. Not this afternoon. Not tomorrow. I'm warning you, son, if you do something stupid you'll regret it. This conversation is over." Stokes looked like a wild animal now and was breathing hard. "And don't ever be insolent to me again. Or you will be sorry."

* * *

LATER THAT MORNING Thomas returned to school just as his father had instructed. He rode in silence, but his brain spun with thoughts of Hannah and his little son. "Wonder if he looks like me," he thought. "Did Hannah have a hard time? What will she do when they take the baby away?" He had not anticipated his strong inner pull toward Hannah. He sighed deeply and ran his fingers through his thick black hair. "Father will never forgive me if I don't do as he says." Thomas pressed the heels of his hands against his eyes, dropped his head backward, and let out a loud sigh. "This is not right. I just want to see her. Why can't I see her and the baby?" Thomas talked to himself and stared ahead. "Between her father and mine … I don't know. But something's gotta change."

Hannah, his baby, future plans and the demands of his father filled his head. His father's ultimatum seemed to be dominating even as he was thinking, "I'll figure out something, find some way to check on Hannah without Father finding out." His shoulders slumped as he continued north, leaving Hannah and his son behind.

Back at school, Thomas was never again into the social scene. He seldom dated, and when he did it was with little enthusiasm. He attended special events on occasion but only because it was expected of him in his fraternity. He thought often of going to Hannah but feared his father would quit paying for school and likely cut him from an inheritance. Showing his father a lack of respect or disobeying in any form would be far worse than fathering a baby. Day after day Thomas chose the same path. It was one that on the surface seemed freer of conflict, and perhaps it was since it was the path his father expected him to take. While his choice gave him a life of privilege, it often nagged at his heart and left him with simmering guilt.

***

THE DREADED DAY arrived. Mr. McMolison returned home from another trip to Leeville and walked through the front door loudly announcing the news: "A family from over in Alabama is willing to take the baby."

Hannah's face jerked toward her father. Her breathing became rapid and shallow as she attempted to speak. "Sir? Who? What did you say?" Even though she knew it would probably be impossible to stop his plan, she had to try.

Her father's attitude was enthusiastic and his demeanor jovial. A friend of a friend, it seemed, had a cousin who had never been able to have a baby. "They really want one and to make things even better, they're known to be fine people, fine Christians, and able to provide a really good home. They'll give him everything he needs. It's great. Everything is going to work out," Bill said. His unabashedly joyful attitude sickened the women and made them mad at the same time. Every word was like a nail being driven into Hannah's heart. Kate had difficulty breathing.

Janie and June Ellen were in the next room and heard every detail. June Ellen held back tears. Janie felt no tears; she was angry. She clenched her teeth and thought sewing Bill McMolison's lips together would give her pleasure—and, God forbid, felt no remorse for the thought. She banged the knife into the chicken she was cutting up, even thinking *it* could be put to better use (the knife would hush him up). Such an action would get her hanged before sundown but might be worth it, she thought.

Bill delivered the final thrust of the one-sided dialogue. "They'll be here on Friday, so have everything ready." He headed outside, allowing the back door to slam shut behind him.

"Everything?" Hannah felt deadened inside. "My baby, my Joseph … he is everything, absolutely everything," she thought. "What can I do? Where can I go? It's Wednesday evening. In less than forty-eight hours some strange couple will be taking him away." She felt completely overwhelmed.

Hannah raced across the hall to her room where Joseph was peacefully sleeping. Her body crumbled to the floor beside his cradle. "He can't. He just can't," she sobbed as Kate entered the room.

"Hannah, please don't do this. We've known this was coming. Get a hold of yourself. You'll make yourself sick," Kate spoke gently.

"Get a hold of myself," Hannah spat, almost screaming as she lifted herself to her feet. "That's my *baby* we're talking about."

"Hannah, shhhhh. Calm down. Don't raise your voice to me."

"*What*? You're telling me not to yell when Papa has made plans to give my baby away in two days. How would you feel if somebody wanted to take one of us from *you*?"

"It's not the same. You know it isn't, and behaving this way is not going to help. Your father is doing what he thinks is best," Kate said, an edge in her voice now.

"But what he does is *not* always best, at least not for all of us," Hannah snapped, looking her mother in the eye. "He would never admit it, never. He's never wrong. He's quote, 'protecting our honor.' Well, you've got to have humility to have honor, and I've never seen much humility from him around here."

"Hannah, stop it. Stop talking like that. Bill is not perfect, but he is your father."

"I know he is, but don't you care at all about what he's doing? After all, Joseph is not just my son, he's your *grandson*." Hannah couldn't ever remember being this angry at her mother, and stored-up resentment at her father poured out. "It's your *grandson* your husband is planning to give away. You understand that, don't you?"

"Of course I do. How can you think I don't? My heart is breaking. I don't want this to happen, but you know as well as I do that your father will dictate what we do in a situation like this."

"*Dictate.*" Hannah hissed, repeating her mother's word. "Right—dictate like he always does. Dictate whatever he wants or whatever he wants things to look like, but this time it's not just some appearance thing. It's my baby we're talking about."

"Hannah, settle down. This kind of behavior isn't like you. Stop being so disrespectful," Kate said firmly. "We're in a bad situation. Being insolent will only make a bad situation worse, and you know it."

"Maybe, but I've never had a baby taken from me before." Hannah paused. "You say not to be disrespectful. Well, I'd like for somebody to respect me and what I want."

"Your father and Mr. Stokes are doing what they think is best. They are trying to preserve your honor and the honor of both families."

Hannah picked up the now-awake Joseph and held him close up under her chin, then looked directly at her mother. "Do you really think it's *my* honor Papa is most concerned about?"

A stricken expression covered Kate's face. "Hannah, yes! What he is doing *is* for you, for all of us. I know it's hard to think about." With her brow still furrowed and her eyes narrowed in their joyless state, Kate continued: "Other than burying Samuel, this is the hardest thing we've ever had to do."

"Oh Mama, please don't do that. Don't say that. Samuel's death was an accident—at least that's what we called it—but you *know* it was Papa's fault, and what's happening now is Papa's fault, too."

"Hannah, stop!"

"You know it's true. The only difference is that he didn't mean for Samuel to die. Now, I know he doesn't mean for Joseph to die, either, but he means for him to disappear—he wants him dead to us. You've heard him. He can't get rid of Joseph fast enough."

Kate was silent. She gripped the end post of the cradle as Hannah's words pierced every part of her. Finally after several seconds, Kate said, "I love you, Hannah. We'll get through this. We'll do it together." She gave Hannah and the bright-eyed Joseph an awkward hug. "I'm so sorry," she whispered. "I hate what's happening—with every fiber of my being—but there's nothing we can do."

Hannah did not respond. She was quiet as she stood swaying gently from side to side.

Kate eased out of the room, but her words lingered. "We'll get through it. We'll do it together."

Hannah returned Joseph to his cradle. She rocked it gently. Her mind was filled with swirling thoughts.

WE'LL DO IT TOGETHER. Hannah kept hearing her mother's words, but a mysterious strength came from within her. "This time *we* can't do it together, but I can," she thought. "I have to. I will." A resolve to do whatever was necessary to prevent them from taking her baby swept through Hannah. She knew her mother, Janie, and June Ellen would help if they could (or knew how), but she would have to do whatever she was going to do without them. Assisting would mean great trouble for them, and she didn't want to cause more hardship than she already had.

She thought about trying to get to Thomas. "If only he could see his baby, he would love him too and would want to help," she thought. That thought was fleeting, though, as she reminded herself that they weren't even married anymore. Mr. Stokes had had the union annulled soon after learning the baby was born, so Hannah knew not to expect support of any kind from anyone in the Stokes family. Mr. Stokes was just as hell-bent on getting her baby—his *grandchild*—gone from their lives as her own father. They wanted life to resume as if Joseph never existed, and for the most selfish of reasons. The thought made Hannah furious at all three of them—her father, Thomas, and Mr. Stokes.

Hannah's hands rested on the side of Joseph's cradle. She looked down at her little baby boy. A hint of a smile crossed his face. "I will save you," she whispered. "I'll never give you away. I'm the one that will be sure you are loved and cared for." Hannah lifted her gaze and stared across her bedroom, out the window and beyond the trees. Her thoughts went back to Thomas. "Thomas, I need you," she whispered. "I need you here, need you strong. I could be strong for you if I just had the chance. I have to believe you want to be a part of our lives.

Maybe someday you will. In the meantime, I have to figure out how to save our son."

"Think," she kept telling herself. What mattered to her more than anything else in the whole world was saving three-week-old Joseph from being given away. Her emotional resolve strengthened, but questions pounded her anxious heart. "What can I do?" she asked herself. "Where can I go? Who can help me?" Then it came to her.

"Katherine!" an internal voice exclaimed. "I'll go to Katherine's. She'll help me figure out what to do after that." Hannah knew she could get to Beaumont, and once there she would ask for directions to Hattiesburg. She knew she could find somebody to help direct her the right way once she reached Hattiesburg.

THE FOLLOWING MORNING, Hannah walked out to where Frank was working. "Frank, would you please hitch Pete to the wagon for me?" she asked. "I'll be back in just a little while."

"You sure, Miz Hannah? You planning on going somewhere by yourself? I don't know if that's such a good idea. Now, I can go and drive you. Wouldn't that be better? You know as good as anybody Pete can sometimes try to show hisself and act up."

"It's alright, Frank. I'll be fine. I'm feeling stronger every minute. I'll be back. Don't say anything to anybody."

Janie saw Hannah wrap a couple of leftover biscuits, a piece of fried meat, and a piece of pound cake in a cloth … but she didn't say anything. In fact, she turned so that Hannah would not know she had seen her. Janie could feel that Hannah was up to something, and she would do anything possible to help her. Maybe, for today, that would mean just staying out of her way.

A few minutes later Hannah came from her room with Joseph all nestled down in a large basket, one he sometimes slept in. Kate was in the room across the hall sewing a baby blanket. Her heart was bursting. The thought of someone else taking Joseph was about more than she could stand. She didn't know whether to cry, scream, or crouch in a corner until it was all over. She knew though, that whatever she did, she needed to stay busy.

Hannah's comments the day before pounded her heart like relentless truth hammers. "What can I possibly do to stop what's happening?" she thought. Her nimble fingers moved quickly, hooking the soft blue thread and pulling it through. "This is the worst of the worst. Watching my daughter with her heart breaking and losing my grandson at the same time. What can I do? What could I say to Bill to make him understand, to make him change his mind?" With her thoughts spinning, she continued to crochet. She would give the blanket to the couple that was coming. Giving them the blanket would be the last thing she could do for her grandson.

"I'm taking Joseph out for a little while," Hannah said as she passed Kate's open door.

Kate looked up. "Oh, Hannah, I don't know if I can stand what's coming, but I'm trying to keep myself together. And Hannah, I'm sorry about anything I said yesterday that made it sound like I don't understand—believe me, I do. I know what it's like to lose a child, and I never want to make things harder for you."

"I know, Mama. I believe you. I don't know if I'll be able to stand it, either."

Tears welled up in Kate's eyes. "I just can't believe this is really happening."

Hannah looked down at the precious eyes staring up at her. "We're going out in the sun for a little while."

"Do you want me to come with you?" Kate started to gather her yarn.

"No, not right now. Come later. Give me just a little time out there by myself with Joseph. I know it's silly, but I want to tell him all about the outside that I know he would have loved—the creek, the chickens, the garden, everything."

"It's not silly at all. You go and I'll come in a bit. I want to hold him, too."

"Then come on out after you finish what you're doing." Hannah walked out the back door, basket in hand.

Janie and June Ellen watched Hannah as she crossed the yard and walked toward the barn. Neither spoke. Neither knew for sure what was going on, but whatever it might be, it would be better than what was planned. They weren't about to stop it.

Pete was hitched to the wagon and ready to go. Frank took the basket from Hannah, lifted it into the wagon, and placed it just behind the seat. Hannah crawled up onto the seat and took the reins.

Frank continued to worry. "Are you sure 'bout this? I can go with you."

"I'm sure," Hannah answered.

Frank pointed to some sacks and said, "June Ellen come to the barn little while ago. She brought couple a quilts, some baby stuff, little money, and some food just in case you need it for anything." He smiled at Hannah. "God bless you, child. I'll be praying. We all will."

Hannah reached for his hand. She squeezed it and said, "I love you, and please tell June Ellen and Janie thanks and that I love them too. Y'all tell Mama I'm fine, but wait as long as you can. Tell them I'll send word as soon as I can."

"Shore will, Miss Hannah. You be real careful, now."

Hannah gently slapped Pete with the reins. Pete responded, and the wagon began to move forward at an even, steady pace down the path, past the yard and onto the road. She turned right. Frank, June Ellen, and Janie watched until the wagon was out of sight.

Chapter Twenty-Seven

245

$\mathcal{B}$LANKET FINISHED, Kate spread it across her lap and smoothed it lovingly with her hands. "Maybe the new parents will use it and will one day tell him he had a mother and grandmother that loved him very much," she thought. She knew that was not likely, but the thought was helping her get through the day. Kate stood, folded the blanket, and headed out to show Hannah the finished piece.

Janie and June Ellen seemed unusually quiet when she stopped by the kitchen. She assumed that—like her—they were doing whatever was necessary to cope with the plan that was to unfold the following morning. No one had felt like talking (much less laughing) since Bill told them he'd found a suitable couple to take Joseph.

Kate went outside. June Ellen and Janie watched just as they had done only a couple of hours before. Kate peered around both sides of the house before starting for the barn. The women could see her talking to Frank. Suddenly her hand covered her mouth, and she just stood there. June Ellen and Janie couldn't hear, but they knew Frank had told her Hannah had left. They hoped he didn't tell her any more than he had to. The less she knew, the better it would be when she told Mr. McMolison.

Kate returned to the kitchen and spoke to Janie and June Ellen.

"Did y'all know Hannah left?"

"Yes ma'am, we know," they said quietly and in unison.

"She didn't tell us, but we saw her leave. She was fine," Janie said after a moment. "I don't think you need to worry 'bout her. She's gonna be fine. She did what she knew she had to do."

"Which way did she go?"

"Don't ask us, Miz Kate. Be better for us all if we don't know which a way."

"Did she talk to y'all before she left?"

"No ma'am, she didn't say nothing to us," June Ellen answered, shaking her head.

"We just saw her talking to Frank. I saw her get some biscuits and fried meat together, but she didn't know I saw her," Janie added.

"She didn't know we did it, but we put couple a quilts, some baby things, extra food and what money we had between us together in a sack," June Ellen said. "Frank put it in the back a the wagon. I'm right sure he let her know it was there."

"We don't really know anything, least wise no more'n that," Janie said.

Kate stood there not knowing what to say or do. She was relieved that Joseph might not be taken from them, but she was overwhelmed with concern for her daughter and her grandson out there somewhere alone. "What was she thinking going off by herself?" she said aloud as her chest tightened. "Y'all know Hannah's never had to fend for herself before—much less herself, a baby, and a horse and wagon."

"Now Miz Kate, we all know she's just doing what she thought she had to. She's got a mother's heart now, and it's telling her what to do," Janie replied, her tone surprisingly firm.

Kate sat down hard in one of the straight-backed kitchen chairs. She gripped the blanket, now wadded in her lap. "I know. But alone out there with a tiny baby? Wish she had told me. I would have gone with her."

"She couldn't. She knows her leaving's gonna cause a problem. She didn't want that to be your fault," June Ellen said gently.

Kate nodded. "I know. I'm proud of her for being so courageous.

Just worried—that's all. I just want them to be okay. Hope I would have done the same."

"You woulda," Janie said confidently. "The way you keep things running round here in spite of what comes, trust me. You'd a done exactly the same or whatever you had to."

Kate stood and clutched the blanket to her chest. She asked one more time, "You sure you don't know where she was headed?"

"We don't," June Ellen answered and then Janie added, "No ma'am—promise we don't."

"Get Frank," Kate said emphatically to both women. "I need for him to go to the mill to see if Bill is there, and if he is, to tell him to come home. I've got to let him know that Hannah is gone." Her voice trailed off as she imagined and feared his response.

"I think we'll wait just a little while, Miz Kate. You told us and we'll see it's done. Just might be best to wait a bit is all I'm saying."

The gossip from the mill grapevine was that Mr. McMolison was in the habit of leaving around three o'clock some afternoons and not returning. The women hoped today would be one of those times. If Frank couldn't find him, then there would be nothing to do but wait until he came home in the evening. They wanted to give Hannah as much time as possible to do whatever she was doing.

Kate spent the rest of the day doing everything and accomplishing nothing. She turned and fluffed pillows in the sitting room, turned the pages in a book without reading, played the piano and checked multiple times on her flower beds. All she could think about was Hannah and Joseph on the one hand … and her husband and what he might do on the other hand.

As the afternoon began to wane, she stood at the window and watched. She couldn't decide if she was anxiously waiting for Bill or hopefully wishing for Hannah. Kate knew Hannah had kept her plan quiet on purpose. She had done all she could to protect those she left behind. They could honestly tell Bill that she had told them nothing.

JANIE AND JUNE ELLEN lingered quietly in the kitchen after finishing their day's work. Frank didn't go home, either; he worked in the barn for a while and then sat at the edge of the woods. All three thought it better if they were around when Mr. McMolison got home. Ever since Samuel's death, they had stayed close.

It was getting dark when Kate, sitting beside a window in the sitting room, saw Bill turn off the main road and onto the path leading to the barn. Her fingers were entwined so tightly that they were discolored. Her heart beat wildly, as if a drum was in her throat and ears. It caused her whole chest and head to pulsate. She stood, ran her fingers through her hair, and walked across the room. She breathed deeply in an attempt to calm herself as she anticipated the inescapable encounter with her husband.

Frank watched from his vantage point in the woods. He hoped he wouldn't have to answer any questions, but he wanted to be close in case Janie, June Ellen, or Kate needed him. Blending into the darkness of the woods, he knew he'd been totally undetected as he watched Mr. McMolison arrive home, put his horse up, and walk back toward the house. Frank breathed a sigh of relief when he was sure Pete was not missed. Nor, apparently, had Mr. McMolison noticed that the wagon was missing.

The knob turned. The front door opened, and Kate walked from the sitting room into the hall to meet her husband. His greeting was friendlier than usual.

"Hi, Kate," he said, giving her a quick kiss on the cheek.

Kate was initially startled, as any type of affection was usually reserved for the bedroom. But she resented that he was behaving as if all was well, and silent anger began to fill her. "He's lighthearted because he thinks Joseph will be gone after tomorrow," she thought. "How could he?"

Frustration, disgust and anger rapidly consumed Kate's whole being. She was worried sick about Hannah and it was his fault she was gone. She followed Bill down the hall and into their bedroom, thinking that his plans for the future—*his* future—and his holding forth on family honor meant absolutely nothing; all she cared about at the moment was Hannah and Joseph.

Bill threw his coat on the bed and sat down to unlace his shoes.

Smiling he said, "We'll get things back to normal tomorrow."

Kate, gathering her strength, reminded herself that if Hannah was brave enough to do what she was doing, she herself would do the same right here and now. "Hannah is gone, Bill."

He looked up quickly. "Gone?!? What do you mean gone?" His stare pierced the space between them. A frown tightened around his eyes and his mouth dropped open.

"I mean she took Joseph and left," Kate answered firmly, looking directly into his face.

Bill pushed his toes back into his shoes. He worked his heels back and forth until they slid into place. "She can't do that," he snapped. "Where would she go? She doesn't know how to go off somewhere by herself! She probably hasn't gone far, probably at a friend's house. Have you checked with her friends?" He bent to tie his shoes.

"No, I haven't. I don't think she would want that. All I know is that she left."

"*How* do you know? Did you help her?" Bill stood and reached for his coat. "Was this your idea?" he said, turning hostile in a hurry.

"No, I didn't help. She didn't say a thing to me. I don't know where she is, and I'm worried about her."

"What about Janie and June Ellen? What do they know? They probably helped. I know Janie thinks the baby ought to stay here no matter what. Well, it's not for her to decide—where is Janie, anyway? She still here?"

"Bill, Hannah didn't say anything to them, either. She did this all alone—obviously did it to keep from losing her baby. Can't you try to understand that?"

"I understand alright," Bill scowled. "I understand you're telling me that a teenage girl and her baby—*your* teenage girl—left this house today, and you knew *nothing*. You saw nothing, you heard nothing, and tonight you announce to me that she's gone. You really expect me to believe that?" he added, throwing his arms into the air and walking out into the hall.

"I do because it's the truth," Kate replied. "And as far as Janie and June Ellen are concerned, talk to them yourself. They're both still here."

He put on his coat. "Good. I will," he thundered as he stomped toward the kitchen. She followed close behind him and resolved that if he threatened the slightest physical action toward any of them, she would not stand by him.

The open kitchen window gave Frank a framed picture of the activity inside. He could see Mr. McMolison's arms flail in one direction and then another as he first talked to Mrs. McMolison, then Janie and June Ellen. Although he could not hear what was being said, he knew what it was about, and he could see that the room was filled with turmoil and anger.

As Kate expected, Janie and June Ellen held their own. They both clearly repeated, "No, sir, she didn't say a word to us, not a word." They stood on opposite sides of the big kitchen table, Janie's hands resting on the surface while June Ellen's hands were pushed into her apron pockets. "Yes, sir. She just went out for a walk with the baby and she never came back. Miz Kate was sewing, June Ellen was doing the wash, and I was getting some cooking done. Time got by 'fore we realized," Janie explained.

Bill restrained himself, uncommon for him even in less trying circumstances. But he stared at Kate through beady eyes, his teeth clenched tightly with anger behind his slightly parted lips. His hands, balled tightly into fists, punched the air beside his thighs. "I don't know what Hannah is thinking or what she is trying to do," he said. "We've got an awful situation here, and what is she doing? She's making it worse."

Kate stood without speaking but looked directly into his reddening face. She followed when he suddenly whirled around and stormed back into the hall. He jerked his hat from the hall tree. "What's wrong with her?" he yelled. "She acts like she's the only one that suffers as a result of what she's done." He kicked a fan that had fallen from the basket and thrust his hat onto his head. He stood close to the door and looked at Kate with his jaw still tight and eyes afire. "She should be thankful for the help I'm trying to give her, but no—she's gone to no telling where." He grabbed the knob and pulled the door open. "Now I have to go look for her. And the fact that it's already dark doesn't help. She refuses to understand the trouble and humiliation her actions cause. And I'll tell you something else, Kate: She *will* do what I say."

"Bill—" Kate started.

Bill cut her off. "I gave my word to Stokes. We had this whole problem solved and now look what she's done." He grew more agitated as he spoke. "Tomorrow is the day. Tomorrow is Friday, and you know Stokes is bringing that family here. They're coming all the way from over in Alabama. This whole mess is pitiful. *Y'all* are pitiful! Three grown women in this house, and all of you just stood by and let her leave. You didn't know a thing. I sure wonder …"

Bill turned and walked out the front door. Then he stuck his head back inside. "I'll find her. If it's the last thing I do, I'll find her and bring her back. She's not going to bring this family down. If we make mistakes, we fix them. We don't run from them. I'll find her."

The three women remained quiet until well after the door slammed shut.

IT WASN'T UNTIL BILL WAS SADDLING his horse that he realized Pete was missing. He had not noticed earlier that Pete wasn't in his stall, or that the wagon shed was empty. "So, she left in the wagon," he said to himself. He hadn't thought before how she'd gone, but he was now forming a picture. "Frank must have helped her … and he knows better." Bill's first reaction was to find Frank and make him sorry he had assisted Hannah in any way, but that would be a waste of time. After all, Kate, Janie, and June Ellen denied knowing anything, so why would Frank be different? And time was wasting—he didn't have long to find Hannah.

With his frustration building, Bill yanked his saddle from the rack, wrestled it onto his horse, and tied the cinch. He lifted himself up and into the saddle and headed toward the road, the same road he'd traveled hardly an hour before.

Four wide and anxious pairs of eyes watched intently to see which direction he would go once he got to the road.

Bill moved with speed and, without hesitation, turned left—toward Leeville. Frank, Janie and June Ellen sighed with relief. Janie, sounding almost giddy, said to Kate, "Hannah turned right, Miz Kate. She turned right." Although none of them knew where Hannah was or what was going on with her, they were all happy that the distance was increasing between her and her father.

As Bill rode, his thoughts raced unrestrainedly. "Leeville is the closest town," his internal voice said. "It's one of only a few places Hannah has ever been. *Has* to be where she would go. She may go to the hotel—I'll go there first. Thomas … is Thomas home now?" Questions but no answers rolled through his mind. "If I can't find her, I'll at least let Stokes know what's happened," he thought as his horse pushed on. "He can tell the couple there'll be a slight delay in getting them their baby. John'll help me think of something." Then: "Could *Thomas* be part of this? Could he be helping her?" Then Bill shook his head. "No, Thomas would never jeopardize his future. He would never go against his father's wishes," he said aloud this time. Then he put all of his energy into riding hard and arrived in Leeville about midnight.

He eased around to the side of the hotel and quietly climbed the steps leading to the private entrance. He knocked several times before the door cracked slightly. Recognizing her frequent guest, Miss Tildy opened the door fully. "Bill, what are you doing here at this hour? What's wrong?"

Bill didn't make a move to go inside. "Hannah left home. Did she come here? Have you seen her?"

"No, I haven't. What do you *mean* she left home?"

"She's gone! That's what I mean. And I need to find her. I need to find her tonight."

"Why do you think she'd come here?" Miss Tildy pulled her robe more securely around her body and retied the sash that held it in place.

"Well, she's been here before and would at least know how to get here. And you know … she's got the baby with her."

"*Baby*? What baby, Bill?" Miss Tildy asked with a puzzled frown.

"Nothing. Just forget I was here. But if you see or hear anything, get word to me, hear?"

The conversation with Stokes was no more informative. Awaking at one o'clock in the morning to find his friend on his front porch caused Stokes such alarm that he almost felt relief when he learned the reason for Bill's visit. However, Hannah's disappearance with the baby did cause serious problems that must be remedied, Stokes told him. It was imperative Hannah be found and the situation resolved.

The men stood on the front porch, Bill pacing in one direction and then the other. "I need to find her, for her sake and for ours." He took his hat off and ran his fingers through his hair.

Stokes stood still. "Not a lot we can do tonight. I'll meet the couple from Alabama as planned, and I'll let them know there's been a little problem that will cause a slight delay. I'll apologize about their having to make the unnecessary trip, so don't worry about that. I'll take care of them." He paused. "You just find that baby."

"Okay, Stokes, but you do understand, don't you, that my daughter is alone tonight only God knows where," Bill replied. "Of course I want to get that baby back, but I want to find *Hannah*. She doesn't know what she's doing." Bill put on his hat. Nervous, he rubbed his palms together as if warming them.

Stokes's mind, though, was still on the Alabama couple. "But if I have to tell them we'll bring the kid in a few days, I will." He opened his door wide. "Come on in and go to bed. You can't do anything else at this hour. You don't even know for sure in what direction she went. I'll get word to Thomas tomorrow to find out if he knows anything. I can't believe he'd have had anything to do with this, but I'll sure find out."

After several restless hours, Bill McMolison again saddled his horse. Just as the new day was breaking, he rode away from Stokes's house and headed for the hotel. If there was news in town, maybe he'd pick it up while having breakfast. But he learned nothing.

Before leaving town, though, he made one more stop. He climbed the three wooden steps to the front door and knocked.

The door opened, and there stood Rosie's grandmother. She was neatly dressed in a blue-and-white print housedress. A few wisps of gray hair had escaped the bun and lingered around the edge of her face. "Mr. McMolison, what are you doing here so early in the morning? Do you want to come inside?"

"No. I just need to know if you or Rosie have heard anything about Hannah. Or if you've seen her." He frowned and rubbed around his lips with his hand.

"Why, no, we haven't. Why are you asking?"

"She's gone off by herself. I don't know where. I've got to find her … she's got a baby with her."

"A *baby*?" the elderly colored woman said in surprise.

"Yes, she has a baby. Just keep your eyes and ears open, and please get me word if you hear anything."

Rosie, dressing in the adjoining room, listened to the conversation and heard her grandmother say, "You know I will. I haven't heard anything; Rosie would a told me if she heard something like that at the hotel. She worked through supper last night."

Mr. McMolison turned to leave. "Thanks, just keep a look out. If you hear something, you can send word to Mr. Stokes, and he'll get it to me."

"I'm sure your daughter is a sweet girl, Mr. McMolison. Always remember problems can be solved easier with love than anger," she said, and held the screen door with an outstretched arm to keep it from slamming. He walked back to his horse without a reply.

From what Rosie could overhear, Mr. McMolison had not been completely clear as to why he didn't know where Hannah was. But the fact that he was there looking for her indicated a problem. As she watched from her bedroom window, Rosie wondered again why there was a relationship between her grandmother and Mr. McMolison. Her past questions were again current questions that bounced around her head. "Why did he come to my grandmother for help? Why does he come here with money from time to time? Why won't my grandmother tell me about him? Why won't she give me straight answers?" Rosie vowed to keep asking, hoping that one day her grandmother would finally decide to provide answers.

Chapter Twenty-Eight

255

The SUN WAS STILL HIGH on Thursday when Hannah made her first stop. After feeding Joseph and getting Pete some water from a nearby creek, she nibbled a little on one of the biscuits and fried meat. "I need to keep moving," she kept thinking to herself as she tried to stifle pangs of panic. She suddenly felt so very alone. No one was with her to tell her what to do or help her make decisions. It was the first time in her life she was totally responsible for everything—not only for herself, but also for her baby and the horse and wagon. As terrifying as it was, she knew she was doing the right thing. There was no choice but to keep moving forward, moving away from Leaf Creek, and away from her father and away from those attempting to take Joseph from her.

The last thought renewed her courage. "I will never allow anyone, not even my father, to take my baby," she said aloud.

It was almost as if Pete heard the vow. He started to pull the wagon forward as if he knew—perhaps better than Hannah—what his role was in the job at hand. And that he was committed to getting it done.

It was mid-afternoon when Hannah finally reached Beaumont. Realizing that darkness was certain to come before she could possibly reach Katherine's, another streak of panic pierced her. She thought of her father and the fact he might already be after her. Her heart rate picked up and sweat covered her palms. Then, by thinking of Joseph and her reason for being there, she was able to regain a small degree of calmness.

She lifted the blanket and peeked at Joseph. "I'm going to think of something," she said, smiling down at him. He squirmed contentedly.

Hannah remembered the great aunt that lived in Beaumont and wondered about spending the night there, but she didn't really know her and feared her father would check there for sure if he was searching in that direction. The possibility of him finding them filled her with chest-tightening dread. She wanted to keep going, to get farther and farther away from Leaf Creek. She desperately wanted to get to Katherine, but it wouldn't be tonight. It was getting dark.

Joseph's pleasant mood soon began to wane, and Hannah began fretting about Pete; what would the horse she was so dependent on require to go the rest of the way? Hannah felt truly alone and overwhelmed as she considered all the responsibility that was hers. She held the reins tight in her hands as her mind raced in an attempt to figure out what she should do. As Pete pulled the wagon slowly down the street, they passed the store where the doctor had his office. Hannah remembered Dr. McLeod's kind words: "Let me know if you need me." She didn't figure what she needed at the moment (to be hidden away for a night) was what he had in mind, but she didn't know what else to do.

"I can do this," she thought. "I'll ask if he knows a place I can stay for the night, and if he knows a place to board Pete." She took a deep breath and pulled the wagon to one side.

Hannah lifted Joseph gently from the basket and went into the store that she had visited once before with her mother. A lady, waiting for the druggist to get her medicine, was sitting alone at one of the ice cream tables. Otherwise the place was empty.

Through the druggist's window, Hannah could see shelves of elixirs and other medicines. With Joseph cradled in her arms, she waited for the kind-faced man with sandy brown hair to notice her.

A minute or two passed. Then, with the woman's prescription ready, he moved to the window and smiled. "Can I help you?"

Before Hannah could answer, though, he called to the lady at the ice cream table: "Emma, here's your medicine. Use it like it says. Won't do what it's s'pose to if you don't."

"I will," the woman answered crossly. "You know I always do what the doctor says. Thanks."

Looking toward Hannah, the man asked, "Now young lady, what can I do for you today?"

"Is Dr. McLeod in his office?"

"He is. And you have a mighty fine baby there. Do you need to see the doctor?"

"Well, yes sir. I kinda do, if he isn't too busy."

"Oh, he is always here for those who need him. Someone is in there right now, but they should be finished real soon. Have a seat, okay?"

Hannah was hardly settled in a chair with Joseph when she heard Dr. McLeod's voice coming from his office in the back. He was giving some final instructions to the man he had just seen. "Use the salve every day, and be sure to keep it clean."

"I will, Doc. Thanks. Be sure to stop by when you're out my way. We always got pie and coffee ready." He walked past Hannah and Joseph, on through the store and out the front door.

The druggist motioned to Hannah, signaling it was her turn. She stood and walked through the opening in the counter that led toward Dr. McLeod's office. Hearing Dr. McLeod's voice and recalling her other visit made her skin tingle, but she kept walking.

Dr. McLeod spoke kindly and remembered her almost immediately. He reached for Joseph and, after looking him over, said, "He is as beautiful and perfect as Jackie reported." He sat in his wooden chair and rocked back with Joseph on his lap.

Hannah was puzzled. "Who is Jackie?"

"Jackie came to see you right after this fine fellow was born. She fixed up your birth certificate for you."

Hannah leaned against the examining table. "Oh, I do remember. A little, anyway."

"That's perfectly alright. I was just glad to learn you and the baby were both doing fine." He rubbed Joseph's cheek with the top of his index finger. His demeanor was gentle and kind and welcoming. "What brings you to see me today?"

Hannah wasn't sure she could say the words. She stood straight. "I'm here because …" she began slowly. "My sister lives in Hattiesburg, and I'm taking Joseph to see her." That sentence was easy, but she knew Dr. McLeod would wonder why she was out traveling alone with such a young baby.

"I'm here because my father doesn't …" She hesitated, took a deep breath, and continued. "My father doesn't think I should keep my baby. He wants to give Joseph to someone else, and I just can't. He doesn't understand." Tears filled her eyes, and her throat burned. "I'm sorry. I don't know what to do. Like I said, my sister lives in Hattiesburg. I'm trying to get to her house, but it's getting dark, and …"

Dr. McLeod stopped her before she tried to say more. He kissed Joseph on the forehead and handed him back to Hannah. "You've had enough to think about for one day," he said. "Get back in your wagon and follow me. I will take care of your horse for the night. And I'll have him ready for you in the morning at whatever time you say."

Hannah followed the kind doctor to a little house just out from town. He helped her out of the wagon, and they walked to the front door of a small, white, wooden house. Dr. McLeod knocked. The woman that answered the door was short, barely more than five feet. Her shoulders were stooped slightly and her hair, a yellowish-gray color, was pulled tightly back into a little bun and held in place with tortoise-shell combs. Her dress was lavender, buttoned down the front. Lace detail peeked out from around the collar and cuffs. She had a ready smile, and her greeting was warm. "Come in!" She opened the door wide and stepped back.

Hannah walked inside and Dr. McLeod followed. Joseph, bundled in a blanket, was sleeping in Hannah's arms. "Miss Maggie, this is Hannah and Joseph. They need a place to spend the night." Dr. McLeod didn't say anything else.

Miss Maggie lit right up. "Oh, I'm delighted to have them stay with me." Her eyes sparkled with kindness as she lifted the blanket that covered Joseph's face. "Precious, he's just precious."

"Thank you, ma'am, and thank you for letting us stay," Hannah said. It seemed obvious that Dr. McLeod and Miss Maggie must have had some unspoken understanding; he had brought her and Joseph here without hesitation, and she had welcomed them in the same manner. Perhaps this wasn't the first time a young girl like her was in this circumstance, she wondered.

Dr. McLeod left to take care of Pete just as he had said he would, and Hannah followed Miss Maggie into the parlor. The room was small but very welcoming. The settee and two chairs had crocheted doilies perfectly arranged across the backs and over the arms. A wooden rocker with a cane back and bottom similar to the ones on the front porch back home sat near a little wood-burning stove. An afghan had been loosely thrown across the arm of the rocker. An open Bible and a cup of tea were on the nearby table.

"I'm sure you're hungry. I'll get you some supper," Miss Maggie said. She walked slowly toward the little kitchen.

"I don't want to put you to trouble," Hannah said timidly as she followed.

"No trouble. You like eggs?" she asked as she moved a skillet over the heat.

The meal was prepared, and Miss Maggie never asked a prying question. Hannah was glad. She didn't want to explain about herself or about her father.

Miss Maggie soon had eggs with grits and a piece of bacon for Hannah and a supply of milk for Joseph.

"Soon as you're ready, I'll show you your bed," she said. "I 'speck you're pretty tired."

Hannah felt completely safe with this stranger. God had His angels, and Hannah was certain He had assigned one named Miss Maggie to her. Love seemed to cover everything she did.

Hannah stretched out on the thin cotton mattress with Joseph beside her. "Feels good to lie down," she whispered to Joseph as she stroked the little fingers wrapped around one of her own. "Just wish I could let Mother know we're okay."

Hannah could only imagine what had occurred at home after she left. She hoped her father had not returned until well after dark. Maybe he wouldn't make an effort to find her until morning. She was confident Frank wouldn't reveal which direction she went. But she knew that with the new parents scheduled to arrive in the morning, her father might feel desperate enough to do most anything, including set out in the middle of the night to find her. Her body gradually relaxed, though, and she soon drifted to sleep.

By six o'clock the next morning Pete was pulling the wagon toward Hattiesburg. The road stretched in front of them like a long, straight ribbon gradually becoming a thin thread and disappearing into the trees and sky. Hannah felt a strong urge of moving quickly. She knew she would be safe if she could just get to Katherine.

CHAPTER TWENTY-NINE

JOSEPH SLEPT MOST OF THE WAY to Hattiesburg. The sound of the constantly turning wheels was a soothing lullaby. It was fall, and the day was lovely. Hannah lapsed into brief moments of enjoying the beauty around her, but remembering her current plight always quickly snapped her back into reality. "What if Katherine and Stephen are not at home?" she wondered, the thought occurring to her for the first time. "Don't cross bridges before you get to them," her mother had said so many times. "Just take the next step."

Reliable Pete was doing just that. He took every next step until he pulled the wagon onto what Hannah assumed was the main street of Hattiesburg.

"Now what?" she said aloud. Her chest tightened, her palms became damp, and her heart beat faster. "What am I going to do? I'm here, but I don't have any idea where to go." The wagon moved forward slowly as she looked from one side of the street to the other. Hannah had never been to Hattiesburg and had only learned about it after Katherine married Stephen. Her mother had talked about visiting Katherine several times, but for one reason or another it never worked out.

Pete pulled the wagon into town and down Main Street a little way before Hannah decided to stop. The buildings were bigger than any she had ever seen. Most were brick with windows on top of windows that were two, three, and four stories high. Katherine had talked about how very different Hattiesburg was from Leaf Creek. She had described the carvings around windows and the big set of steps leading into the courthouse with its fat columns that circled the porch. Katherine had talked about the jewelry stores, the drug stores, the clothing stores and the cafes, but Hannah never visualized the grandness of Hattiesburg until now.

The red Kress sign with gold letters spread across the building with arched windows on the second level and little square ones on the third. Next was a light gray-colored building with a big door and a red awning. Hannah had never seen a door so big. Caught up in the scene all around her, she admired one building after another. The next one was red brick, very beautiful but smaller than the others. The largest building on the street was one of gold-colored brick that appeared to shine in the sun. It had four levels of windows above the doors with carvings above each window, just as Katherine had described.

Pete suddenly swished a fly with his tail. The wagon jerked ever so slightly, and Joseph made a little grunting baby sound. Hannah's full attention was back to her situation, "I'm here," she said, and took in a deep breath. "What am I going to do?"

There were other wagons similar to hers on the street, but most were different in that they had a covered area that protected those sitting inside from the weather. She got down from her wagon and lifted Joseph into her arms. The wagon was stopped in front of a millinery shop. Hannah went inside.

The shop was filled with hats of all colors and all sizes. They were on stands, on tables and on shelves that reached almost to the ceiling. An abundance of flowers decorated the brims of many, and feathers standing tall and proud graced others. Some hats were plain except for flowing tulle gathered from the front, pulled all around and left to drape down a lady's back. Hannah felt as if she were in a whole new world. She wanted to stop and admire every hat (under different circumstances she would not only admire them, but she would emulate Katherine and try every one of them on). A sudden streak of sadness swept through her as she thought of her mother, who would love to be shopping for a beautiful hat but was instead at home very much concerned.

The ladies in the shop were visiting. They were trying on hats, turning their heads from side to side as they looked in the mirrors. A couple of them stopped what they were doing and started oohing and cooing over Joseph. "He is so darling," one said. "How old is he?" Hannah knew that even though the ladies were being kind, they all had to be wondering why she had such a tiny baby out on the streets with her.

"Darling, can I help you in any way?" A lady dressed in navy smiled and spoke kindly.

"Yes, ma'am. I hope so," Hannah said nervously. "My sister and her husband live in Hattiesburg. Their names are Katherine and Stephen Neal. I was wondering if you might know them or have heard of them and know where they live. I have just gotten into town and don't know my way around."

"Do they live in town?" the owner of the shop asked.

"I'm not sure. I have never visited them before. Stephen is a preacher at a Baptist church, but I don't know where it is," Hannah said. She felt embarrassed and dropped her face slightly.

Although everyone in the shop, owner and shoppers alike, tried to be helpful, no one was. One of the ladies said she in fact was a Baptist—but that she belonged to First Baptist Church and wasn't familiar with the church Hannah referred to. Another of the ladies, also a member of First Baptist Church and also not familiar with whatever group Hannah was referring to, suggested the best place to get information would be the sheriff. Following her directions, Hannah headed down and across the street toward the sheriff's office.

The sign on the door read FORREST COUNTY SHERIFF. Hannah felt a little uncomfortable walking into the sheriff's office. She was sure her mother would think it to be a man's territory, but she was also sure her mother would want her to get whatever help she needed, even if it meant doing a few things she would not otherwise do. At that moment the door opened. The man leaving held the door ajar in order for her to walk inside. In an instant she was face to face with a middle-aged man with a strong face and a welcoming smile. He stood up when Hannah walked in.

"Well, hello. I'm Sheriff White," he said. "Come in. What can I do for you?"

Hannah became nervous, causing her to run her thoughts and questions together. "Hello, my name is Hannah McMolison," she said. "My sister and her husband live here, but I don't know where." She tightened her hold on Joseph, her sweaty palms grasping his blanket. "I'm hoping you can help me. I'm coming for a visit, but it's kind of a surprise. They don't know I'm coming. They live in town, I think, but I don't know which part. He did preach with a group that occasionally went to different places, if that helps. I think there is a church he preaches at most Sundays, but I don't know the name. It's not one of the big churches." She paused and took a deep breath. "I think it is on the edge of town."

"Okay, slow down. I'm sure we'll find them. Let's start with their names."

"Oh, I'm sorry," Hannah said, feeling herself turn red. "My sister's name is Katherine and her husband's name is Stephen. Stephen Neal."

"There is a group just a little bit north, actually on the edge of town." He took his hat from the hat tree and placed it on his head. "Let's take a ride and see if anyone out there can help us."

Sheriff White seemed ready to assist, as if he had nothing else to do. Although Hannah knew that was not likely the case, she was most thankful for his willingness to help her.

She was also glad to have company. The sheriff led the way for her and Pete. Even though he was on his horse in front of the wagon, it felt good to have someone with her.

Suddenly, she felt a new wave of anxiety. If her father decided to call or send some kind of wire about her, the sheriff would be the first to know. It obviously hadn't happened yet or the man would have said something. Hannah reassured herself by thinking that her father would take at least two days (or even three) attempting to take care of things himself. She was certain he would want to resolve the issue without any public awareness if at all possible.

"You okay back there?" the sheriff called back over his shoulder.

Hannah nodded her head and said, "Yes sir," although he probably didn't hear her answer over the rumbling of the wagon wheels.

A little church came into view. It was small, white and sat back from the road a short distance. It looked a little like the description she remembered Katherine giving. "Why didn't I pay more attention?" Hannah thought to herself. She wasn't particularly interested at the time, she knew, but now it was important. Because hopefully they lived close to Stephen's church.

"This may be it," Sheriff White said, "but doesn't look like anyone is here. There's a house a little farther up the road. We'll check there. I'll see if they know your sister."

Hannah waited in the wagon, her heart beginning to pound. Sheriff White went to the door. He climbed the three steps and knocked. After a few seconds, the door opened and there in the doorway stood Katherine. Tears of relief filled Hannah's eyes. The stoicism she had worked hard to maintain during the past thirty-six hours was crumbling. She desperately needed her sister.

Katherine looked past the sheriff at the wagon pulled up to her gate. "Hannah," she cried almost breathlessly as she raced past the sheriff and toward the wagon. Hannah was on the ground by the time Katherine reached her. Hannah sobbed uncontrollably as the sisters hugged each other tightly.

"Thank you," Hannah managed to say to Sheriff White as he mounted his horse and wished them a good visit. He tipped his hat toward them as he rode away.

The girls stood beside the wagon, Hannah's right hand holding the side for the support she suddenly felt she needed.

Katherine waved to the sheriff, but her full attention was immediately back to Hannah. "What are you doing here?" she asked. "Did you come all the way alone?"

"I had to," Hannah said. "I didn't know what else to do."

"Who knows you're here?" Katherine questioned.

"No one. I didn't tell a soul."

Katherine put her arm around Hannah's shoulder. "I can't believe you came all the way by yourself. What happened? Thank goodness you're okay."

Joseph began to cry. The sound coming from the basket startled Katherine. She looked quickly at Hannah and immediately moved to the wagon edge. She lifted the little blanket that had been covering the basket. The crying stopped, and Joseph's bright eyes looked directly into hers. "Oh Hannah, he is beautiful." She turned her head sideways to look at Hannah while reaching to pick up Joseph. "You ran away?" Katherine, meeting her nephew for the first time, was filled with a hundred questions. "What happened? What are you doing here? No one knows where you are?"

"No one."

"Well I'm glad you're here, and really glad to meet this special little bundle," Katherine said, cradling Joseph in her arms.

After unloading the wagon and getting Pete settled in a shed out back of the house, Hannah began to pour out the events of the past few days to her sister. She told her everything, from Joseph's birth to the present.

They sat in straight chairs at Katherine's kitchen table. Joseph finished a bottle and nestled sleepily in his aunt's arms. Hannah added with a tone of strong conviction, "And more than anything, I can't give him up. I just can't … I won't. It would rip my heart out. Just thinking about losing him is unimaginable. But I don't know what I can do. Do you think I might be able to stay here a few days until I can think of something?"

"Sure, you can stay here. You know we'll help you all we can. Maybe Stephen will have an idea."

Hannah continued baring her soul to Katherine. "I guess I was thinking that once I had the baby, Papa wouldn't insist that he be given away, or that maybe it wouldn't matter so much to me." Hannah's words were soft. She ran her index finger around the rim of her glass. "After Joseph was born, though, he mattered more than ever, more than I could have thought possible. I could never give him away."

Katherine sat rocking Joseph back and forth on her knees. His little fingers grasped her thumbs. His blue eyes opened and seemed to search her face. She already understood a little of the love her sister was describing.

Hannah sat with her hands folded in her lap. "I'm so glad to finally get here," she said wistfully as she took another swallow of the iced tea Katherine had given her. "Papa hardly looked at him. He never picked him up. He never even touched him." Hannah paused, feeling the sadness and anger mingle inside her. "Instead, he and Mr. Stokes started doing everything in their power to find him another home. Then the other night Papa came home acting really happy." Hannah flipped her head from side to side and added, "It was because Mr. Stokes had found a 'perfect' couple. Oh, Katherine, it was awful. I know I'm not perfect, and I know I don't have a husband, but I love him and will take good care of him."

"I know you will, and I'll do all I can to help you. I'm proud of you for being brave enough to do what you've done."

"They were to arrive on Friday. That's today," Hannah added. "That couple, I mean, that couple that was supposed to take Joseph. I had to do something, and I didn't know anything else to do but leave." Hannah sighed, dropped her shoulders and slumped against the back of her chair. "Now that I'm here, I can't believe I came all the way by myself. You know Papa will be looking for me."

"Yes, I'm sure he will be. And we both know he doesn't allow his family to cross him without consequences, and these consequences could be severe since he already had a plan with Mr. Stokes. I just wish Mother knew you were okay. We will have to get her word somehow."

"I know. I wanted to tell her, but I thought things would go better for her if I didn't."

"You're right. You did the only thing you could do." Katherine eased Joseph into his basket, which Hannah had moved to the middle of the table. She turned to her sister and placed her hands on Hannah's shoulders. "I love you and I'm so proud of you for having such courage."

"Oh, Katherine, I don't feel courageous. I'm scared. I guess Papa was right when he said I'm too young and immature, that I don't know what I'm doing. I've got to figure it out, though. Whatever happens, I'm keeping Joseph."

Stephen came home a couple hours later. While Hannah listened quietly, Katherine filled her husband in on the details her sister had shared with her. All three were keenly aware that their future was uncertain. Regardless, they would stick together. Stephen proved to be as supportive of Hannah as Katherine was.

Before eating supper, the three bowed their heads. Stephen prayed. "God, thank you for giving Hannah and Joseph a safe trip to us, and Lord, please give us wisdom and guidance in the days ahead. Thank you for this food and bless it. In Jesus name, Amen."

CHAPTER THIRTY

IT WAS ALMOST NOON on Friday when Kate heard footsteps cross the front porch. She knew they belonged to Bill. He opened the door "Have you heard from Hannah?" he asked even before getting through the door completely.

"No," Kate answered. "I haven't. Did you learn anything in Lee-ville, anything at all?" Janie and June Ellen had told Kate that Hannah had gone in the opposite direction, but she would never let Bill know they knew. She gripped her hands tightly together against her chest. "I have to think she and Joseph are both okay, or else surely we would have heard. Don't you think we would have heard?"

"I don't know, I don't know." Bill slung his hat toward a chair, but it landed on the floor. "I don't know what fool thing she has done. I'll find her, though. I'll get it fixed." He picked up his hat and hit it against his thigh as if knocking dirt off. "Nobody I asked in Lee-ville knew anything. Stokes is going to get word to Thomas. Guess he might know something. Problem is, we don't want to involve any more people than we have to." He headed out to talk to Frank.

Frank was hoeing weeds from the last of the tomato plants. He stopped when Mr. McMolison got near.

"Frank, you know Hannah's gone?"

"Yessuh, I hear that," Frank said, wrinkling his face and nodding his head slightly.

"Well, Frank, she left in the wagon. What do you know about that? Did you help her?" McMolison's eyes widened, and he nodded his head in Frank's direction with his hands extended and palms up.

"Well, yessuh, I guess maybe so. She come down here early yesterday and asked me ta hitch ole Pete up to the wagon." Frank stood straight, holding the hoe handle like a staff. A sizable tear in the crown of his straw hat caused the brim to dip slightly over his left ear.

"And, did you do that?"

"Yessuh, I did. She didn't tell me nothing 'bout what she was doing. She just asked me to hitch up Pete."

"Where was she heading? Did she say? She must have said something."

Frank, shaking his head slowly from side to side, said, "Nawsuh, she didn't say nothing 'bout where she was heading."

"Did you see her leave?"

Frank wiped sweat from his face with a swipe of his forearm. "Actually, she left all by herself. I got on back ta my work. She didn't tell me nothing."

"My horse is round by the front fence. Get him and take care of him. Got to let him rest."

"Yessuh." Frank laid his hoe on the ground. "I'll get him."

Mr. McMolison turned and walked away. Frank was relieved. He didn't want to tell a lie, but if he had been pressed about seeing Hannah leave, he figured he just might have had to. "Thank ya Lawd," he prayed silently as he walked toward the front yard. "Thank ya for getting me outta that predicament."

THE EVENING PASSED. Kate, anxious about the safety of Hannah and Joseph, sat with a book opened on her lap. Even though she occasionally turned a page, she had no idea what was on the page before.

"Since no one had seen her in Leeville, I'll go in the opposite direction tomorrow toward Beaumont," Bill said. "I'll ask around there and go farther if I have to. Maybe she thought she could go to Katherine.

That would be a long way to go alone, especially with a baby, but who knows what fool thing she's done or tried to do." Bill stretched his legs in front of him and leaned his head back against his chair.

"I can go with you," Kate offered eagerly.

Bill did not answer—he was already asleep. The couple hours he stayed at the Stokeses' house had been restless. He had accepted his friend's offer of a bed, but sleep was far away.

"Bill," Kate called out softly. "Why don't you go on to bed? You haven't slept in two days. You need rest before leaving again."

Bill opened his eyes and sat quietly, as if trying to focus on where he was and what Kate had said. "I will. I'm going to bed. Start again early in the morning."

BILL WAS READY TO GO. Light was barely beginning to show in the distant sky. Kate, too, was dressed. She revisited her question from the night before. "I can go with you. I'd like to."

"In what? The wagon is gone. Remember?" Bill said tersely.

"Perhaps we could borrow a neighbor's horse. Or we could get a wagon from the mill."

"Kate, no. You don't ever ride a horse. We don't want to involve neighbors anyway, or anybody at the mill for that matter. I'll go. You stay here. It's possible Hannah might return."

Bill mounted his horse, rode out of the yard and turned right. He was in Beaumont by midmorning. The little town was filled with people shopping for their weekly supplies. He walked the streets for a while and then stopped in the café for a cup of coffee. Even though he wanted to ask everyone he met if they had seen a young woman with a baby, he couldn't bring himself to be quite so open. He didn't want to reveal his problems to strangers. He did, however, stop by a little church located on the main road.

With his horse tied to a tree branch, he eased the door open and walked inside. He found the preacher sitting in his office, a poorly-lit little room that smelled like old books. Outside light poured through the one large window and made it possible for him to see the sermon he was working on. Bill tapped his knuckles against the open door and took a couple of steps into the small space. "Hello," he said. "I'm sorry to bother you, but I'm wondering if you might be able to help me with something."

The preacher, probably in his fifties, black hair sprinkled with gray and small round spectacles resting on the end of his nose, stood tall and straight and extended his hand. "Have a seat," he said in a voice as deep and dignified as his appearance.

"Thank you, but I can't stay." Bill stood with his hands on the back of a chair. "I'm Bill McMolison from over in Leaf Creek. I've got a little family situation, and I'm hoping you might help me."

The preacher continued to stand on the other side of the book-laden desk that filled the space between the two men. "I'll help if I can. What's the problem?"

Bill, anxious to learn what he could and be gone, was already telling him about Hannah and Joseph. "My daughter and grandson left home as a result of a disagreement, and I need to find them. The baby is tiny, and I'm worried about them being out on their own. I need to locate them and be sure they're safe."

"I don't know that I can help you." The preacher's fingertips rested on the desk in front of him. His voice was compassionate.

"Well, I understand. I just thought maybe you might have seen or heard something."

"You know, though, if anyone ever needs anything around here, Miss Maggie is the one to go to."

"Miss Maggie?"

"Yes. She's a widow, lives just out on the edge of town. She's all the time feeding people or helping somebody with a place to stay. She is the widow taking care of everybody else, rather than everybody taking care of her—if you know what I mean. Might be worth checking with her." He tapped the desk gently with his knuckles.

"I do. Thank you. Can you tell me where she lives?" Bill said hurriedly.

"In a little house just on the other end of town. It'll be the first one on the right after town. You can't miss it. And if you don't find it, ask anybody you see. Everybody knows Miss Maggie."

Bill walked briskly back through the sanctuary and out the front door. He mounted his horse and headed in the direction the preacher had pointed.

JUST AS THE PREACHER SAID, a little house appeared on the right just after Bill passed the last of the town buildings. He pulled back on the reins, threw his right leg over the back of his horse, and stepped to the ground. He was not feeling quite as in control and powerful as he was accustomed.

He walked toward the door with only one thought: "I've got to find Hannah and the baby and get them home. She may *think* she can decide what is going to happen, but she can't. I've already decided. I need to get this situation straight and get my life back in order."

Bill knocked on the door. A neatly-dressed lady with an aging but kind face answered. Bill guessed late fifties.

"Good afternoon, ma'am. My name is Bill McMolison. I'm from down in Leaf Creek. I'm here today looking for my daughter."

"Your daughter? What makes you think your daughter would be here, Mr. McMolison?" Miss Maggie had never met the tall, well-dressed, seemingly polite gentleman who now stood in her doorway, but she was familiar with the McMolison name. She had heard it mentioned in connection with the big sawmill over in Greene County. She remembered hearing a little something about the man who owned it, and as far as she could recall, it had been complimentary. However, her instinct told her to remain quiet and let him to do the talking. When Dr. McLeod brought Hannah, he introduced her only as Hannah. As Miss Maggie stood at her door and listened to the gentleman, she became fairly certain she was now talking to another member of the same family.

"Would you care for some tea?" she offered.

"Yes ma'am. That would be nice," Bill answered calmly, trying hard not to sound impatient or demanding.

"Have a seat here on the porch. I will be right back." She motioned toward one of the rocking chairs.

Miss Maggie went inside and pulled the door closed. Undetected, she watched her guest through the screen. She saw the frown and heard his sigh of apparent frustration before she disappeared into her kitchen.

Bill settled into one of the rockers but didn't rock. He sat, leaning forward, elbows on the chair arms and his hands clasped together between his knees. He gazed at the flowers and shrubs in the well-tended yard but didn't see their beauty. His mind was consumed with Hannah and the purpose of his visit.

Miss Maggie, carrying a tray, eased the door open with her shoulder. Bill stood quickly to help. "Here, let me get that," he said as he reached for the tray.

"Thank you. Just put it there on the table." She pointed to a little table already holding two pots with flowers.

He set down the tray, pushing one of the pots backward to make room. Miss Maggie poured each of them a cup of tea.

Bill sat again but could hardly contain himself. He was drinking tea to be polite and hopefully get in her good graces. All he really wanted was help and information, and he preferred to get it quickly. For him, time was of the essence. Even with the urgency he felt, he allowed Miss Maggie to offer the first inquiry.

After taking a few sips of tea, she leaned back in her chair and said, "Tell me about your daughter and how it is that you came looking for her here."

"I stopped at the church, the one on the main street. The preacher told me you may be able to help me. Can you?"

"Mr. McMolison, I do have people stay with me from time to time. The need, when it arises, is one I can help meet. Years ago when I first started taking people in, I decided I would learn only what they chose to tell me and would never ask questions. Many times I don't even know a name, certainly not a full one. Now, I can tell you with certainty that I have not had anyone recently or otherwise tell me McMolison was their name."

Bill considered her comment and pressed on. "Would you please just tell me if you've helped someone in the last couple of days that could have been my daughter, and if she was alright and where she was heading?"

"I told you I don't ask questions of the people who stay with me. But even if I did, I would never intentionally betray them, either. May I ask a question of you? Why did your daughter leave?"

Bill felt frustrated, sensing this woman knew more than she was letting on. In an attempt to gain her favor, he softened his demeanor. "Miss Maggie, I'm a father. I may have made some mistakes … no, I've *definitely* made mistakes, and I'm sure I will make more in my life." He paused and looked out over the yard. Then, looking back at her, he said, "You know, sometimes I feel like Paul: I do the very thing I don't want to do and wish I didn't do it, yet there I am doing it anyway. My point, Miss Maggie, is that my daughter left home— left with her tiny baby—and I am trying to find her before something happens to her."

Miss Maggie was not impressed by his comparison of himself to Paul or with his shift in tone. Nor was Bill McMolison accustomed to being analyzed and questioned, especially by a woman. He tried his best to continue and get whatever information she might be willing to share.

"Miss Maggie, families have difficulties sometimes," he said. "My family is not immune. If Hannah has been here with you, she had a baby with her—her baby. Hannah is young and unmarried. Knowing it will be in the best interest of the baby to have a mother and a father, I have made necessary arrangements for a fine Christian couple to take the baby to be their own. I'm afraid Hannah's immaturity is not permitting her to think clearly … and perhaps causing her to act some-what selfishly."

Miss Maggie let his words hang in the air before responding. "Mr. McMolison, I haven't said whether or not I've ever met your daughter and grandbaby, but I caution you to remember a mother's love—even if immature—is rarely selfish. It is instead unconditional and often painful. Don't underestimate it."

Realizing it would not help his cause to show impatience, Bill responded as gently as he could: "If you think you have seen my daughter, will you tell me? Will you help me?"

"A young girl and baby did stay with me," Miss Maggie said at length. "She left early in the morning. That is really all I can say."

"Do you know which way she went?" His tone was laced with urgency.

"I think I have said enough," Miss Maggie said coolly. Then she rose to her feet.

Taking her cue, Bill stood. Knowing he wasn't likely to get anything else from the woman, he thanked her for the tea and wished her a good afternoon. Miss Maggie watched the stranger ride away. "Good afternoon," she said.

Bill knew there would be no point in returning to Leaf Creek without at least going on to Katherine's. He had to find out if Hannah was there, or had been. He headed back toward the main street. It was late in the day—too late to continue on to Hattiesburg. He wasn't familiar with the area where Katherine and Stephen lived, so he did not want to get there in the middle of the night. Instead he found a room at a small boarding house and planned to start again the following morning.

Chapter Thirty-One

*H*ANNAH AND KATHERINE knew their father would be coming, that he would not give up until he found Hannah. They both felt that as long as they were together they could face him and do whatever was necessary to keep him from taking Joseph.

Once the decision was made, Hannah, with Joseph snuggled in her arms, attended the Sunday morning service with Stephen and Katherine. The church was small, with only nine short rows of pews on either side of the aisle. Most every available space was taken. Hannah sat with Katherine on the outer end of the second row on the right.

Stephen had prepared his sermon early in the week, days before knowing Hannah would be in the congregation. In God's providence, the sermon title was God's Plan for the Family.

Hannah held Joseph, listened, and wondered what God's plan for her might be. Even though other people (including her father) might insist that what she was doing wasn't right, Stephen seemed to be saying through his words that she *was*—and her heart continued to convince her that what she was doing *was* right. Although Hannah felt uneasy about the next few hours and days, she gained strength from the sweet face cuddled in her lap.

"I don't know how or what I'm going to do to take care of both of

277

us, but I will do it, whatever it is. I'll do whatever is necessary," she thought, hugging Joseph close to her chest. She felt more strongly than ever that loving and caring for him was her responsibility. She had no trouble convincing herself that keeping him was part of God's plan. Her father would just have to understand.

"God Will Take Care of You" was the closing hymn. Hannah heard the words clearly, maybe for the first time in her life. The hymn had been sung dozens of times in church back home, but she had never listened. On that Sunday, though, the words seemed especially for her. She held Joseph close to her heart as the small congregation sang, "… *lean, weary one, upon His breast, God will take care of you.*" She knew the days ahead would not be easy ones, but she felt at peace with the decisions she had made.

After the benediction, several of the ladies welcomed Hannah warmly and made the usual fuss over Joseph. "He is precious. He is *sooo* darling. Aren't they bundles of joy at this sweet age?" The comments were kind, and Hannah loved hearing all of them.

STEPHEN ROCKED JOSEPH while Katherine and Hannah washed the dinner dishes.

"That was all so good. You're a really good cook," Hannah said while drying the plates. "Course, I was starving," she teased.

"Right," Katherine smiled.

"Seriously, though, it's the first time I've felt like eating in days, and it was all so good. Thanks for letting me be here."

I'm glad you came. I want you here, but we've got to decide what to do. Papa will come, and it could be soon." Katherine squeezed the water from her dishrag by twisting it with both hands. She straightened it and spread it over the rounded edge of the sink.

"I know." Hannah sat in a chair near Stephen. Both of her hands gripped the drying cloth in her lap. "I know what I want to do. I just don't know how. I've somehow got to make Papa change his mind. I can't keep running. I don't have anywhere else to go. Maybe with your help he'll give in."

Katherine, standing behind Hannah's chair, patted her shoulders. "I don't know, but we'll do something." She looked at Stephen. "Do you have *any* ideas? Maybe she could stay here. We could tell him we'll help."

The knock on the door interrupted Stephen's response. It sounded unusually loud and echoed through the wood frame house. Stephen stopped rocking, stood, and handed the baby to Hannah. Stepping into the small hall that led to the front door, Stephen gazed with unmistakable recognition at the figure hidden only by the sheer-covered glass panes in the door. "It's your father," he said softly.

A streak of panic pierced both girls' hearts. They stood frozen. Both knew this visit was inevitable, but neither was prepared. Hannah hoped desperately that her father would back down once he learned that Stephen and Katherine were willing and anxious to help. Both girls knew, however, there was a far greater chance he would remain unwavering in his own ideas and plan.

Stephen opened the door. "Why, hello, Mr. McMolison," the sisters heard Stephen say with seeming sincerity and warmth.

"Hello, Stephen." The warmth was not returned—he sounded cold as a stone.

"Come in, sir. Have you had dinner? We've just finished, but I know Katherine would like to fix you a plate. She's a good cook, you know."

Mr. McMolison didn't answer. He looked around the small living room. "Stephen, are both my daughters here? I'm looking for Hannah. She left home without saying much to anybody, and I'm trying to find her."

"Yes sir, she's here." Stephen managed to keep his voice light and welcoming. "She and the baby are both here. Both of them are fine. Katherine and I would like for them to stay with us for a while—at least for as long as she wants or needs to."

"No." Bill stepped close to Stephen. "She's *not* staying here. She is going with me. She is going back home where she belongs, and the baby is going to a proper home, one with both a mother and a father. That is where he belongs. I'll get this mess straightened out one way or another."

"Mr. McMolison, please—"

"Stephen, this is none of your affair. Tell Hannah I'm here."

Hannah and Katherine stepped from the kitchen into the tiny hall and stood a few feet from their father. Joseph was sleeping peacefully in his mother's arms, oblivious to the growing tension that surrounded him.

"Hello, Papa," Katherine spoke first. "Please don't be angry with Hannah. She made a mistake, but she has a beautiful little baby boy—your grandson. She loves him just like you loved Samuel and us. Don't try to make her give him away," Katherine pleaded, hoping somehow to make a difference.

Their father made rules and expected, without exception, that they be followed. She and Hannah had lived under his rod of iron. Katherine knew her wishes were not likely to come true, but she hoped her father would see how much Hannah loved Joseph and would want to love and help them. She wished he would tell them he would be there for them no matter what. She wished things could be like they sometimes were when they were little, when he played with them, hugged them, let them win in checkers—back in the days when there was no doubt he would be there to love and protect them.

Hannah stood clutching Joseph close to her breast. "I'm so sorry, Papa. I'm so very sorry. I know I did wrong. It just happened. I never meant to cause you shame." Tears filled her eyes as she spoke, and her throat began to burn so badly she wasn't sure she could continue. "I love you and Mama. I don't want to cause you any more problems, but I love my baby, too, and I must do what I have to. I have to be sure he knows he is always loved and wanted—"

Before she could say more, Bill McMolison spoke for the first time since the girls entered the room. "That's *enough*," he snapped. "That's enough from both of you. You two are *my* daughters, the daughters I've provided for and loved and still love." He stood straight, unmoving. "You have both defied your upbringing in all kinds of ways. Now we have to make the best and most honorable decision we can." He turned to Katherine. "And Katherine, don't *ever* again compare this baby to your little brother. Samuel was brought into this world in the right and proper manner, into a right and proper family."

Katherine wanted to scream that Samuel may have come into the world in a proper manner, but his death was *not* proper at all. She held her tongue, though. That subject had never been discussed, not before or after her little brother's funeral. When she mentioned Samuel, it had not occurred to her that it would add fuel to the already volatile situation, but it obviously had. Her father looked absolutely fierce now.

Stephen stood quietly to one side of the little hall. He wanted Katherine to know he was there for her without interfering in something that wasn't considered his business. He knew that nothing he could say would be considered by his father-in-law as beneficial, so for the sake of family relations he thought it best to remain silent as long as possible.

"Hannah," their father continued, "we don't need to continue talking. You can't care for this baby. He needs a whole family, and there is one waiting for him. Get your things. We're going home. *Now.*"

Hannah stood unable to move. She had never opposed her father before, at least not while standing squarely in front of him. "No, Papa," she said softly. "I can't go with you. Please try to understand."

"Understand. Understand *what?*" he shouted. "This is not up for discussion. Do as I tell you and get your things. You are coming with me. I'll get the wagon." His whole body became rigid with anger as he strove to maintain his composure.

"No, sir. I can't, Papa. I just can't," Hannah repeated quietly but firmly.

Bill McMolison took a step in Hannah's direction and gestured toward her with his right hand as if reaching for Joseph. Hannah stepped backward, clutching Joseph with both arms. Then Katherine stepped in front of her father, blocking him from Hannah and Joseph.

"*Move,* Katherine! Get out of my way. This has nothing to do with you." He pushed her to one side, causing her to stumble slightly. Defending his wife, Stephen quickly stepped in front of his father-in-law and stood between him and his daughters and grandson.

"Sir, maybe for now you should go," Stephen said commandingly. "We can talk about all this later."

"Young man, you will not now or *ever* tell me how to run my family or when to do it. Step aside *now*!" Bill bellowed. As he started to step forward, though, Stephen put his arm out to indicate that he not come any closer. The very fact that anyone, especially Stephen or one of his children, would attempt to stand in his way made Bill irate. Rage overtook him, and before Hannah, Katherine, Stephen (or maybe Bill himself) realized what was happening, Bill had reached inside his coat and whipped out his pistol. His eyes were hard and wide and he was breathing heavy. His jaw muscles twitched, but his aim on the weapon looked steady. He aimed at Stephen's chest, and he looked ready to fire.

"Papa, no! What are you doing?" Katherine cried out and darted to her husband's side. "Put the gun down. Please put the gun down!"

Bill waved the gun in Hannah's direction for an instant—not pointing it at her but gesturing for her to come toward him. "Go to the wagon. Go, *now*. We're going home." Hannah, though, turned her back, dropped to the floor and covered Joseph with her body. And Stephen, sensing an opening, tried to grab the gun away from Bill McMolison and got his hand on his father-in-law's arm instead.

The men battled, the gun pointed toward the ceiling. Then Bill, a much bigger, stronger man, grabbed Stephen's hands with his left hand while making every effort to pull himself free. Stephen wouldn't relent, though, and the struggle became fierce as arms flailed back and forth and up and down. Katherine lost sight of the gun, as it was hidden somewhere between her outraged father and her husband. She tried to intervene, but both men screamed her away. Hannah was paralyzed with fear. She couldn't speak, look or move but stayed folded like a ball in the corner of the hallway. Her only conscious thought was to keep Joseph protected. Katherine, oblivious now to Hannah, watched in horror as each man continued his desperate attempts to gain control of the firearm. Within seconds they fell to the floor. The intense struggle became more frantic. Katherine thought Bill might be gaining control when—

The sound of the gunshot was deafening. It bounced with growing intensity off every wall. It exploded in Hannah's and Katherine's ears. The fear that had been gripping them turned into panic and terror.

Katherine stared at the clump of unmoving flesh before her. The sudden stillness caused Hannah to turn and lift her eyes. She gasped in disbelief at the sight. Blood began to seep into the cracks between the wooden floor planks. It had only been a couple of minutes since the nightmare began with Bill's loud knock on the door, but it seemed to Hannah and Katherine as if it had been an eternity.

As Katherine knelt beside her father and her husband, Stephen lifted himself slowly off the floor. His hands and arms were covered with blood. He leaned against the wall, and with Katherine's help he slowly slid down until he was sitting and holding his face with his bloody hands.

Bill McMolison was lying on the floor with his gun, covered with his blood, as his life slipped away and death slithered in. Holding Joseph with one arm, Hannah knelt beside her father. She put her free hand on the side of his face. He responded ever so slightly with a grunt, but it was clear Bill McMolison was dying.

"Oh Papa, I'm so sorry," Hannah said. "I love you. Please don't go. Please, please forgive me." She bent over so that her face touched his and whispered again, "I love you, Papa."

Bill didn't respond. Tears ran down Hannah's cheeks as she sat beside his body and stared into his sightless eyes. She had wished most of her life for understanding and kindness from him. The few joyful and fun times that occurred when she was very young had almost faded from her memory. At that moment, all she could remember were his rules and expectations. Guilt spread over her like a giant wave as she said again, "I'm so sorry. If only I hadn't done what I did. But, oh Papa, why couldn't you listen to me? Why couldn't you have tried to understand?" It was too late. Her father lay lifeless on the floor.

"What have I done?" Though barely audible, the words came from Stephen as he remained crouched against the wall. His face, hands and arms were covered with blood. Katherine hugged him as she would a small child. "I was trying to protect my family," he whispered, "and I've ended up destroying part of it. Katherine, I'm so sorry."

Hannah stood and turned to face Katherine and Stephen. "It's not your fault, Stephen. It's mine. I shouldn't have come."

Katherine, now on her knees beside Stephen, looked up at Hannah. "You know it's not any of our faults. This is all horrible," she said, looking at her father's body. "I wish everything was different, but it's not your fault and—" Katherine took Stephen's hands in hers. "—it's not yours, either. Papa could have shot Hannah or the baby. Please, both of you, stop thinking about blame. Maybe all of us could have done something different, but I don't know what it would have been. He never listened to us, not even Mama. Right now we have to think about what to do. We must get word to Mama," Katherine said, taking charge of the situation. "We have to tell her what has happened."

Stephen pushed to his feet and went to the basin on the back porch to wash the blood from his hands and face. He changed his clothes, saddled his horse, and rode into town to get the sheriff and undertaker. Katherine and Hannah didn't know what they should be doing, so they sat on the floor near their father. It seemed respectful to stay near him, although everything about the last hour seemed to them surreal. Their insides felt numb.

Sheriff White walked up the steps. Following him were Stephen and the undertaker. The sheriff had been there just two days before and watched the joyful reunion of two sisters. No one could possibly have predicted that he would soon return because their father had died from a gunshot.

"He pulled the gun out and swung it around," Stephen said dazedly. "I just wanted to take it from him. I didn't want anyone to get hurt. We fought—it just went off. I don't know. It all happened so fast."

Katherine and Hannah were still sitting on the floor near their father's body. Joseph slept in Hannah's arms. Even though the danger was over, she was afraid to put him in his basket. Holding him close protected him, and it comforted her.

"Why don't y'all come sit in a chair?" The sheriff extended his hand to help Hannah up from the floor. Katherine stood and moved to the sofa beside Stephen. Hannah, holding Joseph, sat nearby.

"I think Stephen has pretty much filled me in on what happened, but I need to hear from everybody." Sheriff White looked to Katherine and Hannah. "First, tell me why he was here today."

"It's my fault," Hannah started but Katherine put her hand up.

"It's not your fault. It's nobody's fault," she said, holding Stephen's hand.

The sheriff nodded for them to continue. "He came today because …?"

"Because I left home," Hannah said. "He didn't want me to, and he came to take me back."

"Came to take you and your baby back? Is that right?" Sheriff White asked gently.

"Yes, sir. He was so angry. I've never seen him point a gun at anyone before." Hannah couldn't hold back the sobs that filled her throat. "I'm so sorry."

"Where was the gun when it went off?" The sheriff looked toward Katherine and Stephen.

"We were in the hallway," Stephen said. "I was just trying to get it away from him."

"I couldn't see it," Katherine added softly. "I don't know why he would have pulled out a gun in here with us. It was just us."

After talking to both girls and again to Stephen, Sheriff White was satisfied that the death was the result of a sad family tragedy. The coroner arrived, and after hearing the same details he came to the same conclusion. There would be no further investigation into the incident, and Sheriff White instructed the undertaker to take the body and prepare it. He would be along later to help make arrangements to get it to Leaf Creek.

The undertaker took Bill McMolison's body, and Sheriff White took his gun.

Chapter Thirty-Two

COUNTY HERALD OBITUARIES
October 17, 1918

Accident Claims Life of
Greene County Supervisor

One of the saddest tragedies that has occurred in this vicinity in many a day happened last Sunday. The occurrence about which the people of Greene County are so saddened did not actually take place in our county but rather in the city of Hattiesburg. It was at about the three o'clock hour that in the twinkling of an eye, the life of Mr. William McMolison was snuffed from him.

While Mr. McMolison was not a native of Greene County, he had made his home here for many years. He served the county in the capacity of supervisor, served his church in the capacity of deacon and elder, and has been identified with the large milling concern in Leaf Creek. Mr. McMolison dedicated his life to serving the people and making this area a better place to live and to raise families. His friend,

Mr. John Stokes, said, "Bill McMolison was my good and faithful friend. I am going to miss him terribly, but more importantly the county is going to miss him. He was tireless in his efforts to improve every aspect of this county's life. He was a faithful husband, a good father, a fair boss and a loyal friend."

Mr. Charles Echols, pastor of Leaf Creek Presbyterian Church, remembers Mr. McMolison as a true God-fearing man who was always ready and willing to help in whatever activity or capacity the church needed. "He is going to be sorely missed."

Mr. McMolison came to his untimely death after falling victim to an accidental gunshot from his own pistol. At the time of this fatal accident, he was visiting in the home of his daughter and son-in-law.

He was preceded in death by his loving parents, Martha and Lawrence McMolison and his young son, Samuel. He is survived by his wife, Kate Brannon McMolison of Leaf Creek, his daughter and son-in-law, Katherine and Stephen Neal of Hattiesburg, and his daughter, Hannah McMolison of Leaf Creek.

The wake will be at the family's home on Wednesday evening. The funeral service will be at 11:00 o'clock Thursday morning at Leaf Creek Presbyterian Church, with the burial to follow at the Leaf Creek Cemetery.

THE NEWS SPREAD quickly once Sheriff White got a message to the Greene County sheriff. The unanswered questions remained just that—unanswered. Sheriff White related the tragic accident as he saw it. No other details were available.

A CLOSE FRIEND OF THE SHERIFF was Fred Davis, one of Hattiesburg's wealthiest timber men. He was a member of Stephen's church and the owner of a new, five-passenger Ford Model T. Arriving at Stephen and Katherine's house shortly after Bill McMolison's body had been taken away, Mr. Davis offered to give them a ride to Leaf Creek.

"I don't know." Stephen stood with his left hand holding the edge of the open door. "That's a big imposition."

"I want to help." Mr. Davis stood just outside the door. He held his hat with both hands and tapped his chest gently with the brim. "I know this is a hard time and you're traveling with a baby."

Stephen, still dazed, sighed deeply. "Actually, I'd appreciate the help. Thank you."

"I'll get a couple of the men to take the wagon and your father-in-law's horse to Leaf Creek. Don't worry about anything here."

Arriving home in Leaf Creek four hours later, Hannah and Katherine soon felt as if they were going through the same motions they had gone through eleven years before. People and food filled the house. The events surrounding wakes and funerals in Leaf Creek hadn't changed. The only difference was that they were a few years older and would likely be asked questions they didn't want to answer. Some folks were never timid when they surmised there was more to a story than they'd heard.

Kate invited Mr. Davis to stay the night before returning to Hattiesburg, but he declined. He did accept her invitation for supper. After enjoying several helpings of the food that had been brought to their home, he stood to leave. "I hope y'all will forgive me for rushing off right after eating, but I do need to get started back to Hattiesburg."

"We understand," Stephen assured him. "Never be able to thank you enough for giving us a ride."

"Mrs. McMolison, thank you so much for supper." Mr. Davis reached to shake Kate's hand.

"You're more than welcome," she said. "Thank you so much for bringing my family."

Before releasing her hand, he said, "May I speak with you alone before I go?"

"Certainly." Kate turned to her family with instructions. She was polite as always, but firm. "Y'all finish eating and don't get up. I'll walk your friend to the door, Stephen."

"Sir, I appreciate your helping my family," she said when they reached the porch. "It means a lot to all of us. And please let me pay you for your trouble."

"Oh, no ma'am," Mr. Davis replied. "That's not why I wanted to speak to you. And I'm sorry to be the one bringing this to you, but the sheriff asked me to." He reached inside his coat and pulled out a cloth-wrapped bundle.

"Oh, my," Kate said, startled. She felt her heart quicken and knew what she would find beneath the wrapping.

"The sheriff said Stephen and your daughters were so upset that he just didn't have the heart to give it to them. He cleaned it up and gave it to me to bring to you. I'm so sorry."

"I understand." Kate's hands trembled as she took the gun.

"Since it belonged to your husband, it's rightfully yours. So sorry to be handing it to you out here like this. Can I put it someplace for you?"

"No, I'll take care of it." Kate didn't unwrap the cloth. She could feel the barrel and the handle. She knew what the weapon looked like and had no desire to see it ever again. "Be careful driving back home."

Back inside, Kate went straight to her bedroom. She opened the bottom drawer of her chifferobe, lifted the folded undergarments inside, and shoved the gun beneath them. She would bury it as soon as things settled down. She sure didn't want it in sight to remind her children of what they'd been through.

SEVERAL FRIENDS lingered throughout the house when Kate reentered the dining room. Stephen, Katherine and Hannah were all sitting around the table. "Come with me for a minute," she said to the three of them before leading the way to her bedroom. She closed the door. She sat down in the chair beside the bed, her hands clasped together on her knees. She looked up, a worried frown on her face. "Can y'all tell me what happened?"

"It's my fault." Hannah said. "I shouldn't have left." She trembled and felt close to crying as she sat on the edge of the bed with Joseph in her arms.

Kate moved to sit on the bed beside Hannah. She put her arm around her shoulders. "Whatever happened, it's not your fault. Mr. Davis told me Bill had an accident with his gun? Said that was all the sheriff had told him."

Katherine and Stephen told Kate the truth about what had taken place. She covered her face with her hands and sobbed. "Oh, what was he thinking to pull his gun out like that?" She wept with her daughters as they told her of their father's final moments. Hannah apologized again and again about being responsible, and Stephen kept saying that he should have been able to prevent it. Kate hushed them both. "There was nothing any of you could have done."

When the family conversation was over, Kate instructed her girls and son-in-law to make no mention of the events that led to her husband's untimely death. She wiped tears away with her fingers. "People will wonder and probably ask questions," she said quietly. "I think we should say only that the gun went off after he took it from his coat, so awful, just don't know exactly how it happened."

HANNAH FELT LIKE a distant somebody that she barely knew. She just kept putting one foot in front of the other and doing the next thing that seemed to be expected. She had to face not only inquiries about her father's death, but questions about Joseph. The probing about what happened to her father was, more often than not, an open-ended question or a statement such as, "Your father was more than comfortable handling his gun. Strange how something like this could possibly have happened." She gave the same answer as her mother, Katherine, and Stephen: "Yes, it is all so hard to believe." They had shared the truth about what happened with Janie and June Ellen, and no one else needed to know.

The questions about Joseph were harder to deal with. Only a few people had known about him, but suddenly people (not only from in town, but from the whole county) were coming to their house. The ones who saw him always commented on what a pretty baby he was—but swiftly asked who he belonged to. Hannah cringed inside the first time or two she tried to answer. Then she became a little bold and was able to say "He's mine" without feeling her throat start to close. Most of the time those asking the questions realized the situation was a delicate one and shifted to comments about how old he was, whether or not he was sleeping well, or whatever other topic they could think of.

Kate greeted each person and accepted condolences with the stoic grace that her husband would have expected. The others followed her lead and went through all the appropriate motions at home, the church, the cemetery, and then back home.

Throughout the ordeal, Hannah saw faces without really seeing them, spoke to people without hearing her words or theirs, and responded to hugs almost unconsciously. As she followed her father's casket back down the aisle of the church, she looked upward toward the balcony. Men from the mill were there. They, no doubt, were already wondering what would become of their jobs. Frank, Janie (holding a bundled sleeping baby near her heart) and June Ellen stood together in the center of the group, but there in the midst of the sea of dark faces was an unexpected but familiar one—it was Rosie from the hotel in Leeville. She stood beside an older woman that Hannah did not remember seeing before. The two women appeared especially somber. Hannah wondered why they would come all the way to Leaf Creek to attend the funeral, but her attention to the two women was only fleeting. Her sad heart allowed no room for prolonged interest in other mourners.

Back at the house following the graveside service, Hannah felt smothered by the dozens of people who were there to share her family's difficult time of loss. Some of the ladies helped June Ellen and Janie in the kitchen, but most folks just stood around eating, drinking, sharing memories of the departed and talking about the tragedy and what a sad time it was for Kate. The haze in Hannah's brain seemed to grow thicker. She fed Joseph and put him in his cradle for a nap. Watching him sleep peacefully, she thought how wonderful it was to be oblivious to all that was going on. She eased out the back door, down the steps, and walked across the yard with no destination in mind. She wished for a momentary reprieve from the oppressive feeling that filled the house.

Hannah neared the barn and saw Frank tending the horses, some of which were still hitched to wagons. Then she saw them. Rosie and the older woman from the funeral were sitting in the back of the wagon that belonged to Mr. Stokes. Thinking they must be waiting on Mr. Stokes to finish paying his respects, Hannah walked toward them. She liked Rosie and wanted to be sure the two women had something to eat and drink before starting the trip back to Leeville. At the same time, she had no desire to be anywhere nearby when Mr. Stokes came out. Hannah's brief conversation with him earlier in the day had been stiff and cold. He had actually mentioned the Alabama family coming for "the baby," and she'd quickly and confidently told him Joseph was staying with her. Stokes, giving her a mean look, said that she was never to interfere with Thomas and never to expect help from him. Showing no interest in even seeing his grandson, he'd spun on his heel after his warning and strode away.

"Hello," Hannah said to Rosie. The women had not seen Hannah approach and were startled when she spoke.

"Oh, hello," Rosie said as she and the older woman both eased from the back of the wagon and stood side by side. "We didn't hear you coming. This is my grandmother. We're sorry about your father."

"Thank you. It's kind of you to come. Did you both know my father?"

"I worked in the hotel up until a couple of years ago. Mr. McMolison has been a regular for a long time." The older woman smiled and nodded when she responded.

"You appear to be waiting for Mr. Stokes. Did you come over with him?"

"Yes. Yes we rode over with him," Rosie said hesitantly, almost as if she knew it would not be what Hannah wanted to hear.

"Do you work for Mr. Stokes?" Hannah knew there had to be a good reason for him to allow two colored women to accompany him, even though they rode in the back of the wagon.

"No, we just know him from the hotel. He and your father have been at the hotel many times together. They always seemed like good friends. We knew he would be coming over today. We asked if we might ride in his wagon," Rosie answered.

"Your father was always a good man. He was a friend to us, and we wanted to be able to come and pay our respects," the grandmother added.

"Do you know Mr. Stokes's son?" Hannah asked, hoping to hear any news about Thomas. Even if she never fit into his life, she so much wanted to hear about him.

"Yes, he comes by the hotel when he's home," Rosie said, but offered nothing else. She laced her fingers and rubbed the side of her hands with her thumbs.

"Do you know if he is at home now?" Hannah continued.

"Haven't seen him lately," Rosie said. "Here comes Mr. Stokes," she added, which Hannah took as a cue not to mention Thomas further. Hannah was thankful for the warning, but her frustration over his earlier indifference toward her pushed her to anger. She had hoped to not see him again, but if she had to, she would just pass him by with a look of disdain. She wheeled around, and he was right in front of her. She looked at him with a furrowed brow, set jaw, and tightened lips—but said nothing. She had no idea the depth of *his* anger at *her*, and nothing could have prepared her for his parting shot.

"You two sisters consoling each other?" he sneered. "It's time you got to know the rest of your family, Hannah." He motioned with his hand toward Rosie. "Rosie came to bury her father today, just like you. The difference is that Rosie's grown up knowing her place and doing what she's supposed to. You and Katherine ..." He paused. "Well, that's just another story. I hate to even think about what you and your sister put your poor father through. Now my friend is dead. Your father is dead. What are you going to do now?"

All three women stood in stunned silence while Mr. Stokes climbed onto the seat of the wagon. "Rosie, you and Granny get in the wagon." His voice snapped with anger and bitterness.

Hannah, her chest pounding, didn't move. She watched as the wagon went down the worn path and onto the road. She saw Rosie, stunned in disbelief, look wide-eyed at her grandmother as the grandmother looked back in Hannah's direction. Her sad eyes made Hannah wonder if what she had just heard could possibly be true. "I have a colored sister? Impossible," she thought. "My father was a lot of things, but he would never …" She couldn't finish the thought. "That just can't be true. Mr. Stokes has been mean to me, but surely he wouldn't … but what if it *is* true? Rosie's grandmother didn't say anything different."

Mr. Stokes had delivered a powerful blow, suddenly making Hannah angrier with her father than she had been before. "How could he have been so judgmental and intolerant of me?" Her thoughts spiraled up and down in a vicious cycle. "He did the same thing I did, only worse. He was married, and he was with another women—a colored woman—and had a child by her." The idea was unfathomable. "I can't believe he made me feel so guilty, so responsible for destroying family honor. How could he do that?" Looking toward the path of Mr. Stokes's wagon, she stood motionless, crossed her arms and hugged her shoulders. "And he must have stayed connected with his colored daughter. That's why her grandmother brought her all the way to Leaf Creek today. It must be true."

Hannah's head and heart were spinning. She tried to grasp what Mr. Stokes had said but nothing made sense. Had her father acknowledged a colored daughter, but barely acknowledged—and never touched—his white grandson?!? "Who was he?" she asked aloud. But it was impossible to comprehend at the moment. Every inch of her body and soul and mind felt more tired than it had ever felt before.

* * *

THE MANY DISCREET VISITS and conversations Rosie had witnessed between Mr. McMolison and her grandmother suddenly made sense. The two women were silent as they rode home that evening, but once they were home and away from Mr. Stokes, Rosie didn't let her grandmother rest until she filled in the blanks. Rosie learned for the first time that her mother and Mr. McMolison had shared an ongoing relationship. "I saw what was happening," her grandmother said to her. "I tried to caution your mother against always being available for

Mr. McMolison, but she was in love with him, and he acted like he really cared about her, too. He brought her things and treated her nice. Of course it was always in secret. He never let on when he was in the dining room, and she didn't either." Her grandmother sighed deeply and leaned back in her chair.

Rosie sat on the edge of a small sofa. She held her hands still on her lap. "Did Mama know he was married? I mean …" Rosie hesitated. "I mean, I know if he wanted to be with her at the hotel, she didn't have a choice. But still, did she know? Did it matter?"

"Oh, Rosie, it always matters, but most times with the white men, we didn't have a choice. But with your mama and Mr. McMolison, it seemed different. Now, it still wasn't right, but he kept sending for her, and she was happy to go." Her grandmother shifted her position and gazed across the room, not really looking at anything in particular. "She tried to keep it from me for a long time, but I knew and finally she told me." She paused, then looked back at Rosie and said wistfully, "You know what? I worried at the time, but I'm not sorry about it at all now because I'm so thankful for you."

"I'm thankful for you, too, and I love you. But why haven't you told me any of this when I've asked before?" Rosie asked.

"Because after your mother died, it just didn't seem that it would serve any good purpose," her grandmother replied. "Not for either your mother's memory or Mr. McMolison's reputation, so I stayed quiet. Just so you know, he has always known you were his, and he has helped us ever since you were born. He even paid for your mother's funeral. It was an awful time, and I didn't know what I was going to do." Her grandmother closed her eyes and leaned her head back on the chair.

"Didn't people wonder why he helped you?" Rosie asked, not wanting her grandmother to stop talking. She wanted her to tell everything about her mother and about Mr. McMolison.

"No, not really. Three or four of the white men that were regulars at the hotel came to the house. I took in washing for a time, you know. Also made a few cakes to sell. It's just that when Mr. McMolison came, he slid an extra envelope full of money into my pocket. He has been regularly bringing envelopes ever since."

They both sat quietly for several minutes. Rosie tried to grasp all her grandmother had just told her, and what her grandmother tried to recover from—not only the physical strain of the day, but from the emotional strain as well. Rosie could see that her grandmother had been truly saddened by Mr. Stokes's actions when she said, "I am so sorry for the hateful way Mr. Stokes spoke to you and Hannah today. I never knew for sure if he knew the truth, but I *never* would have thought he would have done what he did. I'm so sorry you found out that way, and I'm sorry for Hannah, too. Mr. McMolison wouldn't have wanted things to happen that way either—I know he wouldn't. Anger got the best of Mr. Stokes today. He betrayed his friend and us."

Rosie went to bed that night with answers she had wanted for a long time. She had been serving her own father in the dining room and never knew. She wasn't sure how she felt. Her grandmother had kept the secret. She would too. She lay awake most of the night, allowing her mind to go over and over the events of the day.

Chapter Thirty-Three

SELLING THE MILL was Kate's only option. It was a man's world, no place for a woman (at least not for her). One of the Neal sons from the Neal sawmill family—no relation to Stephen, of course—bought it two weeks after Bill McMolison's death. He kept all the men and added more.

Kate got a good price. The transaction wasn't difficult, as an attorney friend did all the negotiating and paperwork. The house, the furnishings and ten acres of land were hers, free and clear, and the sale of the mill gave her money for security. But it would have to last. She was only in her early forties, Hannah was barely sixteen, and Joseph was a baby. No money was owed, but very little had been saved. She was acutely aware that for the first time in her life no money was being made by her family.

Kate, with a strong but quiet resolve, began to deal with the changes her husband's death caused. Having to think about money (or the possible lack of it) was new to her. It made her cautious, but she didn't worry. She took every next step necessary to provide for Hannah and Joseph, as well as herself.

For Kate the most difficult place to scale back was the help. Frank came inside and stood with Janie and June Ellen in the kitchen. All three knew the mill had been sold and had been worried about what she would have to do.

Tears stung Kate's eyes when she started talking. "I know y'all all realize how everything is. There just isn't money to keep things like they have been."

Janie leaned against the table. "We pretty much knew it was coming. Are you saying not at all, or what?"

"Frank, you have a place at the mill if you want it."

"I do. That'll be good." Frank nodded his head and shifted from one foot to the other.

"Kate looked at Janie and June Ellen. "I would love for you to be here one day each week if you want to, but I'm sure neither of you will have trouble finding work. If someone has a job for you full time, I want you to take it—if you want to. Just don't forget to come from time to time to check on things here."

"I'm gonna keep my day with you," June Ellen said first.

"Me too," Janie added emphatically.

"June Ellen and Frank, y'all can stay in the property house where you are—that is if you want to. I hope you will. I would like having you close by," Kate continued.

Janie walked over to Kate, put her arm around her and said, "We understand. Wish it wasn't this way, but we knows it has to be." Janie rubbed tears from her cheeks with the tail of her apron.

June Ellen and Frank continued to live in the little house on the property. Frank started full time at the mill but helped Kate late each afternoon. Janie and June Ellen's other four days were quickly filled. All three, thankfully, had jobs.

Janie also stopped by now and then for an extra afternoon. She usually whipped up a meal, visited a bit, and planned something special for Joseph, just as she had done years before for Hannah and Katherine. Hannah watched as she let Joseph help make cookies and draw faces in the dough with a spoon. She watched as they laughed together and Janie hugged him close. She watched and remembered the love of those hugs. It was long ago, but the memory still gave her a wave of security and warm feelings of comfort.

Mr. Mallett, one of the men from the church, brought his mule and helped Frank plow a small area for Kate and Hannah to plant vegetables. Mr. Dickson, another church member, built a second chicken house where Kate eventually added more laying hens. These new efforts provided not only food for them, but also food to sell for income. Life continued to be a cycle, but it was a new and different cycle for Hannah and Kate.

Joseph was a constant joy to both his mother and grandmother. His black hair was thick and curly. His blue eyes sparkled as he "helped" do chores. To Kate's dismay, he loved shooing the chickens and causing all manner of extra cackling and commotion. But most of the time she just stood back and smiled as she watched him bend over laughing. After Lost, the family dog, joined them, Joseph spent many afternoons running and playing with him or throwing sticks for him to fetch.

Seasons came and went. Spring flowers bloomed; the creek ran cool in summer; the fall leaves glowed with colors of red, orange, and yellow; the cold of winter drove Hannah, Kate, and Joseph to the coziness of the sitting room's welcoming fire. Hannah loved seasons. She loved their faithfulness to come, stay a while and then to leave, making room for the next glories of nature to march onto the scene.

Chapter Thirty-Four

As CHRISTMAS APPROACHED in 1924, Kate, out of the blue, said to Hannah, "Let's do something special during the holiday season. Joseph is six years old. He would love to see the Christmas decorations in Leeville. We haven't been in such a long time. We'll all enjoy it. We can stay at the hotel."

Hannah's heart quickened. The current that ran through her was one of both anxiety and excitement. "That sounds great. It would be fun to take Joseph to see the decorations … but are you sure about going to Leeville? I guess I mean we just haven't been since Papa died."

Hannah thought of Rosie, too. She had never revealed anything Mr. Stokes had said that day at the barn because she hadn't wanted to add to her mother's burden and heartache. And as days passed into months and months into years, it seemed easier to let it stay buried in the recesses of her mind and not mention it at all. She had not even told Katherine.

The possibility of actually seeing Thomas caused Hannah's chest to tighten. She thought of him often. She still looked at and lingered over his picture from time to time. She couldn't help but wonder what he would be like, what they would say to each other, and—most of all—what it would be like for him to meet Joseph.

Kate, giddy with enthusiasm and seemingly unaware of Hannah's concerns, answered jovially. "It will be fine. We can do it. I'm sure we can," she said. "We will go one day, show Joseph the decorations and visit the shops the next day, and then return home the next. We'll only be away two nights. I'll ask Janie or June Ellen to tend the chickens, and everything else will take care of itself. I'm looking forward to going already." Kate clapped her hands a couple of times and smiled broadly. "Katherine and Stephen will be coming for Christmas, so let's plan to go the week before." Kate hummed continuously as she finished cooking supper with an energy she usually didn't have.

Hannah kept her thoughts to herself, though. It was good to see her mother so excited, and it was contagious. Hannah was not about to let her father, now in the grave a little over six years (or Thomas, who she had not heard from in that long) put a damper on their plans.

* * *

THE TOWN WAS MORE BEAUTIFUL than Hannah remembered it from their last Christmas visit. Wreaths with red bows hung on every door. Santa Claus, surrounded by stacks of packages wrapped in pretty paper and tied with Christmas ribbon, filled window displays.

A liveryman, doubling as one of the hotel servants, greeted Kate, Hannah and Joseph. "Afternoon, ma'am," he said to Kate and then nodded toward Hannah, "ma'am," before lifting Joseph from the wagon: "Yes sir, a mighty fine young man you are." He carried their trunk inside and made the necessary arrangements with Kate regarding the care of Pete and the wagon.

Evidence of Christmas was everywhere in the parlor. Many of the decorations were just as Hannah remembered from six years ago. The open Bible, pine cones, and bowls of fruit were in almost all the same places. There was one new addition, a beautiful Nativity scene on one of the side tables with fresh greenery tucked around the outer edges. The pieces were carved from wood and had been meticulously painted. The baby Jesus was wrapped in a white blanket. Mary wore blue, and Joseph wore a dark brown robe tied at the waist with a rope.

There were two shepherds, both dressed in tan-colored robes that were belted with dark green ties. The wise men, also beautifully painted, wore royal colors of red, purple, and gold. "Joseph, come see the little sheep," Hannah called to him. He ran over beside her and watched as she pointed out each one tucked down in the straw.

Joseph stood mesmerized by the nativity scene. His curiosity led him to check out every detail. Hannah, looking down at his thick black hair, was reminded of the night she had looked in Christmas store windows with his father. Her eyes became misty. She blotted the tears as inconspicuously as she could. "You're missing so much, Thomas, so much." The words crossed her heart but not her lips.

The decorations were much the same but, for Hannah, life was far from the same. Much water was under the bridge since her last time in this room. Six years before, she would never have imagined that she would be returning with her son and *without* her father.

Hannah took Joseph's hand as they entered the dining room for supper. Her heart beat faster and her breathing was rapid and shallow. She took a long, deep breath as she got to the door. Then she scanned the room—Thomas was not there.

She didn't see Rosie either, but she knew the girl might be in the kitchen. She wanted to greet Rosie warmly. They both, no doubt, vividly remembered Mr. Stokes's announcement to Hannah on the afternoon after her father's funeral. With his cutting words, Mr. Stokes had betrayed his deceased friend, as well as Rosie's grandmother.

Hannah's silence after the incident with Mr. Stokes was part of the reason she was nervous about seeing Rosie. She had lived with a nagging feeling that she should have reached out to her years before. As it turned out, Rosie was not there (or if she was, she didn't serve in the dining room that night).

Supper proved to be a special event. The food was delicious, the atmosphere delightful, and Joseph very much liked the lazy Susan. He tried to keep it turning throughout most of the meal. The other guests were patient with him and even asked him to turn the table for them. He was the star of the evening, and he relished every minute.

WHEN HANNAH WOKE the following morning, her thoughts went immediately to Rosie. She wanted to see her. After she and Joseph dressed, they left for an early morning walk. Hannah began to do what she felt she must, and that was to find Rosie and talk to her.

Hannah and Joseph began skipping down the stairs, hand in hand. "I would like to ask about someone in the kitchen. Let's go by there before we go outside," Hannah said to Joseph, who had started jumping flat-footed down one step at the time.

"Okay," he said happily. Stopping by the kitchen was as good a plan as any, he thought. Turning the tabletops the night before had been fun, and he hoped to be turning them again soon at breakfast.

Hannah held Joseph's hand as she led the way through the dining room and into the main kitchen. There was a bustle of activity. Two colored women were making biscuits, frying ham, and cooking grits. Eggs sizzled in a big black iron skillet coated with bacon grease, and the baking cinnamon rolls filled the air with a most inviting aroma. The women didn't notice Hannah and Joseph at first and were startled when she spoke.

"Good morning," Hannah said softly. She knew she was not where they expected her to be.

Joseph tugged Hannah's hand and whispered up at her, "Can I have one of those?" He pointed at the cinnamon rolls.

Hannah was explaining that it wasn't quite time to eat when one of the cooks handed Joseph one of the rolls. "Best right now while they're hot. We don't always have pretty little boys here, so you can have anything you want. That is, if ya mama says it's okay."

"What are you going to say?" Hannah said to Joseph.

"Thank you, ma'am," he said while licking icing from the top of the roll.

The woman turned her attention back to Hannah. "Yessum, good morning. Everything will be ready soon. We'll be ringing the bell."

Hannah, realizing she had made them a bit uncomfortable by suddenly appearing in their space, quickly answered, "Oh, I'm sorry to be interrupting your work. I know you are busy. I was just wondering if a girl named Rosie still works here. I met her when we were here several years ago. I wanted to ask if you might know her, and if you can tell me if she still works here."

"Oh, yessum, Rosie's still here. She's out back with Twila getting a little more stove wood."

"Twila?"

"Yes, Twila, her little girl." The woman paused and tightened her eyes, causing her forehead to wrinkle. "Why you're Mr. McMolison's daughter. I remember when you were here last time. Heard 'bout your papa. I know it's been a while, but I'm real sorry for your loss."

"Thank you. You said Rosie is out back?"

"Go on out there. You'll find her. Sometime it takes a while with Twila helping."

Hannah eased out the back door, holding tightly to Joseph's hand. The grip was more for her own security than for Joseph's. He was six years old and perfectly capable of walking alone. There was nothing around to cause him harm. She wasn't as sure about herself. She needed his steady little hand

Hannah could see Rosie over by a pile of stove wood. A little girl, probably about four or five, stood beside her. The little girl had her arms outstretched in order to hold the wood that was being gently loaded onto them. Her skin was even lighter than Rosie's. From Hannah's distance, the little girl could easily have been mistaken for a white child. The two made a pleasant scene. They were singing, "… do Lord, oh do Lord, oh do remember me … way beyond the blue." They neither heard nor saw Hannah and Joseph approaching.

"Hello Rosie," Hannah said when she and Joseph got close.

The singing stopped as both pairs of eyes turned to look at them. "Hello," Rosie replied cautiously.

"You must be Twila," Hannah said. "You certainly are pretty."

"Thank you," the girl said shyly.

"Miss Hannah, this is Twila, my daughter," Rosie said, looking first at Hannah and then to Twila. The introduction was polite and gracious, sounding almost as if she had recently completed a session with Mrs. Russell Parsons, the etiquette expert of 1890. Kate had given Hannah newspaper articles on the proper way to eat, dress, write, walk, and talk, all written by Mrs. Parsons. Rosie sounded as if she had been given the same articles.

"It's nice to meet you, Twila. This is my son, Joseph. He is six years old. How old are you?"

"I'm five, almost. My birthday is March thirty-first."

"That's wonderful. I heard you and your mother singing. It sounded lovely. Do you like to sing?"

"Yes, ma'am. I want to sing for people."

Rosie smiled at Twila and added, "Miss Tildy teaches us new songs, and we have a radio, so we listen and sing along. Twila knows all the words to 'Ida! Sweet as Apple Cider' and 'Down By the Old Mill Stream.' We have a good time."

Twila looked up at her mother. "Tell her about the ragtime song," she said timidly.

"Miss Tildy gave us an article about a man named Irving Berlin and told us to listen for his songs. She thought he would be famous one day," Rosie said. "We've heard 'Alexander's Ragtime Band,' and Twila really likes it. She says she is going to play or sing on the radio someday."

"That sounds exciting, Twila. I would like to come hear you sing." Hannah looked back to Rosie. "How's your grandmother?"

Rosie dropped her eyes to the ground. "She passed away. It's been almost a year ago. One day she said her arms were kind of tingly and then within the next hour, she couldn't move or swallow or speak. She died three days later without ever waking up." Tears filled Rosie's lower lids. Twila moved close to her mother and put her arms around her legs.

"Oh, Rosie, I'm so sorry." Hannah's impulse was to hug her, but she didn't. She wondered to herself what was wrong with hugging someone who was a different color, especially if she was your half-sister. She had hugged (and been hugged by) Janie and June Ellen lots of times. She thought it made no sense to feel the way she did. "I can't even reach out and touch Rosie," she thought. "Why is this so hard?"

"Twila and I must get the wood inside. They will be wondering what has happened to us," Rosie said after a moment.

"Could we visit sometime later today, perhaps between dinner and supper? I expect Joseph will be ready for a short rest with my mother sometime between two and three o'clock. Would you have time then?" Hannah wasn't sure what she wanted from a conversation, but she was sure she wanted to talk.

"Sure, I can do that. Twila has a cot in the back hall, and we usually read for a little while middle of the afternoon. She has to get up early to come to work with me, so she is ready for a nap by that time. I will meet you on the back porch."

Hannah imagined that sitting beside the fire on that December day would be far more inviting, but as soon as she thought it, she realized sitting beside the fire in the festive hotel parlor was not an option for Rosie. "I will see you then," Hannah said, and they all went inside.

Hannah and Joseph met Kate, and together they entered the dining room to enjoy a wonderful breakfast. Rosie deposited the wood in the wood box, washed her hands and prepared to serve the guests. Twila, her rag doll in tow, went to the space between the wood stove and the wall. The space, warm and cozy, was a perfect place to play on cold days and ideal for her make-believe world. It was the corner where Rosie had played when she was a child, and the same corner where her own mother had played before her.

Chapter Thirty-Five

"You want to know about me, don't you?" Rosie said, speaking first as they sat together on the back steps.

"Yes, I suppose I do, and maybe I don't. The truth is I really don't know. I don't want to do anything to hurt my mother." Hannah looked down at her hands, which were palms together and pressing her skirt between her knees.

"I wouldn't want to hurt your mother either. I didn't know what you would do after Mr. Stokes said what he did the day of your father's funeral. I was as surprised as you were. My grandmother would never have wanted to make what was already a difficult day for you even more difficult." Rosie gazed out across the yard. "I can't tell you truthfully that I'm sorry he said what he did, because part of me is glad. I wanted to know the truth, and I think maybe it's good that you know the truth. But neither of us should have learned like that."

"It's okay, at least now it is." Hannah looked over at Rosie, whose eyes were still fixed on the back side of the yard. "It was hard to hear at the time given the circumstances, but Mr. Stokes was angry with me. I guess he still is. He just couldn't help himself, I suppose."

Rosie turned to face Hannah. "You're right. He was *furious*. He and your father always met at the hotel. They never paid much attention to my being in the room, so I overheard a lot, at least enough to know what was happening. I know it was a bad time for you."

Hannah steeled herself and asked, "Can you tell me about my father and your mother?"

"Not very much." Rosie shook her head slightly. "Everything was a mystery to me growing up. I never had real answers as to who my father was. There were other colored children in similar circumstances, so it didn't seem much out of the ordinary. The difference for me was that my mother died when I was born. My grandmother raised me. She buried her daughter and took on another."

"How did you come to know my father?" Hannah asked. "How can you be sure about him?"

"I didn't know anything more than who he was from his being at the hotel often. I never knew anything else except that he came by our house from time to time. He always brought my grandmother an envelope. I suspected it was money, but I didn't know for sure until the day of the funeral. Occasionally, he brought something—like a book or candy—for me. When I asked why he came, my grandmother always answered, 'Don't be so inquisitive. He is just a nice man.'"

"Did you ever ask who your father was?"

"Yes, but she always answered, 'Child, your heavenly father is the one that is important, and He will always take care of you. Don't worry so much about one on this earth.'"

"So, when did you know more?" Hannah said, wanting to learn as much as she could without making a pest of herself.

"Well ..."

"Please continue, Rosie."

"When we got home after your father's funeral, I begged my grandmother to tell me what Mr. Stokes meant when he called us *sisters*," Rosie said softly, as if someone might hear. She wrapped the folds of her skirt around her knees, hugged them with both arms, and again looked away from Hannah and toward the back of the yard.

"She told me it was true," Rosie said at length. "But she had kept the secret to protect my mother and Mr. McMolison." She sighed deeply. "It's strange. He's still Mr. McMolison to me. I can't think of him as my father. My grandmother told me a lot that night after we got home, but then it was after Twila was born that she was willing to tell me more. I really cared about Twila's father. He was from up north somewhere, came here and spent a summer visiting family. He talked all about traveling and music and books. It was exciting. My time with him was wonderful. We were together for a few hours every day for five weeks. Then he was gone, headed back to where he came from. I never heard from him again. Twila was born eight months later."

"Did you try to reach him?" Hannah asked, recognizing all too clearly the familiar pain and heartache.

"No, I really didn't know how. And it wouldn't have been a good thing. I was foolish, and it hurt my grandmother more than I could have imagined. She had hoped I would eventually leave Greene County. She wanted me to have opportunities she didn't. And in one summer, I let myself and her down in every possible way," Rosie said, practically whispering now. She looked into her lap and fidgeted with the fabric of her skirt. "Twila will be different. She is learning to read, and she already sings like a mockingbird. I will get her to a stage one day."

Hannah sensed Rosie didn't want to talk anymore. She couldn't help but wonder, though, if Twila's father was white. She suddenly felt sure he was, but Rosie didn't volunteer that information and it didn't seem right to ask.

"So when Twila was born, you asked again about your own father?"

"Yes. I wanted to know more. You know I wanted to know if I was born out of love. I know what I'm saying probably doesn't make sense to you, but I wanted to know for sure if my mother was loved or just, you know … convenient. I pleaded with her, and she finally told me either all she knew or all she chose to tell."

Hannah waited while Rosie paused. Rosie clearly seemed to need a moment to collect her thoughts. "Please go on," Hannah said after a long moment.

"Well, my mother worked at the hotel. She had been there since she was a little girl, just like I have. She was very beautiful, and apparently your father was attracted to her. You know he came to the hotel often, and she often joined him in his room after she got off work. I'm sorry."

Rosie, looking into the distance, spoke so quietly Hannah strained to hear the words. Then, turning to face Hannah, she added, "I know this is not easy to hear. It's not easy to talk about. They're both dead, and I'm talking about them this way."

"It's okay," Hannah said as compassionately as she could.

Rosie again looked away from Hannah and out across the back lawn. Almost as if talking to herself, she said, "You see, I was born out of love. That matters to me. Even though he never acknowledged me, he helped take care of me. He cared enough about my mother to do right by me, and he didn't have to. He did it because he cared. He cared about me."

Hannah had trouble grasping what Rosie meant by saying *cared about me*. She wondered how Rosie could feel that way when their father had basically ignored her. Hannah believed it was probably true that he gave money to Rosie's grandmother, and maybe it was also true that he cared about her mother. It was obvious to Hannah that Rosie's understanding of the relationship between her mother and their father meant a lot to her. There was no reason to suggest it was anything other than what she thought.

Hannah mulled all this over and recognized a common thread between the two of them. Bill McMolison had provided things for both, but had given little of himself to either. "I was acknowledged to make an impression," she thought, "and Rosie was kept secret to preserve an impression."

"Thank you for meeting me, and thank you for being discreet about my father," Hannah said to Rosie. "I have not told my mother or my sister about you, and I would like to keep it just between us, at least for the time being."

"I have never talked to anyone about it except my grandmother, and I had not planned to until you asked."

"I know," Hannah responded. She was getting chilly and felt as if her brain was being overloaded, but she didn't want the conversation to end. The two continued to sit on the cold back steps. Hoping for more answers she asked, "What about Mr. Stokes? Do you think he has ever said anything to anybody else?"

"The two of them, your father and Mr. Stokes, were best friends. I don't think he would do anything to cast ill on your father, especially after your father's death. I know he said what he did to us that day after the funeral, but I really don't think he would have spread it in the community. Anyway, he was busy getting his son far away."

Hannah's heart rose to her throat the way it might if she'd just been thrown from the barn loft, but she managed to get her next question out. "Do you know anything about Thomas? Do you know where he is, or what he's doing now?"

Rosie winced. "Oh, I'm so sorry I mentioned him, Hannah," She looked at Hannah and spoke even more softly than she had been. "Nothing I know will make you feel better. You still love him, don't you?"

"Tell me please," Hannah insisted. Her chest felt tight and her heart raced.

"After your baby was born, he wanted to go see you. I heard him telling his father—almost pleading with him—but Mr. Stokes wouldn't listen. He wanted him to get back to school. Then a year or two later, he went to study to be a doctor. I think it was Atlanta or someplace like that—pretty sure it was Atlanta he sent him to school."

"Does he have a family? I mean ..." Hannah hesitated before continuing. "Do you know if he is married?" She was asking for information she both wanted but didn't want, all at the same time.

"I think so." Rosie's soft answer dashed any lingering hope Hannah's heart had been guarding. "He came to the hotel about a year ago. He came with his mother and father and another woman and a little boy, three or four years old. I heard them introduced as his wife and son. That's really all I know. Except I did hear Mr. Stokes a while back telling some other people that his son would soon be moving to Leeville. They may already be here. I don't know. I'm sorry, Hannah," Rosie added kindly.

They parted that December afternoon with a mere touching. Hannah reached over to cover Rosie's hands with her own and squeezed them ever so slightly. "Thank you for sharing with me," she said. "I will always remember you, and I'd like to see you when we're back in

Leeville." Hannah didn't know what else to say. She rose to her feet, walked around the side of the hotel and up the steps, where she disappeared through the wreath-clad front door. Rosie said nothing. After sitting in silence perhaps another minute, she, too, rose to her feet and disappeared into the hotel through a different door, the one marked "colored entrance." Inside, the reality of their differences once again took its place. Rosie assumed her job to serve, and Hannah joined her family to be served.

AS HANNAH WAITED for her mother and Joseph to get ready for supper, she sat looking out one of the windows of their room. The many thoughts that crowded her mind piled one on top of the next. She thought of Joseph, Twila, and Thomas's child—three children with an absolute connection but with whom contact was unacceptable. "Joseph has a half first cousin. I guess she is a half first cousin since her mother is my half-sister," Hannah reasoned, "and he has a half-brother, but since Joseph is to remain forever unknown to them, he has no siblings and no cousins." The realization made her sad. Hannah continued to grapple with all Rosie had said. "Even if I wanted to acknowledge Rosie and Twila, how could I?" she thought. "My mother has suffered enough. I could never let her know about them. It would be hard enough if they were white, but for her to learn that her husband had a colored daughter would be worse."

Without realizing it, Hannah had slumped down in the chair and rested her head on the tall cushioned back. With her eyes closed, she thought back on the difficult days and weeks after Joseph was born. Having Joseph without having a husband was hard, especially at first. Most people never said anything, but she knew they had questions, the biggest one being *who is the baby's father*? She knew that no one from Leaf Creek could recall ever seeing her with a boy. So far as they knew, Bill McMolison had never let her date. She remembered how glad she was when things had settled down. Although at the time everyone was curious, no one wanted to be party to rumors or innuendo about anyone in the McMolison family. Every person that lived in and around Leaf Creek was thankful for the leadership Mr.

McMolison had given the community before he died. They respected the man they had thought him to be, respected him far too much to pry into his family's private affairs.

Hannah opened her eyes and looked at the tongue and groove ceiling. The cream-colored paint was beginning to chip in the space just above her head. "Oh me," she sighed deeply. "I don't know what to do." No one would ever stop talking if they learned about her father's colored daughter. The people's high regard for him would plummet, and Mother would be hurt even more than she already has been. He is dead and gone; what purpose would it serve to talk about it now?" Thinking of the whole situation caused a lump to form in her throat. "It's just too awful to think about." Not recognizing Rosie made Hannah feel guilty, but she just couldn't. She couldn't tell her mother anything that would cause her to hurt all over again.

"Hannah," we're ready," Kate said.

"Yay! Come on, Mama, let's go," Joseph added excitedly. He was anxious to turn the lazy Susan again.

Out of necessity Hannah had become adept at managing her mind, so she shifted gears, stood, offered her hand to Joseph and said, "I'm ready. Let's go." They pranced from the room with their hands joined and their arms swinging back and forth like a clock's pendulum happily ticking in a new day.

ONCE SEATED, Joseph began to manage the lazy Susan as he had the evening before. In the midst of cautioning him to wait for the other guests, Hannah's greatest fear came true. Coming from behind her she heard the voice she had so longed to hear. Hannah took a deep breath, but her heart felt as if it would beat right out of her chest. She listened as greetings were exchanged between Thomas and people at the other two tables. Then:

"Mr. Thomas, is the first table going to be okay? It's the only one with three empty chairs right now." Hannah overheard the server's question and strained to hear his response. She didn't hear an answer but heard the server continue. "Yes sir. I'll get your tea."

She, Joseph and Kate were seated at the first table. Her heart raced.

She waited for the inevitable. As she tried to calm her breathing, the three available chairs filled. They were directly across from her. She looked up and into the blue eyes she had first met in that very room. They were beautiful, as beautiful as in her dreams and as beautiful as she remembered. But with him was a lady … a well-dressed, pretty woman with blond hair. Between them was a little boy, also with blond hair. "His family?" she thought. "Is that his family?" The tension in Hannah's chest was making it difficult for her to breathe.

Thomas settled the little boy into a chair. He sat down and pulled his own chair up to the table. He then began to glance around and speak to others. He met Hannah's gaze. His stare froze for several seconds before being drawn to the little boy beside her. She knew he was seeing a younger image of himself. He was seeing his own black hair, his own blue eyes. He was seeing what Hannah herself always saw. He dropped his fork. Was it possible his heart was at a pace matching her own?

"Thomas. *Thomas*. What's wrong? I asked you to get a roll for me. Didn't you hear me?" the blond asked, wrinkling her brow. "What's wrong? Are you okay?"

"I'm sorry. I guess I didn't hear you." He handed a roll to her and to the little boy between them, never taking his eyes off Hannah and Joseph.

"Thank you, Papa," the little boy said as he pulled the roll apart and began to eat.

Hearing the exchange, hearing *papa,* cut through every cell of Hannah's heart. Kate, having finished her conversation with another guest, suddenly became aware of Thomas Stokes. "Hello, Thomas."

"Hello, Mrs. McMolison," he managed to answer.

Aware that Hannah was not eating—that she had her fingers laced together in a tight fist—Kate continued her attempt at polite conversation. "How are your parents?"

"Fine. They're fine. Thank you for asking." Thomas nodded slightly toward Kate, but immediately focused again on Joseph and Hannah.

Hannah felt she had to flee. She couldn't watch the family seated across the table. "Mother, will you stay with Joseph until he finishes?

I think I would like to go on back to the room," Hannah whispered.

"Yes, that's fine. I'll bring something in case you feel hungry later."

Hannah eased her chair from the table and walked quickly toward the parlor.

"Excuse me. I'll be right back," Thomas said to his wife as he pushed his chair from the table. He, too, walked toward the parlor.

Hannah had just started to climb the stairs when she heard him call her name. "Hannah, wait. Can we talk just a minute?"

Hannah had hungered to hear her name in that voice. She had waited for so long. Now she stopped, then slowly turned and faced the man she had fallen in love with. He walked toward her. Her heart pounded, her mouth dry.

"Hannah, I wanted to see you," Thomas said. "I wanted to come. I'm so sorry."

"I'm sorry too," Hannah said softly. "Why didn't you? You said you would."

"I know. Please forgive me. You know my father would have cut me off. I wanted to go to school, but ..."

"And you did. You did what *you* wanted." Hannah's eyes narrowed. She gazed directly into his eyes and set her jaw as she spoke. "I hurt, Thomas. I waited because I believed in you. I even thought you cared."

"I did," he said haltingly. "I do."

"Thomas, don't." Her voice stayed calm and even. "Look where we are. I'm where I was when you left me. The only difference is that I now have a beautiful son—*your* son. The question is, where are you? Is that your wife with you?"

Thomas dropped his eyes from Hannah to the floor. "Yes, I met her in Atlanta. Her family is important there." Thomas paused, then added, "Father was pleased. It seemed right at the time."

"Oh, Thomas," Hannah said, really feeling the familiar pain now. "Money, power, and appearances drove your father and mine. But I thought you were different. I really did. I believed you."

Thomas gazed into space beside Hannah and back toward the floor. "I know it doesn't help for me to say I'm sorry, that I wish I had done things differently, but I do, Hannah, with all my heart." Thomas paused. Hannah said nothing. There were a few seconds of silence. Thomas lifted his eyes to meet hers. "Please tell me about you and your son. Are you married?"

"*Our* son," Hannah said firmly. "His name is Joseph. No, I'm not married."

"Joseph. I like his name. It's hard to see him because he looks just like me."

"He does and I'm glad. He's handsome and a very special young boy. You would be proud of him. He's a joy. I'm sorry you don't know him. You're missing out."

"I'm sorry I didn't do things differently. I know I keep saying the same thing, but I don't know what else to say. I hope you believe me. You're the most special girl I have ever known, and I messed up. I'll never forget you."

"You did mess up. I *loved* you," she said. "I wanted to be a family with you. I waited because you said you would come." Hannah's hands were clasped together in front of her. Thomas reached out and covered them with his. For a few fleeting seconds she saw and felt the longing in his eyes. There was no smile, only an expression of earnest appeal. Then Hannah, suddenly needing to be alone, withdrew her hands and said, "You made your choices." She turned, walked up the steps, and into her room.

Hannah eased the door closed and leaned back against it. His closeness and touch had sparked a familiar flutter in her chest. In that moment she wanted to hate him, to blot him from her mind forever. Instead the familiar desire for him was rekindled. She still ached for him. There was a hard truth that punctured her heart—he was married. She had known from having spoken to Rosie, but seeing Thomas with his family was like salt being poured into her wound. The grains were rubbing unmercifully against the rawness.

THOMAS WATCHED Hannah until she disappeared from his sight. "If only I could turn back time. I'd do things differently no matter the risk," he thought. He turned away from the foot of the stairs and returned to the dining room. He sat down, one son beside him and one son across the table from him. He had no appetite for the food before him.

***

ONCE BACK IN LEAF CREEK Kate and Hannah began plans for Christmas and for Stephen and Katherine's visit. Sometimes thinking of Samuel and Bill and her parents caused Kate twinges of sadness, but six years had passed since the most recent death, and for the first time joy and fun were overriding any hint of melancholy. The holiday season seemed especially happy. Everyone had a light heart and a festive spirit. Stephen and Katherine stayed a full five days, and while the women cooked and visited, Stephen gave his undivided attention to Joseph.

Katherine and Stephen did not have children of their own, though they wished for them desperately. When the subject arose during past visits, Katherine always bravely said, "God will give me a child when He is ready." There was really never anything else to be said.

Singing and laughter filled the house. Hannah participated fully, but her heart was full of Thomas, and her mind often replayed snippets of her conversation and time sitting on the hotel steps with Rosie. Her position with Thomas seemed clear (though not the one she desired and dreamed of), but what about Rosie? What had she accomplished in talking to her? She mulled the question over and over. There was no answer to her pondering questions, and yet the visit had seemed right. She felt a deeper respect and affection for her half-sister and a relief that she had finally spoken to her.

The exchange had been incredibly exhausting for both women and, for Hannah, even rethinking it a week later drained her emotionally. Harboring such weighty facts deep within her soul and being unable to speak of them was burdensome. She kept wishing there was something she could do.

Then, several weeks after they returned from their December trip, Hannah approached her mother with an idea. Kate sat with her legs extended, bare feet toward the fire. She was holding a book but wasn't reading. Kate didn't look up when Hannah entered the room. Her attention was focused toward the dancing flames.

Hannah pulled a second chair up close to the fire. She, too, removed her shoes and stuck her feet out to enjoy the heat. "I've been wondering," she began. "You know Rosie, the girl at the hotel? Well, she told me her grandmother died, so she lives alone now with her own little girl. I keep thinking that I would like to do something for her. I was thinking about it for next Christmas, maybe, but I just remembered that her little girl's birthday is in March. Sending a birthday present might be fun. Would you mind?"

"Not at all. It is a lovely idea. We can send something for her birthday and then we'll think about Christmas, too. We can't do a lot, but doing *something* will be nice and will be a good lesson for Joseph."

A book, *The Rhythms of Childhood*, was mailed in March with happy birthday greetings from the McMolisons in Leaf Creek. In April they received a note with THANK YOU written in big block print. It was signed TWILA in the same penciled letters. Written at the bottom in neat cursive was a note of thanks from Rosie.

THE FOLLOWING CHRISTMAS a new tradition was started, and each year Joseph helped Hannah with the special Christmas box. Three Christmas packages had now made their way to the hotel in Leeville, each one addressed to Rosie and Twila. The packages usually contained an assortment of gifts. There was always a book for Twila and sometimes one for Rosie. Something pretty to wear in their hair was always included as well. The first year it had been hair ribbons, with barrettes and combs in other years. Joseph chose the hard candy, wrapped it separately, and tagged it as if it came just from him. Kate always made something sweet-smelling, most times a sachet for Rosie. Hannah did her best to have an extra dollar or two to stick inside the package. In the most recent package she had enough money to put a five-dollar bill in a pair of socks that she tucked under a pencil and tablet Joseph had added.

Preparing the Christmas box became the highlight of the season. Hannah, Kate, and Joseph often began to plan for it long before the holiday arrived. As Joseph got older, his interests changed, but he never lost interest in helping prepare that one special gift. Then after Christmas they all three anxiously awaited the note that always came.

Dear Mrs. McMolison and family,

Twila and I received the Christmas box you sent. Thank you very much for always thinking of us at this special time of year.

We love everything you sent, especially the books. Miss Tildy at the hotel has always shared hers with us, but it's especially thrilling to own some ourselves. And the ribbons are beautiful. Twila feels so pretty wearing them.

The hotel looked really beautiful at Christmastime. I wish you could have seen it.

Twila and I hope you had a very Merry Christmas, and we wish you a Happy New Year.

Again, I thank you for your kindness to us.

Sincerely,
Rosie and Twila

The notes from Rosie were well-written. Miss Tildy had encouraged and taught her since she was a little girl; Rosie had been attentive and eager to learn. The letter changed a bit from year to year, mostly regarding the contents of the package. Hannah was always disappointed that she never included news about the people or happenings in Leeville; she had not forgotten her lost love and would have loved to hear anything about his life. She especially wondered whether or not Thomas ever thought of her, and of the son he had seen only once. Joseph was getting old enough to begin wondering why he didn't have a father. He had never pressed her, but Hannah knew the day would come when he would. She prayed for wisdom when answering him. She would be truthful. She would not withhold from Joseph what he had a right to know.

Chapter Thirty-Six

THE WIND GENTLY WHIPPED the ribbons of her butter-yellow hat. The friendly breeze wafted ever so courteously from the south and stroked Hannah's face like a soothing balm as it parted and moved on past her. She felt sensations of warm comfort that not only danced on her face but also filled her entire being. Her heart was light as she walked past the general hardware store and toward the Mercantile. She needed fabric. She had designed a pattern for pencil and ruler holders and planned to make one for each child in school.

Joseph, now nine, would be ending his third year soon. He loved learning to read. Hannah had encouraged him by starting 'Joseph's Library.' She promised him they would add a book every two or three months. Arithmetic was also "pretty fun," he said, but trying to write like the teacher instructed was much too time-consuming. Hannah continued the walk through town and smiled to herself as she thought about her little son and all his special attributes. He was intelligent, charming, and thoughtful. His sense of humor often provided a laugh for Kate and Hannah as well as his teacher and friends.

HANNAH'S FELICITOUSNESS had sprouted and grown from events that occurred a year before. One Sunday Hannah and her mother were sitting in church with Joseph between them. The preacher prayed, and then everybody sang "Amazing Grace." The piano, as always, had that kind of tin-like, strident sound. It was tuned occasionally, but the notes were never mellow and solid. Even with the instrument's shortcomings, voices always rang out with enthusiasm. *"Amazing grace, how sweet the sound,"* bounced from every rafter in the church. After singing came the announcements from the preacher.

"… Dinner on the Ground is planned for next Sunday after the morning service. We will have a second service at two in the afternoon. All you ladies are encouraged to bring lots of good food for this special time of fellowship together. You always do. We look forward to the dishes you prepare. Don't forget that plans are getting underway for children's catechism and choir school to be held for one week during the summer. If you can possibly help with this program, let me know. And now, I want to introduce a newcomer to our community. He is visiting us in worship today, and we certainly hope he will come again. His name is Lex Reeves. Lex, please stand so everyone can see who you are. Lex moved to Leaf Creek last week from up in Hattiesburg. He is the new president over at the bank. I know all of you will want to welcome Mr. Reeves after the service."

"The Grace of our Lord Jesus Christ be with you. Amen," the preacher concluded, pronouncing the benediction.

Kate always encouraged Hannah to get out more, so as they rode home after church, Kate asked her if she'd met the new bank president. "He seemed really nice. Didn't you think?"

"Yes, I guess. I didn't pay much attention," Hannah answered. "I shook his hand and spoke to him. At least he'll look good sitting behind the desk, better than the last."

"Hannah," Kate said sharply. "That was not nice, and you've just left church."

Joseph snickered.

"I'm sorry," Hannah said through a smothered laugh. "I just meant he was nice-looking enough." Then her voice took on a bit of an edge. "But if you're thinking he's eligible and I should pay more attention, don't."

EVEN THOUGH HANNAH was still young, she spent almost no time dwelling on men and romance. It was as if she had built a protective wall that guarded her from any such potential relationships. She had no desire to ever care about a man again. She had given her heart, soul, and whole being once before. Except for the wonderful joy of having Joseph in her life, that giving had caused nothing but heartache for her and for her family. She convinced herself that the love she had felt could only come once in a lifetime. For her, it had come and gone. She would not allow herself to be vulnerable to such pain ever again.

Mr. Reeves began to settle into Leaf Creek and small town life. He was a handsome man and, in fact, did look distinguished behind his desk at the bank. His appearance was not something he ever thought much about, but the tellers were delighted to have a good-looking man in their midst. The number of new accounts increased rapidly as every single woman in and near Leaf Creek suddenly had a little money to save. The bank reaped the benefits, and the women were all charmed by his attention.

Lex found a room at Miss Massey's Boarding House. Included was a hot supper every night and breakfast on weekends. Biscuits with gravy, ham, and eggs were served on Saturday mornings and pancakes with sausage on Sunday mornings. Boarders were welcome to use the kitchen on weekday mornings but had to purchase what they cooked and were required to leave the kitchen cleaner than they found it.

Mr. Reeves found his living situation quite pleasant. The occupant of Mrs. Massey's other room was a teacher named Joe Gordan who was in his second year of teaching at Leaf Creek School. He was quiet, and for all Mr. Reeves could discern, was an agreeable sort of person. Their respective jobs took them in opposite directions during the day, but in the evenings they often sat together on the front porch while waiting for supper. Joe's habit was to retire to his room to read or grade papers after eating, but Lex most often returned to the porch to enjoy either a chorus of crickets or the quietness of a hushed still night. In the tranquil surroundings, he felt far removed from the profits, the losses, the loans and the hardship stories that were ever present in the banking world.

The following Sunday—the one with dinner on the ground, book-ended by sermons—found Lex back at Leaf Creek Presbyterian. He sat in the same spot he had the Sunday before. Presbyterians often sat in the same place Sunday after Sunday, as if changing pews would result in grave turmoil to their eternal soul. Truth was, it could cause a scare if an unsuspecting newcomer sat in one of the histori-cally staked-out pews. After only two Sundays, though, the new bank officer had claimed his space and had been wise in his choosing. He'd unknowingly avoided all pews (and portions of pews) that had for years—or in some instances generations—been claimed by others. Most folks would not ask a newcomer to move, but some would … and had. When a guest sat in the wrong place, witnesses held their breath, waited in anticipation, and prayed the guilty party would be spared embarrassing treatment. Most times the inner frustration was hidden behind a welcoming smile and a gracious greeting: "It's *so* nice to have you worship with us today. *Do* hope you will come again." Unspoken, of course, was, "But don't sit in my pew next time." On occasion, however, a newcomer having to endure a raised eyebrow or huffy shoulder shrug was inevitable.

Hannah, her mother, and Joseph were in their usual spot, about two thirds of the way down the right side next to the aisle. Hannah had particular difficulty concentrating. Mrs. Pearson, who was sitting immediately in front of her, wore a new and slightly oversized hat. Mrs. Pearson's hats were fun to see because they were never plain. There were flowers, ribbons, feathers, pins, bows, or a combination of all. They were invariably colorful and always matched her dress. Hannah especially admired her hats with net streamers; she sometimes tied the streamers beneath her chin while at other times allowed them to flow behind.

Her hat that day was made of carnation pink felt. Deep pink, rose and ruby-red feathers extended forward and back from a large cluster of carnation pink peonies on the right side of the crown. Loops of matching pink ribbon were tucked in the midst of the blooms, and streamers fell gracefully around the green stems and leaves. Mrs. Pearson was always as elegant and delightful as her hats, and on that morning one of the resident church flies found her elegance to its liking. It would walk slowly up a loop of ribbon, fly quickly to another loop, and then hurriedly cross a petal before disappearing momentarily down between the flowers and bows. For Hannah, the morning sermon was lost somewhere in the hills and valleys of adornment as the fly traversed every inch of the ribbon road. It would flit off occasionally and come to rest on another person's shoulder or the back of a pew, but after taking only a few steps, it always returned to the festive landscape sitting atop Mrs. Pearson's head. Suddenly, the organist began to pump the pedals and the postlude began to ring out. Hannah had completely missed the sermon.

"HANNAH," KATE BEGAN, "go on and begin getting the food from the wagon. I will be there in a minute." The ladies' accommodations were in a two-seater located a short distance into the woods behind the church.

"Yes ma'am," Hannah responded. She and Joseph headed out to begin helping unload the food that would soon fill the long wooden tables.

"May I carry your basket?" came a male voice from behind. Hannah turned and saw the visitor who had been introduced last week.

"Yes, thank you," she said.

"My name is Lex Reeves."

"Hello, I'm Hannah, and this is my son, Joseph. I remember meeting you last week. Glad you were able to visit our church again."

"A friend at my church in Hattiesburg told me about this church and suggested I would like it. So far I have. I really liked the sermon this morning."

Hannah couldn't continue with that line of conversation, since she knew far more about the morning's activities of a fly than she did the sermon. "Here, let me spread the cloth and then you can put the basket down," she said instead. She took the folded tablecloth from the top of the basket, unfolded it, and spread it next to the cloth that Amy

Mack was just smoothing the wrinkles out of. The table would soon be covered with the usual variety of cloths and colors. The edges were most often hanging at different levels, but the irregularity made no difference to anyone and added to the charm. Dinner on the ground was about food and friends. There was a great supply of both.

Hannah's mother walked up just as Lex Reeves put the basket on the table. "Hello, Mr. Reeves. So glad to have you back with us today. How are you liking Leaf Creek so far?"

"Fine, ma'am. I like it a lot. It's a little different from Hattiesburg, but everyone has been really nice. Is there anything else I can do to help? If not, I am going to step over here out of the way."

"No, we're fine, but thank you. We'll be ready to eat soon," Hannah answered as he walked over to where a group of men were standing together. Hannah watched as he shook their hands and joined in the conversation.

"Nice man," she thought, as she helped get the food on the table.

As soon as he walked away, Amy Mack came shoulder to shoulder with Hannah. She tipped her head and said discreetly, "He's handsome and seems really nice. You need to think about him." Amy Mack, one of the schoolteachers, was happily married with two older children and was always busying herself with anyone who wasn't.

"Amy Mack, shhhh. Please be quiet. Don't call attention." It seemed to Hannah that Amy Mack had spoken loudly enough for the entire world to hear. She bumped Amy with her whole right side and said under her breath, "My family is fine just as it is. Mother, Joseph, and I are quite happy. I don't need anything or anybody to stir the pot."

"You're hopeless," Amy replied with a smile, bumping her back.

"Maybe so," Hannah responded. She had given little thought to the newcomer. He was polite and had helped her carry their lunch, a gesture most any of the men would have made. That was it.

Chapter Thirty-Seven

*I*T WAS EARLY FALL, not long after Lex Reeves arrived in Leaf Creek and began attending church, that Amy Mack invited him to speak to her class at school. She was always coming up with something extra for her class. Having Mr. Reeves tell a little about the bank would show the children they needed arithmetic for more than counting egg or bean money.

Lex enjoyed being at the school. He spent extra time afterwards with Joseph and a couple of the other children who showed a special interest in learning how money got bigger in the bank. They were fascinated by the interest rate that Mr. Reeves told them about. He invited them to come by the bank, told them about jars of stick candy, and offered to give them a piece when they came.

Joseph didn't forget the offer. He loved the brightly-colored sticks of candy in the glass jars at the Mercantile. His mother always bought a piece for him when they were shopping, but Mr. Reeves said he would give him a piece for free. Every day when he left school, he turned left and walked home, but on that day he really wanted to go by the bank even though it was in the opposite direction. Joseph reasoned that it wasn't far, and he hadn't had candy in several days. He plunged his hands in his pockets, pivoted right and headed for the bank.

He opened the door, and sure enough, there was Mr. Reeves over to one side behind the great big desk that sat by the front window. He was talking to a man who sat across the desk from him. A lady was sitting at another desk closer to the door, and there was one man and one lady in the cages to his left. Joseph thought the bank seemed much smaller than it had when he was there with his mother or grandmother. All eyes felt close and looked directly at him as he let the door slam behind him.

He winced at the way the sound echoed through the bank and could hear his mother's voice telling him not to slam the door. He looked around, and there was Mr. Reeves walking toward him. The lady at the desk closest to him was smiling.

"Hi, Joseph. I liked being at your school today," Mr. Reeves said. "I'm glad you stopped by, but I'm with someone else right now and will be busy for a little while. Is there something special on your mind?"

"Well, yes sir, I was hoping for a piece of the stick candy you said you would give us if we came by."

"Oh, absolutely." He walked over to one of the cages and asked for the candy jar. He held the jar down to Joseph. "What color would you like?"

"Yellow, please." Joseph liked all the colors. He would have liked one of each but knew requesting more than one would be rude.

"Thank you," he said as he departed the bank without slamming the door. The lemon tartness of the candy stick was delicious as he walked home. He decided he would stop by the bank again soon.

JOSEPH LIKED SCHOOL and did well. Four grades in one small room could be chaotic, but not in Miss Amy's room. She believed in discipline as much as she believed in reading, writing and arithmetic. The dreaded paddle, whittled for her by one of her previous students, was rarely used; its presence was all that was necessary. No student ever doubted she would take it from its nail if a circumstance warranted. Then, too, most students knew that trouble at school meant trouble at home, so misbehaving was rarely a problem.

Miss Amy, a little more lax when out of the classroom, managed to come up with a handful of school field trips. Shortly after Mr. Reeves visited, she chose the bank for their monthly outing. Hannah and another mom went along as chaperones.

Mr. Reeves, as well as the other bank personnel, were all waiting for them. Hannah held the door for Miss Amy, the students and the other chaperone to go inside. She followed and fell into the group in front of Mr. Reeves. His eyes met hers. She felt a hot flush and her palms dampen. Embarrassed by the unexpected feelings that swept through her, she looked away and feigned interest in something across the way.

"Learning to save is very important," Lex said a moment later, his voice resonating through the small room. "We're going to give you a nickel today." The children, sitting on the floor in a semi-circle, gasped in pleasant surprise and, with eyes wide, looked at each other. Lex smiled at their response and continued: "You may take the nickel home. Ask your parents if it is okay for you to open a savings account. If they say yes, bring it back, and we will put it in the bank in your name. Now, let me show you how it works." Lex put a nickel on the table in front of him. The children, wanting to see what he did with the nickel, scrambled to their feet and pushed in around the table.

Hannah leaned against a nearby wall and watched the children crowd around with their elbows and arms covering the tabletop.

"What do you think?" Amy whispered. She leaned into Hannah, almost knocking her off balance.

"What do I think about *what*?" Hannah squinted her eyes and frowned as she regained her stance and looked around at Amy Mack.

"*Him*! Isn't he handsome and *soooo* nice?"

"Shush," Hannah said firmly. Some of the children heard and turned to look at her. "Amy Mack, be quiet. Don't say another word or I will leave."

Amy grinned from ear to ear. "But I think he likes you. Did you see the way he looked at you when we first got here?"

Hannah gave Amy a cold stare and walked to the other side of the room.

Lex picked the nickel up from the table and, with all the children close behind him, walked to one of the bank cages. He gave it to the lady whose face they could see through the bars. Seconds later she gave him a piece of paper with $ .05 written in the balance column.

Lex's manner was lively and happy. "Okay, let's move back to the table so I can show you what happens next," he said. Amy and Hannah helped Lex herd everyone back in the right direction. Once the class was gathered around him again, he held up a calendar and turned it to December. "It's Christmas and someone gave me a nickel," he said excitedly. "Does anyone have an idea what I might do with it?"

Arms flew into the air, many with hands shaking wildly to get attention. Lex pointed to a little girl wearing a brown jumper whose hand had eased up rather timidly. "What is your name?" he asked.

"Eliza Kate," she answered quietly.

Standing a few feet away, Amy Mack started whispering again to Hannah: "Don't be mad at me. At least be willing to have some fun. I bet Joseph would like it, too." Lex glanced their way, lifted his eyebrows and smiled—he seemed to be telling them that he would appreciate it if they would quiet down. Hannah blushed, feeling almost as if she had been caught doing something wrong. Vowing never to help Amy Mack chaperone another field trip, she concentrated on the answer Lex was giving the little girl in the brown jumper.

"… well, that's a lovely name. Now what do you think I should do with my Christmas nickel?"

"Bring it to the bank?" she answered questioningly.

"Yes, you are right! Bringing it to the bank is a wise thing to do. But now … let's just say I *really* wanted a piece of the penny candy from the candy store. What could I do?"

Everyone was quiet for a few seconds. Then one of the little boys, forgetting to raise his hand, shouted, "Bring what's left!"

Amy couldn't resist stepping close to the group and reminding them to always raise their hands when they wanted to speak.

At the same time she was correcting the youngster, Lex was laughing and saying, "That's exactly what you can do. Bring the pennies you have left and deposit them into your savings account. Money can be put in any time. At the end of the year, the bank adds interest."

"What does that mean? What is interest?" an enterprising third-grader asked. "My grandma said she has interest in everything I do. How does that make my nickel bigger?"

"The interest from the bank means *bank money* is added to your money, and then it is yours," Lex answered with a smile. Lots of questions followed; some of the children were interested in how to make their nickel bigger, but most of them were interested in the jars of colored candy sticks sitting on the counter. After questions, each child was treated to his or her flavor of choice.

Hannah enjoyed watching Lex and listening to him interact with the children, but she would never in a million years admit it to Amy Mack. Lex looked distinguished in his navy blue suit, white shirt and dark red tie, and he seemed so comfortable with the children. She admired how patient he had been as each child deliberated (some for several seconds) on which flavor candy to choose. She liked his voice, too, and kept hearing it.

"I'M GOING TO OPEN an account at the bank," Joseph announced that night as he was eating supper with his mother and grandmother.

"Oh?" responded his grandmother. She didn't know all the details of the day's field trip.

"Yes ma'am. Mr. Reeves gave me a nickel at the bank today. This is it." He pulled the nickel from his pocket and held it out in his palm for her to see. "I'm going to take it back tomorrow and get my account."

"That's wonderful," Kate continued. "That is really a smart idea. You can earn money from time to time and add to it. Saving is very wise. I'm proud of you."

"Would you like me to go with you after school tomorrow?" Hannah offered, thinking to herself she might like an excuse to go back to the bank.

"Sure," Joseph responded. "You can if you want to." He pushed the nickel deep into his pocket, picked up his fork, and shifted his focus back to his supper. "I think Mr. Reeves will help me if you can't go."

Kate chimed in, "I think it would be nice for you to go with Joseph tomorrow. Mr. Reeves seems like such a nice man." Kate glanced at Hannah, tilted her head to one side ever so slightly, and raised her eyebrows. "Joseph would like to have you go with him, I'm sure."

"Mother!" Hannah said the word a little too emphatically, causing Joseph to look up at her.

"What's wrong?" he asked.

"Oh honey, absolutely nothing is wrong. Your grandmother made a funny face at me for some reason. Let's plan on going to the bank together. I will meet you after school."

Supper was finished, and Hannah did the dishes with a song in her heart.

***

SEVERAL WEEKS LATER Amy Mack maneuvered Fall Festival assignments so that Lex and Hannah spent the evening together at the Go Fish booth. The two, fast and furiously, tied tiny boats, planes, trains, dolls, lollipops and candy canes to the fishing lines dropped repeatedly over the sheet attached to upright two-by-fours. Lex joked with every child, talking to them from behind the sheet as if he were a fish under water avoiding getting caught. The children laughed and so did Hannah.

"He really did a great job of making each one feel special," Hannah told her mother later as she described the events of the evening. What she didn't tell her mother was that as the two of them worked frantically throughout the evening to attach treats and trinkets to the never-ending poles, the occasional brushing together of their hands or their shared laughs filled her with delight.

"We've never had him over to eat. I think we should. Should have had him before now," Kate said matter-of-factly.

"I don't know. I don't want you or him to think anything," Hannah said cautiously.

"It's just Sunday dinner," Kate grinned mischievously. "What is there to think?"

LEX HUMMED and smiled all around the bank the day after the festival, and that night he wished Hannah was with him to share the beauty of the moon and stars he witnessed from his front porch. He leaned his head back against the rocker and closed his eyes. "I'll ask if I can visit. I'll ask her Sunday." His plan was settled.

The following Sunday afternoon was the beginning of Lex and Hannah spending many hours together. He often came by after closing the bank and tried to help with some of the chores. He was more willing than he was adept at the tasks, however; he had never gathered eggs, milked a cow or chopped wood. Joseph taught him to gather eggs, and Hannah tried to teach him to milk, but was never successful. He wasn't sure if it was fear of the cow or a lack of rhythm in the squeezing. Whatever the reason, he couldn't seem to get the hang of it.

Frank, though, was available to teach the art of chopping, splitting and stacking wood. It was hard work for any man, especially for one who had never chopped wood at all. Lex was willing to try, though, and he had the blisters to prove it.

IN WASN'T LONG before Lex began to suggest more and more frequently that he and Hannah slip away alone. They strolled in the woods, picnicked on the creek bank, or rode into town to pick up some supply or another.

One of their trips into town suddenly put them in the midst of white robes, white hoods, and the sound of thundering horse hooves. Lex and Hannah were walking on the wooden sidewalk in front of the stores when the group came riding down Main Street. One man, without hood or robe, was circled by the others and was obviously the object of their chants. Words like *fornication, adultery, wedlock, Christian*, and *our town* rang through the air from the dark holes in the white robes.

"What is it? What's happening?" Hannah's heart raced as she backed against the wall of a store.

Lex reached for her hand and led her inside. "Come on. Let's get off the street."

"Who are they? What's happening?" she asked again.

"I don't know who they are. Maybe people we know, maybe from church, even."

"Have you seen them before? What are they doing?" Hannah stared through the window.

"It's a group taking the law, mostly *their* law, into their own hands. I hear they are big on family—morals mostly, against Jews, coloreds and Catholics. Come on, let's get outta here." Lex again grasped Hannah's hand, and together they hurried back in the direction they had come.

"Oh, Lex, I'm glad you were with me. So glad Joseph didn't see that. Do they do that often?"

"I've never seen them in town. Just heard about them from other men at the bank."

Once back at the McMolison's, the two sat together on the back steps, both attempting to talk about more pleasant things than what they had just witnessed.

HANNAH DIDN'T DREAM often (or didn't remember them if she did), but that night she did dream, and it was real and vivid. She was a little girl again but wasn't sure how old. She and Katherine were hurrying toward the Mercantile when the horses came. They were close to her and snorted loudly as they rocked their big heads up and down. Dust rose from the street, spreading upward like a cloud covering the white robes. It filled her nostrils. Whiteness seemed to balloon in all directions. All she could hear was *fornication ... sin ... HELL.* Suddenly there was a strong wind that lifted the hood from the rider directly in front of her. She screamed, "Papa!" The scream woke her.

Hannah sat up. Her heart was racing and her whole body was damp. She sighed deeply, thankful to be awake. "Papa, you can't do this to me," she whispered. "You may wish you were here to be one of those men, but you're not. You're dead. I'm fine. Joseph is fine. Leave me alone." She resolved not to think any more about her father or the men in town. Her father was in the past and the men had nothing to do with her. She wasn't at all sure why but she felt unexpectedly calm. She changed her gown, went back to bed and slept.

***

LEX AND HANNAH rarely mentioned the white-robed men. Occasionally they heard tell of activity (mostly deep in the woods), but they were never aware of anyone they knew being tied to the group. Instead they talked mostly about Lex's work, about Joseph, and about flowers and chores. Then one day when deep in the woods themselves, Lex stopped mid-stride. He reached for both of Hannah's hands and held them for a moment before pulling her toward him. He lifted her chin with his hand and looked down into her face. He leaned in until his lips slowly and gently met hers. His eyes closed and his arms tightened around her back and waist. She did not resist.

"I love being with you," Lex whispered close to Hannah's ear. "I want to be with you forever."

Hannah's heart skipped. Being kissed felt good. She kissed him back. Emotions of both desire and betrayal surfaced, though. She questioned the relationship she was allowing to happen. Lex was wonderful to her and to Joseph. She admired and respected him and had been enjoying his company … but was that enough? What could she do about the thoughts of Thomas that kept creeping into her mind? The more seriously Lex talked about the future, the more often Hannah's memories of Thomas overshadowed most everything Lex did. When he walked, she thought of how Thomas walked. When he talked, she imagined the words Thomas might have used. The phantom Thomas that dwelt in her brain would not go away.

HANNAH SAT ALONE on the creek bank. It was a cool spring afternoon. She felt guilty. She did not want to continue allowing Lex to think he had a future with her if he didn't. He was too nice a person. She felt certain he would soon ask her to marry, and she asked herself if she should say yes for Joseph's sake. As difficult as it was to think about, she wondered, over and over, if she was going to let the memories of Thomas drive her for the rest of her life. She hadn't intended to mislead Lex. Then a letter arrived.

Dear Hannah,

I've thought of writing so often. I've wanted to. It's been two and a half years since I saw you here at the hotel, and I can't stop thinking about you. Over and over I've wished to see you again. I even made one trip to Leaf Creek hoping to see you. I waited at the school thinking you might be there to pick up Joseph, but I didn't see you. Joseph walked by with a classmate. Seeing him again made the ride worthwhile.

Hannah, I'm so sorry for the heartache I've caused you. I want you to know you will always be special to me. I didn't do what I should have done, what I wanted to do. My father won, and after a time in Atlanta, I got married. Sometimes I think my wife knows she doesn't have my heart, but she doesn't say anything. She's a good person, a good wife, a good mother. She always tries to make the best of every situation, but I don't think I can ever tell her about Joseph. I'm sorry.

Yet as I know I never want to hurt Sadie, I am always trying to devise plans to see you, to be with you. I shouldn't be writing, but after wanting to for so long, I'm giving in. I think of you often, imagine being with you and felt I had to tell you.

I wish the very best for you and Joseph. If you need anything, please let me know. Also, the next time I'm in Leaf Creek, I plan to stop by your house. I hope that will be okay.

Fondly with Love,
Thomas

Hannah lay back on the moss-covered ground and stared at the sky overhead. Hearing from Thomas had given her fluttery nervous feelings just like ones she felt when hearing from him in years past. Even before the letter, she had been dealing with the hard question of why she couldn't throw away the picture in her letter box, why she still removed it from time to time to remember and relive that special time from so long ago. She knew it was not right to give Lex only the unused portion of her heart. He was deserving of someone better, someone whole.

HANNAH'S LONG CONVERSATION with Lex was painful for both of them. Hannah was hurting someone for whom she cared greatly, maybe even loved. She knew she might be ending an opportunity to marry, but even if she was making a mistake, letting Lex go was something she had to do.

Hannah and Lex had barely entered the edge of the woods when Hannah suggested they stop to talk. "Let's sit here for a minute." She dropped to her knees and sat back on her heels. "Lex, I've got to talk to you."

Lex sat, Indian style, on the ground in front of her. "Talk away. I'm always glad to talk to you," he said with a happy lilt and a smile.

"Oh, Lex, you're too wonderful. I don't even know how to say what I'm about to say."

Lex leaned forward and frowned slightly. "Can't be that bad. I'm sure we can fix whatever it is."

Hannah reached for a pine needle and twisted it in her fingers. She took a deep breath. "We can't fix it because it's me. I know you want someone to spend your life with, but I'm not the right one."

"I don't understand what you're talking about. What have I done? Haven't things been good?" Lex leaned forward and covered her hand with his.

"Yes, everything is good. I've loved being with you but ..." Her voice trailed off to silence.

Lex tightened his hand over Hannah's. "I love you, Hannah. And I love Joseph. Please don't do this." Lex withdrew his hand and sat straight. "At least tell me what's wrong."

"Nothing's wrong. At least nothing's wrong with you. You're wonderful. You deserve more than what I can give. It's me. It's all me."

"What do you mean? You can't just tell me we're over without some kind of explanation." Lex scrambled to his feet and looked down at Hannah, frustration and anger etched in his handsome face.

"It's better this way, Lex. Please believe me. I'm sorry. I really am."

Hannah managed to look up into Lex's eyes before standing herself. "Please know I care about you. I care a lot."

"Well, you've got a funny way of showing it. If this has anything to do with Joseph, with you having a son … well you know I don't care." Lex, devastated, kept his composure as he reached to take Hannah's hands in his.

"It does and it doesn't … I don't know." Hannah looked at the ground. The words didn't make sense to her, and she knew they didn't make sense to Lex. But she knew she had to do this. "I just know I can't be all you deserve right now."

"Where is Joseph's father? Is he here? Is that what's causing this?" Lex's voice was low and tense.

"No, no, he's not here," Hannah said softly. "I haven't seen him in a long time, but Lex, I still care about him. I care about him a lot."

"Has he said he's coming? Has he ever been here for Joseph? I've never known about him if he has."

"Don't be angry. I'm trying to be honest with you."

"Maybe you are, but are you being honest with *yourself*? I mean …" Lex hesitated before continuing. "Well, you know I love you. And I love Joseph, and I know somebody is in your past. But I've never said anything or asked because it doesn't matter."

She looked beyond him into the distance at nothing. "It does matter. It matters to me. I hear from him sometimes. I don't know what the future holds, but I know I can't get married." She brought her gaze back to meet his. "There is a part of my heart that's locked. The locked portion keeps me from being whole for you, and that's not what I want in a marriage. It's not what you deserve."

"You know, you should really let *me* decide what I deserve," Lex said, hurt permeating his voice. "I don't know what happened that caused you to start thinking like this, but I can give you time. I could give you a good home and provide whatever you and Joseph need."

"Lex, please don't make this harder than it already is. I've loved being with you. Joseph loves being with you. But talking about marriage changes things."

"I don't see why. If I'm willing to simply plan for the future and not dredge up the past, why can't you?" Lex stood firmly planted in front of Hannah, staring at her.

"That's just it, Lex. The past is still with me. I'm not saying it is good or right, but it's the truth—I don't want to get married." Hannah knew her relationship with Thomas had left an indelible mark on her heart. Tears filled her eyes, and her voice softened. "I'm so sorry. Please try to understand."

Without another word, Lex turned and walked away.

CHAPTER THIRTY-EIGHT

BRANDON WAS JOSEPH'S best friend. They went to church and school together and fished whenever Brandon's father could take them.

They both continued to make regular trips to the bank even after finishing third grade. They liked having interest added to their pennies and nickels, and they were always hungry for stick candy. After making their deposits, the lady in the cage smiled and lowered the jar so they could get a good look before making their choice. Mr. Reeves waved at them when they went in, but he wasn't especially friendly.

On one of their trips, Joseph said, "Mr. Reeves used to come to our house a lot but not anymore. I guess Mama got tired of having him around all the time. Maybe that's why he's not as friendly as he used to be."

"Grown-ups are weird sometimes," Brandon replied, wrinkling his face. "Come on, let's hurry."

Brandon's father had a seed store and the boys had gotten in the habit of going by there almost every afternoon after school. Mr. Fisher always had something for them, but the year they were ten years old, he started having the best thing ever—he had a big brown crock filled with bubble gum. Both boys thought stick candy was good, but the new pink Double Bubble gum was fun. With daily practice, their bubbles grew bigger, often leaving a layer of sticky pink goo all over their noses, cheeks, and lips after they burst. Mr. Fisher just laughed.

***

JOSEPH FIRST ASKED about his father when he was only four years old. Hannah had felt he was too young to understand, but she always tried to answer his questions as simply and directly as she could.

One afternoon that year Joseph went fishing with Brandon and his father. At supper that night, he told Hannah and Kate all about the afternoon. "I had a long fishing pole," he said excitedly, holding his arms as far apart as he could manage. "Mr. Fisher had worms—a *lot* of worms—in dirt inside a bucket." He wiggled all his fingers at one time as he described the worms squiggling around in the dirt. "We put them on hooks." He hesitated just long enough to spoon mashed potatoes into his mouth. "I did it myself. I put a worm on. It was real wiggly," he said, moving his right index finger back and forth to demonstrate. "But Mr. Fisher showed me how, and I did it. I caught a fish, too, but Mr. Fisher said it was too little, so we put it back in to catch next time." He took another bite of potatoes. "Mr. Fisher caught one, but he threw it back in. Since he caught only one, he said it must not be a good day for fishing." Joseph shrugged his shoulders.

"Sounds like you had a fun afternoon," Hannah said, smiling.

"He said he would take us again."

"Well, that's great, and I bet you'll catch something next time," Kate said encouragingly. She reached for the plates and started clearing the table.

Then out of the blue—and in the same four-year-old tone he'd been describing his fishing trip—Joseph said, "Mama, do I have a papa like Brandon?" Hannah's heart skipped a beat as she felt it rise to her throat. The day had come that she needed answers.

"Yes, you do have a papa. He just doesn't live here." Hannah began. "He's smart and very handsome, just like you."

"Where is he? I want to see him. Maybe he would take Brandon and me fishing some time."

"Well, he doesn't live close by, but maybe we will see him

sometime. I would like to see him too." Hannah, of course, shared Joseph's wish more than he could possibly know.

Kate added, "Sweetheart, you just remember your papa has a very special son."

"Okay, but I would still like it if he came and took me fishing," Joseph replied as he finished his supper.

"Maybe one day he will," Kate answered.

Hannah leaned over and kissed the top of Joseph's head. "Yes, I hope one day he will."

* * *

WHEN JOSEPH STARTED SCHOOL, the teacher didn't ask Hannah his last name. She wrote Joseph McMolison on his papers, and Hannah never corrected her. After Joseph learned his letters and began to print his name, he printed "Joseph McMolison." Hannah thought it would be easier and less confusing for Joseph if she just didn't say anything. He continued using the name right on through junior high school and after.

Joseph's wishes for a father usually came on the heels of doing something fun with a friend and the friend's dad. Hannah always answered him softly, saying, "I know. I wish he were here too." Hannah's response usually ended the conversation. As Joseph got older, he sensed that asking about his father made his mother uncomfortable (she got very quiet), so he quit asking. He didn't mention him for almost three years.

Then, in the beginning of ninth grade, Joseph's social studies teacher gave an assignment that included drawing their family tree. Hannah sat at the kitchen table with him. As she answered his questions and gave him the information he needed to fill in the blanks, he suddenly blurted a question that had been on his mind for some time. "The other boys—and girls, too—all have the same last name as their father. Why don't I, and why don't you? We have the same last name as Grandma. I've seen what some of the other kids have written so far, and I'm the only one with the same last name as my mother's mother. Doesn't make sense. What is my last name supposed to be?" He stared at his pencil, one hand on either end. "Did my father not even want me to have his name? Did he not want me?" He slapped the pencil down on the table, pushed his chair back, folded his arms and looked at Hannah. His tone was suddenly full of resentment.

Hannah's heart broke into pieces. She had thought the assignment might raise questions, but she didn't know they were the ones he'd long wanted to ask. She had allowed herself to live under the pretense that if Joseph did not ask about his father, he was not ready to find out about him. He had seemed satisfied with her simple answers, and she was always thankful he didn't press her. She had not realized, however, that her reactions on those long ago days made him think his asking made her sad—which, in turn, made him stop asking. On that day she understood for the first time that his quietness had been for her sake; he was a young boy trying not to hurt his mother. The thought made her feel sick. "How could I not have known?" she wondered. A knot of blame and sadness filled the pit of her stomach.

"Oh, Joseph, I love you so much." Hannah leaned across the table, both hands extended toward Joseph. "Please, please always remember that. I would never do anything to hurt you, and I never meant to keep anything from you about your father. I've always planned to tell you anything you want to know. I guess I just thought it was right to wait until you asked. I didn't know you weren't asking because of how you thought it would make me feel." Hannah wished she could hold him and make the pain go away.

"Will you tell me about him now?" Joseph sat stiffly, his arms still folded across his chest.

"Of course. I loved your father, and a part of me still does. I think of him often. You look so much like him, and I'm glad because he is very handsome." Hannah hesitated as she searched for the right words. Joseph sat quietly and waited for her to continue. "When you were born, your father and I were both young. He was in college and had plans to go away to medical school. Our marrying caused both our fathers to get extremely angry. His father insisted that a wife and baby would get in the way of his medical school plans and made him return immediately to school. And my father wanted you to have another family."

Joseph frowned as he looked at his mother. "What do you mean, another family?" He pulled his chair close to the table and leaned forward on his forearms.

"Your father—his name was Thomas—went back to school at Ole Miss, and my father thought it would be better for you to live with a family where you would have both a mother and a father. You know, some people don't think a single mother is a nice person. Or a good mother." Hannah's eyes filled with tears as she continued. "But I couldn't. Maybe I was selfish, but I just couldn't let you live with someone else. Both my father and Thomas's father were adamant that you would. They said it would destroy the honor of both families for me to have a baby and not have a husband that stayed with me." Hannah paused. She leaned back in her chair and smoothed the fabric of her skirt with her hands. Then clasped her hands in her lap and looked at Joseph.

"Being honest, fair and sincere make us honorable, Joseph, and I hope your grandmother and I have instilled those values in you," Hannah continued. "Your grandfathers, both of them, were strong and proud men, but the honor they lived by was flawed. They lived by one standard while demanding another for everyone else, especially their families. For them it seemed honesty, fairness, and integrity were mere bywords to be pulled out when circumstances threatened who they were, who they intended to be, or what they wanted." At some level she couldn't believe the words had come from her mouth. But Hannah knew it was long past time for the truth to be told.

"Weren't they nice at all? And what did that have to do with me living here?" Joseph had clearly waited a long time for information. He was eager to get as much as Hannah was willing to share.

"Oh yes, they were nice in a lot of ways, Joseph. They both did a lot of good all over the county. People everywhere believed in both of them because their public presence was wrapped in honorable talk and proper appearances. What most folks didn't know was that they hid or manipulated circumstances and decisions they didn't like. We really didn't know much about what they did. We just knew that what other people thought was … not always the way things really were."

"What was it like for you and Aunt Katherine? Was he mean to you?"

Hannah hesitated before answering. "Sometimes it was hard, at least after we got older. Father was very stern and ruled harshly here at home. He demanded we be where he wanted us to be, that we look as he wanted us to look, and behave exactly as he thought proper. He preached honor and living honorably from the time we were very small, but the truth is we lived only in the *shadows* of honor—not in an environment of honor. Never the real thing, is what I'm trying to say. Appearances and well-chosen words don't bring true honor. Your life in word and deed is what matters."

"I'm glad you didn't send me to live with someone else. I would never want to live with anyone but you and Grandma."

Hannah's eyes misted. "And we would never want you to live any-where else. That's why you are right here, and we love you so much," she added.

"I guess my father didn't want a son?"

"Your father's name is Thomas Stokes. He was very special to me, but like I said, *his* father was very demanding. I just don't think Thomas had the strength to go against his will."

"Do you know where he is?" Joseph asked.

"I believe he moved back to Leeville where his family lived. I learned several years ago that he had married. That may be why he has not come to see us. His wife probably doesn't know about you, or me. I imagine he is trying to live the life that was expected of him. Maybe you will meet him someday. I hope you will forgive us both for not providing a proper family."

"Well, he shoulda come. Shoulda come to see you and me. He was crazy not to do whatever he had to do to be with you. I wouldn't *ever* do like he did." Joseph's words carried a hint of anger. He pushed his chair from the table, stood, and looked at Hannah. "And thanks for not giving me away. I'm glad I'm here." He walked from the room.

Hannah was quiet. She was concerned that she'd said more to Joseph than she should have. Either way, though, the conversation she had dreaded for years was finally over.

Chapter Thirty-Nine

"Ten in a row! Wow. Here give me the ball," one of Joseph's friends said cockily after watching Joseph shoot ten free throws through the bottomless peach basket nailed high on a pole. "I'll drop eleven."

Joseph pitched him the ball and stood under the goal to rebound for his friend. "Okay, let's see you," he retorted. The ball went through cleanly four times before the fifth toss hit the edge of the basket and bounced back toward the shooter.

"Ahaaa, heck," he said. "I'll get you 'fore the year's out. Just wait."

"I'm waiting," Joseph said teasingly as the two pitched the ball back and forth a few times before heading home. "Wish we had a team."

"Me too, but I don't want to go stay at Pine Level just to play basketball, and that's what we'd have to do." His friend tossed the ball up and down in the air as he spoke.

"Me neither," said Joseph. "I wouldn't want to live in Pine Level."

Even without athletics, Joseph's days were busy. There were books. There were chores and, equally important, there was fishing. His time was filled, causing his high school years to seem to fly by. He graduated from high school in the spring, and with the help of Katherine and

Stephen, he was able to attend State Teacher's College the following fall. He was only sixteen years old.

"OH ME, THE HOUSE seems empty without Joseph," Hannah lamented to Kate. She measured cornmeal into a bowl for cornbread. "Hardly worth cooking for just us."

Kate was turning pieces of ham she had frying in an iron skillet. "Things are quiet, but we'd get hungry if we didn't cook at all." Looking around at Hannah, she added, "May be quiet around here, but I bet Katherine loves having Joseph with her."

Hannah stirred buttermilk into the meal. The metal spoon clicked against the side of the glass bowl. She sighed. "I know. I want him to go to school. Glad he has Katherine and Stephen to stay with and the cafeteria job to help pay the fees. I just miss him so, so much."

"Well, we have a lot of work to keep us busy." Kate strained to loosen the metal ring on a jar of canned peas.

"I'm glad." Sizzling sounds filled the air. Hannah poured the cornbread mixture in a hot skillet and pushed it into the oven. "Work helps fill the time."

DURING JOSEPH'S FIRST YEAR away, Hannah and Kate packed the Christmas box for Rosie and Twila.

"I still love doing this, but do you remember how much fun Joseph had helping when he was little?" Hannah wrapped a bottle of perfume and tied it with red ribbon. She wrote Rosie on the label and added the package to the stack of gifts she and Kate were making.

"I know, and he still liked helping even after he was older. If you remember, it was Joseph who chose the books for last year's box." Kate held up two broaches, one for Rosie and one for Twila. "Aren't these pretty?"

"They are. Hand me one to wrap." Hannah took one from Kate and began wrapping it with gold paper.

Hannah still carried the secret of Rosie alone. The holidays made her wish her mother and Katherine knew the truth, but there never seemed to be an appropriate time to tell them; when she thought about revealing everything she always backed out. The pain the truth would cause her mother always outweighed the benefit, so the years had passed with only the pleasantries of the Christmas exchange.

For Hannah and Rosie, though, there was an invisible bond that traveled back and forth with the packages and the letters. Some years there might even be something tangible such as a few dollars—or maybe as many as five—that Rosie would find hidden in a sock. Because of the unspoken understanding she and Hannah shared, she never spoke about it in her letters. But she seemed to know the extra money was a special gift from Hannah meant just for her. Neither took the initiative to make changes. Rosie never asked for recognition, and although Hannah felt guilty about not acknowledging Rosie, she remained quiet.

AS USUAL A THANK YOU LETTER arrived from Rosie that year, only this time it arrived a little later and with a surprise. The return address was not Leeville. Instead, it was New York, New York.

February 28, 1934

Dear Mrs. McMolison and family,

I know you have wondered why I have taken so long to write and thank you for the wonderful Christmas box. I suppose it takes a long time for a package to come so far. We received it a couple of weeks ago and were just as excited as we would have been if we had received it on Christmas day. It was hard this year to be so far away during the holiday. Some of the people here invited us to have Christmas dinner with them, and we did, but it's just not the same as it is back home.

Receiving your package lifted our spirits. Just knowing we are thought about means a lot.

Hannah read while thinking to herself, "Rosie, I think of you more than you would ever imagine."

I know you wonder what we are doing in New York. It all started last spring. A man visiting our church heard Twila sing and asked about the possibility of her entering a contest in Mobile; he even offered to take her. It seemed like a real good opportunity, so I agreed as long as I could be with her. It turned out she won and got a job with a band that performs at different towns around the country. She's done real good. I'm so proud of her. They started her singing jazz music, and she just seems to be a natural. For the past several days she has been performing at a place called the Apollo. The people really seem to like her. I think she has found the stage she has always wished for. Hopefully she will never have to spend her days and nights working the hotel kitchen.

I'm going home to Leeville soon. Twila is sixteen—almost seventeen—and is very much on her own. I've worked at different jobs to be able to stay here, but it is time I get back. I can't even imagine how much I am going to miss her. My heart tightens to even think about it. This life she has chosen is a hard one, but I know she will be alright and one day, maybe other young colored girls will see her and know that a dream can become real.

I didn't mean to ramble so much. Thanks again for the lovely presents. We loved everything as always. Twila wore the pretty jeweled broach last night.

Miss Tildy says I can come back to my job at the hotel, so if you do come to Leeville, maybe I will get to see you.

We hope all three of you are well and are having a good year.

Sincerely,
Rosie and Twila

JOSEPH SETTLED into a routine at State Teacher's College, a routine that changed very little during the almost three years he had been there. He lived with Katherine and Stephen, worked in the cafeteria, and studied. Hannah and Kate settled into their own routine. Not only did they keep up the chores at home, they were both active in the church and in a ladies garden club. Kate quilted with her friends, Hannah helped at the school, and they both cared for the sick and the shut-ins.

Twice a month their church had dinner on the ground, the church-wide fellowship time that both Kate and Hannah still looked forward to. Baskets were being put on the table when the newspaper that covered Mrs. Pierce's basket caught Hannah's attention. The heading of an article on the front page stirred her heart. Almost fourteen years had passed since she'd last seen Thomas, but her heart still quickened at the sight of his name. Hannah and Kate didn't take the county paper, but Mrs. Pierce, one of the other ladies, had used a recent edition to cover her food.

Prominently displayed in the center of the basket was the headline, MEACHEM THOMAS STOKES ATTENDS OLE MISS. The article began, "Meachem Thomas Stokes, an honor graduate of Leeville High, has been accepted to The University of Mississippi. He is the son of Thomas and Sadie Stokes and the grandson of ..." Hannah's beating heart muffled the words as she read. The story listed the boy's accomplishments, plans, and on and on. She read no further.

"Would you like to have the paper?" Mrs. Pierce lifted the rest of the issue from the basket and handed it toward Hannah. The movement of the paper and her question startled Hannah.

"Oh, no, that's alright," she managed. "Thank you though."

Hannah felt a mix of lost love and righteous anger, and for the moment anger was winning. This son of *her* son's father seemed privileged in every way. Meachem, if that was what they called him, would not likely be working in the cafeteria in order to pay tuition fees. It was far more likely he'd be following in his father's footsteps. He would be living in the dorm, having free time to spend with friends, and joining the *right* fraternity. His clothes would be the latest style, and his hardships would be none. Hannah was thinking of all the things she wished she could provide for Joseph.

Hannah, putting all of this out of her mind for the moment, forced a smile at Mrs. Pierce. "I'm finished with it. The article about the women in the First Presbyterian Church in Leeville is interesting. Maybe we could do something like that here." Hannah was thankful she had noticed the headline of the adjoining article. She didn't think Mrs. Pierce would give a second thought to her being interested in Meachem Thomas Stokes, but she might. There was no way to know, and Hannah did not want to discuss the Stokes family at all.

Chapter Forty

KATHERINE WAITED IMPATIENTLY at the train station for Hannah and Kate. It was May, and she had not seen them since Christmas. She finally heard the train whistle blowing in the distance. It got louder and louder until it sounded full blast as the train rounded the final curve coming into Hattiesburg. She wanted to leap onto the train but waited instead until she saw her mother and sister assisted onto the platform. She ran to meet them. "I could hardly wait for y'all to get here! It's so great to have you," she said as she hugged them both. Barely stopping to breathe, she continued, "Joseph was scheduled to work this afternoon's shift in the cafeteria, so he couldn't come with me. He was so disappointed not to be here, but he'll come to the house as soon as he can. I hope he'll be home in time for us to have supper together. I think he will."

Joseph's graduation from college was exciting for the whole family. He had completed his studies at State Teacher's College with a degree in history and a license to teach school. Hannah never returned to school after Joseph was born. She read and studied at home, but she did not have a diploma; Joseph was the first in the family to not only finish high school but also to get a college degree.

"Oh, shucks, I'm disappointed, too, that he couldn't be here,"

Hannah replied. "You know I still miss him after all this time. I just can't believe we're here for his graduation. It's just wonderful. I'm so proud of him." A gust of wind blew over the platform. Hannah reached up to hold her hat in place.

"Don't get gushy and mushy now," Katherine said. "We're all proud of him. Come on, I want to show you our car." Katherine walked between her sister and mother and circled her arms through their elbows.

"Your *what?*" Kate asked. "Oh my. Well, before we see Joseph or your car, we need to be sure the porter has our trunks." Kate stopped walking and looked back toward the luggage area. A man, pulling a dolly with their trunks, was following.

"Wow," Hannah said as they came to a dark green, two-door sedan with white side walls, chrome bumpers, and two headlights perched on the fenders like sentinels on duty. "Looks like it probably cost a lot of money."

"We didn't buy it new. It belonged to a man in our church, and he made the price one we could afford. He thought it would help Stephen be able to visit church members more easily," Katherine explained as she opened the trunk for the porter.

"And you can drive?" Kate asked.

"Yes, Mother, I *can* drive," Katherine said emphatically. "Come on. Get in."

"Well, I hope we make it because I really want to see Joseph graduate," Hannah said sarcastically as she climbed in the backseat.

They were soon on their way down the same street Hannah had traveled with Joseph when he was only a few weeks old. This trip was her first time to retrace her steps. It was hard to believe so many years had passed. Most everything was the same, except cars had replaced wagons, and this time she wasn't alone.

As they pulled the car up in front of Katherine's house, Stephen was walking up from the church. "Glad you are here safely," he said with a big grin. "You never know with Katherine at the wheel. Sometimes I think she wants to be a race car driver."

"That doesn't surprise me," Hannah replied, smiling as she hopped out of the car. She threw her arms wide to hug Stephen. "Katherine has always been full throttle at everything. We all know that."

After helping Stephen get the trunks inside, Katherine directed Hannah and Kate to the kitchen with her. "I need to get our supper started, and I don't want to miss a minute with you. Come visit with me while I cook."

"Hey everybody!" The shout rang down the little hall and into the kitchen where the three women were putting supper on the table. Joseph was beaming. He grabbed his mother and swung her around in a big hug. Kate was next. Everybody in the room was laughing. Joseph had just set his last table and washed his last dish in the cafeteria. The following day he would be a real college graduate. "I have great news." He could hardly get the words out fast enough. "A few weeks ago I talked to a principal about a teaching job, and he came to see me today. I got the job! After tomorrow I will be a teacher—I start this summer. I can hardly believe it."

"Oh, that's wonderful." Hannah cupped his face in her hands and kissed his forehead. "You have a job even before you graduate. That must be a very wise principal. He recognized what an extremely smart and special young man you are. I'm so proud of you. Now, where is the school? Of course, *any* school would be fortunate to have you." Hannah's heart was bursting with pride and joy for her son. She had assumed he would be home during the summer, but for him to have a job even before graduating was wonderful. "Where will you be living?" she asked again, hoping his answer would not be some place too far from Leaf Creek.

"Pine Springs. Isn't that great?" he answered. "I'll be about halfway between Leaf Creek and Hattiesburg. I can visit you, and I can visit Aunt Katherine and Uncle Stephen."

THE FOLLOWING MORNING they all dressed for the exciting day of graduation activities. "Is my hat tilted right?" Hannah leaned her head to one side for Katherine to inspect.

"It's perfect. It's beautiful, and you look beautiful. Joseph will be very proud of you."

The women all had new dresses, hats, and gloves. Hannah chose a peach color. It was straight and fitted with a big square collar. Her hat was off white with peach flowers nestled in a bed of tulle. Katherine's entire frock was shades of lavender. It had a ruffled stand up collar, pearl buttons down the front to the waist, and a full billowy skirt. Although the dress was completely different in style, the color immediately reminded Hannah of the one Katherine requested so long ago for the school chapel program. Katherine was beautiful on both occasions, but both times she reminded Hannah of an Easter egg (an opinion that would never be spoken aloud). Kate, older but still beautiful, wore a dress and hat of black and white—she'd always dressed in a classic and sophisticated style, and her style did not change, even when there was very little money to spend. Classic suited her, and her dress on that day was black with bold curving white insets that ran from the shoulder seams diagonally until they met in the middle at the waist.

Joseph and Stephen looked handsome in their suits. The five of them drove to the campus in Stephen and Katherine's car. The sky was blue and the temperature was comfortable. It was a perfect day for the grand occasion, one of the most exciting in any of their lives.

As they drove to the auditorium, Kate peered out her window. "Look at the dome on top of that big building. Isn't it beautiful?" She motioned toward an octagonal-shaped building in the center of five red brick buildings. "Oh, and look over there," she added, pointing in the direction of a big clump of azaleas that still had blooms. "Aren't those pretty? I'm surprised they still have blooms this late."

As Joseph gathered with the other graduates, Hannah, Kate, Katherine, and Stephen found their seats. The ceremony started. Tears of joy dripped from Hannah's eyes as Joseph marched in wearing his cap and gown. To her, he looked more handsome than ever. "Pomp and Circumstance" filled the space. Seeing Joseph march in with his head held high and the gold tassel swinging with his every step filled her with delight. She watched him as he attentively looked toward the speaker, and she remembered the fun days watching him grow and learn and fish and chase chickens. He was graduating from *college*, she reminded herself again. Her heart almost burst with pride. "That's my little boy up there, all grown up," she felt like shouting.

That wasn't all she thought, of course. "I can't imagine my life without him. What if I had done what my father wanted?" Reflections and questions flashed in Hannah's mind. She closed her eyes and suppressed what was nearly an audible sigh as an old but familiar pang of fear and anxiety shot through her. Opening her eyes, she rebuked herself for allowing her thoughts to digress to that horrific time. "How could my own father have ever demanded I give him to someone else?" Hannah pushed the terrible memories from her thoughts. She smiled and clapped her hands along with the rest of the audience, although she had no idea what had just been said.

Joseph received his diploma, moved the tassel to the other side of his cap, and smiled a smile that reached from ear to ear. Hannah sat with her hands folded together just under her chin. Sheer jubilation filled her whole being. Her elated heart beat in a joyful rhythm. Thoughts of her father were quashed. She would not allow him to mar the day.

Thinking of Thomas and the life he shared with another son did not dampen her spirits, either. What she thought more about was the joy he had missed by not sharing the life of the exceptional young man that looked so much like the picture in her letter box.

Chapter Forty-One

JOSEPH WAS STRICT, but he was fun and a favorite teacher. The students never knew what to expect. Guns fired and cannons blasted as the Civil War came to life in his classroom. Robert E. Lee spoke with a southern drawl, and Ulysses Grant was abrupt and ill-tempered. He complimented strengths and never publicly admonished weaknesses. Field trips to stores, mills, farms, and factories were an important part of the schedule.

His students were older than he had been when his class went to the bank in Leaf Creek, but to Joseph that did not matter. On the day he and his students went to the bank, he filled his pockets with stick candy. He demanded much but gave even more. The love he learned from his mother and grandmother he unselfishly gave to every student in his class.

Joseph had been teaching at Pine Springs for one year when Nita Glass was hired to teach third grade. Nita had actually had two job opportunities, but she knew Joseph was a teacher at Pine Springs. She remembered him working in the cafeteria. She had noticed him chatting with every student as they came through the line. He seemed fun, and he was definitely handsome. She thought it couldn't hurt to accept a position at the same school.

"Would you mind helping me move a table in my room?" Nita smiled as she casually asked Joseph for help after they sat through several faculty sessions together.

Joseph remembered Nita from school (he thought she was pretty) but didn't know her. "Delighted to," he happily responded. The table, along with a few chairs, was moved quickly with the help of another male teacher. Joseph lingered and waited for the other teacher to leave. "Where are you from?" he asked as he and Nita walked from the building together.

"Actually, I'm from Hattiesburg," Nita said with a sheepish grin. "Didn't have far to go when I left for college."

"Wow, I guess that was nice being so close to home. Did you live at home?"

"No, I stayed in the dormitory after my first year. My parents thought the experience would be good for me." Nita was short with brown eyes and dark hair. She had a ready smile and a pleasant cadence to her Southern accent.

"Was it?" Joseph asked, and explained that he had lived with his Aunt Katherine out of necessity but often wished he could have lived with friends in the dorm.

"It really was fine. Where did you live?" Every word Nita spoke was stretched out with an extra syllable.

Joseph told her about his Aunt Katherine and Uncle Stephen. During the next few months, he told her all about his family (at least the part he knew). He told her about Leaf Creek and even included the tradition of packing a Christmas box for Rosie and Twila. From Nita, Joseph learned about her family and things about Hattiesburg he never had time to discover on his own.

Nita got high marks from Hannah and Kate when the couple visited during the Christmas holidays. They were drawn to her cheery personality and her bright and ready smile, but most of all they could see that Nita's focus on Joseph was matched by his focus on her. A loving marriage for Joseph had been on Hannah's prayer list for a long time, and she felt certain she was seeing and meeting the answer. The school policy that forbid faculty members to marry stood between them, but Hannah encouraged them to let love rule. "Where there's a will, there's a way," she said often, reminding them that she was solidly on their side.

Next, Joseph took Nita to see Janie, June Ellen and Frank. He got hugs and whispers of approval from all three.

After several meetings with people in authority and serious pleadings with the school board, the marriage policy was changed. Joseph and Nita were married the following summer in Hattiesburg in the beautiful old Methodist church on Main Street. The sun shown through the stained glass windows with such magnificent timing that it seemed God was giving His sign of approval in a most glorious way. Nita was radiant, and Joseph beamed with happiness.

Bethany was born two years later and Joseph Luke fourteen months after that. Bethany's little face, like Nita's, was round with delicate and beautiful features, but her black hair and blue eyes reminded everyone of Joseph. Nita's mother, having suffered a black widow spider bite, was unable to help with new baby duties. Kate and Hannah, of course, filled in quickly and eagerly. Kate's enthusiasm about being *great* grandmother and being called "Gran Kate" was equaled only by Hannah's joy with her new title of grandmother.

A FEW WEEKS after Bethany's birth, Kate and Hannah returned home to find that neither Frank nor June Ellen were well. The fatigue they were experiencing made it difficult for them to do anything. They had done their best to keep the work caught up until Hannah and her mother returned, but their condition worsened with every passing day. They were tired, weak, and running high fever at night.

Frank moved his head wearily against the pillow. "I'm sorry, Miz Kate." He started to get up.

"Don't try to get up, Frank. Stay where you are," Kate said kindly.

June Ellen was in a rocking chair. "He can barely get out a the bed and I don't do much better. We sweats so much, the bed stays plum wet. Ev'er night it's wet."

Kate went immediately to Beaumont to talk to Dr. McLeod. "The coughing is awful," Kate told him. "They're coughing so much they're completely exhausted, and I'm afraid what they're coughing up may be blood. Please come as soon as you can."

"I will head your way in the morning," Dr. McLeod said. He shook his head from side to side and wrinkled his face with concern. "I'll do what I can, but from what you're saying, things don't sound good."

Kate returned home. She and Hannah sat up with Frank and June Ellen, ready to do whatever they could to help. Kate took chicken broth, coffee, water and whatever vegetable liquor she thought they might like. "I can't eat," Frank said. "Just can't swallow." He let his head sag back into the pillow and closed his eyes. "I'm sorry, Miz Kate," he whispered between coughs and catching his breath.

June Ellen took a few spoons of chicken broth, but then she, too, exhausted herself in a fit of coughing.

Dr. McLeod came just as promised but told Kate there was not much he could do. He left an elixir for the cough and told Kate to give it to them as long as they could swallow it.

Three days passed. "Go to Janie's," Kate said to Hannah, "Tell her Frank and June Ellen are getting worse, and we need her help. *Now.*"

Janie came. One of her knees was swollen, and the pain caused her to hobble along as if one leg was shorter than the other. Her bad leg, as she called it, wouldn't stop her from helping Kate take care of Frank and June Ellen, though. The women bathed their faces with cool rags, and did what they could to keep the cough controlled and the fever down. In spite of all their effort, Frank and June Ellen got worse and died within a week of each other. Both had remained faithful to Kate and Hannah until their deaths.

Chapter Forty-Two

"Oh, HANNAH, look at this brooch," Katherine said to Hannah. "I think it belonged to our grandmother. Isn't it beautiful? Look at the lovely cameo surrounded by gold filigree and rhinestones. You should wear it and then be sure to give it to Bethany."

"It would be nice for Bethany to have it someday, but right now why don't you take it. You're the oldest. I'm happy for you to have it. Mother had another really pretty silver pin with a blue stone in the center. It should be here somewhere. Maybe I could keep that one." Hannah wiped away a tear that ran down her cheek.

"What is this?" Katherine said to Hannah as she lifted a big box from the bottom of the quilt box.

Hannah looked up from the pieces of jewelry she was sorting to see Katherine holding a box, the bulging top tied down with string. "I don't know. I don't remember seeing it before."

Katherine loosened the string and removed the lid. Letters addressed to Mr. and Mrs. Bill McMolison, Route Two, Box Sixteen, Leaf Creek, Mississippi filled the box. The return address was Darathea Brannon, RR Five Box Sixty, Ashwood, South Carolina. Katherine and Hannah both opened letters and began reading news written many years before, penned by the grandmother they never knew. "Listen," said Katherine as she began to read aloud a portion of one of the letters. "*We had two new baby calves born this week. I wish you could be here to see them, because you always loved watching the little ones. Both of these are red with white faces and both healthy and already running alongside their mothers.*" Katherine looked at Hannah and said, "I wish we had learned more about Mama's family back in South Carolina. When she mentioned her life growing up, I never paid much attention. It didn't seem important to me at the time."

"I know," said Hannah. They sat on the floor and read two years of news from their grandmother in Ashwood as well as tidbits about the life their mother had left behind when she moved to Mississippi. At the bottom of one of the stacks was the letter Kate had received from the preacher informing her of her parents' death. They read the words Kate had read and felt an additional heaviness in their hearts.

GREENE COUNTY HERALD
Thursday, May 24, 1941

Kate Brannon McMolison Dies In Her Sleep

Friends, family, and all the residents of Leaf Creek are grieved to endure the passing into Glory of Kate Brannon McMolison. Her daughter, Hannah, with whom she shared her home, was unable to wake her mother on the Friday morning just passed. The date was May 18, 1941. In only a short while, the sad news was known all over town.

Mrs. McMolison was born in South Carolina where she spent her young years. She wed Mr. Bill McMolison, and together they moved to Leaf Creek where they raised their family and contributed greatly to the betterment of the community. Kate was a loving mother. She was always ready to render assistance in all church undertakings. She was faithful to give her time and resources toward the care of anyone in a difficult situation or to anyone suffering illness. Her tireless gifts of love to many in Leaf Creek will always be remembered.

The funeral service was conducted at two o'clock on Saturday at Leaf Creek Presbyterian Church. The mourners were comforted by words from the Holy Scripture and the tender singing of The Holy City, to which the spirit has been taken. A large concourse of sympathizing friends, having formed the cortege, followed the remains from the church to the graveyard and brought with them many fragrant floral tributes.

Mrs. McMolison was laid to rest beside her dear little son, Samuel, who preceded her in death. The remains of her husband, Mr. McMolison, who also preceded Kate in death, rest on the other side of their youngest child. As Kate's remains lie beneath a flower-laden mound, the sweet soul of this most noble woman rests in the arms of her Savior.

In addition to her husband and young son, Mrs. McMolison was also preceded in death by her mother and father. She is survived in this life by two daughters, Katherine McMolison Neal and her husband, Stephen, of Hattiesburg, and Hannah McMolison of Leaf Creek. Also mourning her departing is one grandson, Joseph, his wife, Nita, and one great-granddaughter.

To the bereaved, the citizens of Greene County, and especially the people of Leaf Creek, we extend sincerest sympathy.

Kate had died quietly and peacefully in her sleep. She usually went to the kitchen first thing and started the stove heating and coffee brewing before Hannah joined her. But one morning she was not in the kitchen. Hannah was alarmed. It was unusual for her mother to oversleep. Concerned that her mother may not be feeling well, Hannah knocked gently on the bedroom door and eased it open.

"Mother," she said softly at first. "Mother?" Her voice, a little louder, bounced off the wall. Kate did not move or respond. Hannah reached to gently shake her shoulder. She gasped and withdrew her hand quickly. Her mother was noticeably cold. She looked as if she could be sleeping, but there were no breaths—no movement at all. Fear swept through Hannah. She dropped to her knees beside the bed, buried her face in the crisp white sheets, and sobbed. Flashes of a similar scene from years before flew through her mind. Only this time she was kneeling beside her mother, her rock. Her mother was gone. Hannah was alone.

The suddenness of her mother's death brought an overwhelming sense of loss. In less than six months, her emotional pendulum swung far right and far left. The joy she had felt when first seeing her new granddaughter had been indescribable, and in holding her she had been overwhelmed with the incredible truth that she was, without a doubt, fearfully and wonderfully made. On this day, death had come and snatched her mother away, giving her a poignant sting that burned her heart for a long time.

JOSEPH, NITA AND THE BABY stayed a couple of days after Kate's service. Stephen and Katherine stayed longer.

A few days into the sorting through of Kate's things, Hannah and Katherine were both emotionally drained. Katherine put the jewelry on the dresser and the letters back in the box. She stood up, her hands on her waist and thumbs forward. She arched her back and stretched. "Come on, Hannah. We need to stop for a while." Katherine had insisted on a previous visit that she teach Hannah to drive. The lesson on that day had not gone particularly well; it was more a comedy than anything else. Katherine took Hannah's hand and helped her from the floor. "We need to figure a way for you to get some kind of car, and when we do, you need to know how to drive it. So let's go practice." The last two days of their stay with Hannah were taken mostly with her driving up and down the road, jerking every foot of the way. Her feet just did not want to cooperate with each other in operating the clutch, brake and gas.

"It's the clutch's fault, always pushing my left foot up too fast," Hannah called out to Katherine as she laughed and gripped the steering wheel with both hands.

"You'll get it. Just ease out real slow and give it a little gas."

Katherine was laughing as she tried to give instructions. Stephen leaned against a fence post with his arms folded across his chest. He shook his head from side to side and laughed as hard as Katherine. Finally, just before Stephen and Katherine left for Hattiesburg, Hannah enjoyed a small measure of success. All of them needed the diversion from the sadness.

As the sisters hugged each other goodbye, Katherine's words lingered. "I can hardly stand to leave you," she said. "You're going to be in this big house alone. Are you *sure* you want to stay? You know you're always welcome to come with us."

"I know. Thank you, but I want to stay here. You know this is still home for me. Let me just see how I manage before I start making changes," Hannah answered softly.

The sadness, however, was something Hannah had never known before. For the first time in her life, she was totally without the support and unconditional love of her mother. It left her with a heartache that for a long time was rarely consoled. Her mother's touch, smile and even Kate's scent were all missing. Hannah cherished the memories and often buried her face in one of Kate's shawls, deeply inhaling her essence.

HANNAH SOMETIMES sought the solitude of the kitchen pantry. The whole house was empty, but the small space was comforting. One day a couple of months after her mother died, she stood propped against the door facing. Rambling thoughts ran through her mind, and she thought about the words from the preacher's sermon the previous Sunday: "… *For what is your life? It is even a vapour that appeareth for a little time, and then vanisheth away*?" Everything was vanishing, Hannah thought.

The month showing on the feed store calendar was July 1941. She remembered her mother saying—more than once in recent years—that life seemed to go by faster and faster. At some point for Hannah, the sentiment had become personal and real. She wasn't sure when.

She inhaled deeply, leaned her head against the wall, and closed her eyes. She was feeling more wistful than usual. "Maybe I should have been willing to marry Lex," she said aloud—there certainly wasn't anyone to hear her talking to herself. "At least I wouldn't be here alone. *He* surely didn't want to be alone. He found someone else—quickly, or so it seemed." She sighed again and pursed her lips. "What am I even thinking about all this for? I did the right thing." She gave a half chuckle, scoffed at herself, pushed thoughts of Lex from her mind and squashed her pitying. She reached for a jar of beans to cook for her supper. "I've no regrets on that front," she said to her surroundings. "Wrong to marry one man while wishing you were marrying another one."

"COME LIVE WITH US," Joseph encouraged Hannah during one of their visits.

"Well, I don't know. I'm not sure I need to leave Leaf Creek and home. Lot to think about." Hannah looked down into the face of sleeping Bethany as she rocked.

"Just think, you could do this all the time." He put his hand on the back of the rocking chair and leaned over to kiss Bethany's forehead.

"Certainly tempting, but you may not always be teaching at Pine Springs."

"Well, if we had to move, Mother, you would move with us. You could help Nita with the children. She'd like that, and you would too."

"I'm sure I would, but let's think about it a little longer. I'm doing fine. I really am."

"If you change your mind, all you have to do is let us know." Joseph sat in the rocker nearest Hannah and began to rock back and forth.

"I will, but what I would like to do right now is take little Miss Bethany here out to see Janie. She would love a visit. It's Wednesday, and I usually go every Wednesday. Plus, I have a few things I want to take her."

"I'll go with you," Joseph said, and stood.

Janie's bad knee slowed her to a hobble, but she still got around well enough to cook, take care of herself, and get to church most every Sunday. Hannah and Joseph stepped across the wood porch of Janie's house and eased the door open. There was a loud squeak. "Janie," she called. "Janie, where are you?"

"In here, y'all."

Joseph put the box he carried on the small painted table that centered the kitchen.

"Coffee, tea, sugar, fruit." Hannah gestured toward the box. "Look who I have." Bethany, happily riding on her grandmother's hip, had one hand on Hannah's shoulder and the other fingering a button on the front of her dress.

"I see that pretty girl." Janie sat down in a straight chair with a wooden slat back and a cowhide bottom. "Now come here to Janie, sweetie pie." Bethany looked at Janie with bright, wide eyes. Janie tapped the tip of Bethany's nose, rubbed her cheeks and bounced her on her knees. Bethany smiled and clapped her hands before reaching for one of the bright blue buttons that held Janie's housedress together.

"What are you cooking, Miss Janie?" Joseph lifted a lid from a pot on the stove.

"Dumplings. Thought you might like some for supper." Janie grinned and handed Bethany back to Hannah.

"Sounds great, but I think Nita is fixing something for supper." Joseph sat down on a tall stool that he pulled to the edge of the table where Janie worked.

"Then you just take some home and add to whatever she's fixing, and next time bring Nita with you." Janie turned to Hannah and cupped her chin in her hand. "Love you, girl, and this precious family." She ran her fingers through Bethany's hair as she talked.

"Love you too, but we probably need to get going. Nita will wonder what has become of us. Tell Janie *bye bye*." Hannah waved Bethany's arm and repeated, "Bye, bye."

On their way home, Joseph commented on how glad he was to see Janie and how well she seemed to be doing. Then he added, "What have you heard from Rosie and Twila? Anything new?"

"Well, yes, some exciting news, actually. Twila has become famous—enough to be traveling and singing on stages in big cities like New York and Las Vegas."

Joseph looked over at his mother. "*Really?* That's great."

Bethany, standing and bouncing on Hannah's lap, kept trying to put her fingers in Hannah's mouth. Hannah talked around the little fingers. "She performed in Mobile recently, went to Leeville afterward, and spent a whole day at their church leading a celebration in song. Rosie wrote that it was great. She was so proud of her."

"I know she is. I'd like to have heard her," Joseph said.

"Me too," Hannah said, still maneuvering her lips around Bethany's fingers. "Rosie wrote that several white people, having heard about Twila's success, went for the night program. She said they mixed in pretty good and gave lots of compliments to Twila. I couldn't help but wonder where they sat—if the whites were on the back pew." Hannah smiled at the thought and at Bethany.

"Interesting," Joseph said with a chuckle. "I'm happy for her, that's for sure."

"I'm happy for her too, and proud of her. She'll be a legend among future generations of colored women, no doubt," Hannah replied. In the silence of her heart, she added an unspoken thought: "Yes, I'm very proud of this daughter of my half-sister. Your cousin, that is, and kin you will never know."

They drove up beside the house. Joseph turned the switch and killed the engine. He turned to face Hannah, who was fighting the battle between bouncing little feet and trying to keep her skirt somewhere close to her knees. "Mother, I want you to really understand that we—Nita and I both—will be happy to have you with us at any time. You know that, don't you? You would never, ever be a burden or in the way."

"I do, and I love you for saying that, but this is home and I want to stay. I'm making it fine. Don't worry. I've gotten rid of most of the animals. I only have one cow to milk, a few laying hens and the garden is *really* small." Hannah paused. "You know all that already, and I like substituting at the school. I have enough. I know you and Nita can't come as often as you have been, but that's okay."

"That's what I'm thinking about—that we can't come as often as you may need us to." Joseph's words were filled with concern.

"Well, we'll think about that when we have to. I'm not *that* old, you know. I am fine and I want to be here for the time being. I love you for caring, Joseph. Now, you and Nita get on with your life." Hannah opened the car door. "Get Janie's dumplings from the back, and let's get inside and see if we can help Nita."

The thought of leaving the only home Hannah had ever known was successfully pushed into the recesses of her mind once again.

CHAPTER FORTY-THREE

AFTER GRADUATING FROM OLE MISS, Thomas Stokes left for medical school in Atlanta. His new environment, his difficult studies, and the infrequency of his visits home had dulled the past in his thoughts. Greene County seemed a world away, another life.

During his first year a lovely girl named Sadie (daughter of one of his professors) got his attention. She was pretty. She was sweet. She was easy to be around. Coffee in the hospital cafeteria turned to an occasional supper outside the hospital. The two found themselves content and comfortable with each other. They married. Sadie had never lived in a small town nor had she ever been to Mississippi, but she thought she was ready to follow him anywhere, even to Leeville.

After medical school, he and Sadie moved into a spacious house in town. Built only ten years earlier, it had all the modern conveniences: running water, indoor plumbing, and electricity. It was located on a side street shaded with oaks and close to downtown, where Thomas set up his office next to the drugstore on Main Street.

Their son, Meachem, was two and a half when the couple moved to Leeville. Other than the joy Sadie felt as a mother, though, she never felt satisfied or happy living in a small town, and Thomas never regained the lust for life he'd had as a young man. His medical practice kept him busy, but he showed little interest in anything else. They both found themselves living a rather quiet and uninspired life. Thomas cared for ill parents until their deaths. He attended church, participated in a few community activities, and loved Sadie the best he could. He was more than successful financially. His medical practice thrived even though he often cut his fees by half all the way to nothing, depending on the amount people were able to pay. He and Sadie lived a frugal lifestyle, as they constantly saved for a rainy day. They faithfully planned the inheritance they could leave to the grandchildren they wished for—but never had. Contributing more to his financial wealth than anything else was Thomas's inheritance. The Stokes estate was large, and his share was significant in land, timber, and money.

Thomas was comfortable but never truly content. He lived his life feeling as if a part of him had been broken and was never mended.

* * *

HANNAH WAS SWEEPING the front porch when the strange car pulled off the road and stopped in front of her house. It was getting late in the day and though she was never really afraid, she had gotten more cautious in the weeks since her mother died. Living alone had brought several changes, and this new level of caution was one of them. She moved close to the front door as she watched to see if the driver would get out of the car. The glare of the late afternoon sun on the windshield blinded her ability to see inside the automobile. Then the driver's door opened.

There was no mistaking the man now standing just outside her gate. It had been eighteen years, but he was as recognizable to her as he would have been had she seen him every single day. A grip, old and familiar, tightened around her heart. She inhaled deeply in an attempt to relax. He walked toward the porch. She stood, unmoving. He was almost exactly the same, save for a slight thickening around the waist and a sprinkling of gray in his black hair. As he got nearer, she saw wrinkles that creased his temples, his forehead, and even the edges of his mouth. His eyes seemed tired and sad. Was his spirit gone?

It appeared that the life of privilege Hannah had imagined Thomas having had not served him well. She was glad she had just done her hair and applied rouge to her cheeks and lips as concerns for her own appearance flashed into her mind. She thought seeing that she was still beautiful might, in some way, cause him regret for not coming back to her. Regardless, she knew without question that even though he had privileges and material wealth, he had missed the riches of knowing his eldest son.

Since seeing Thomas with his wife and little boy in the hotel dining room all those years ago, Hannah had received exactly one letter. She had hoped for more. She had hoped that Thomas seeing Joseph that day would prick his heart and push him to make contact, even if the contact was in secret. Contact was never made. Hannah was not naïve, however. She knew that complicating his family with a past life would be extremely difficult. Yet her hope, though on occasion diminished by reality, was never completely extinguished. She never stopped thinking that Thomas would want to know about Joseph and what kind of man he'd grown into … and how she had actually fared all these years. She never wanted to believe that he'd simply forgotten about them.

She'd sometimes thought, too, of what it would be like to run into Thomas again, but there had never been much chance of a second incidental meeting. Hannah and Kate had made only a couple of trips to Leeville, and after Joseph left for college they rarely left Leaf Creek at all. When they did, it was toward Beaumont or Hattiesburg, both in the opposite direction of Leeville.

In addition, Hannah never forgot the demands of Mr. Stokes and her father. Their ultimatums had driven her to life-changing action— and led to the death of her father. She had always imagined that their demands had been difficult for Thomas too, but Thomas would have long ago become his own man making his own decisions. Even so, there had been no more word from him.

Suddenly, though, there he was walking up the path to the porch, getting closer. Hannah propped the broom against the door facing and walked to the edge of the top step. She stood and faced him.

"Hannah, I was hoping I would find you at home," he said, sounding stiff and awkward to her ears. "How are you?"

"Well I'm … I'm fine, Thomas. And you?"

"Well … I drove over because I wanted to see you, see how you're getting along. I heard a few days ago that your mother passed away. I was sorry to hear." He stepped onto the bottom step, and Hannah wondered if he wanted to be invited inside, but she didn't offer.

"It was sudden," she said. "I won't deny that it's been hard, but I'm fine. How's *your* family?"

"Okay. Everybody is okay. Tell me about Joseph."

"Really, Thomas? Now?" Hannah's eyes tightened and her brow furrowed. With a hint of frustration she said, "Tell you about Joseph. After all this time, you want to know about your son?"

"I've always wanted to know. I just couldn't."

"There is *always* a way to do what's right, Thomas. You just never did."

Thomas dropped his chin. Then he motioned with his hands in front of him, palms upward. "Please, Hannah. I really don't want to rehash all I've done wrong. I heard about your mother. I wanted to come, and I do want to hear about Joseph if you'll tell me."

Hannah stared at him and didn't say a word.

"Do you hate me so much you can't tell me about our son?"

"I don't hate you, Thomas," Hannah said quietly. "Maybe I hate myself for *not* hating you, but I've loved you for what seems like my whole life. And I realized long ago that you have no idea what that really means—for me, for Joseph, even for you."

"Hannah, I don't know what to say. I don't—"

"Don't," she said firmly. "Don't even try, okay? I don't think there is anything you *can* say, and you don't need to search for words you think I might want to hear. You know it really doesn't matter because nothing you could say or do will change the past. But, sure, I'll tell you about Joseph." And for the next several minutes Hannah talked all about him—fishing with friends, good student, graduation from high school and college, his profession as a teacher, his wonderful wife, his beautiful two children, and the fact that he was known far and wide as a thoughtful, respected man and a good husband and father.

"Maybe it was a bad idea to come today, but I'm glad I did," Thomas said, looking her straight in the eye. "I think of you. I do, Hannah. And I think of Joseph."

"Maybe this *was* a bad idea, Thomas. Seeing you reminds me so much of questions and disappointments from a long time ago. Your words today sound just like your letters from college. 'I think of you often.' What really hurt was you not coming to see me when you learned Joseph was born. I thought, for sure, that you would want to see your own son."

"I *did* want to see him. I should have come, but my father was so adamant. I let my father rule me, but you know that. And now I'm having to live with it."

"And when my father was killed? I thought *surely* you would come then. Just to see if I was alright, to see if your son was alright or to tell me you cared or that you were thinking about me."

"Hannah, I didn't even know until several weeks later! My father didn't *tell* me. I know that's no excuse. I should have come when I did find out."

"Yes, you should have." She had no desire to offer ready forgiveness or to continue belaboring what couldn't be changed. "These are old wounds, Thomas," she said quietly. "Doesn't do much good to open them again. I wished for you, but you didn't come. You never came."

"All I can do is apologize. I can't undo the regrets. I've wanted to see you. I've wanted to know about Joseph. Then, after hearing about your mother …"

Thomas trailed off. Hannah didn't help him finish the sentence but let it hang in the air.

"I suppose I should go," he said at length.

Hannah managed a constrained, but polite response. "It was nice of you to stop by."

"Hannah," he said suddenly, "before I go, I want to ask if there is any way I can help you or help Joseph. Money, maybe?"

Hannah's mind flashed to Joseph working in the cafeteria at Teacher's College and living with Katherine because they couldn't afford the dormitory fees. But she answered calmly and without a hint of the jealousy she'd once felt toward the child Thomas had with Sadie. Shaking her head slightly and with a half-smile, she sighed deeply. "Fixing things with money. Sounds like something your father would do."

"I didn't mean to suggest it would *fix* things. Just maybe … it might be helpful. I'm sorry. I never meant to offend you."

"Everything is fine. Joseph and his family are all fine. Maybe if you had come sooner."

"I know. I just let days and months … and years … get by."

"I know you had a wife and another little boy, but Joseph wished for you. He wanted a father to take him fishing, to do things the other fathers did. Thomas, your son worked *the whole time* he was at State Teacher's College," Hannah said, angry now. "He lived with Katherine while he worked. Yes, I wish you had been here for him and for me. It's not just that things have sometimes been hard—it's the *brokenness* from living our lives with a piece missing. Can you imagine what that's like?"

Thomas backed away a step. "Again, I'm sorry. I can't fix the past, but I hope you will find a way to forgive me. Maybe somehow in the future we can find a way to mend." He continued before Hannah could manage a response. "I probably need to start back toward home. Take care of yourself, Hannah."

"You too." Her words followed him as he walked back across the yard and got in his car. She watched the blue-gray fender disappear around the same curve she had watched his wagon many years before.

"Mend?" she said aloud. "I'm not sure what that means, not sure what I would want it to mean." She felt pensive and sad as she thought of what might have been. Then she took a deep breath, picked up her broom, and continued sweeping.

Chapter Forty-Four

Thomas, STRIVING hard to not be at all like his domineering and strong-willed father, almost never gave Meachem parental guidance, much less any rules to follow. So Meachem followed his own guidelines which, thankfully, were polite and orderly for the most part. He graduated from Ole Miss as his father had done but had no interest in medicine. He went to work for a drug company and traveled around Louisiana and Mississippi extolling the benefits of penicillin, the new wonder drug.

Meachem Stokes could have lived anywhere, but he chose New Orleans. He never married but lived with another man with whom he shared interests. His flamboyant lifestyle was difficult for Thomas and Sadie. His pastel pink jackets with lavender and celadon trim were foreign to both their tastes. Even so, they were eager for his visits, though infrequent they were. Thomas and Sadie, with sad hearts, feared that their son's life was not one that would ever meld with their own.

OUT OF RESPECT for his father and mother, Meachem chose a black coat, gray tie and white shirt for the funeral of both of his parents. He wore his black patent leather shoes that were, no doubt, the only pair of men's patent leather shoes in Greene County. Several of Meachem's high school classmates attended one or both of the services.

"I tell ya. That family's snakebit," one old classmate said to another as they stood outside First Presbyterian Church after Dr. Stokes's service and waited to go to the family plot. "I've been up in the north part of the state helping my brother build a house and a barn. Didn't even know the Stokeses were sick. What happened? Do you know?"

"Yeah, I know a little," the second one answered. "My sister was helping take care of both of 'em." He leaned against the car and folded his arms. Folks were slowly coming out of the church, and it was too hot to wait inside the car. "Dr. Stokes had that stroke a couple months—no, probably been four or five months back. Not sure just when. He was only like forty-five, but it left him partly paralyzed."

"I didn't know. That musta happened before I left, but I didn't know about it. Living out from town like I do, sometimes I don't learn things till they're said and done with. What happened to his wife?"

The men walked over to stand in the shade of a big oak. Perspiration glistened on both their foreheads. The second man pulled a white handkerchief from his coat pocket and swiped it across his face.

"She had help at their home, of course, but she did most of the caring for Dr. Stokes, at least till she got sick—Dr. Fish, the new doctor in town, said pneumonia. You met him?"

"No, I haven't."

"He's nice," the first classmate said. "Folks like him. Anyway, he told her he thought she was overly tired and would require several weeks rest. Nurses were hired to care for both of 'em, but what I heard was that Mrs. Stokes lost her will to live."

"What does that mean?"

"Well, according to my sister, seems she took the recommendation for bed rest more seriously than the doctor intended. She went to bed, and in spite of the nurses trying to coax her up, she refused to get *out* of bed or even to eat by the end. Truth is, I think she and Dr. Stokes worried over Meachem a lot."

"Doesn't Meachem sell that new drug …?"

The first classmate lowered his voice. "Penicillin. You know he went to college. He's been going 'round peddling that stuff ever since. His daddy wanted him to go to medical school, but he didn't want to. I heard they gave Mrs. Stokes penicillin, but my sister said in spite of it she got worse and worse—maybe she would have gotten worse faster without it. My sister said it was pretty awful, her propped up trying to breathe, high fever, gurgling, coughing and sweating. She didn't live but two weeks. And now here we are burying Dr. Stokes."

"Does seem like they've had their share of troubles. You say Dr. Stokes died from a stroke?" the second classmate asked, waiting until after a clump of people walked past.

"*No*. Had one but didn't die. Just the other morning he had a bad stomach pain, wouldn't let my sister call the doctor at first. Kept saying it would pass but finally gave in."

"Sounds like your sister's had a time of it lately. Think we ought to be getting in the car? Looks like the hearse is about ready to pull out." The men left the shade and walked back toward their car.

"Yeah, my sister had a pretty rough day with Dr. Stokes. She said she pulled a chair close to the bed and tried to keep his face wiped with a cool wet rag, but he hurt worse and worse and finally vomited a bunch. Said she was quick though—she grabbed the water bowl and caught it."

"She call the doctor?"

"Yes, and the doctor called the sheriff and they all headed to Mobile. Operated on him that night—it was appendicitis. He woke up from the surgery, said the last thing he remembered was the counting—ten, nine, eight … very slowly as ether filled his nostrils—funny how they tell you to do that."

"Did he get out of the hospital?"

"No. His appendix had ruptured. Bad infection. They gave him penicillin too, but he died six days later. I think he had turned forty-six."

The two men got in their car, closed the doors, and rolled down the windows. Meachem Stokes was getting in a black Ford two cars behind the hearse.

"And look at Meachem." The classmate from out in the country nodded his head toward him. "I don't know what's wrong, but he looks pretty bad to me."

"Could be just losing both his parents has him down. I mean, it's been less than six months since his mother died. Wonder what he'll do. Reckon he'll ever come back to that big place they've got here?"

The conversation continued as they pulled into the procession. "I doubt he'll come here to live. Think he's got a whole new life in New Orleans."

"Well, I'm no doctor, but I tell you something is wrong. Look how thin he is, and his color is so bad. My grandmother would say he looks mighty sallow."

Six months later Meachem was diagnosed with tuberculosis. Before he could be committed to a sanatorium his condition had worsened, and he died a year after his father.

There were several large bank accounts, hundreds of acres of timber, and hundreds of acres of farm land bearing Thomas Stokes's name, but Thomas, Sadie, and Meachem were all gone. No family ever shed more truth to the folly of laying up treasures on earth.

Chapter Forty-Five

$\mathcal{M}$EACHEM THOMAS STOKES had six first cousins. Five attended his funeral. Before the service they sat on the front pews of First Presbyterian Church. Three stained glass windows, all brightly lit with representations of Jesus, glowed down upon them as they whispered and wondered among themselves what was to become of the Stokes family fortune. With Meachem's death, they considered themselves the next of kin. One of the women sat on the edge of the pew and turned sideways toward the others. She spoke just above a whisper: "Do you know if Meachem had a will? I know Uncle Thomas left everything to him."

Each woman shook her head, but before any of them could answer further, the funeral director appeared in front of them. "The family, please come this way." He directed them through the door beside the chancel. The preacher waited in the room behind the sanctuary.

Dressed in a black suit, white shirt, and black bow tie, the preacher smiled slightly. "Is there any more family here? I'd like to pray with you before we go in for the service."

"No, this is it, all that's left of us, anyway," one of the men answered with a tone that was somewhere between gruff and solemn.

"Then let us pray." The preacher bowed his head. The cousins followed suit. The preacher then led the cousins around the outside of the church to the front door and down the aisle to the pews they had previously occupied. A couple of prayers, a hymn, a short eulogy and a long sermon later, the cousins retraced their steps as they followed the casket and the preacher out of the church, to the waiting cars and to the family graveyard.

Most of the people who attended the graveside service left promptly when the preacher finished his final thoughts, but the group of five (along with a couple of their spouses) stood huddled in the cemetery. A male cousin spoke up first: "Well, I don't know for sure about a will, but Uncle Thomas spoke to me some time ago about being executor. He was worried, I think, that Meachem may not take care of things. I mean, he wanted Meachem to get everything. I was just supposed to kind of guide him." The man's hands were pushed deep in his pockets. Looking down at the ground, he kicked a clump of dirt with his foot, doing so just hard enough for the clump to break into small pieces and cover his brown leather dress shoe with a layer of beige dust.

One of the women stepped sideways to keep the dusty shower from landing on her navy pumps. "Be careful," she snapped, and stomped her feet against the ground a couple of times to knock the dust off.

"Sorry. Don't get in a twit."

Playing together growing up had not prepared the cousins to share oversight of a fortune. They had never had problems getting along, but the possibility of one having more power than another quickly created tension.

"That's interesting," a second female piped up, her tone carrying a hint of anger. She hadn't flinched when he kicked the dirt clod but stood firmly planted, feet slightly apart, arms folded together across her protruding stomach, a black handbag dangling from her left wrist. "When I was with him after Aunt Sadie died, he asked if *I* would be sure to take care of his estate."

"I guess we'll see," her male cousin replied. He walked toward his car and snapped at his wife: "Come on. Let's get outta here."

Another cousin spoke quietly but firmly: "Probably we all need to wait until Uncle Thomas's lawyer reviews whatever he has available. He'll contact us if there's a reason."

***

TWO MEN AND FOUR WOMEN did receive official letters—the two male cousins and the four females. The Stokes estate was indeed settled, and the date and time for revealing the will had arrived.

The table was mahogany and polished to a bright shine. It sat in what was probably the most impressively decorated room in Leeville. There were a couple of original paintings hanging on the walls, but the artists were unknown except to locals. The artwork would have never won awards, but giving it prominent space was good for business. Stored in a closet were several other pieces that were rotated on and off. It was the secretary's job to remember who had appointments and to change the pictures if one of the artists or family members was coming in.

Chairs circled the table. They were made of the same dark mahogany and were quite sturdy with thick arms and polished to the same shine. Three large, clear glass ashtrays were strategically placed so that anyone seated at the table could reach one. Other than the ashtrays, the sweat from the anticipatory palms that surrounded the table was the only thing that marred the perfect shine. Three hands that rested on the table left damp streaks each time they moved. Two women sat stiffly with hands folded in their laps. The tension in the room was almost palpable as Meachem's cousins and three of their spouses surrounded the table.

One chair remained empty. There was an estranged cousin out in the world somewhere whose place it would rightfully be, but he'd disappeared some years before. He cut off contact with the family, and if he kept up with family matters, he did so from a distance. If he knew a chair was available for him on that day at the hotly-anticipated event, no one else was aware he knew. No one but the lawyer had planned for his presence, and certainly none of the cousins desired it. They knew an extra person would only dilute the pot.

The cousins and spouses had all arrived at the law office in Leeville a little before the scheduled time. No one dared be late. They had each been summoned to the occasion for the reading of the will of their deceased uncle, Thomas Stokes. Since their cousin, Meachem, had died shortly after his mother and father, they were now the fortunate heirs of all that had been stashed away and invested and banked. Their aunt and uncle had accumulated enough wealth to provide for all their wishes quite easily. They knew the assets were significant. None of them knew just *how* significant, but they were about to find out.

"Do you have any idea how much money we're talking about today?" one of the women whispered to the cousin next to her.

"I don't. You know they never spent any to speak of. It makes me feel kind of sad to be here like we all are," the cousin whispered back. "Seems almost indecent, as if his money is all we can think about or remember."

"You're right. I shouldn't say anything. But … we could really use the money right now."

The cousin who kicked the dirt at the gravesite service sat looking downward. His hands were in his lap with his fingers intertwined and his thumbs pushing hard against each other. Every few minutes he moved his thumbs to where one rolled quickly over the other. He'd grunted a hello to the others as they all entered the room but didn't take part in additional conservation.

Different cousins were silently pondering different questions: How many bank accounts were there? What are the balances? How many stocks and what kind? How much timber? There was speculation, speculation, speculation. They could hardly contain themselves because every one of them had made plans for spending his or her share. One man had even checked on the price of a new truck down at the Chevrolet place. He convinced his wife that he'd really need it in order to properly care for his portion of the timberland. One of the women quietly hoped her share would cover debts she and her husband owed, and another had mapped out a trip to California. Their minds were teeming with questions, plans, and wishes as they waited.

Even though two of the cousins had had a heated verbal exchange about handling their possible inheritance, they remained cordial as they sat in the conference room, though cool and stiffly polite toward each other. One of the women remained poised, though. Her greeting to the others was warm and courteous. There were nine people: five cousins, three spouses, and one lawyer in attendance.

Lawyer Morrison finally entered the room. He was dressed in a dark navy three-piece suit that stretched tightly around his generous girth. His graying hair was almost to the collar of his white starched shirt. He wore a red plaid bowtie. His silver-rimmed spectacles were perched close to the end of his nose, and a diamond-studded wedding band indented the skin of his left ring finger. One of the women thought to herself that he would need fat, soap, or oil if he ever wanted to take it off. His attire fit his position, fit their surroundings, and fit the occasion. His entering with documents in hand increased the contractions of every coronary muscle in the room … except his own. Like children making Christmas lists, the cousins had made their plans, and those plans would be limited only by the actual dollars that lined their pockets when they exited the room.

"Good afternoon," he drawled. "I'm sorry if I've kept you waiting. My previous meeting lasted a little longer than expected." His previous meeting had actually been lingering too long over dinner, but suggesting he had been tied up with something important was what came out of his mouth.

Several of the cousins tried to make proper greetings, but most of those around the table simply needed and waited for the recitation of the will to begin—that's why they were there. They were all ready to get down to the business at hand.

"Well, as you all know, you have been asked here today so we can clear the matter of the Last Will and Testament of Thomas Carlton Stokes—or, actually, *Meachem* Thomas Stokes. Your uncle was a fine man, a respected citizen who meant a lot to this community. I will always remember him fondly." There were clenched fists under the table and on top. They were ready to hear the balances, not a eulogy.

"Please just continue on with the will," one of the cousins said after a second.

Lawyer Morrison looked at the paperwork, which lay unopened

on the table. "Yes, of course," he said. "I realize you are all anxious. I know Mr. Stokes loved his wife and son dearly, and he made total provisions for both of them if he predeceased them." Lawyer Morrison glanced again at the unopened folder where his right hand rested. "He was a realistic, thoughtful, and far-sighted man, as you all know. I did his legal work for many years, but I know you have known him all your lives, so I don't suggest I can tell you something you don't already know." The anxiety level in the room was increasing swiftly.

"Please, Mr. Morrison, I don't want to be rude," said one of the male cousins from near Hattiesburg, "but is there any way we can speed this up? I would like to get back home before dark."

"Oh, again, I apologize. I just wanted to extend to you my sympathies for your loss of a fine uncle, but we do need to proceed. I said he was far-sighted, and we see an example of that here today. He, with Meachem's knowledge and agreement, prepared a will for Meachem that would become effective if Thomas predeceased Meachem. Meachem could have made some changes after his father's death, but he never did." Lawyer Morrison paused. "Meachem, of course, inherited everything from his father, but there were restrictions and stipulations. Thomas asked that there be a clause in Meachem's will that at Meachem's death—if he remained unmarried, which he did— all remaining assets would be given to the closest living relative, or divided equally if there was more than one of the same kinship."

Lawyer Morrison sighed deeply and leaned back in his chair, as if to stretch his back. Then: "It's obvious through his generosity that his nieces and nephews meant a great deal to him." Hearing the word *generous* caused mouths around the table to become dry and hearts to quicken again. Lawyer Morrison hesitated as he adjusted his spectacles, only adding to the tension. Then he leaned forward, both his forearms on the table. The will was between them. He started to lift the top page but stopped. "Oh, I am sorry. I forgot to offer you coffee. Would any of you like a cup?"

"Please get on with it," muttered the grouchy male cousin who kicked the dirt clod at the graveside service. "Nobody here needs any coffee or anything else, Counselor."

Lawyer Morrison started to flip over the top page of the will. There was a gentle tap on the door, and the door opened slightly. Every cousin slumped in his or her chair with the interruption. It was Lawyer Morrison's secretary. She had been his secretary for twenty years, and she took care of everything in the office and knew if and when interrupting a meeting was important.

"Excuse me, sir. Could I see you a minute please?" she asked.

"Can it possibly wait? We are just getting started." Morrison knew it was *not* something that could wait, though (or she would never have knocked), but he wanted to keep up appearances. Morrison excused himself, and when the two were in the hall and the door was securely closed behind them, she said, "Greg Jones is here."

Morrison frowned. "You called me out of a meeting because of Greg Jones? This doesn't seem like you. What does he want?"

Greg Jones was a ragtag lawyer in town—the *only other lawyer* in town, actually. He worked some, fished a lot, and drank a lot depending on the day. He was a nice sort of guy. Most everybody liked him, but they didn't often seek his legal advice. He didn't worry much about money or appearances. He was not a colleague that Morrison chose to be seen with. That afternoon was definitely not a good time for him to stop by. Morrison's fees from the afternoon's activity were going to be sizeable, and he did not want delays any more so than the anxious cousins who waited in the adjoining room.

"He has something I think you need to see," his secretary said quietly but firmly, "and information I think you'll want to hear."

Morrison walked into his office where Greg Jones was waiting. Jones was wearing a pair of khakis and a white shirt. The green pack of Lucky Strikes showed through the worn fabric of the pocket on his left chest. The red circle on the front of the pack pushed tightly against the pocket's front, almost like a bullseye right over the heart. His hair looked as if he had ridden through a windstorm. His unpolished boots were the same ones he had worn for the last ten years, and his brown leather belt was fastened in a hole that had obviously been added to make the size more generous. Only the tip of the belt was visible beyond the buckle. The two men were as strikingly different as a chipped jelly glass and a Baccarat crystal goblet. Jones started the conversation. "Hello, Morrison, I hear you've got the Stokes clan gathered," he said rather nonchalantly.

"That's right, but I'm not sure why that concerns you," Morrison responded arrogantly. His forehead was creased, and his eyes squinted at Jones over his spectacles.

Jones was not fazed. "Well, I'm here on behalf of my client, and I'm also here to keep *you* from making a very big mistake."

"You're going to keep *me* from making a mistake? You know, Jones, you really are absolutely ridiculous."

"I'm here because it has been brought to my attention that the rightful heir to the Thomas Stokes estate is not in that room."

"What?" Morrison said incredulously. "Is this some sort of *joke*? What are you trying to pull?"

"Just standing for the truth and the law and doing what's right. Isn't that what we're supposed to do?" Jones held his arms out with palms facing upward and shrugged his shoulders, adding his own touch of nonverbal sarcasm. He then plopped down in a chair. Morrison walked to the front of the chair and looked down at Jones.

"Well, tell me then. Get on with it. What are you talking about?"

"Morrison, this information came to me in an unusual way, so I wasn't sure about it," Jones said, dropping the boastful blustering the men were doing. "I would have come to you sooner, but I wanted to check it out first. I have just finished reviewing all the records. I believe the information is true."

"Go on."

"Last night the minister from the little Baptist church out on fifty-seven came to my house," Jones explained. "He said he had just taken a call from a minister friend of his that lives in Hattiesburg. The man's name was Stephen Neal. Neal claimed he has a nephew that is Thomas Stokes's son and is the rightful heir, and that it could be proved by a birth certificate."

"How did he—this Stephen Neal, I mean—know about today's meeting to read the will?" Morrison asked, beginning to pace back and forth.

"Well, that's a mystery, even to him. He got a call late yesterday telling him about today's meeting, and that some other people were going to get everything that belonged to his nephew—Joseph Stokes— unless he did something. All he knew was that it was a *woman's* voice. She refused to give a name and hung up quickly. He said at one fleeting instant when she was talking, he thought she *may* be colored but he could never be sure."

"Well, that is one intriguing story, but we can't go changing wills on the basis of an unknown voice in a telephone call."

"I know," Jones said. "That's why I went looking. The minister knew about how old Joseph Stokes is supposed to be, so I've been searching boxes of records at the courthouse all morning. I finally found this."

He handed Morrison a folded piece of yellowed paper. It was a midwife's record that clearly stated BABY BOY, JOSEPH, BORN TO MOTHER, HANNAH MCMOLISON, AND FATHER, THOMAS STOKES.

Jones gave Morrison a second piece of yellowed paper to read. It was a record of the annulment of the marriage between Hannah M. Stokes and Thomas Stokes. It was dated just a little over a week after the baby boy's birthdate.

It became clear to both attorneys what had taken place those many years before: a marriage was arranged so the baby would have a proper name and a father, at least for a time. The two lawyers were unified on the one point that mattered—the cousins who had eagerly assembled themselves that day were not the rightful heirs.

Both lawyers knew what they had to do. Together, they walked back into the room. The case was presented. The room quickly filled with angry tension. Three or four seconds passed as each member of the group looked at them with their mouths parted slightly and their eyes wide open. "That's a lie!" one of the men screamed as he clenched his fists tightly and held them, knuckles to knuckles, on the tabletop.

"Who forged those documents?" another man said angrily, almost shouting.

"Don't you think we would know if whoever you are talking about was real?" another cousin ranted, pushing his chair backward and almost knocking it over.

"This is unreal. You can't possibly believe what you're saying. We'll get another lawyer," the cousin who kicked the dirt clod said, and hit the table with his fist.

"Yes, that's a good idea. Surely we can find one that knows what he's doing. It will be better than what is going on here today. This is a joke. Little town, little lawyer mentality, I would say," one of the women added.

"You said yourself that you have a proper will. You can't just be changing it because you want to," one of the men said.

It would take time (perhaps more time than some of them had left in the world) for the anger to subside. Only one lone cousin maintained a sense of dignity. That cousin was disappointed, too, but she responded with the grace of a genteel southern lady.

The will clearly stated that the heir was to be the closest living relative, meaning that the son—Joseph Stokes—would, in any lawyer's office, come before nieces and nephews.

Chapter Forty-Six

Joseph had a myriad of questions. The will, the mystery surrounding its discovery, and the identity of the father he had never known provoked a swirl of emotions. The visit to his mother's house by Mr. Morrison and Mr. Jones had left him reeling as he tried to reconcile the loss he felt with the exhilaration of sudden wealth. He walked through the kitchen and out the back door, allowing the screen door to slam—something his mother never allowed. He didn't even hear the noisy bang as wood met wood.

He walked onto the back porch, down the steps, across the yard, and headed down the hill. A clump of dried dirt shattered into a thousand bits as he kicked it hard with the toe of his shoe. It was almost as if no part of his usually in-control self knew how to react to the news the men had brought him. He reached for a stick that in years past he would have thrown for Lost to retrieve, but today he twirled it in his fingers and tapped, sometimes hard and sometimes gently, on trees and bushes that dotted either side of the path. As he neared where the creek runs, the sound of gently-flowing water reminded him of fun, happiness, his mother and grandmother. He had a thousand questions about his father. He did not have answers and knew it was possible he never would. Everyone was dead that could have shed more light on Thomas Stokes's absence from his life. Well, everyone was dead except his mother, and she had told him so little. Would she tell him more? Maybe one day. He would never push her to discuss things she didn't want to share.

Joseph sat cross-legged on the bank, threw little pebbles into the water, and watched the ripples glide across the surface. Twinges of unexplained confusion and sadness he'd felt began to subside. He dropped his head backward and gazed at the blue sky overhead. With the sun shining brightly on his face, he suddenly said aloud, "There's so much money, all from a father I never knew." After a moment he bounced back to his feet, brushed dried leaves from the back of his pants, and shook his head in dazed amazement as he continued to process all the lawyers had told him. The news was almost more than he could fathom, but he was beginning to enjoy trying.

"Life will be easier for all of us, that's for sure," he said, more quietly this time. He snapped a twig from a little red oak as he walked leisurely back toward the house. His heart was light. His mother could spend time with her grandchildren and enjoy hours with them at the moss-covered respite. She could watch them swim in the cool flowing water and play hide and seek on the footpath as they made their way back up the hill. Never again would she have to worry about chores or provisions. His father, without knowing, had made it all possible. He had provided for all of them in a manner they would have never before considered.

Nita was quiet during the lawyer's visit, and she stayed quiet as she sat with Hannah on the big front porch. She felt as if the news and events were somehow intruding into a private time in her mother-in-law's life. She would ask no questions. Respecting Hannah would be a priority. As she rested her head on the back of the rocker and closed her eyes, a little smile formed on her lips. She couldn't help but think, "Enough money, extra money, even …"

Hannah sat in one of the big old rocking chairs. She rocked slowly. Joseph Luke was sleeping peacefully on her lap. Bethany, in a chair pulled as close to Hannah as possible, was singing "Rock-a-bye Baby" to her own sleeping doll. The lawyers' visit had been an unbelievable surprise, and the dollar amount was more than Joseph could have earned in ten lifetimes. Katherine and Stephen, afterward, told them the story of the mysterious telephone call, and Hannah had smiled to herself and thought of Rosie—always quiet and listening as she worked in the hotel dining room. Hannah's life had certainly not been as she once dreamed. Her heart had planned the way, but her path had been directed otherwise. Through it all she had been given the strength to take every next step. Now, a prayer of thanksgiving fell from her lips.

The only man she had allowed herself to love was gone forever. She had wished for a life with him, but he married someone else. She had hoped he would someday meet their son, but that was not to be. The news of his death had brought her sadness; the loss she felt was incredibly real. For a long time thoughts of Thomas had coated the impulses of her heart, sometimes causing it to race uncontrollably and other times burdening it to a near stall.

Death, Hannah knew, was final. The imprint on her heart would fade but never completely go away. The memories would last. Joseph Luke squirmed slightly in her arms. She leaned over and kissed his soft black hair. He opened his eyes and smiled, reminding Hannah of her tomorrows and the mercies that would be new every single morning.

$\mathcal{E}$PILOGUE

ONE YEAR LATER

$\mathcal{H}$ANNAH'S HEART still carried the lingering sadness that had come over her when she first learned of Janie's passing. It was only a month earlier that Janie died in her sleep, just like her own mother had done. Katherine and Stephen came for the funeral, and the three of them sat together with Janie's surviving sister and several of her nieces and nephews. Janie's death brought an abrupt end to Hannah's link to her childhood in Leaf Creek—everyone else had died or moved away. A feeling of aloneness had enveloped her, and that aloneness kindled a desire to embrace her family—her whole family—even if it meant exposing buried secrets and hidden truths.

Following directions given to her by one of the cooks at the hotel, Hannah took a sharp right off the main road. The blacktop turned to dirt as she eased her way into Leeville Quarters. She passed laundry on fences, boards covering broken windows, a tire filled with purple and white petunias, painted houses, and unpainted houses. She stopped, cut the engine, took a deep breath and pulled the key from the ignition. "I should have come long before now. I hope she's home," Hannah thought. Her heart was light; she was excited and yet nervous as she walked the short distance to the front steps.

The house was painted white, the windows all in good repair. Two rocking chairs looked welcoming, and two ferns hung from rafters on either end of the porch. Hannah opened the screen and knocked gently on the dark brown wood of the front door.

The door opened. There was a moment of awkward silence before the surprised voice from inside filled the void. "*Hannah!* What are you doing here? Is something wrong?"

"Hi Rosie. Nothing's wrong. I hope it's okay that I came. I just wanted to see you, maybe visit a little. Do you have time?"

"Yes. Sure," Rosie answered tentatively. "Would you like to come inside? Or if you'd rather, we can sit on the porch."

"Either is fine with me."

"Inside, then." Rosie stepped back and opened the door wider. "Several curious neighbors would likely join us on the porch if we stay out there." They both laughed. "Would you like some lemonade? Just made some."

"Sounds delicious. Can I help you get it?" Hannah offered.

"If you want to." Rosie led the way to the kitchen—yellow Formica countertops, white appliances and a small oak table with four chairs welcomed them. "Also made some oatmeal cookies."

"I love oatmeal cookies! My favorite," Hannah said enthusiastically.

"Mine too. Wanna sit here at the kitchen table?"

"Sure. This is perfect." Hannah smiled as Rosie handed her a glass of lemonade, a napkin and a plate of cookies.

Sitting in the chair across from Hannah, Rosie took a sip of lemonade. She nibbled on a cookie and turned her glass in little circles as she waited for Hannah to tell her why she had come.

"I know you wonder why I'm here," Hannah started. "Well, I should have come a long time ago. So first off, I apologize for not coming sooner. I'm sorry I excluded you for so long. Somehow I just couldn't tell my mother, but she passed away several years ago, and I still didn't come. And I haven't told my sister—"

"Hannah, it's okay. I understand. I really do. I never—"

"No, it's not okay," Hannah interrupted. "I want Katherine and Joseph to meet you, have a chance to know you. Who they decide to tell—and who *you* decide to tell—is up to them and you."

"I don't know, Hannah." Rosie sighed deeply. "I just don't know."

"Look, I know it was you that made the anonymous phone call that led to great benefit for Joseph and his family. He needs to know it was his aunt and so does Katherine. I want you to meet them."

"Are you sure? I've never told anyone else, and you haven't either. We need to be sure we wouldn't be doing something we'd regret."

"I've thought about it, and I've waited too long already," Hannah said firmly.

"Well … if you're sure."

"I'm sure. I'll bring them wherever you say—here, the hotel, wherever." Hannah was feeling a long-carried burden being lifted. It was incredible.

"The hotel, I think," Rosie answered. She still sounded unsure.

"That's perfect. I'll write and let you know when. We'll have tea and cake—all of us together."

"Hannah, we don't need to plan on tea and cake. I'll meet you on the back steps like we've done before, and I'll be ready to meet Katherine and Joseph when the time comes. If you still want me to."

Hannah's heart felt crushed. For the first time she truly faced the reality of what their differences really meant. In the past she had only thought of the scandalous actions of her father, but the reality was that whites and coloreds just didn't mix regardless of the circumstances.

"I'm sorry," she whispered. "I just didn't think when I said that, Rosie. I would never want you to be humiliated or embarrassed. I hope you believe me. We will meet on the back steps, and we'll meet quietly."

"I believe you. And thank you for wanting me—I mean that. But Hannah, I really think we need to be quiet after that. Quiet for my mother's sake, your mother's sake, and your—*our*—father's sake. I really don't want to do anything disparaging to any of our parents, and I'm sure you don't either." Rosie's voice was soft and pleading. "There's a lot of good that we can remember. Don't you think we should leave it that way?"

Hannah clasped Rosie's mulatto brown hands in her ivory white ones. "I'm glad to know you, and after I share you with Katherine and Joseph, we'll keep our secret."

"That will be good, and I hope you'll come back often. I'll make lemonade."

"I'll definitely be back." Hannah hugged her and asked, "Can we have more oatmeal cookies, too?"

"Sure." Rosie smiled. To Hannah it was a beautiful smile.

As Hannah walked away from Rosie's front porch, she waved in the direction of the next-door neighbor who was peeking between the curtains in her front window.

Rosie laughed as she walked back inside. "Sisters," she said to herself. The idea felt good.

TWO YEARS LATER

*H*ANNAH LISTENED TO THE BUZZ of chatter and happy talk that filled the room. The Mississippi Art Association was hosting its spring show, and her very own "The Respite" was hanging in a prominent spot. It was a watercolor of the creek, the moss, the ferns, and the surrounding woods.

"I told you people were going to love your work," the man said. "You're a natural, with your fluid strokes and pleasing colors."

"I love hearing your compliments even though I know they're not always true," Hannah whispered in response. "But I am really glad you were able to come tonight."

"Me too. I wouldn't have missed coming. And it's true—people do love your painting. Watch them admire it."

Hannah looked up at the deep brown eyes and silver hair. A smile covered her face. "Right. And I guess you know what all these people are thinking," she said mockingly.

"Well if they don't know it's the best painting here, it's their loss." He leaned over and whispered, "Only thing better is you."

"*Shhhhhh*. You sound like a teenager."

"Feel like one."

Hannah laughed. "Right. A forty-eight-year-old teenager—a widower with grown children—with me, the forty-five-year-old teenager and grandmother of two."

"Yes, sounds like a delightful pair." Hollis's eyebrows lifted and his head tilted sassily to one side.

"Won't argue, but you are a principal—the principal where my son works and has worked for the past two years, so you must behave. You know, proper decorum. Never know who might be watching."

"Right, right. You know, the best thing I ever did was hire Joseph."

"Of course I know. He is the best."

"True, but the best part is that his beautiful mother helped him move and then started coming weekly for art lessons."

Hannah couldn't keep from smiling. "Aren't you filled with flattery tonight?"

"True, true. All true from one teenager to another."

In hurried Joseph and Nita. "Wow, Mama, this is great. Paintings everywhere and yours is right there in front."

"I know. It makes me nervous. But an excited nervous." Hannah folded her arms in front of her and pulled them tightly into her body. "It's just that there are some really important people here. I don't know why they put my painting right in front."

"Guess we should go on and look around since we were late getting here. Took us longer to get to Jackson than usual and then I didn't know where on State Street we were coming," Joseph explained.

"Doesn't matter at all," Hannah assured him. "You're not late. People just mill around and look at everything, come and go. Oh, wow

… that's Marie Hull!"

"Where?" Nita asked as she looked across the room.

"That's her talking to the lady in the blue and white polka dot dress. She's such an encourager to an artist, does a lot to make these shows happen."

"Katherine!" Hannah exclaimed a little too loudly when she spotted her sister walking across the room toward her. "I'm so excited you and Stephen are here. Your coming makes the evening perfect."

"Look at my little sister," Katherine answered excitedly. "My little sister all the way from Leaf Creek showing her very own work in the big city. I'm so proud of you."

"Thank you," Hannah answered. "I can't believe it either. I'm trying to be calm, but I'm about to pop I'm so nervous and excited."

"Who knew all those little drawings you always liked to do would lead to this?" Katherine scanned the art covering the walls.

"I certainly didn't." Hannah stood tall and clasped her hands together over her chest. Her eyes widened and her lips pursed in an expression of joy mixed with surprise. "You're right, all that doodling and sketching I did," she said under her breath. "Now I'm trying to paint, but I never thought I'd be here at one of these shows, actually showing a painting."

"Well, you're here!" Katherine squeezed Hannah's shoulder. "Only two years of formal lessons and look where you are."

With a teasing grin, Hollis chimed in. "You know why she really started those weekly lessons in Hattiesburg, don't you?"

"Hollis." Hannah, smiling, countered firmly and quickly. "I started because I wanted to take art lessons, and Hattiesburg was the perfect place. I could visit my grandchildren and learn to paint all at the same time."

Joseph laughed. "Actually I thought it was because you wanted to be out traveling the countryside in that new dark blue 1943 Fleetmaster Sports Coupe."

"That, too," Hannah said with a smile. "For sure."

Stephen nudged Joseph. "Come on. Let's look around before they kick us out."

"That's a good idea. There's a lot to see," Hannah said with a grace-ful wave toward the artwork. She watched as they visited with other guests. She smiled as she watched them appreciate (or not appreciate) one piece after another. "What a special family I have," she thought. "Everything they said is true. I like going to Hattiesburg. I like my lessons. I like seeing all my family, especially my grandchildren. I like driving my car, and Hollis … yes, I like Hollis too. I like seeing Hollis in Hattiesburg, and I like introducing him to Leaf Creek, to my flowers, my woods … I like sitting with him where the creek runs, still cold but ever welcoming and peaceful."

Hollis appeared at her side. "What are you smiling about?"

"Oh, was I smiling? Didn't realize. Just happy, I guess. Happy to have everyone here."

"How does the Mayflower Café sound for supper? We can cele-brate," Hollis said as Joseph, Nita, Katherine and Stephen walked up beside them.

"Never been, so wherever you say," Hannah answered with a lilt in her voice.

The six were soon honoring Hannah's success with good company and good food. Without missing a beat in the conversation and without the others noticing, Hollis eased his knee against Hannah's knee and moved his hand from his lap to hers. Welcoming his touch, she laced her fingers through his and gave his hand a tender and agreeable squeeze.